The Initiative

Book One
Of
The Eleusis Cycle

D. Brumbley

Content Warning

This book contains content that some readers might find triggering, such as:

Mentions of suicide (off-page, not depicted)
Combat violence
Mass casualty events
Sexual content (explicit)
Arranged marriage
Genetic experimentation
Medical trauma
Mentions of pregnancy complications
Apocalyptic scenarios
Pandemics / disease

Read with Care

To all of you
who love someone
who doesn't know it.
Yet.

CONTENTS

1

The temporary silence and solitude before dawn gave Anna the chance to think. Anna's days rarely started at sunrise, so the gradual brightening of the sky through the small attic window was what Anna saw first when she opened her eyes. She enjoyed the quiet with a sense of relief as she rubbed at her eyes and forced herself awake. Soon the house would be busy with all of her siblings going about their chores around the farm, and she wanted to cherish the silence for as long as she had it.

Anna scooted to the end of her bed and leaned toward the window so she could push the curtains aside and see more of the sky. Her room was the highest and smallest room in the house, just a tiny space that had been made into a room on the east end of the attic. Small as it was, it was enough for her, and it gave her the privacy she wanted. Being the oldest of seven children, privacy was a difficult thing to come by. The grey sky and the unaccustomed silence were eerie reminders that the usual lack of privacy inherent in a big family might be something she would miss someday. Maybe even one day soon.

The window at the end of her bed was small, but when she pushed it open she was greeted with a sweet, fresh prairie breeze. She smiled as she ran her hand through her brown hair and looked up into the last remnants of the night.

Above her through the diminishing darkness floated not just the familiar morning constellations, but also one of the many giant space stations that had been a permanent feature of the sky since long before she was born. The station in the dawn sky looked like half a dozen stars had clustered together to have a party. A hundred childhood nights spent with a clear sky and a telescope had shown her all the details the naked eye couldn't, but most of the older stations she could identify on sight.

One look at the space station brought the previous night to her mind, and she turned slightly to glance at her desk where her laptop was still open, staring back at her.

Anna Prince,
We are pleased to inform you that your application to join the Eleusis Initiative has been accepted . . .

Accepted.

She couldn't even think about the rest of the brief message she'd been sent, since that single word kept swirling around in her mind.

What would her family say? What would her father say? What would they do?

Anna looked out her window again, chewing on her bottom lip as she thought about the day she had gone to answer the call in the first place. The Eleusis Initiative was looking for very specific types of people. She knew they wanted a variety of skill sets, different personalities, and that no one from Earth older than twenty-five would be accepted. She also knew that not many had actually applied from her home territory, but they were wanted by the Initiative. Farmers. Problem-solvers. Mechanics. People who could live life without complex computers or technology if necessary; and build what they needed. She still hadn't expected they would accept her.

Did she really want to go? Would she? It would mean leaving everything behind, everything and everyone she knew. Possibly forever. She usually tried to avoid anything with a duration of 'possibly forever'.

It was for the greater good of humanity. Wasn't it? Wasn't that what they told her? It was what she wanted to believe. She was twenty-one, and not once married. Twenty-one, and still living in her father's house, with no prospects. Maybe, just maybe, this could be her purpose? It turned out to be too much to think about before the sun was up.

Anna jumped out of her bed and rushed from her room down two flights of stairs. The bathroom with the big shower was hers today, and she would not have to wait or fight anyone for it. She had a long day ahead, since harvest season waited for no one. Not even a confused farmgirl wishing desperately for time to think about the rest of her life. Thinking would wait. The crops would not.

She rushed through her shower and dressed quickly, piling her wet hair into a bun on the top of her head so it would be out of the way. Anna didn't waste time with makeup or primping, which her father told her was part of her problem, but she knew she didn't need it. She knew she was pretty, but she also knew she was bullheaded and sharp-tongued. *That* was her real problem, not the lack of makeup on her face.

When she got to the kitchen she wasn't surprised to see her father already at the table drinking coffee. He had most likely spent most of the night awake, coughing, not sleeping. His illness was getting worse, but ever the farmer, he was still up long before the sun.

He looked up at her over the rim of his coffee cup as she went to get a cup for herself, adjusting his glasses once before looking back at the tablet in his hand to read the news. "I figured you'd be later getting up, late as you were up last night. Light under your door was on past midnight." Joseph Prince's voice had been put through a meat grinder in recent years by his constant and continual cough. He hardly even sounded like the father who had raised her anymore. The stress lines on his face changed him more and more with every passing year, though they didn't stop him from keeping himself clean-shaven every morning of his life.

"And suffer Ben's wrath if I slept in? No thank you." She laughed as she finished pouring her coffee, then went to sit by her father, savoring both the coffee and company before she had to get out and get to work. She grabbed a muffin from the middle of the table where Ben's wife left them out the night before. Before she took a bite, she leaned in and gave her father a kiss on the cheek. "I might've been born the oldest, but somehow he always acts the part. And sometimes he can be scary."

"Only sometimes?" He asked with the smallest hint of a grin before he had to turn away and cough, burying his face in his arm to keep from waking the younger members of the household. "I think," he continued as if he hadn't had to stop, his voice sounding temporarily even more broken than it had been before, "he's scary a hell of a lot more than sometimes. You're just braver than the rest of us."

"I think the word you're looking for is 'scrappy', not brave. That's what people call stupid, small, people who pick fights, right?" She joked, but there was definite concern in her eyes as her father coughed. It sounded worse than usual, but she hated to think about it. Let alone talk about it.

Her father was dying. They all knew it. He knew it. Talking about it wouldn't change it. Death came. Death took people every day. It was a beast no one on Earth could tame.

Her father looked like an old man worn by years, but he was only a few months shy of fifty. He had been worn down by the same illness that would take them all in the end. There was no cure, and life on Earth was short because of it.

Anna tried not to think about it much, even though her mother was already gone. She put her hand on her father's arm but used her other hand to bring the coffee to her lips for a sip. "Were they still fighting when you went to sleep?" Ben and his wife were having a difficult time of it recently, but Anna was hoping that they would work it out. They were perfect for each other . . . most of the time.

All he could do was roll his eyes and return to his own coffee as if the taste would push the memory farther away. "They stopped yelling when Ginny went to sleep, but yeah, they were still fighting last I heard. Going in the same circles about all the same things . . ." He sighed, which triggered a small racking cough, then he looked back at her. "Just remember when you get married, it's not worth it. If you're going to fight about something, tell them what you think, listen close to what they think, then work it out. Don't waste the time you have spinning in the same place over and over again."

"You sound so certain I'm gonna get married." Anna picked at the muffin she grabbed but she couldn't convince herself to take another bite when her mind was elsewhere. Her mind wasn't on marriage, it was on the acceptance letter haunting her from the night before. Her thoughts made her stomach twist into knots, but she kept quiet about it. "I don't see anyone lining up for the opportunity."

"Well, a line would mean you'd have to break some hearts. You're much better at breaking other things. Like their arms or legs. Or collarbones, you've done an impressive number of collarbones." He grinned at her again and drained what was left of his coffee cup, sighing in satisfaction at the end of it.

Anna's lips quirked into a small smile at the sight of her father's grin. Despite the fact that he was dying, he still smiled more than she thought any dying person usually did. It made her love and respect him even more. She knew he was determined to enjoy life with his children as long as he had the chance. "Exactly the reason why it might be wise for you to give up on the idea that you're gonna get rid of me that way. And as for the arguing in circles thing, that's just because Ben is a stubborn asshole who . . ."

She stopped mid-sentence when her brother came into the kitchen, but she couldn't help but giggle anyway. Anna didn't want to start a fight with her brother so early in the day, but that didn't change the fact that he was, in fact, a stubborn asshole who didn't listen to his wife nearly as often as he should.

Ben glared at her as she cut off, but just nodded at her as he went to get his own coffee and start a second pot. "Well, go on, I'm a stubborn asshole who what? You're the second person to call me an asshole today, and I've only been awake five minutes. I might as well get some constructive criticism to go with it."

"Second? Wow, you really did make her angry. The Susan I know doesn't often use words like that." Anna shook her head. Her brother's wife was usually a very soft-spoken and tender woman, but recently there had been a truckload of tension between them. Susan wanted Ben to take a second wife because she was having trouble conceiving another child. They had one healthy little boy, but time was never in anyone's favor, and Susan didn't want to be the woman that gave her family only one child. Susan and Ben were in love, though. Anna could understand why Ben fought Susan on the idea, but it was clear that Susan wasn't going to give up on it.

"You're a stubborn asshole who should just listen to his wife and make her happy if you can. If this is something that she wants, and clearly she hasn't changed her mind about it, then you should talk to Logan."

"Only thing I'm gonna talk to Logan about is borrowing some of his miracle farm equipment for harvesting next week, if he can spare it." He glared even after he had taken the first sip of his coffee, since he clearly didn't need the caffeine jolt to be awake enough to get angry. "It's barely been a year since Matt was born, and you're all talking like the damn sky is falling."

Anna sighed and continued drinking her own coffee in silence for a moment before she decided to say more. "It's hard, having expectations and feeling disappointment and guilt over and over again. She feels like she's failing, and sometimes that can drive someone to want things they wouldn't normally want. She's only suggesting it because she loves you. It's not like she'd think about you with another woman by choice."

Ben drank his own coffee in silence for a while before he shook his head. It wasn't an idea he could bring himself to stomach, even if he knew Susan's motivations were only from a good place. "I've said I won't, and I won't. If my mind changes in the future, then that'll be the future. But right now, it's not going to happen. That's the end of that."

Joseph sighed, but nodded slightly, with a warning glance over at Anna. "It's your family, son. You've got to do what you think is right by them, whatever that is." He got up to get himself another cup of coffee, leaving his tablet on the table with the headlines still marching across it in their slow procession.

The North American Territories Commemorate 250th Anniversary of the NATA. World Census Office of the Orbital Consortium reports growing population in the American territories, North and South, and in African states, but declines elsewhere. Estimates expect total North American census counts to surpass thirty million by year's end for the first time in four decades.

"You gonna help me with the livestock before we get started on the rest of the day?" Ben said without entirely looking at Anna, clearly done with the previous conversation.

Anna was so caught up in reading the headlines and letting them spin her thoughts that she barely registered her brother's voice, but when he repeated himself, she snapped her head up to look at him. "Help . . . oh, yeah, of course. Long day ahead, right?" Anna knew she sounded distant and distracted, since she was, but she couldn't help it. The message she received the night before was definitely beginning to take over her mind.

"They're all long days." Ben's look turned from a glare

to mild concern, and his eyes scanned the headlines before looking back at her. There wasn't much by way of actual news there, to his mind, but if Anna was concerned by it, that was her business. "You feeling alright?"

Anna nodded at first but then looked up at her brother with a weak smile. He was bigger than her by a long shot and in every way he looked the part of the older sibling, which always amused her. He was always looking out for her, even though Anna definitely knew how to take care of herself. "I, um, I heard people started getting acceptance and denial letters yesterday for the Eleusis Initiative. I was just curious if there was anything newsworthy about it."

That seemed to confuse Ben even more and he let out a sudden laugh that sounded more like a cough or a bark than actual amusement. "Yeah, sure, they're gonna advertise that on the front page. Anybody walks into that suicide mission, government's gonna keep that to some kind of Top Secret, need-to-know bullshit. We'll only hear about it after they launch and plow into an asteroid or something equally stupid."

Anna winced, though admittedly, she wasn't entirely convinced that it *wasn't* a suicide mission. She wanted to believe that it was something good, something that would help humankind, but she didn't live in a world where that kind of hope and idealism thrived.

Earth was harsh, and hope had an even shorter life expectancy than people. It was a miracle if anyone made it past fifty, and to keep humankind alive on Earth, it meant having as many kids as could be had. Anna was definitely behind on that. Ben was nineteen and already had one kid, showing her up as usual. A twenty-one-year-old woman, single and childless, was decidedly in the minority. "It might not be a suicide mission. I mean, it could be a good thing, being the first people to go to Eleusis."

"First person to do anything in this world, or any other world, for that matter, always gets a bad day for their trouble. Can you imagine trying to be the first person to break a horse? First person to try all this grass and get poisoned for your trouble before somebody finally figured out that wheat and oats might actually be edible?" Ben took a muffin, but clearly intended to stay on the move as he shook his head. "I'll take second place in line any day. First mouse can have the cheese and the ass-kicking that comes with it."

"I would hope the Consortium would take better care of its people than sending them off into some kind of trap." Joseph said with a skeptical look up at Ben. "They've certainly been working on this Initiative long enough. If they say they're nearly ready to go, I can't think of any reason they'd lie about it."

Anna nodded in agreement while he spoke. "It would give someone purpose, anyway. If they felt they didn't have any." She was afraid to say too much else in case they guessed her thoughts before she was ready to talk. Anna glanced over at her brother for a moment, gauging the impact of her words, but the moment was broken when she heard footsteps barreling down the stairs toward them. The rest of her siblings were on their way.

Cory, her eighteen-year-old brother, came rushing in first, followed quickly by Danny, who was only a year younger. "Grab something quick, boys." Ben was already prompting as they ran. "We've got a lot to do."

As soon as the rest of the family was moving in the morning, the kitchen became a swirling mass of people trying to eat and getting yelled at in turn to go get showered and ready for the day. Emily, at fifteen years old, was sent off first so that she could take care of Ginny whenever she woke up. Their ten-year-old sister was the youngest of them all, but easily the most energetic. Only Cory really gave her a run for her money.

Susan and Matthew didn't come down until after the rush, the one-year-old tottering across the floor to grab at anything that was put within his reach. He found himself picked up by Joseph before too long, and squealed in protest a few times before Joseph managed to settle him down with a spoonful of oatmeal from his own dish. The smile on Joseph's face was that of a very happy grandfather, even if the man behind the smile knew he only had a short time to hold his grandchild.

"Oh, Anna." Her father spoke as she finished washing out her mug and wiping down the kitchen after the breakfast madness. "I almost forgot, Liam sent a message last night, sounds like he's coming down to help out for the day. Just wanted to warn you."

Anna's initial reaction was to roll her eyes, but she didn't have a huge problem with Liam. Nothing more than a chronic annoyance, at least. His twin brother Logan had been her childhood best friend, and for years, people had teased her and Logan that they would end up together.

It hadn't worked out that way.

Logan married someone else, Melanie, a beautiful, quiet girl who was nothing like Anna, and life had moved on.

Until his wife had killed herself nearly a year ago.

After that, Logan's life had changed drastically, along with his personality. Changed or not, though, Anna would always be there for Logan whenever he needed her. That included dealing with his playboy twin brother on occasion. "I guess I don't really need to worry too much about him making a visit. Emily and Ginny are too young for him."

"I think Emily's got her eye on the Roth boy. Steven or Steffan or some such." Joseph rolled his eyes and got up to go with Anna out into the morning. The sun still wasn't up, but it was time to get to work anyway. "And no, I'd worry more about him being a bad influence on Ben than anything else. Even if that bad influence goes both ways sometimes." Ben was as loyal a son as any father could ask for, but his bad temper still caused more problems than it solved. "And I'm not even thinking about Ginny's matchmaking yet. That'll be your problem to deal with one of these days, not mine."

"I'm not thinking about my ten-year-old sister getting

married. I'm not even there yet myself. That's just wrong." Anna gave her father another kiss on the cheek once they were standing outside the house. "Don't stay out here too long. I don't want you to get worse."

"Uh huh." He gave her a quiet look at that, but he wasn't going to give her the same response that he had always given her before. Worse was the only thing he was going to get for the rest of his life. What was killing him wasn't the kind of thing anyone got better from. "Come find me and let me know what Liam wants later when he gets here. I have to drive Emily and Ginny up to see Doc Weber later for their checkups."

Anna nodded slowly but she stared at her father a little longer. "See what Doc can give you too while you're there." She let that linger between them before she headed off quickly to the barn to help with the cows.She found Cory there, already busy with the milking. "You beat me out here. How did you do that?"

"Oh, I'm actually a mutant. Forgot to tell you. Superspeed. Forgetfulness is a side effect." He smiled up at her as he worked, then nodded to the cow beside him, which already had a stool and a pail set in place for her to start helping. "I also woke up like three hours ago and broke into Susan's muffins, so I wasn't hungry."

"Three hours ago? What in the world were you doing up that early?" She went to the stool and immediately sat down, since there was really a lot to do. "You didn't sneak out to see a girl, did you?"

He looked guilty at her comment, but then shrugged. "I got stood up. Nancy Baxter. She said she'd leave her window open for me, but she wasn't there when I got there." He shook his head and sighed dramatically. The Baxter estate was their closest neighbor, at five miles away, but apparently Cory and his bike had been dedicated to the midnight meetup. "So if I pass out later, just try not to judge me."

Anna laughed softly and shook her head. "I have a truck

that you know how to drive, even if you're not good at it. Five miles isn't too far, you could have asked." She smiled at him, turning her attention back to the cow. "Nancy, huh? She doesn't really seem like your type."

"I don't need a type, I need a girlfriend. Freaking Danny . . ." he looked around for a moment just to make sure they were actually alone in that section of the barn before he continued in a lower voice, "freaking Danny's already got his girl talking about what they're gonna name their kids, and I can't even get Nancy Baxter to hang around for me instead of jumping out with somebody else?" Cory didn't usually have a problem with self-confidence, but Danny and his girlfriend had recently gotten serious. He was definitely feeling the pressure of being behind his game.

"That's disturbing. Mostly because Danny should not be talking about kids already." She looked cross as she looked back at Cory, but she knew she shouldn't say much. Sooner rather than later she would be turning twenty-two, which meant Ben would soon be twenty, Cory nineteen and Danny eighteen. No one would bat an eye if Danny got married, and it turned her stomach. Her siblings all seemed so young, even though she knew they weren't, not by any Earth standards. It was commonplace in their life, commonplace on Earth. Start young, grow families fast.

"Forget Nancy Baxter. There are other girls. Prettier girls. Hell, even Larissa is about your age." Larissa also happened to be the girl that Susan wanted Ben to consider as a second wife. Larissa was young, but her personality matched Susan to a T. She was also Liam and Logan's younger sister. "I know it feels like a race. But I'm not married either."

"I know, and I want to personally thank you for not leaving me here to deal with Ben all by myself." He gave her a sarcastic grin, knowing that wasn't her reason for not being married. He wasn't going to bring up that can of worms, though. "It's just different. I don't know. I don't think I've ever actually talked to Larissa outside of schoolwork. But that's not exactly talking either. She seems nice, I guess." It was hard to make any real connections with people when all their schoolwork was done by online correspondence and two weekends a month in each other's physical company at a school four hours away.

"Well, maybe you should." Anna didn't want to interfere with Susan's plans to try and bring Larissa in as a second wife for Ben, but she had more than one brother to worry about. Especially as she considered the acceptance letter still haunting the back of her mind. "Liam is coming over today. Maybe the next time I go visit, you can come with me. Or I can talk to Logan about it. I know she's quiet, but she's incredibly smart and pretty."

Cory scrunched up his face at the mention of Liam. "Yeah, but then Liam would be my brother-in-law. That's . . . blech."

Anna briefly thought about all the times that she had *hoped* Liam would be her brother-in-law. It wasn't much of a secret that she'd had several crushes on Logan throughout the years, but anytime she wasn't seeing someone or she was interested in him, he had been with someone else. When he ended up getting married, she knew it was the universe telling her that she and Logan would never be a thing. "Liam isn't *that* bad. You already have Ben as an actual brother. At least Liam can be funny now and then. And since when does a brother-in-law trump the idea of a pretty girl? What's wrong with you?"

"There's nothing wrong with me. It's just weird." He made a face, but she could tell he was clearly thinking about it. "I guess let me know what Logan says. I'll brush up on my love poetry in between . . . everything else around here."

"Poetry? Why doesn't anyone write *me* poetry?" Anna smiled at Cory and continued milking the cow. "I'll put in a good word for you with Logan."

"Make it a few good words. I need all the help I can get." He finished with the cow he was working on and patted the animal's back a few times as he moved away, heading to the next in line. "I um . . . I heard from Holly last night." Anna didn't even have to turn and look at him to see how red his face got every time he talked about this particular friend. The fact that Holly lived quite literally on the far side of the world hadn't stopped him from developing a ridiculous crush on her by the time he was fourteen, nor had it kept him from staying in touch over the years. The distance also hadn't stopped him from getting mopey a few months earlier when he found out she had a boyfriend. "She and her boyfriend got their acceptance letters for Eleusis. Both of them."

"Oh yeah?" Anna tried to seem as surprised as possible so that she didn't give anything away about her own letter. She definitely wasn't ready for that conversation yet. "I heard that they sent out the letters yesterday. You can't be too mad at her for it, though. You didn't want to apply."

"I still don't." Cory didn't sound completely convinced of his own opinion, and he must have taken it out on the cow, since he had to stop and calm the animal before he continued. "She said they have to go to space for like, a year. And that's before they even launch. And then after that, who knows what's gonna happen."

"I don't think it sounds terrible." She admitted softly, but loud enough for him to hear. "I mean, these people are going to lead the way to Eleusis. For the rest of the world. She could have a life longer than forty or fifty years on Eleusis."

"Or a life shorter than forty if she never actually gets there." Cory shook his head. "There's no guarantees. I know there aren't any here either, but it's just . . ." he huffed in frustration. "I tried to talk her out of it. She wouldn't listen."

Anna quietly continued milking the cow in front of her, clearly conflicted about what she should say. She didn't like keeping secrets from her family. Secrets about her lovers and sex life, sure, she wasn't going to share those. This was bigger than that. "What did you say to her to try and change her mind?"

Cory gave her a confused look at that question, but Anna was his big sister. She could interrogate him however she wanted. "I asked what her parents would feel like watching her run off to the other end of the galaxy with no guarantees and no idea what she's really in for. I asked her if she really wanted to throw away her life for that. That's what it feels like she's doing."

"What if it isn't throwing away her life? I mean, maybe she feels like it could be important. Maybe she feels like she could make a difference?" She patted the side of the cow in front of her, then closed her eyes for a minute. "I'm sorry. I know you have feelings for her."

"I do. But it's been impossible since I started talking to her. I always knew that." He tried to shrug off the thought, but it wasn't going to leave. "And if anybody can make a difference, it's her. She's probably the smartest person I've ever met. No offense."

"No one would say that I'm the smartest person they've ever met. That's for damn sure." She eventually got up from her stool and picked up the bucket of milk she collected. "I'm sorry you don't get your dream girl, and that she's leaving for Eleusis with someone else. But I hope it will work out with Larissa. Even if she's not your dream."

"I'm realistic enough to have flexible dreams." He grinned over at her and took the pail from her to combine them into one for processing. "I'll take care of this. Ben and Danny could probably use your help out on irrigation. Tell Danny he still owes me for the other week. Which makes it his turn to muck out after the horses." He added with a smug smile of satisfaction.

"I'll tell him." She smiled at Cory and gave him a quick hug, grateful he wasn't quick-tempered like Ben. Cory was going to be a good husband and father. Ben was already those things, but he always looked pissed about life.

Anna walked out of the barn only to see Ben in the distance standing next to a truck that wasn't one of theirs. The truck belonged to the Bickford farm and Ben was talking to Liam, who clearly hadn't wasted any time getting down to their farm. Anna made her way toward them, crossing her arms against the morning breeze when she got close. "Hey, Liam. You're out early. I didn't know you could be anywhere by sunrise."

"I can be all kinds of places before sunrise." Liam promised with a wicked grin. Pleasant a day as it was, he hadn't bothered with anything resembling a shirt, and his hair hung in shaggy waves around his clean-shaven face. Liam and Logan were identical twins, and it was incredible how much he could look like and yet *be* absolutely nothing like Logan at the same time. For all they shared in DNA, they shared almost nothing in temperament. "And yes, that's a promise. Ow!"

"That's my sister you're talking to, asshole." Ben pulled his hand back from the punch he'd given Liam's arm, but he was smiling anyway. "Behave. You've got bimbos aplenty already without bothering decent women. Knock it off."

"I'm going to mark this day as a triumph. My brother called me a decent woman." Anna grinned, since she was grateful for the punch on her behalf. "Liam, you are not even a little bit tempting, so save it for your women. My legs will never open for you."

"I'm heartbroken. Really." He just rolled his eyes at her with another grin. He'd known Anna just as long as his brother had, and in all that time, they had never been what either of them would call friends, but he didn't have any reason to dislike her either. He was closer with Ben, and she was just too easy to mess with.

He nodded to the back of the truck, which was loaded with half a dozen massive water tanks. "I meant to bring these back a month ago, but I just kept getting sidetracked. Your dad said he wanted them hooked up on the south reservoir. Once we're done with that, I wanted to see if you'd be willing to be borrowed for a few days. Logan's marching out the harvesters and could use your help. I just build the things, I could never drive them worth a damn."

Anna consented with a nod. She knew their own lands had plenty that needed tending, but there were more members of the Prince family than there were of the Bickfords. Logan's parents were both gone already, which left Logan, Liam, and Larissa running the whole farm. Not to mention the Bickford property was several orders of magnitude larger than the Princes'. "Dad wanted to see if we could use the machines as well, so maybe once we get your farm done, Logan can bring them over here?"

"That's a plan." Liam agreed without hesitation, which meant Logan had already had the idea and told Liam about it before he left to come down to the Prince farm. "If they work half as well as Logan seems to think they will this year, harvest should be done in a couple of days and we'll get this place finished in time to spend the rest of the season partying like we were born to do it."

"Partying. That's all you ever think about." Anna shook her head, but she secretly agreed that she could do with some alcohol and a good time. It would help her forget about the letter and the conflict still brewing in her head. "Can we get to work? You can focus on planning your party later. It's going to take you time to map out how you're going to manage a party with all of your girlfriends."

"Hey, the logistics are tough to keep up with, alright? Show some respect." He pointed a finger in her face, then put the truck in reverse to drop off the water tanks, leaving Ben and Anna to follow.

"He's got three now." Ben said as soon as Liam was out of earshot. "He picked up another one not that long ago. Crazy bastard."

"Three?" Anna's voice cracked incredulously. "What three women would agree to that circus, and how good must he be in bed to convince three women to date him at once?" She shook her head. "I just talked with Cory. I'm going to help with both of your problems and talk with Logan about Larissa for Cory. What do you think?"

"For Cory?" Ben stopped walking for a second and

looked back and forth between her and Liam, who was still maneuvering his truck into the right place. "God, that would be crazy. Two people that quiet? Married to each other? Their entire life would just be one long string of silence."

"It would *not*." She glared at Ben, since she thought that Cory and Larissa would be good together. "Larissa is only quiet until she gets comfortable with someone, then she can talk your ear off. I think they would be good together and good for each other. Better than some Nancy chick who stood him up and some girl across the world who's going to Eleusis and already has a boyfriend."

"So his girl did get accepted." Ben said sadly, shaking his head as he ran a hand back over his hair. The hat he replaced on his head afterward had been beaten up by time and at least three generations of Princes, but at least it kept the sun off him. "That's a shame. I swear Cory's been about ten steps from trying to hop on a plane and fly halfway around the world ever since he met her. She goes upstairs, she'll be a little out of his reach."

Anna felt guilty she hadn't paid close enough attention to know that Cory was *that* into the girl across the world, but she didn't want to admit Ben had been paying closer attention than she had. "That and the boyfriend he said she has. Anyway, Cory doesn't need to go across the world to find someone good for him. He said he tried to talk her out of going."

"Well, yeah, of course he did." Ben said with a laugh, giving her another look as if he was wondering if she was really awake yet or not. He was too perceptive for his own good sometimes, even if he wasn't always aware of what he was seeing. "If he cares about the girl, why would he want her to hightail it off-planet like that?"

"If he really cares about the girl, why wouldn't he consider going with her?" She countered, but not to start a fight, only to try and see what Ben thought about the whole Eleusis issue. "Maybe it's been her dream to go."

"Well, if it was this girl's dream to go up and live her life in a big open sky of icy nothing, I say it's a good thing she and her dreams are on the other side of the world. Might leave Cory heartbroken, but leastways he can find somebody closer to home with dreams worth having." Ben very rarely made eye contact with anyone when he was talking. He instead spent the entire conversation examining the plants growing along the side of the long dirt road that led from the main thoroughfare in the county to their house's front door. The beds to either side were all planted with flowers and herbs their father was teaching Emily and Ginny how to work with. Many of them looked like nothing more than weeds if someone didn't know what they were looking at. Ben clearly knew what he was looking at.

"They're both young still. Cory and his mysterious girl across the world." Anna on the other hand wasn't as young as she used to be, and she still wanted to make a difference. It was the reason why she had applied to the Initiative in the first place. Even if the acceptance had seemed like an illusion at the time. "Anyway. I better get a move on if I'm gonna head to the Bickford farm."

"What do you think he'll say?" Ben asked as he paused with her. Together they stood watching Liam at a distance fighting with the harness he'd used to secure the water tanks. "Logan, I mean. About Larissa and Cory."

Anna knew Logan wouldn't want to even entertain the idea about Larissa with Ben, but she figured he would probably agree that Larissa and Cory would make a good match. It just hadn't been an obvious one, apparently. "I think he'll leave it up to Larissa. If Larissa approves, I think he would agree it would be a good match. Logan's a softie when it comes to his baby sister. He just wants her to be happy and to be with a good man."

"Well, Cory's that. Or he will be, once he gets a little taller." He shrugged it off and turned back toward Liam. "Keep me posted. I'll talk to Dad once he gets back with the girls, let him know what you're working on. I'm sure he won't have a problem with it."

She nodded and started moving away from Ben. "I'll have my communicator with me. Call me if you need anything, or if anything happens." Anna didn't have to say the rest, 'if anything happens with dad'. They knew it was coming. They didn't know when he would take a turn for the worst, or how quickly things would change and the end would come, but they were as prepared for it as they could be. The end could be weeks. Months. Maybe a year or two more. It was never easy to tell. "I'll be home in a couple of days when the Bickford harvest is done."

"I'm sure they'll be uneventful. Unless Danny decides to leave the door unlocked on the chicken yard again." Ben rolled his eyes and waved, then moved quickly to help Liam unload the water tanks. Ben wasn't a particularly large man, and certainly not a match for Liam, but between them they managed the work. Liam's inability to take anything in life seriously had Ben actually smiling before Anna even walked away, which was a rare accomplishment in her perpetually-grumpy brother's life.

The walk to the house allowed her to be alone with her thoughts again. Solitude was turning into a dangerous thing. Not only was she feeling even more conflicted about her acceptance, but she was headed to see Logan, and that always gave her a twisted feeling in the pit of her stomach. Seeing him had never been easy, but *not* seeing him had always been worse.

Anna packed a quick overnight bag (and a few more of Susan's muffins for the road), before she climbed into her truck and checked its charge levels before she put it in gear. She needed to *stop* thinking about what her feelings had been. She needed to *stop* thinking about her own problems finding and holding onto a relationship. She needed to think about Eleusis, and her acceptance to the Initiative. She needed to decide if she was really going to leave her family and set off for a new world.

2

It was over an hour drive from the Prince farm to the Bickford farm, and Anna didn't see a single car on the road the entire way. It was as empty as it was ordinary, and that fact alone was testament to the desolation of the world around her. She drove past long-abandoned houses that had crumpled in on themselves in the centuries since they had last been reliably occupied. Fallen telephone poles and tangled stretches of wire along the side of the road were relics of a utility grid as defunct as the communities that had once used them.

There was a small cluster of homes between her family's farm and the Bickford estate that had once been a much larger town. Half a dozen houses, two shops, and one tiny hotel were still occupied. The rest had been bulldozed into piles of rubble long since and allowed to go to seed, though the bones of long-empty streets still remained.

Anna tried to keep herself occupied by looking for radio stations worth her attention, but she didn't find much by the time she actually arrived at the Bickford farm. The quiet and the empty road didn't usually bother her, but when she had so much weighing on her mind and nothing to distract her from it, it left her a bundle of nerves. The attempted optimism of news radio shows from one coast of North America to the other didn't help.

Once Anna arrived at the Bickford farm, she jumped out of her truck so fast it almost seemed like something was chasing after her. It was still early in the morning, and even though the sun was up, there was still plenty of day to fill with work, and yet never enough to get things done.

"Logan!" She yelled out as she approached the house. There was no way of knowing where he was, but yelling had always been a good go-to for her, especially when she was nervous.

Using the word 'house' to talk about the Bickford home was like calling Hong Kong a town or the Pacific Ocean a large puddle. Even Logan and his siblings didn't have a clear and confirmed answer as to who had built the monstrosity in the first place. The most popular rumor was that someone in the area had gotten obscenely rich in the years after the Crisis and had built a massive palace for themselves. They then left no family behind to inherit it, leaving Logan's many-many-great-grandparents to snatch it up. There were wings and underground bunkers and entire courtyards that couldn't even be seen from the outside, and that didn't even include the massive hangar a hundred meters away that housed all the estate's vehicles and farm equipment.

It rose in no fewer than five stories for two dozen windows in either direction, and wrapped around itself in twisting, layered branches, always more to discover the moment the eye thought it had taken it all in. The mansion was beautiful, if more than a little on the ostentatious side. It was clear, however, that it wasn't kept up to the level at which it had been designed to be maintained. The paint on the exterior was dull and cracked in many places. The flower beds leading up to the front door were half-full, and far from thriving. All that remained was the sheer size of the place to speak of its intended grandeur.

There was, however, a man and woman who turned around at Anna's shout, both of them hanging from the roof by a cable and harness in order to get to the exterior of the windows on the upper stories. Lenny and his wife tended to do odd jobs for everyone within a few hundred kilometers of the Bickford estate, and it was hardly a surprise to see them washing windows even in the early morning. "Morning, Ms. Prince!" Lenny called down from his harness. "Mr. Bickford's in the hangar, been there since last night."

Anna approached Lenny and Karen so she didn't have to yell, but she obviously didn't intend to have a long conversation. "He's been in the hangar? He slept there?"

"He set himself up a cot out there when he started working on the equipment a few days ago. Been going at it non-stop since." Lenny looked every bit as worried as he sounded, throwing concerned looks at the hangar as he dangled along the wall. "He's usually got music going, but maybe he's not in the mood today, I don't know. We heard the machines starting up and stopping a while ago, though, so he's awake, whatever he's doing."

"Thanks, Lenny." She was worried, but she gave a reassuring smile before she headed over to the hangar. Anna hesitated before she yanked open one of the giant doors, mostly because she had to prepare herself to see Logan. All she saw inside were the hulking machines waiting to be used for harvesting, and no sign of their owner. "Logan? You in here?"

More silence answered her at first, but then in the stillness of the hangar, she could hear heavy booted footsteps moving across the smooth concrete floor.

"You got here fast."

She could hear Logan's voice before she saw him. He came around the side of a massive harvester, looking every bit the mess Lenny had given her cause to worry about. He wore a pair of jeans that would either need to be washed half a dozen times or just condemned on account of the oil and grease that covered them. The rest of him was no better, but there was no way Anna would ever think it needed condemning. He wasn't wearing a shirt and most of his skin was either singed or covered in the oil and dust from the hangar. He was a mess, but that had very rarely made him less attractive as a specimen of mankind.

He was a good deal taller than she was, and built large, with the kind of imposing physicality that never made it to a movie screen. He had never showcased chiseled abs or rippling muscles, but the sheer strength the man possessed was evident in everything he did. His dark brown hair was a mess that didn't quite reach his ears, and was pushed out of his way just enough to let him work without being bothered by it. His beard had clearly caught its share of sparks in the course of his work, but defined the hard lines of his jaw. His sharp grey eyes were the only part of him unaffected by the occupational hazard of his environment and his work, looking back at her with a hint of a smile on his face. "I didn't expect you until this afternoon, if then. I'm glad you were free."

The fact that Logan was shirtless made her heart beat faster, but she was glad he wouldn't be able to tell. Probably. Even filthy from work, she had to go back to practicing the same self-control she'd been building up all her life where he was concerned. Look, don't touch. She was there to work. "It was either hightail it out here or attempt to survive helping Liam and Ben with the water tanks. I will always pick spending time with you over that." She smiled at him and looked him up and down, though she was making a show of it and hoping that he wouldn't suspect the thoughts in her head. "No offense, Logan, but you need a really, *really* long shower."

Once, he would have laughed. Once, things would have been easy and simple between them and they could both expect the kind of comfort that came from making fun of each other freely. Instead, Logan just smiled and looked himself over. "Once I'm done out here, believe me, I'll get one." He was working a rag between his hands to scrape off as much of the grease and oil that coated them as possible, but it looked like a losing battle.

He nodded toward the machine he'd clearly been working on before she came in, and started walking back toward it with her. "I came out here at the beginning of the week and found out almost none of the cooling ducts got drained the right way at the end of last year. Seeing as the summer was hot as hell, every damn one of them ruptured, so I've had to replace every single one of them and re-tune the engines. This is the last one, though. It's been a long week."

"You could have called me sooner, you know." She moved just a little bit closer to him, but she wasn't about to hug him or even touch him when he was so filthy. Anna had to wonder if that had been his intention, to make himself repellant to anyone who might want to get close to him. "You don't have to do this kind of stuff alone. You know I'd come out and help you anytime you need me."

"Liam's been out here with me most of the time, but he was the poor bastard who had to make the run to St. Louis to get parts. Plus, I knew things over at your house have been busy with your irrigation going crazy and whatnot." Even the way he stood with both hands braced on one of the machines had him framed in ways that did bad things in the back of Anna's imagination. "I knew you'd be here. You always are."

He sighed as they went to the opened engine of the massive harvester he'd been working on, obviously not looking forward to getting back into the belly of the beast immediately, but there was nothing else for it. "How's everything going for you guys out there? Liam said it looked like things were starting to get locked down, at least."

At least he knew she was dependable, that was something. Dependable until she made a decision about Eleusis, and then . . . Anna felt physical pain at the thought of never seeing Logan again. Maybe it would be a good thing to never see him again. The attraction, the *attachment* to him was only getting worse.

For the first time in their lives, they were single at the same time, even if it wasn't by choice for either of them. Anna had men she hooked up with occasionally, but it wasn't anything serious. As she looked at him in his current state, though, she wondered if he would ever move on from Melanie, or if he would be . . . broken, for the rest of their short lives. "Oh, um, things are going good. Thanks for asking."

"Glad to hear it." He nodded and started climbing up into the engine, since it was large enough that he had to get his entire body inside to get to where he needed to go. "How about your dad? I haven't seen him in a while."

Anna wasn't sure how he wanted her to help him, so she moved closer to the machine as he climbed up into it. "He's . . . well, he's not getting better, obviously. But he's not getting worse too quickly. Not yet, anyway." She sighed and tried not to pay too much attention to his ass. "Do you need me in there too?"

"Just grab the end of this hose to make sure it doesn't pop off." He struggled with the other end that was further up in the engine. The way he was contorted inside made it obvious just how crazy the last week had been for him, trying to do the same thing on dozens of similar-sized machines. A few patches she could see on his back (when she wasn't staring at his ass) looked almost like skin, but were shaded just a little differently to show a patch of medicinal spray he'd put on himself to help speed healing along. They were big machines with a lot of violent moving parts. 'Safe' wasn't a word that could be applied to many things Logan did. But that was life.

She immediately did as he asked, eager to help, though she felt pathetic just watching a hose. "I'm smaller than you are, you know. It would be easier if I climbed in there instead." It killed her to see how unaffected he was by her, but even when they were younger, she had always felt as though she had been busier looking at him than he had been looking at her. "But I'll stay put if you say so."

He fought with the hoses through a round of grunting and swearing until he finally popped it free, making even more of a mess than had been there before. He fell back against another part of the engine in the process, which just brought about more swearing, since he'd clearly done the same thing more than once in the past week, but he pulled himself back up again quickly. "Yeah, actually, can you see if you can untangle that mess? It always gets hooked and shredded behind the alternator." There wasn't much room left inside the engine frame where he was, but there was a tiny gap between him and the part of the hose that had gotten caught just barely out of his reach.

"Yeah, of course." Anna climbed in quickly and deftly shimmied into the gap. It put her flush against Logan, but she refused to let her brain freak out over it. There was work to do, and it was Logan. Her best friend. Nothing more. No matter what her body was trying to say about it.

He had been panicking at the moment that he asked her for help, but he managed to stabilize himself slightly better once she got into place. That cleared up his thoughts to take more notice of the situation he had gotten himself into. Her brown hair was up in a bun, but the scent of her shampoo was a powerful contrast to the oil and burnt rubber of the rest of the hangar, as was the softness of her t-shirt and jeans sliding into place between him and the rest of the machine. He groaned at the sensation, and immediately hoped she would mistake it as him trying to keep his balance inside the machinery. "You, um, you got the tangle?"

It was so hard to focus, but Anna was doing her best as she wiggled and struggled, since even though she was smaller, it also meant that her arms were shorter. She wanted to die by the time she actually got it untangled, since she had been rubbing against Logan the whole time. "Yeah, I got it. This one goes over . . . here . . . there, that should straighten them back out." The dirt on her clothes was starting to compete with his, but she didn't really care. All she could think about was feeling Logan's body pressed back against her.

"Great, thanks." He let her wiggle out first, which didn't make his situation any easier, then took another moment pretending to work away at another part of the machine before he dropped down next to her and tossed the shredded tubing aside. "Right, well, that takes care of the last of them. Let's do status checks and see about getting this party started."

"I forgot how complicated these machines are. You're too smart for your own good sometimes." She teased as they headed to the control room, since Logan had designed the beasts and built them piece by piece. He then controlled them from a separate place. They were all remotely operated, huge machines that they were. Anna was decent at fixing things, especially when someone gave her instruction, but she was better at handling the controls. "My dad keeps telling Ben we should just pay you to make one for us too."

"No chance. I won't sell." His half-smile returned as he brushed off his hands and headed with her up to the control room that sat above and to the side of the hangar. "Besides, Liam and I picked up a flatbed a couple months ago. Junker that he had to rebuild the engine on. Now I don't have to drive the harvesters down to your place one by one, we can just load them up and tell everybody to get the hell off the road." He pointed to the back of the hangar where a much-abused tractor trailer was parked with a broad flat bed attached to the back of it. "Means we can take half a dozen of these things down to your place once we're done with them here and get your farm swept and cleared in just a couple days. Save you folks having to hire anybody."

"Wow. That would be so great, I, um . . . thanks, Logan." She stared at the truck and avoided looking at him long enough to eventually convince herself to turn around and move closer to him. The control room was cozy enough for her to easily reach out and give him a side-hug, even though he was too distracted to notice her make the initial approach.

He flinched when she touched him, but only because he hadn't been expecting it, and he put an arm around her quickly to hold her. "Yeah, of course. Whole reason I designed these hunks of junk in the first place. Give everybody around here a little more peace of mind and maybe a little more peace and quiet instead of driving themselves crazy trying to get anything done." He didn't let go of the hug immediately, but she did feel him chuckle rather than hear it. "I thought you liked this shirt?" He plucked at the back of it as he let go of it, since it had clearly seen better days after her assistance in the engine.

"It's already dirty now. It won't hurt to get a little more of your dirt and grease on it." She actually looked up at him and smiled, but she knew it was a mistake immediately. She was so close. Anna glanced at his lips for just a moment, and it was long enough. Long enough to bring all sorts of fantasies to mind that she had spent years trying to banish.

Logan's smile got a little wider than it had been since she arrived, and he moved around her to get one of the stations up and running, dancing past her in the tight confines of the control room. It was built for one person to use in operating all the machinery inside and just barely outside the hangar. Maneuvering past her involved a lot of contact transferral of the dust and oil covering him, and did nothing to silence the thoughts she'd been trying not to have.

He had to clear his throat again as he brushed past her in exactly the wrong way, and he quickly turned away to face the panel closest to him. "I've, um, got one through twenty-three going, but I need to check through their scans. Can you run startup tests on the rest?"

"Sure." Anna did her best to keep distance between them as she worked, mostly because she was going crazy every time they brushed against each other. Anna took a minute to reacquaint herself with the system to run the tests, since Logan had shown her how to use the beasts as soon as he had finished building them. She caught on pretty easily with machines anyway. "They look pretty good . . . only one that isn't responding."

He stepped over to take a look at the one she was talking about, and growled a little. "I just fixed that piece of . . . oh well. I'll go take another look once we get the rest of them out on trial runs in the near field." He had to get up close against her back to take a look over the harvester's internal scans, and he ran his fingers just above the screen to take in everything that needed to be addressed. "Always something broken in the world, I guess. Some places more than others. One out of thirty-four ain't bad."

"No, I'd say that's pretty damn good." Anna unconsciously pressed her backside into him and barely stopped herself before a groan could escape her lips. "What, um, what else do you need me to do?"

Logan didn't answer immediately, and pretended to be engrossed in the technical specs on the screen in front of him. Oh, there were a lot of reasons he had kept himself away from people for the past year. Anna in particular. It was just too easy to be around her, and too difficult at the same time. "I um, I'm gonna go back down and take care of our non-responsive friend. Power that down for the time being so it doesn't start while I'm wrapped up in it. If you can start mapping trial runs for all of them just to make sure all the moving parts still move right, we can get them going. Then we can get inside and get cleaned up. Nothing else should really need engine grease once they're all moving."

"Alright." Anna responded softly as he moved to get away from her like she was on fire. She supposed she deserved it, since she was getting all bothered by his presence. Clearly he must have realized it. Anna didn't even look away from the screens as he exited the control room, but once he was gone, she ran her hands over her face, dirty as they were.

What was she doing?

She wiped her face off with the bottom of her shirt and went back to doing as Logan had instructed. Apparently her sticking around the Bickford estate until the harvest was completed was going to make for a long few days.

Repairs and routing the harvesters took most of the morning, Logan did most of the work on the ground while Anna kept an eye on things from the control room. Eventually all of them were up and running and headed to work on the closest field as a trial run for the rest of the harvest. It left Logan waiting for Anna at the bottom of the steps leading up to the control room. He didn't look any dirtier than he had been when they got started, but it would have been hard for him to get much worse without actively trying. "What I should really do is just let you run this place. You handle them better than I do, and I designed the damn things."

Anna laughed as she climbed down, and she hopped down to the ground without his help. She never was the type to ask for help, even when she probably should. "Well, you're a man and you designed them, so it makes sense that a woman can handle them. What man do you know that doesn't like a woman all up in his controls?" She smirked and shook her head. "I hear your brother now has three."

He rolled his eyes so violently his head rolled with them, then started walking next to her toward the house. "Yeah, he picked up a strawberry blonde a while back. Brianne. Nice girl, pretty freaky, according to him, which is a change of pace from the two he's already got hanging around. Crazy idiot."

"Freaky, huh? I guess your brother likes all the flavors he can get." She shook her head and kept walking, though she really couldn't look at Logan and even briefly talk about sex. "I'm surprised that he can convince three girls to stick around. Your brother must really know what he's doing in bed."

"Well, Larissa and I did finally exile him to the north wing of the house. It's nothing a few soundproof doors couldn't fix." Logan looked over at her with a smile, though it was followed by falling back half a step so he could look her up and down without her knowing. "I just hope he doesn't whip any of them into the kind of frenzy where they're really gonna come and kill him for stringing them along like this. I know I used to joke about that as a possibility, but it feels more real every freaking year."

"Well, I know Margo pretty well, and I started to get to know Rachel at the last get-together in town. They don't seem the type to actually want to hurt him." She looked down at her dirty hands, and at the mention of Larissa she felt as though she needed to talk about Larissa and Cory. Especially because she didn't know what kind of chance she would have if she was going to go for the Eleusis project. "Since you mentioned Larissa, I have something to ask, actually."

"What, to borrow some of her clothes for the next couple days? I figured that went without saying." He looked her over again with some of her playful best friend behind the smile, for a change.

Anna looked down at her clothes again and laughed. "No, I came somewhat prepared with a few changes of clothes. But I wanted to talk about something else, actually. I was talking with Cory this morning and I actually thought it might be a good idea if Cory and Larissa . . . get to know each other."

That made Logan miss a step, but he recovered fairly quickly, looking her in the eye just to make sure she was being serious. "Cory? Last time Liam talked to me about it, it sounded like Ben was the one who was interested." In the majority of cases, whether Ben or Cory was interested wouldn't have mattered, only what Larissa was interested in. Logan still had his sister's desires as the top of his priorities. There were broken bones and rearranged faces scattered across the district as proof of how protective an older brother he was, all of them belonging to men who had decided their interest in Larissa was more important than her interest in them. "Whose idea is that? Yours, your dad's, or Cory's?"

"Mine. And for the record, Ben isn't actually interested

in her. Susan thinks he needs a second wife and that Larissa would be a good fit for our family. While I agree Larissa would be a good fit for our family, she wouldn't be happy with Ben. Ben is moody as fuck. He wouldn't ever hurt her or anything, but I don't think he would make her happy. He loves Susan. Cory, though, I think Cory and Larissa would be good together. He's sweet, and he would be sweet to her."

She finally looked over at Logan, since she couldn't believe she was trying to get Cory with a Bickford when she had wanted one nearly all her life. "I hate to take her away from you and Liam, but I would also hate it if someone else snatched up your sister. Cory doesn't need to be hung up on some girl across the world bound for Eleusis. He needs someone like Larissa."

She knew him well enough to read every thought he had in the smallest gestures and expressions. Acknowledgment, consideration, pros, cons, anxiety over the choice itself, resolution to make it anyway. "He seems like a good kid, from the little I've ever seen of him. And if you think the two of them would be good together, I trust your judgment. I'll talk to Larissa and see what she thinks about it. But I'm on your side, I don't like the idea of her with Ben. I like him just fine, just not for my sister."

"They would both be happier *not* together. Susan will forgive me." She smiled at Logan again, then sighed. "Never thought Cory would beat me to it." She mumbled, her eyes stubbornly forward.

Logan couldn't bring himself to smile at that, and stayed quiet as they walked. "I assume Jamie hasn't exactly been rushing to get down on one knee? Or is that not really happening anymore?" It had been months since he had last actually inquired about her love life, and a lot longer between the last time and the time before that. Thoughts of Anna with anyone else had never been welcome in Logan's brain.

"I could never marry Jamie." She shook her head quickly

to dismiss the idea. "He's good looking. That's about all he has going for him as far as I'm concerned. I'm sure he's chasing all sorts of tail, and I haven't seen him in over a month." Jamie wouldn't matter anyway, if she was going to Eleusis. "I've been thinking a lot about what else I might have to offer the world if not babies. I don't have much of a purpose here. Babysitter, maybe."

"You're good for a whole lot more than just babysitting kids." Logan replied with a glare as they finally reached the house. "Everything looks great, guys!" He called up to Lenny and Karen. "Pretty sure those windows haven't been cleaned since the last time you were here."

"I know they haven't." Lenny called back with a smile. "You look like shit, by the way. In the fight between you and the machine, looks like the machine kicked your ass."

"Yeah it did." Logan agreed with a chuckle and a wave, not missing a beat. "Don't stay out too much longer, Larissa's gonna have lunch set up here in a little while, I'm sure." He opened the front door to the house for Anna when they got there, and sighed when it closed behind them like a bank vault door, every bit as huge and every bit as secure, thanks to the house's paranoid builders.

"What are you thinking about, then?" He finally looked back at her, obvious concern on his face. "Head out to the city somewhere? St. Louis? Try your luck out in the Rockies district?"

Even Anna's shrug lacked the necessary energy for real uncertainty, since she didn't have anything else on her mind other than Eleusis. "Who knows, maybe I should try to go to space or something."

For the first time that day, her mention of space wasn't met with immediate amusement or scorn. The look in Logan's eyes was deeply thoughtful as he looked back in hers, and she could see wheels turning in the storm of his irises.

"You think so?" It was a good thing he had lived in his house his entire life and didn't need to look where he was going to navigate. He moved around to one side of the fountain in the grand entry hall that they had never once activated, and headed down a broad hallway toward the part of the house he and his siblings actually occupied, all without looking away from her. "What would you do up in orbit, do you think?"

Anna shrugged again. "I heard they need people who know how to farm, and I'm pretty good with learning how to use machines. I think I could be handy up there with those soft Orbitals. I don't know. Working toward Eleusis sounds like a worthy cause. At least for someone like me who isn't doing shit for the benefit of Earth."

"You don't have to be a saint ending the world's problems to be doing good in the world." He bumped into her side as he said so, just to shove her briefly off-balance. "Eleusis seems like a dream to me. I want it to be true. I want it to be real. Or just possible. Possible would be enough."

"I want it to be real too." She didn't bump into his side in return or seem at all playful, since Eleusis weighed so heavily on her mind. "Everyone else seems to think it's a cruel joke waiting to happen, but I . . . I don't know. I don't think it would be so terrible to investigate my options. My family doesn't need me as much as they think they do, and there's nothing else tying me here."

"I don't think it's a joke." His voice almost sounded sad, for some reason. "I think if somebody wants to go to space, go to the city, go to the bottom of the ocean, for all I care, then they should do it. If Eleusis works out . . ." he hesitated, giving a short, humorless laugh, "*if* it's real, and that's a big if, then it would be worth any sacrifice."

"So you think I should go?" Anna actually stopped walking, looking over at him and adding hastily, "I mean, do you think I should apply?"

They had finally gotten all the way down the main hall of the wing containing his family's main rooms, passing a spacious kitchen that actually looked used, as opposed to the other three they had passed along the way. There was a wide lounge with one wall devoted to entertainment projection, comfortable couches, and papers scattered over the available table space. Logan paused at a smaller hall that led away from the lounge toward the bedrooms, looking back at her with an eyebrow raised and his voice lowered, in case Larissa was around.

"I think, if you're asking me, it sounds like you've already asked everybody else. I also think if you're asking me, you've already applied." Most people would have thought he looked angry as he said so, but Anna knew Logan too well to make that kind of assumption based on the fact that he wasn't smiling. "And my next guess would be that you've already gotten accepted. Otherwise you wouldn't be asking at all."

Anna didn't respond immediately, which she knew was giving it away before she was ready to talk about it. She wasn't going to lie to Logan, but at least she knew he wouldn't tell anyone if she asked him to keep it quiet. "I applied . . . more than a year ago, and I never thought they would accept me. I felt like I needed to get away from here, and it sounded like a good cause to work toward. I didn't tell anyone, and I still haven't. No one else."

The storm in his eyes was quiet for once as he turned and started toward his room, beckoning her to come with him without saying anything else.

It was hardly the first time she'd ever been in his room, but it was the first time she'd seen it in a long time. It was cleaner than she remembered, which was always a bad sign. It meant he was keeping himself busy on purpose.

The wall across from his king-size bed was kept blank for projection, brightening as Logan went to the terminal by the bed. It only took a few taps to fill the blank wall with words. Familiar words.

Logan Bickford,
We are pleased to inform you that your application to join the

Eleusis Initiative has been accepted.

Attached, you will find introductory documents regarding the expected timeline and initiatory procedures of the project to which you have applied. It is expected that the contents of these documents will remain confidential, as they are intended only for Eleusis Initiative personnel.

You will also find contact information for your local recruitment officer, whom we ask you to contact within two weeks of receipt of this confirmation, to claim your offered place in the Initiative. During this contact, you will receive further information about your role in this great endeavor.

From all those at the Eleusis Initiative and the Governing Board of the Orbital Consortium, we thank you, both for your willingness to participate in this Initiative and all that you will do for the human race. We hope to see you soon.

With Sincerest Gratitude,

Hugo Vance, Initiative Director

Anna had to read over the letter twice just to believe that she was looking at something real, since she wasn't entirely convinced that even her own letter was real. After the second read-through, she met Logan's eyes. "You applied?"

His voice was still low when he spoke, and he took every excuse not to look her in the eye, instead focusing on shutting off the screen and closing up the computer again. "After Mel . . ." He had never said out loud that she died, and certainly not that she had killed herself. For Logan, it was only after her, as if she was a movie or an event that had ended. It was easier to think about her that way.

"You already know I ran off for a month. When I came back, getting back into anything here just seemed . . . wrong, for a while. So I applied the day before they stopped taking applications. I figured if I could just go through the motions until I got accepted, maybe I could go upstairs and be useful as a pair of hands repairing whatever ends up getting broken. Things always do. I never expected them to be dumb enough to think I'd actually be worth having along."

Although she knew he certainly hadn't applied to hurt anyone, Anna still felt a knife twist in her chest, thinking he would just leave them all behind, even if she understood why. At least in her case, she had applied because she wanted to be working toward something instead of running away from everything. Still, she had considered at the time that it would be nice to run away from seeing Logan with his wife all the time. "So have you decided, then?"

"No, I've got no idea." He finally looked back up at her when she asked that question. "I really didn't expect to get in. Certainly didn't expect to know anybody else who made it. They said they were only taking two thousand people. Worldwide."

"I know." She said softly, but she hadn't expected to be accepted either. At least from her acceptance, she was assured that she was actually fertile, since she had started to wonder after so many years childless. Birth control was illegal on Earth, so Anna was amazed that some of her ill-timed hookups hadn't resulted in anything. The Initiative wouldn't have accepted her if she wasn't capable of helping further a colony.

"I guess you'll have to let me know what you decide." It was the only thing she could say without giving her opinion either way. Logan's future was his to decide, and she didn't have any say in the matter. As his best friend, it was simply her job to be supportive, no matter what.

"Well, what I'm deciding right now is that I need a shower. That's about as far into my future as I can see." He gave her a weak smile, and stepped closer, reaching out to tug at the front of her shirt where she'd gotten it dirty by being around him. "I don't know if Larissa's in her room or not, but even if she's not, I'm sure she won't care if you go use her shower. We can run these through the machine a few times and have them as good as new by tomorrow."

"Thanks." Anna replied without looking at him, but she put her hand on top of his as he tugged at her shirt. Only when she was actually touching him did she look up, but she was holding her breath, thinking about a thousand scenarios at once that would never happen. Eventually she let go of the breath to respond. "I'll go find something to wear and use the shower for a quick rinse."

"Sounds good." He actually tightened his grip on her shirt for a moment rather than letting her go, but he forced himself to uncurl his fingers slowly. Would it be so disastrous to say what he was thinking? Ask her if she would rather share his shower than go find her own? Ask her whether she ever got tired of putting on clothes and would rather just walk around naked all the time instead? Would it be . . .

Yes, it would be, the voice of reason in his head replied. It *would* be disastrous. It would eventually mean the end of Anna, as his best friend or anything else. He didn't deserve to have that with her. Didn't even deserve to have her as his friend after everything that had happened, but they had been friends long before either of them had ever been mature enough to question what they did or didn't deserve in the world. Even entertaining the possibility of it wasn't worth the risk. Not if Anna was the risk.

"I'll see you in a bit, then. Um, if you see Larissa, tell her I promised Lenny and Karen lunch. I'm sure she's already got something going, but just so she knows."

Anna's chest tightened in pain as he let her shirt go and all she could do was nod as she backed away from him. She didn't know what to think anymore about Eleusis. She wouldn't be leaving everything behind if Logan went.

She did know one thing.

She couldn't watch him with someone else, and eventually he would find someone. He was gorgeous and caring. He would find someone again. Anna turned away sharply so he wouldn't see her eyes burning with tears as she started to walk away. "I'll meet you downstairs in a bit."

He couldn't stop himself from watching her before he turned to go to his own shower. It felt good to be out of his clothes, mostly because it allowed him to be free of the confines of his pants. Being around Anna too long and having her so close had made that freedom an urgent need that wasn't going away anytime soon. Being under the hot water felt even better, and he stood there a long time just letting it heat and soak away all the grime and grease of the preceding week.

Thoughts of Anna never left his mind. She was somewhere else in the house, possibly naked already herself, standing under her own stream of hot water . . .

He groaned at that thought, half in pleasure, half in frustration at himself. He couldn't and wouldn't stop himself from imagining what she would feel like in that shower, pressed between him and the wall, but he hated himself for it, having her so close but still unwilling to do anything about it. Still, his self-hatred didn't stop him from getting lost in the thought. It never had when it came to Anna.

Standing outside the shower afterward, Logan let himself air-dry in front of the open window of his bathroom. It was every bit as oversized and opulent as the rest of the house, letting in sunlight and an afternoon breeze that whipped around him and set the towels fluttering on their racks. If Anna went along to the Eleusis Initiative, would he still go? Would he want to go even more? That was a stupid question, of course he would want to go, even if it was just to be around Anna. He'd gladly go to the other end of the universe for that, even if he wouldn't go down the hall and tell her what was really on his mind.

He looked up at the sky just in time to see one of the massive orbital Stations coming into view, crossing his window along the longest arc of the sky overhead. It was low enough in orbit that he could make out the arms that gave the place its distinctive shape. He could even count how many there were.

Eight arms. That meant it had to be one of the lower-numbered Stations. The most massive of them, the earliest developed and the longest spinning. That much he knew from his history classes. Who was up there, looking down at him? Anyone? Did people in orbit even look down at the world they had come from? The world their grandparents and great-grandparents had come from? How much did they think about Earth? About people like him or Anna?

He had no way of knowing.

Would he be able to make a difference on Eleusis? Would his life have more meaning there? Or would his presence alone be enough to drive more people around him to end their lives?

He was toxic. Everything he touched, everything he tried to do, ended up hurting people. Eleusis had to be different. It . . . it had to be.

3

There was never a day when the halls of her hospital were quiet, and Mercury preferred it that way. Modern medicine or not, people still got sick. People still died and people were still born, every single day.

Mercury had just stepped out of an intense labor that ended with the birth of twin boys, both huge and healthy. She washed up and paused to fix her hair, since a few strands had pulled free of her efficient tie. She pulled it all back again into a long, brilliantly red ponytail before she hurried toward a nearby nurse's station.

Before she asked the question she wanted to ask, she updated the file on her most recent patients, then looked over at one of her fellow doctors and friends. Greg worked in the neonatal intensive care unit, but by the look of the coffee in his hand, she figured he must be between patients.

"So? Any news?" She'd been on pins and needles all night during her shift, but she'd had no updates on her communicator. Eventually she had given up even checking.

Greg gave her an amused smile as he shook his head. "Not for you or the other twenty people who've asked me in the past half hour. Why am I the repository of all information on this subject, exactly?" He glanced down at his coffee, but was also surreptitiously checking the communicator he held in his other hand.

"You're the senior doctor on call at the moment. I just assumed that if anyone would get information first, it would be you." It almost seemed silly to attach the word 'senior' to someone like Greg, since he was only a little older than she was, and she was twenty-three. Just in the last year, she had finished her residency and became a practicing obstetrician and gynecologist. Half her days were spent in an office examining and the other half were running around the hospital for various purposes. Mostly delivering babies. "Am I wrong to assume that you would know first?"

"Nope, not wrong." He replied without even looking back at her, still refreshing something on his communicator. "A little birdie *may* have told me that they're sending out the letters tonight. May have. I'll deny it under interrogation."

"Tonight?" Mercury deflated. She had to be patient a little longer. "At least I will find out while my parents are still here." Mercury moved toward a snack dispenser in the wall behind the nurse's station. When it scanned her hand, it selected a healthy snack within her remaining calorie allotment for the day. Out popped a sliced apple and a bottle of water. "I'm supposed to meet a potential match tomorrow. If I don't cancel it tonight."

"Oh, wow, I didn't realize you had one lined up already." He finished the rest of his coffee slowly. He didn't bother to try and hide the slight look of disappointment on his face, but he knew she had submitted her name to be matched. It wasn't like it was out of nowhere. "How does his profile look?"

"He matches almost all my requirements, and even several areas where I didn't think I would find a match. He's significantly taller than I am, which isn't always easy to find." For a woman, Mercury was tall, and she had a full figure to go with it while still maintaining a healthy weight to height ratio. She knew she had qualities that made her physically attractive, curves in pleasing proportions, or so she'd been told, but she wasn't particular about an attractive match. She wanted someone who matched her intellectually and someone who was loyal and resourceful. Someone who would challenge her mind more than anything.

"He's a high ranked pilot, top of his class. I just don't know if I want to go through with this whole matching process. I don't really have much time, and if I get accepted to Eleusis, I would only be able to pursue this man if he is accepted also." Almost everyone she knew had applied. It had never once occurred to her that her match might not have. Everyone wanted to go to Eleusis. "My parents are sickeningly cute together and they were matched, but I don't know if I'm ready for it."

Greg himself was just barely Mercury's height, so long as she wasn't wearing heels of any kind, so he understood just how difficult it would be for her to find a man taller than she was. Especially one *significantly* taller, as she'd described. "Your parents are pretty cute. Even if the whole secretary thing takes a little getting used to." He chuckled against the rim of his coffee cup. "I'm sure the system took Eleusis acceptance into account when making its decision on him for you. I doubt it would set up a match just to have to completely recalculate the thing later."

"That's true. That would be illogical and a waste of everyone's time." She agreed as she munched on a piece of apple. Mercury looked over at Greg, staying quiet a moment as she considered what to say next. "Do you think I should meet him?" She valued Greg's opinion and friendship, even though she was somewhat aware he liked her more than she liked him. She was more about practicality and sensibility, and he liked her for more than that.

The only time they had engaged in sexual behavior had been to satisfy a curiosity of Mercury's, though she knew that hadn't been the reason for him. In the end, though, he was still her friend and she wanted to know what he thought.

"I . . . am skeptical." He said with a laugh. He motioned down the hall to where he was going to be heading for surgery soon, so that she could walk with him. "I've never trusted the match programs, but like you said, your parents are happy and I know plenty of other couples who are too. I'm too much of a romantic for my opinion on the subject to be entirely clinical." He bumped into her shoulder as they walked, but he doubted it would get much of a reaction from her. Nothing else he'd ever tried ever achieved a desired reaction. The woman's focus was a thing of legend.

"But, I will say he sounds like a dream come true for you. Especially with the height. I know maybe two men taller than you. Total. And one of those . . . would not be interested." He shook his head and tossed the empty coffee cup into a nearby chute for reclamation and processing. "I do think, no matter what, that you should make the time for it. Whether it's the guy you're matched with or anyone else, you need to make the time for somebody. You deserve that. So if you trust the system, yeah, sure, give the guy a shot. Nothing to lose, as they say."

"Statistically there are definitely more than two men I could match with and who would also satisfy the height requirement." She replied to that first, since she wasn't typically a romantic and she knew the match program was a very fine-tuned algorithm that had enough data to produce more success than failure. "As for *needing* to make the time for someone, I don't feel as though I need to. Biologically, I have plenty of time to start a family without any fertility concerns. Mostly it comes down to the fact that my parents harassed me enough for me to fill out the necessary information and to have my file uploaded into the program. Though it would be nice to have someone to talk to and spend time with when I go home after my shifts."

"It's not just about having somebody else to take up space." He knew better than to try and convince her of anything like the divinity of being in love or the greater metaphysics of the universal human need for it. "It's about sharing your life with somebody. Sharing somebody else's life with them. Being there for them when things go wrong, when they go right . . . office parties and promo celebrations can only go so far."

"I know it doesn't seem like it, but I want that too. I want to be important to someone and I want someone to be important to me. I hope to be that person for someone else, but I'm not going to tie my thoughts and desires up with that. That might be difficult to find and maintain." She looked over at Greg again. "Maybe my feelings will change if I meet the right match. That's part of the point of the program, right? I would never meet a pilot otherwise."

He doubted she would see the flinch that crossed his face, but that didn't mean it wasn't there. It stung more than a little to hear her talk about just needing to meet the 'right one' when he had been trying for a long time to *be* the right one for her. "That's true, I can't think of any reason why you would, really. And I hope that's what happens."

It wasn't until after her entire explanation and his flinch that she realized she had hurt him. "I'm sorry, I didn't mean to hurt your feelings." She hesitantly reached out to touch his arm in a pathetic attempt at reassurance. "This is why my parents pushed for me to enter the matching program. I don't know what to look for or what to do when it comes to a partner. It's not something I understand easily."

"I know that." He said as gently as he could, still giving her a quiet smile. "What I do hope you understand is that I want you to be happy. And it sounds like this is a good chance for that. That's important to me."

"Thank you." Mercury smiled and patted his arm gently, then stepped away from him slowly. "I saw you have a surgery. I hope it goes well."

"So do I." He reached out to take her arm as well, then stepped in and gave her a kiss on the cheek. Yes, they were on shift at work, but there was no one else in the hallway, and even if there had been, he wouldn't have cared. "Keep me posted about your match. I don't think we're on shift together again until Friday. Unless you end up taking the next two weeks off for Introduction, of course." He did his best to make his smile playful when it came to that possibility, but it clearly wasn't one he really wanted to imagine.

"I don't think that's likely, I'll be surprised if the first meeting goes without some kind of hitch." Mercury gave him a small smile, but she didn't kiss him back. She wasn't interested in him that way, and she didn't want to give him the idea that she might be. That would be unkind of her and she didn't want to do that to a friend. She did promise to keep him updated, though. "Let me know what you hear tonight. I hope both of us are accepted."

It was several more hours before Mercury's shift was over, leaving her exhausted, but she was glad to be able to go home and see her parents for one more night before they returned to their station. She enjoyed having them with her for a visit and she missed them often. She could already smell her mother's cooking as the door to her unit opened.

"Good evening, Doctor." Her father said from the side of her living room. He had commandeered one corner of the room the week before when he arrived and turned it into a makeshift office for himself while he was away from Station Six. He still had a job to do, after all. "How's the saving-lives business?"

"You mean the life-making business?" She teased, since she spent more of her time with expectant mothers than patching people up. "It was a busy day. Lots of crying babies." She went to get a glass of water (since she wasn't allowed any other beverage according to her daily food log), then sat down at the table with her communicator. "Word is that the Eleusis notices are going out tonight."

"You have good sources." He said with a smirk that some had told Mercury all her life she had inherited. Marcus Finnegan was an intimidating man, government official as he was, standing just slightly taller than his one and only child. His hair had once been close to the same red as hers, but had faded over time, and had turned more blond than red, well on its way to white. A lifetime of public service tended to have that effect on people, he was fond of saying.

His Irish accent was thicker than her own, but he had also lived on Six nearly all the sixty-odd years of his life, whereas Mercury had left for Station Seven when she had been accepted into medical training at age fifteen. "Should be heading out any minute now, I'd expect. I tried to requisition some popcorn for the show, but my privileges don't work here the way they do back home."

She pouted a little, since she would have enjoyed some popcorn, but she was used to her restrictive diet. Doctors were expected to maintain the best health possible and so her health was heavily monitored daily. "I wish I could at least order a piece of cake or something. If I get accepted. Or even if I don't, I suppose. I haven't had any sweets in months." She checked her communicator again, but she still didn't see any new messages from the Initiative. "I think I'm going to meet my match tomorrow." She said to distract herself while she waited. "I'll fly out in the morning."

Her father's eyebrows went sky-high at that, and he shared a quick look with her mother before he gave a quick laugh. "Has anyone ever told you that you're a master of subject changes?" He was smiling as he shook his head at her, putting away some of the screens he used to monitor business back on Six. "I thought you were on the fence about it. What changed your mind?"

"I'm trying to distract myself from my anxiety about hearing from the Initiative, so I changed the subject." She said it as if it was obvious and made perfect sense, but then went on to answer his question. "I *am* on the fence. But I asked Greg what he thought, and he encouraged me to meet this match. I know you both want me to as well. It won't hurt to meet him, and tomorrow is my day off."

"I didn't realize it was that time of year already." Her father replied with a good-natured smile, since teasing his daughter about her intensity only went so far. She had gotten it from somewhere, after all. "It's true, we are excited for you to meet him. Skeptical, but excited. I did some digging of my own once you told us his name. Without divulging anything about what kind of digging or any other details, I'll say that I haven't found anything to put me off my ease. Yet."

"Really? If you haven't found anything, then I'm impressed. Either he's good at hiding things, or he really is just a genuinely good man. Fighter type or not." She drank her water slowly and thanked her mother for the plate of food she had prepared, even if it was only a lightly seasoned chicken breast and steamed vegetables. She had burned most of her calorie allotment on her breakfast, which usually she knew better than to do. Eleusis was making her nervous. "Do you think he will like me? I know I'm strange and a bit off-putting. I didn't even realize that I had offended Greg today until it was too late. I didn't realize he still had feelings for me. I only went on a date with him one time."

The complete lack of surprise on her parents' faces at that announcement was all the confirmation she needed about her own oddness. Even so, her father looked optimistic. "If the match program chose him to be yours, then it knows what he thinks strange looks like and whether he likes it or not. Everything about you and everything about him the program could glean from your calibration sessions will already be factored in. It may end up that you both find each other remarkably strange, and that will be the basis of your relationship. I've heard of worse beginnings. I'm sure he will like you. He went looking for this the same as you did, keep in mind."

Mercury sighed but she nodded, since she knew her father was right. Orion Al-Jabbar hadn't canceled the meeting from his end, and neither should she. "I need to have more optimism going into this initial meeting. You two are happy."

"Very." Her mother added with a smile as she put down a plate in front of her husband. "The program has more successful matches now than it ever has. You will be happy, I am sure of it." She smiled wider as she looked across at her daughter, then she went to grab her plate last. On her way across the small unit, she heard both her husband and daughter's communicators ping at once. "I bet that's . . ."

"It's from them!" Mercury felt adrenaline pump through her body, but her hand remained steady as she held onto her communicator. She slowly exhaled a nervous breath as she set down her utensils, then put both hands on the communicator and opened up the notice.

Mercury Finnegan,
We are so very pleased to inform you that you have been accepted into the Eleusis Initiative. Your skills and high marks as a doctor . .
.

Mercury couldn't breathe as she stared at the screen, then she turned her green eyes to look at her mother and then her father. "I got in. I got in!"

It was a rare moment to see something that could put their stoic daughter off her cool, and both her parents were grinning from ear to ear as she very nearly squealed. Their daughter, the genius wonder-child baby-doctor, squealing at her acceptance letter.

"Of course you did." Her father didn't seem surprised at the acceptance either, but he had been in government for the past twenty years. If he was surprised by something, it meant he wasn't getting enough information from the right people. "They'd be idiots not to come begging for you, and they'll be richer for having you as a part of them."

"This is incredible! They are only taking two thousand people this time, and with all the people that applied . . ." She was still stunned but ecstatic as she read over it again. "I just . . . Eleusis . . . a brand new world . . ." She jumped out of her chair, then rushed over to her father and wrapped her arms tightly around him. "I can't believe it!"

"You deserve it." Marcus hugged his daughter tightly and kissed her cheek before he let her go. "You've worked since you knew how, so that you could be the best. And that's what you are. Stands to reason you'd be going to the best of places, to make it even better. We're proud of you, Mercury."

She did a little jump-hop dance as she moved over to her mother and hugged her as well. "This is incredible." She repeated, as she ran her hands over her face. "Wow. Eleusis." Mercury eventually made it back over to her seat, and she sat down quickly. "I suppose I will have something to discuss with my match tomorrow. This must mean he was accepted also."

Marcus nodded confirmation. "He was. You'd not have been matched if he hadn't. I'm sure he's doing his own happy dance right about now, wherever he is."

"I hope so. I want someone who is as excited about it as I am." Mercury settled enough to cut into her food, but it was obvious by her grin that she was still overflowing with excitement. "Is there more you know that you are keeping from me?"

"Always." His smile had covered up a lot of things in her life, and while she knew it was covering a lot even in that moment, her parents' secrets were one of the great constants of her existence. "Most of them will be more fun for you to figure out than to be told by me." He cut into his own food after pulling his wife in for a kiss to thank her for the meal.

"Oh wait, that's not true. I do know that the Initiative is actually planning on starting with the accepted recruits a little earlier than they originally thought. The earliest estimates I've heard are just a month from now, but nothing that's been confirmed officially. Even so, you may want to plan accordingly."

"A month?" She stabbed her fork into a piece of chicken. "Wow. That's fast. I wasn't expecting that. But if they want to get started that soon, then I will certainly be there. Matched or not."

They ate the rest of their meal in relative silence, each of them pondering the implications of the impending future.

When everyone was nearly finished, Marcus spoke up again, a little more quietly than before.

"Whether it's one month from now or six, there is one thing I want to tell you, about what to do when you go. Not some kind of intelligence I've gathered on it or anything, just . . . some unsolicited advice, if you'd be willing to take it into consideration." Their daughter was very much her own person, and sometimes their advice had been completely rejected, even if that rejection had never been out of spite or some kind of teenage rebellion. That just wasn't their daughter.

"Of course." She gave her father her full attention, since she was always willing to listen, even if she didn't always agree with them. "What advice is it?"

He swallowed the bite he'd taken before he spoke, still obviously weighing exactly what he wanted to say in his mind before he said it. "There are going to be people already appointed by the governing board of the Consortium to make sure things run smoothly in the Initiative. Some of them may be going with you to Eleusis when the time comes, but for the most part, I'm guessing they're going to be administrators who'll stay behind when you leave."

"They're going to have a way of doing things already in mind, probably already laid out in very convincing detail, with structures and hierarchies and all kinds of very official-looking trimming. These people, who aren't ultimately going to be going with you, are going to have their own agenda and they're going to want you to follow it." He knew nothing he was saying would be surprising, but he wasn't finished. "My advice? Don't."

He let that sink in for a moment, since it was, so far as he could remember, the first and only time in her life that he ever suggested Mercury disobey someone in authority. "The people who are *actually* going with you are going to be the ones who are important in determining how things are run. Not the admins here. Don't lose sight of that."

"I'll . . . try to keep that in mind." She replied hesitantly, not because she didn't think what he said was important, but because dealing with life and death often meant it was better to follow rules, protocols, orders. "I'm not usually a rule-breaker. Or a rule-bender. You know me."

"I do know you. Which is why we're having this conversation." He grinned over at her and pushed away his finished plate. "But you're also incredibly perceptive when you're looking for something, and you know how to improvise when things get dicey. I'm telling you this now so you can be on the lookout for things that come from leadership. If they're not going to work for the Initiative, for the people actually going to Eleusis, they should be disregarded, at best. It's going to be your world. Yours and the others who are going with you. No reason to take any baggage along from here you don't have to."

Mercury nodded again, since she agreed with her father's logic and rationality. Sometimes leadership needed to be challenged if it wasn't for the greater good, and Eleusis was a different planet that would be led by different rules. "I hope it won't be too long before you both can come to Eleusis too. I want you there with me."

"Oh, we'll follow eventually. The last we were told, we'll be on the third or fourth wave behind you. So, you know, I expect our house to be fully built, hot tub ready, ocean view, the works."

"I will do my absolute best to make that happen, Dad." She laughed softly and grinned at him. "You deserve nothing but the best."

"So do you, Mercury." Her father said with another smile. He would make sure she had everything the universe could give her. No matter how many strings he had to pull, no matter what favors he had to call in, he would make sure she was taken care of. Always.

* * * * *

Orion loved the burn in his muscles every time the

momentum of the ship shifted. He loved the feeling of the controls under his hands, the way everything moved when he said move.

What he didn't love was when people didn't follow protocols and left him to improvise his way out of a catastrophic collision.

"Fitch, I need the landing cables out, now!" He didn't have half a second to spare, even just to look away from the window at the controls. The massive carrier had disengaged almost right on top of them, and their inertia was going to kill both ships in just a few seconds. Not only that, but from the way the other ship was moving, it was obvious the other pilot had no idea what was going on.

"I've engaged the landing cables, stop yelling at me! You are incredibly bossy." Kameron Fitch didn't like traveling with Orion as his second, mostly because he knew so much and it made her feel like an idiot every time. She really was a good pilot. He was just a better one. They were friends, usually, unless they were in the cockpit together.

"Oh, I'm sorry, did I hurt your feelings? I was trying not to get us killed!" He yelled without looking at her, grabbing the landing cable controls to latch onto the rapidly-approaching ship.

Since he didn't have the momentum to thrust away from it, he grabbed onto the underside of its hull and used the cables to cushion the impact and shove away from the carrier to get clear. He imagined it was a shock to the pilot of the other ship, but he didn't really care about that. He cared about keeping his crew and passengers safe.

The maneuver threw them all around in their restraints, but at the end of it, the transport ship he was piloting pivoted right around the far end of the larger freighter into more or less open space. Enough for him to maneuver safely, at least.

He let out a heavy sigh once it looked like they were clear, and retracted the landing cables so he could get back to the actual docking portion of the Station where they had been about to land. "Anybody from that freighter tries to talk to us, tell 'em where they can shove it. I'll go see the port authority as soon as we get capture. Any casualties?"

"Everybody's fine." Kameron mumbled as she worked through her own portion of the checklist, even after a near-miss. They happened more often than people liked. "You're just wound up because you're going to meet that doctor. Thank god I'm doing a jump right after this to Station Two without you."

"Yeah, well, you would be too." He shot back quickly, working through his own half of the procedures. "If you ever actually decided that being my copilot wasn't your favorite thing in the world anymore and you left me to get matched yourself."

"It's *not* my favorite thing in the world." She said honestly, still flipping switches and recording flight information. "I look like a dumbass next to you. And I know that's why you're barking at me. You think that's how you're gonna look next to this prestigious doctor. I don't know why you're going to meet her if you think you're not gonna be a good match."

Orion glared over at her and finished the last few steps of his checklist to get them on their way toward the unoccupied docking bay they'd been assigned. "You're not a dumbass. I don't have a real high tolerance for dumbasses, and I've tolerated your ass for a long while now. You just hesitate when you shouldn't. Bad habits I'm trying to break you out of."

She wasn't wrong, though, and he didn't bother contradicting her on the rest of what she'd said. He was going to look like an idiot next to the doctor, and he didn't consider himself an unintelligent person. She was just . . . very intimidating. At least her record was.

"When do you actually have to meet her?" Kameron looked up from her computer screen and smirked at him. "What if she's a hideous beast of a woman? That would make me laugh so much."

"Yeah, that's because you're kind of a bitch." He returned the smirk, and shrugged as if to say he wasn't going to apologize for it. Not that she would have expected him to. She knew him better than that. "And I told the system that physical attraction is important to me. Not critical, but important. I doubt it would completely leave me hanging like that. Program set a 'high confidence' label on us. So I'm gonna take this woman's hotness on faith."

"Well, aren't you shallow." Kameron scoffed with her eyes on the controls. As his close friend, though, she already knew physical attractiveness mattered to him. "What if there's this fantastic match out there for you and you're being a dick by thinking with your dick?"

"I am not thinking . . . entirely with my dick." He managed to sound at least half-defensive as he said so, pushing away from the control console to let her run the rest of the docking sequence on her own. She needed the practice. "And don't pretend like you know all my reasons for wanting to get matched. If the doctor and I start getting along and things go well, then she'll be for me and I'll be for her. I'm not gonna make it complicated with soulmates and metaphysical bullshit."

"I don't know if I believe in soulmates, but I believe in falling in love. That's a thing. And it doesn't have to be with someone supermodel gorgeous. I mean, your sister *is* a model. I would think you of all people would want something more substantial than that." Kameron worked quicker the moment he left it up to her to finish. "You didn't say when you were actually going to see her."

"Half past second bell." He said with a nervous sigh he didn't bother hiding. "So, you know, in about forty-five minutes. No big deal."

"Oh. That's soon." She looked up again and laughed a little. "Did you even get a gift or anything?"

"Did I get a gift. You really don't know me." He flipped himself upside down, since there was no up or down to be had at the moment there in the cockpit, working on some of the sensors along the surface above their heads. He wanted to be sure they weren't going to have any more surprises. "I've got a gift and I even remembered to pack along my Class A getup. In about twenty minutes, I'm gonna look so good, even *you* might actually like me."

"Uh huh. *Doubt that.* You know you're not my type." She looked him up and down anyway as she finished up her procedure. "Good luck."

"Not necessary." He grinned at her as he pushed his way out of the cockpit, disengaging his bag from the storage compartment on his way. The crew was busy talking to the passengers and assuring them everything was fine, and Orion knew he should probably step in and do some of the talking himself, as the pilot for the trip. He had more important things to do, though, and talking to nervous passengers wasn't going to help make him any less nervous.

Once the shuttle docking port opened and Orion floated down into the linking corridor, he started getting even more nervous. There were two people with Port Authority insignia on their uniforms coming toward him. He'd never once been actually approached by the PA people before. He thought they just sat in offices and yelled at people they saw getting out of line on their monitors. Seeing them in motion was actually a little eerie. Was Station Nine's security really just that hyped? "Everything in order, officers? I'm not used to you folks making housecalls."

"Everything is just fine, Lieutenant." A severe-looking woman responded, though she barely even looked at him. "That was quite a landing you made." The woman seemed distracted, but she was trying to make small-talk anyway, which meant she was thinking about something else but didn't want to be obvious about it. "I'm impressed."

"Well, that makes two of us. I'm impressed by how outside of protocol the other guy was. It doesn't take much presence of mind to look behind you when you're backing out of the dock. That pilot needs a write-up, whoever they are."

"I'm sure someone is dealing with it." She looked over at her partner and then down at the communicator strapped to her wrist. Clearly she was under a time crunch. "Must get moving. This is a busy port today, so I wouldn't linger too long."

Orion managed to look confused at her comment, but he was accustomed to being hurried along. What he wasn't used to was people looking nervous when they did the hurrying. "Yes, ma'am. I doubt I'll be here more than a couple hours, one way or another." He gave them a brief and informal salute, since he was on their turf, after all, and moved on down the corridor toward the central space of the docks.

Station Nine was a secondary Station, rather than Orion's home back on Three, but the overall fundamentals of the design were similar. The secondary Stations had six arms instead of eight, but they were still fixed to a central hub that housed the docks and the main storage facilities for the Station, where the rotation caused the lowest artificial gravity. Orion emerged from the access corridor into the main vault of the docks, and smiled at just how familiar the place was. Some things were always the same, no matter where he went in orbit. There would always be someone having an argument over timetables, always a pack of regulatory officials standing off to one side doing their best to look menacing while doing as little as possible. Most importantly, there was always a bar, which was what he needed at the moment.

The open space of the Station's heart was crisscrossed by support beams and intricately laced guide columns, to make movement in near-zero gravity a little less problematic. He found one such beam and pulled himself along until he got close to the decorated hole in the ceiling/wall/floor that served as the bar. He latched his bag onto his back as he pulled himself up/down/over to the rim of it, and twisted himself around to orient in the same direction as the woman on the other side of the opening.

"Good morning, beautiful." He gave the woman one of his more charming smiles as he looked around, still taking in the unique appearance of the Station and marveling at how different in their similarities all of them could be. "Bit of help for a poor, helpless stranger to this Station?"

The woman with at least three different colors in her hair looked at Orion and laughed, not buying his self-identification for a moment. "You don't look like the type to be poor or helpless, Stranger." She went about her task, organizing the bottles in front of her. "I know my badges, and you didn't get yours without provin' you definitely ain't helpless." She nodded at his shoulder as she moved his direction.

"Well, there are different kinds of helpless." He insisted with a grin, since he certainly wasn't ashamed of his rank or his station. He had worked hard to get where he was, and he enjoyed it as thoroughly as the next guy.

"I need three things, in no particular order. First, I need a shot of Shine without being judged for drinking in the morning," he chuckled at that, since he really was fairly nervous about what he was heading into. "Second, I need to know if there's a travel hostel setup in here where a guy can shower and change, and third, I need to know the best way to get down to . . ." he looked down at the communicator strapped to his own wrist to make sure he got the right information, "Arm four, deck fourteen, corridor seven-C. And I need all that within the next . . . forty-two minutes."

"Just so happens I'm the answer to all your prayers, then." She smiled a flash of perfectly-white teeth at him, then started extracting a shot of Starshine as he had requested. It had to be drawn from a spout into a tube and then into a small glass that was covered at the top so all the liquid would stay inside.

"Here's one object of your desire." She floated it out to him and looked down at her communicator. "Name and ID? I'll set you up with a temporary room easy enough. It's a daily occurrence that I have to float some drunk into one anyway. I'd much rather be floating you."

"Beautiful. I won't need it for long." He let the shot float in the air between them while he tapped his wrist against a panel to transfer all the information she needed along with flipping her his ID card. He took the shot, sliding back the covered lid as he moved it in practiced fashion to toss the liquid straight down his throat.

He gave a pleased growl at the way it burned all the way down, and tossed the glass gently toward the collection bin behind the bar, slightly magnetized as it was, to make sure it stayed put. "What about the directions? Far to go?"

"About twenty minutes out from here." Once she had his information in her system, she punched in the room ID he asked about and sent the directions to the station's own navigational system. "I've loaded up the final location for you, so it should guide you when you ask." She looked him up and down before she came out from her spot so she could lead him to get cleaned up first. "What's got a pilot like you all up in knots? Don't tell me you're here to get matched. I've seen a few people wandering around here today for Introduction, but surely a man like you doesn't need help in that department."

He let her lead the way, floating just behind her along the guide-bars. "It's not about needing help so much as it's about . . . something different." He didn't bother to hide the fact that he was looking her over as they moved through the dock, since she *was* gorgeous. A great deal shorter than he generally liked, but still gorgeous nonetheless. "Finding somebody for a night? Or even a few months? No problem. Finding somebody who's actually gonna go the distance? That's a trickier picture. I figure the match program's got a pretty good track record, might as well see what it can do."

"I don't know if I trust it. I've seen some major fuckups. It's still a bit of a gamble. But I've heard a lot of sob stories in general, it just comes with the job." They didn't go far before she opened up a hostel room for him with her own ID card. Inside he could see a cot, a shower and a toilet.

Definitely a temporary space. "Good luck. You're gonna need it."

"Good luck? That's all I get? These are possibly my very last moments of singlehood, here." He tossed his bag into the tiny compartment past her, but was still grinning as he held onto the doorframe.

The woman tucked a strand of purple hair behind her ear to join the blue and green of the rest of it. It suited her with her piercings and a few visible tattoos, all of them accentuating her natural beauty rather than obscuring it. "You don't even know my name, big guy." He was big. So tall. She could only imagine what he was hiding beneath the belt.

"Maybe not, but you know mine." He was still holding the ID card she had handed back to him, and he flicked it through the air from one hand to the other between long and obviously-nimble fingers.

"My name is Lila." She said as she moved a little bit closer to him. "Is my debt paid, or are you looking for more than that? You asked for three things." Lila chewed on her bottom lip slightly, and she seemed perfectly fine with the idea of giving his lips an introduction, if he was looking for it.

"I'm always looking." He reached out and took a handful of her shirt to draw her in against him. "And actually, Lila, I think I'm the one who owes you, setting me up with a room and directions and all." He pulled himself slightly into the small compartment she opened up, taking her along as far as the doorway before he brushed her lips with a teasing kiss. "Just wish I had longer to stay and settle up."

Lila wasn't going to simply accept the light brush of a kiss, so she grabbed onto his uniform and kissed him heatedly. He'd started it, after all, and she had a thing for men that seemed like trouble. He definitely seemed like trouble. "You're dangerous. I hope this woman knows what she's getting into. I also hope you hate her so you'll come back for a few more . . . well, a few more drinks, to start."

He grinned against her lips and returned her kisses with every bit of the enthusiasm he was glad to have inspired. It was easy. It was something known. Something familiar and practiced, even if she was a stranger.

It was also everything he wanted to get away from in coming to be Matched in the first place.

"You know, I've never actually been to Nine before. I think I'm gonna like it here." He chuckled and kissed his way back along her jawline, doubling up his grip on her shirt in the process as he spoke into her ear. "If I hate her, I'll be back, and not just for drinks. That's a promise."

Lila drew one of her hands down his body to get an idea of what she was encouraging in front of her. She liked what she was feeling. "I'm gonna hold you to that." She groaned softly as she imagined more about this dangerous stranger in front of her. "I can only imagine what you're hiding under these."

"Well, that's what imagination is for." He pulled her into a last kiss and spun her around so she was facing the bar they'd left a moment ago, then settled one hand firmly on her ass to get her lined up. "Until later, baby. If I don't see you by tonight, have a shot on me while you put that imagination to work."

He kissed her neck and let her drift for a moment before he shoved her back by her ass toward the bar with a laugh, sending her spinning in mid-air along the pillar they used to guide on. She worked in near-zero, she would be fine. And it was fun to watch her tumble the whole way, even if it got a whole slew of judgmental stares from the other more-serious occupants of the dock.

Orion couldn't care less. He had to prepare for a potentially very important meeting.

4

Mercury wasn't usually prone to fiddling, but she found herself tapping her nails over and over again as she sat in the room where she was waiting to meet her match. She had shown up a half hour early because she needed to feel as though she was prepared to meet this mysterious pilot. While she knew everything available about his health, genealogy, education, and hobbies, she knew nothing about the way he looked. She hadn't included much concerning appearance in her profile requests, because she didn't really have a preference. As a result, she had no idea what she was getting into, even though she was incredibly impressed by the information she did know.

Mercury had dressed up for the occasion, since she had somehow let her mother talk her into a new dress. It felt odd to wear a dress and heels instead of scrubs for a change, but she agreed that it looked good on her and complemented both her figure and her coloring. She was pale, not just because she lived in space, but because she was Irish to the core, as reflected by her slight accent and dark red hair. She was taller than most women, but she hadn't investigated where that genetic change had originated in her family line. Whatever else she inherited from her mother, it hadn't been that.

In her anxiety she sipped her water constantly and tugged at her long hair because it wasn't pulled back like usual and it gave her a distraction. The dark green dress fell just above her knees, cut in a deep V in the front to accentuate her ample chest, and was open halfway down her back to expose her silky fair skin. Her mother also insisted on giving her a gold necklace and stud diamond earrings to wear. They had been passed down in her family, and her mother cited that they were necessary for good luck.

Mercury didn't believe in such things. Luck was a silly, simple way to explain the unexplained. If it was a good match, it would mean the system had done its job, not that she was lucky.

Orion found the room just ninety seconds before the appointed time, and stopped just outside to give himself another once-over. He wasn't the only well-dressed person he had seen in the last few minutes, but none of the others he'd seen had red hair. That was the only thing he knew about his intended match when it came to physical appearance, and he'd been on the lookout for redheads ever since. When his nerves were as calmed as they were likely to get, he let the door take his handprint and stepped into the vestibule.

The outer door closed behind him, leaving him in a space of only a few square meters, with a frosted fiberglass screen between him and potentially the rest of his life. The lights were on in both parts of the chamber, but all he could see from his side was the vague outline of a low table and a couch against the far wall, with someone sitting on it. A hint of green, nothing more.

There was another handprint panel to the side of the frosted glass barrier, and he took in what he hoped was a quiet breath before he reached up to key himself in. No going back now.

"First Lieutenant Orion ibn-Sayyid Al-Jabbar. Fleet pilot second-class, graduate of Station Three Flight and

Navigation curriculum with full honors. And very glad to meet you." The last part wasn't technically part of the formula for Introduction, but Orion couldn't adhere too precisely to regulations. It just felt wrong, especially in the context of that meeting. He hoped she could hear the smile in his voice, and she knew he was sincere when he said he was glad to meet her. Whoever she was.

Mercury got up from the couch and set her water aside as she stepped up to the barrier. She took a deep breath before she put her hand up to the panel and hoped that she sounded confident. "Mercury Finnegan, M.D., Practicing in gynecology and obstetrics, graduate of Station Seven, magna cum laude. Glad to meet you as well."

It was a rare occurrence when Mercury had to really look up at anyone, but when the frosted glass slid back with a pleasant *ding* of acceptance, she had to crane her neck a little to look Orion in the eye. He stood well over two meters tall, head, shoulders, and then some taller than Mercury, and was smiling as if he expected the surprise that usually came along with seeing someone his height. His black hair was cut close against his scalp, immediately screaming military, as if the rest of the uniform he was wearing didn't do the job sufficiently. His skin was a deep shade of warm bronze, the features of his face lean and narrow. There was something sharply observant about his dark eyes, darting over every aspect of her appearance before locking onto her own with intense focus.

His uniform was the deep blue of the Consortium's official colors, with his patches of rank and station clearly placed along his upper arms. There were a few small colored markings against one side of his chest that looked like awards of some kind, but Mercury couldn't identify them, having not had cause to spend much time around members of the military unless they were in the room with their wives for the delivery of their children. The uniform was of stiff fabric, but it was easy to tell even with the uniform that the man in front of her was lean, lithe, and more than a little dangerous.

"Good morning." He said it not so much as a greeting, but as if he was passing judgment on it and it would be a good morning no matter what anybody else had to say about it. "Wow, you look amazing."

Mercury certainly wasn't expecting a man so much taller than she was, since she honestly didn't think they really existed. She looked up into his sharp eyes with her green ones for a full breath before she thought of an appropriate response. She was still stunned by his appearance, how attractive she found him, and the simple fact that they were both actually meeting, to know what she should say. It hadn't felt real until the moment she was staring up at him. "Thank you. You're . . . you look good as well. You're a lot taller than I ever imagined you would be. I read that you are 'significantly taller' than I am, but I honestly didn't imagine you being quite this tall. It's . . . refreshing, actually."

"Significantly taller. Computers have a talent for understatement." He chuckled and stepped into the space the partition had vacated, putting them a lot closer together and making it even more difficult to look all the way up at him. "I'm glad you think it's refreshing. Your neck might disagree with you after a while. I try to stay sitting down as much as possible so as not to send too many people to a chiropractor."

He reached out tentatively and put a hand along her waist once he was close. He was a very comfortable person, physically speaking, and he had been encouraged by every other matched person he knew not to try and put on any kind of act during the first part of the matching proceedings. They were there to find out who the other person was and to be known for themselves. That wasn't going to happen if he acted like a reserved person when he was really anything but.

"It told me about your red hair and I saw you were Irish, but I didn't realize that still came with an accent. I like it." He had a slight Arabic accent himself, harsher on some consonants and slightly different stresses in his words, but it was by no means thick enough to make him difficult to understand.

Mercury certainly wasn't expecting him to touch her, but she wasn't the type of person to initiate physical contact, usually. She didn't pull away from his touch, but she did motion toward the couch so maybe he would want to sit down and talk. "Both of my parents are Irish, and there's an intact community of Gaelic speakers on Six. I left for the beginning of my medical training at fifteen, though, so my parents say that my time spent on Seven has 'watered down' my accent."

"My parents complain about the same thing with mine." He went with her to the couch, and sat down near her with an arm along the back of the cushions, mostly facing her. "My mother's family is Egyptian, my father's is Saudi. My Arabic isn't what it used to be as a kid, but I haven't been back to my parents' station in years except to stop in and say hello when I'm running shuttles through there."

"Years? Doesn't that make you sad?" She couldn't imagine going years without seeing her parents, though now that she was part of the Eleusis project, she knew it could be much longer than that before she saw them in person. "I saw my parents just yesterday." She looked down at her dress. "My mother encouraged me to buy this dress for this meeting, though most of the time I spend my time in scrubs or something much more relaxed than this. It's just easier that way. Though I did agree with her that it is a beautiful dress. It would just get messy in my normal life. Delivering babies is a messy business."

"Not for the faint-hearted." He said with another laugh, looking over her dress. "It is a beautiful dress, and you look incredible in it. So I'm glad in this case that you had your mom's encouragement. I got this . . ." he looked down at his uniform with the same playful smile on his face. "Oh, about . . . six years ago? The rank patch came through just last year for First, but the uniform's been around a while. I'm actually the same way when it comes to dressing up. If I'm not in a jumpsuit flying somewhere, I'm at home in something comfortable or in jeans and a t-shirt hanging around the station. I don't really feel the need to be more formal than that unless I'm around somebody I'm going to have to salute. Or somebody I'd like to try and impress." He indicated her with a grinning nod.

"Clearly we both were dressing to impress." She tugged on her hair nervously as she sat close to him, though the situation still felt strange to her. She was acutely aware of the beginning of some responses in her own body that were becoming mild distractions. Her nervousness had her cheeks flushed and her pulse racing more than she knew was typical for her. Was that nerves or arousal? She wasn't sure. "I feel as though I know a lot about you, but also not very much at the same time. I'm not good at dating. I've never had the time. So I apologize in advance for not knowing what to say or do, since I've had such limited experience with the opposite sex."

She couldn't miss the fact that his eyes widened when she claimed not to have much experience. "You've got nothing to apologize for. It's other people's loss." His arm along the back of the couch moved so he could caress along her shoulder lazily as they talked, just to keep her close and because he really didn't want to put any distance between them. His fingertips and the touch they brought with them was lighter than she had expected from someone with a military background, precise in their playfulness.

"I think in that respect, I'm coming to this from the opposite end of the spectrum. So if we're going to apologize for how we're starting, I'll apologize for that. I've dated . . . pretty extensively, but never for longer than a few months and never seriously enough to consider making things permanent. That's my track record, but that's not the way I want things in my life."

"I couldn't possibly hold your past against you. But I do want a relationship with someone who can be a faithful partner. I am a busy woman and sometimes it can get in the way. I don't want to come home to someone who is with someone else because of my job as a doctor. I take it seriously." Everything in her life, she took seriously. "I can promise complete fidelity, I would only want the same thing."

"I can promise fidelity. I'm more of a serial monogamist than I am actually promiscuous." He had been called that in the past, but it wasn't a completely fair label. He just had a long train of failed relationships or non-starter relationships. "And we'll be a fine pair when it comes to being home or away. Pilots aren't known for being the stay-at-home type, and if we're going to Eleusis, I doubt we'll have a lot of free time on our hands, either of us."

"If? I'm definitely going to Eleusis. I received my letter of acceptance last night." She raised a rust-colored eyebrow as she looked at him, their knees just centimeters apart as they faced each other. Sitting down made her dress hike up higher on her thighs, but she didn't notice. "You haven't heard? Maybe they haven't sent everyone's letters yet."

"No, I got my acceptance last night, same as you. I figured they wouldn't match us if we weren't both accepted." He continued his slow caress over her shoulder absent-mindedly as they spoke, still looking down slightly at her even when they were sitting down. "I just feel skeptical of the entire thing. There are too many secrets and contradictions in what I've read about the program for me to feel rock-solid about it. But it's too good an opportunity not to take the bet and go to be a part of it."

Mercury briefly thought about her father's warning about authority, but she didn't say anything to Orion about it. They were still strangers, and she had no reason to trust him yet. "There's no way I'm going to miss out on going to Eleusis. I feel like I've been working toward it my whole life."

He smiled at the ambition he could see in her and nodded as he thought back over some of the things he'd read in her file. "I can see that." His caress moved up over her shoulder to the back of her neck, running along her hair in slow strokes. She was so focused, he wasn't sure if she was happy about the touch or not, but he was ready to pull away if she showed any sign of not being enthusiastic about it. "When I was fourteen, interest in Eleusis was just starting to heat up again. They'd suddenly started getting all the probe data and whatnot, you remember how it was. The Alperts and the rest of the Board couldn't shut up about it."

He settled a little against the couch, but in spite of the slouch, he was still so tall that it did nothing to detract from the dignity of the uniform he was wearing. "Anyway, I was up to my eyebrows in gravitational propulsion around that time, so our instructor handed all forty-two of us full access to the Consortium cosmography database. Told us to get from Earth to Eleusis as quickly as technologically possible. There were contests on Earth and over in Station Sixteen around the same time."

"So I went down and took a sleeping bag, stayed in the lab for the whole two weeks we were allowed access, and I managed to get our travel time shaved to seventy-four years, four months, twelve days, fourteen hours and twenty-seven minutes. Between take-off and landing at the chosen site on Eleusis. Next runner-up behind me was at eighty-six years and change." He smiled, since it was still something he was fairly proud of, though he was conflicted about it at the same time.

"One of these days, I'm gonna find out who managed to beat my time and take first place, but they classified the winner and the plan proposal both. All they would tell me is that it left my plan completely in the dust. Fucked if I know how. Anyway, I'm pretty sure that silver prize is what got me on the list for inclusion."

"Wow." Obviously she had seen the award in his qualifications, but there hadn't been a story along with it, and she was glad to hear the explanation from him. "I was surprised when I was matched with a pilot, not because I don't think you are intelligent, but because I feel like our intelligence is so vastly different. Listening to you tell the story, though, I find it fascinating, what you can do. We both have to be quick thinkers. I think it would be beneficial in a marriage." There was no sense in taking time or talking about 'dating' without considering the end goal. The whole point of being matched was to find someone to be with permanently. Not to find someone to date casually.

"I think it would be." He agreed, since that was part of what had impressed him about her in the first place. Being a doctor at her level had to involve a lot of quick decision-making, and he appreciated that about a person. "There's a lot about you that I'm impressed by, even just on the descriptors I already know. Curing Farrier's Syndrome when you were what, nineteen? I read about that at the time, but I hadn't remembered your name from the headline."

"There was a lot of research that was already in place before I made the key discovery, but honestly, it was more fun than altruistic. I liked working toward solving the biological puzzle. It just happened to cure a disease." Sometimes she was honest to a fault, but she didn't often make apologies for it. "I'd like to cure more diseases. Birth more babies. When they cry and complain, it's cuter."

"You and I have very different definitions of the word 'cute,' I think. I'm a fan of kids, but mostly I like them once they're big enough I can throw them around a little without worrying about breaking them." His touch on her shoulder jostled her a bit as if she was the one he was throwing around, setting her necklace swinging against her chest. "When they're all factory-fresh and wobbly, I feel like they're just way too fragile for me to get away with handling."

"Imagine if you had to catch them covered in slime several times a day." She teased as she smiled across at him. "I still think they're cute." Mercury laughed softly and moved just the tiniest bit closer to him. "Do you mind if I ask what prompted you to enter yourself to be matched?"

His smile dimmed, but it was the difference between mischief and seriousness, nothing more. "No, I don't mind. Full disclosure is the best policy, I think. It was my last breakup. Which was six months ago, you should know." The mischief in his smile came back for a brief moment.

"It was just . . . sort of symptomatic of every other relationship I've had in the last few years. Quick start, good times, talk about getting serious, meet the family, start fighting, keep fighting, make up, start fighting again, make up again, keep spiraling until eventually it just doesn't make sense anymore to try because we've gotten too far onto each other's bad side and can't take it seriously anymore."

He went through the recitation so easily that it was clear he'd been around that misery-go-round more than a few times. "I figured it was time to stop wasting time with things that weren't going to go the distance. My parents were matched, my brother was matched, my sister is matched, all . . . well, I was gonna say all happily matched, but that's not really true. My sister fights with her match all the time. But two out of three ain't bad."

"My parents were matched too, and they are sickeningly cute together. My mother worships my father, and my father adores her." She searched Orion's eyes before she reached out and tentatively ran her fingertips across his cheek. She could feel the smoothness of a recent clean shave, the quirk of his smile in the muscles of his cheek beneath her fingertips. "The program must know more than I have ever given it credit for, I've never found anyone as attractive as I think you are."

He searched her eyes after that just to see if she was being serious, but he was quickly learning that his match was close to being incapable of saying anything she didn't absolutely mean. It was so unlike anyone else he'd ever dated that he wasn't sure he would know how to deal with it if it really was just the way she was. "Well, right back at you."

He turned his face slightly to kiss her fingertips, then pulled her in closer by way of his caress along the back of her neck. "Most of the women I've dated have been connected to the runway industry on Three. They tend to be stick figures. If they do eat a cheeseburger from time to time, they're incredibly short." He reached out with one hand to run his fingertips over her knees, then pulled them over one of his legs to sit closer. "I can't tell you how happy I am to have come past that screen and seen you standing there, divine as you are."

Divine? That was quite a compliment, and she wasn't sure how to take it. "I don't eat many cheeseburgers. I don't believe I've had one since before I started my studies. The diet regimen on Seven is very strict for medical personnel. I feel like celebrating when I'm actually allowed a little chocolate every few months." Mercury looked at his hand on her leg, and she found that his touch actually affected her.

Interesting.

Her heart rate had increased slightly, but she wasn't sure if it was his appearance or simply because she was aware of their situation and that he might become her husband. It was amazing what the mind could do and how it could affect one's physical state. When he ran his fingertips across her knee again, she spoke up. "I've only had two sexual partners. Neither experience was particularly interesting. The first time was because I felt a gynecologist should not be a virgin, and the second was to see if the second experience would be similar to the first. When I say I am inexperienced, I do mean it. However, I learn quickly."

That brought back the mischief in his smile, and his touch along her knee grew more scandalous, his long fingers tracing what could have been some kind of signature over her thighs. "Nothing interesting? That . . . that is a damn shame. And not what anyone should have to say about their sex life."

"I didn't feel as though I was missing out on much of anything." Though now she wondered if maybe she *was* missing out on something. The man beside her was convincing her body that it wanted something as his fingers explored her leg. She knew what arousal was, certainly, but she had never experienced it herself in such a way. Apparently fellow doctors didn't spark arousal in her. "I'm usually too busy to find much interest in sexual activity."

"With that kind of experience, I can't say I blame you." His eyes dipped down to take in the sight of her slowly. As they moved up from her knee along her curves, his hand followed, walking up along the cut of her dress. He left a slow caress over the laces that covered her stomach and didn't stop as he trailed over her breasts, moving up her neckline to her cheek, when he met her eyes again. "Well, you said you started out with a mind to investigate, to see what all the fuss was about. It's possible that with a little more data, you may find the conclusions of your earlier experiments require some slight revisions."

Mercury's breathing quickened as he ran his hand over her body, frozen briefly to savor the sensation, since she couldn't convince her mind to think of anything else other than his long fingers exploring her.

So interesting.

Mercury leaned closer, which only made her heart beat faster. "I was hoping to get to know you. I did not anticipate that you could have this kind of effect on me physically, and so quickly."

"I'm glad not to have been anticipated. I can't say I anticipated you either." He pulled some of her hair forward over her shoulder and ran it between his fingers as the back of his knuckles caressed back down the way they'd come. "I thought I'd come in here, have an incredibly awkward conversation, and walk out of here feeling conflicted about the prospect of being matched up with a stranger."

He leaned in and kissed her cheek near the corner of her lips, but it was nothing like the other times she'd been kissed on the cheek in her life. It was a promise and a threat at the same time, both of which he seemed fully capable of making good on. "I hope to get to know you too. But there's a lot of ways two people who are going to be matched together should know each other."

She felt a chill of excitement run down her spine as he kissed her, but it was unsettling how much he could affect her. She barely knew the man. "Is it wrong to feel this intense attraction only moments after meeting you? Do many matches start out this way?" Mercury ran an exploratory hand down his arm. "There's so much I already know about you, agree with, and appreciate. Your health and family history is clean and clear. You're smart and successful. Is it a risk to just jump with two feet and hope that the program is what everyone says it is?"

"A risk? Absolutely." His hand continued its caress down to her waist, at which point he pulled her roughly into him so that she was actually sitting in his lap instead of just halfway there. "Everything when it comes to being with another person is a risk. But you should know, you've been matched with a gambling kind of guy. Not to the point of addiction or self-destruction, but a gambler nonetheless." He put his arms around her waist once he had her close, but kept his eyes on hers, finally level with him as she was. "From everything I know about you so far, I'd bet on us. I'd bet a lot on us."

"Really? Why?" She wasn't a gambling type when she didn't have to be. Sometimes the odds were not in her favor for a patient here or there, but most of her decisions were calculated and backed by logic and research. It was difficult to think about anything other than the closeness of Orion's body once he had pulled her into his lap, though. There wasn't much logic or reason behind that. No man she had ever known would have done such a thing, but she wasn't offended. She was just surprised and unsure how to behave.

"Because I can see why the program matched us." He leaned back into the couch to look up at her, his hands working over her back in a constant caress that hadn't stopped from the first moment he touched her. "I came in here, after looking over your profile, wondering what in heaven or Earth I would have that I could offer you. I'm a pilot, and I'm a good one, but you don't need a pilot. So you don't need that part of me."

"But I'm from Three. They call it the Edge for a reason, and most of that reason is that it's about as far from Seven or Prime as it's possible to get. We work hard, we play harder, and bending the rules isn't just encouraged, it's rewarded. I may be military, but that's still the way I work, and it's gotten me pretty far, in my sights." His grin turned not just more mischievous, but outright wicked as his hand moved down over her thighs again in his constant exploration even as he continued.

"I respect everything about you and what you've made yourself. You're the best at what you do, and you always will be. I'm getting the impression that's just who you are. Being with you, belonging to you, would keep me focused, in the program's eyes, on what's important. I get that, and I can admit that I need somebody who's going to help me do that from time to time. As for what I can do for you . . ."

This time, when his hand moved up over her dress, it was no light caress or subtle touch, but an easy, casual pass of what felt almost like ownership, smoothing the fabric of her dress all the way up to her neckline where he pushed her hair back over her shoulder again to keep her as exposed to him as possible.

"I like to enjoy this life we're living. And if you're used to living life in rigid lines, if you've only had sex twice, with disappointments both times, then that's something I can definitely be for you. Something I would like very much to be for you. Not just when it comes to sex, but just taking the time to enjoy the world. All of it."

Mercury's body was starting to ache in places that had never really ached, but she didn't say anything immediately as his hands left his invisible mark all over her. It was intoxicating, his touch, his closeness, and she was beginning to wonder if she should put more study and research into the power of pheromones. It was happening so fast, she could barely apply logic to it. She couldn't stop her heart from racing, and she knew her pupils had to be clearly dilated, which would show him easily how much every touch made her even more aroused.

"I'm often told that I'm too focused. I don't feel as though I am missing out on life, but maybe I am." She wiggled on his lap in response to a powerful chill that ran up and down her spine again. "I am often awkward and strange. I know everything there is to know about my field and my focus, my research, and I try to know everything I can about medicine more broadly. I might embarrass you. I've done that to my parents, even though I'm aware they are proud of me regardless. I might make you angry and not know immediately, or hurt your feelings." She thought briefly about Greg, but any experience with Greg paled in comparison to even sitting on Orion's lap. "I just want you to know that I can be difficult."

"I didn't come in here expecting the rest of our life to be easy." He moved to run his touch down her arm to her hand, where he laced their fingers in her lap. "While we're on disclaimers, I'll give mine a shot. I am not a shy person. It is very likely that I will overstep at some point, joke about the wrong thing, push something too far, ask more questions than I should and then be confused when there's no answer until I figure out how exactly I'm fucking up. I'm almost certainly going to end up flirting with somebody else at some point without really thinking about what I'm doing, and I'm going to say I'm sorry in advance for that right now. That's gonna be one habit that'll be hard to break, but I get the impression you're worth it."

"Also, my family should come with its own rider to my disclaimers. My parents and sister-in-law are very fundamental, and that's off-putting for some people. My sister Khadi and I went more secular as we grew up, but we still own it as part of our heritage. Basically, I come with complications." He admitted freely, since that was part of what he'd been concerned about in being matched at all.

"But I'll do my damnedest to make sure the majority of the ways I complicate your life are the kinds you like, whatever we discover those might be."

Mercury gave him a warm smile for his own disclaimer, as it made her feel more at ease about all the things that she knew would be difficult about her. A flirtatious, somewhat religious man who had trouble keeping his mouth shut didn't really bother her. There wasn't much that did bother her, as long as someone was being genuine. "I'm not religious, but I have nothing against those who are. I'll apologize if I don't always understand your jokes, and flirting doesn't bother me. If you promise me that you're going to be faithful to me, then unless I learn somehow you haven't been, I don't care about flirting. It's a natural expression of emotion for some people, and it is healthy. There's nothing wrong with that."

The next time she had to wiggle on his lap to reposition herself, she felt something that was distinctly not a part of his uniform. He just pulled her in to lean against him afterward, though, one arm around her back leaving the other free to explore her. "I think we're going to get along well, Mercury." It was the first time he had said her name out loud, and his accent shaped the word differently than most, rolling the Rs and accenting it strangely in his gentle baritone voice. "What do you think?"

"I would definitely like to get to know you better, and work in the direction of making something here. I like . . . being with you. I feel at ease." Her body certainly liked him more than she thought was possible, especially as his hands wandered all over her. She couldn't quite convince her muscles to keep her still where he was holding her, something in her hips wanted to move of their own accord and dig into the man.

When his fingers trailed along the exposed skin of her back, she leaned into him even more, pressing her breasts into his chest. She hesitated, her lips hovering close to his, but she didn't know what she should do, or even how to do anything well. Even kissing someone seemed like a complicated thing in her mind.

He thought at first that she was going to kiss him, but he could feel her hesitation in the way she moved, and he smiled, renewing his caress along her back. "I like being with you too." He whispered against her lips, right before claiming them with his own.

'Claimed' was the only word that came to mind as sufficient to describe the feeling. He was clean-shaven, unlike Greg and her one other sexual partner had been, so kissing him was a very different sensation than either of them had been. Most of the difference came from the fact that while both of her previous lovers had been nervous or awkward in their own ways, no such emotion came through the touch from Orion. His lips took hers slowly, easing her into the kiss gently as his arms held her body tightly pressed against his. It was like gravity, drawing her entire body in against his with the heat in the single kiss, a slow, patient burn to go along with the low moan that escaped him at the taste of her.

Mercury remembered the noises her previous lovers made when she was with them, but no noise they made impacted her the way Orion's moan worked through her body. It made her ache for him even worse, but she tried to focus on his lips. She didn't make any sound until his hands moved down to grip her backside and press her body into his while his tongue teased the seam of her lips. She felt needy instantly and the whimpers and moans that escaped her chest had quickly forgotten any measure of her usual control.

When the kiss finally broke, Orion was breathing heavily and his grip on her had gotten rougher, raising questions about what the man beneath her might be like when he really got going. "So." He finally said without pulling away from her lips, kissing her gently between words as he spoke. "Mercury" *kiss* "Finnegan, will you do me" *kiss* "the great honor and pleasure" *kiss* "of marrying me for the next month?"

A typical Introduction trial period was two weeks, but a month wasn't unheard of. They would only be given two weeks of liberty from their jobs to get to know each other more thoroughly and meet family, but Orion wanted to see what they could be together even beyond that initial period. A contract was nothing if it was only beneficial when they had the leisure time to devote every moment to each other.

Even a month of being someone's 'wife' was a huge adjustment to consider, especially for someone as singularly focused as Mercury. She wasn't sure how it would go, but she wanted to try the experiment. Especially if he was going to kiss her like that again. He needed to teach her how to kiss like that.

Mercury nodded as she lifted a hand and caressed his face before her hand rested at the back of his neck. "Yes, Orion Al-Jabbar, I want to be your wife. At least for the next month." She gave him a small smile before she kissed his cheek innocently. Mercury didn't know much about being anything else. Certainly not seductive or sexy. "I really hope your confidence in the match is not unfounded."

"So do I. I hate being wrong. Good thing it doesn't happen often." He teased as his hands wandered down over her spine to her backside again, since he had very much enjoyed the whimpers he had gotten out of her before. "I'm licensed to take private pods at the major Stations for personal use back and forth between them. They're cramped, but they're fast and they don't require waiting for another carrier heading for Three or Seven. I made sure to clean up my cube back on Three before I left, in case you'd be coming back with me, but we can go to whichever first that you'd prefer."

"I don't want to be tempted by work or my patients if we go to Seven. Pregnant women have a lot of things that concern them, and I always want to ease their minds when I'm around to be on call." It almost sounded like a joke, except the expression on her face was serious. Pregnancy was not an easy time, and even though she had never been pregnant, she wanted to comfort her patients as often as she could. Although in her absence, the other doctors on staff could manage. "I'd like to see your home. If your body doesn't drive mine crazy before we get there." She was definitely feeling all sorts of aroused, and she didn't know what to do about it. Whenever he kissed or touched her it made things so much better and somehow so much worse at the same time.

"I think I'd be okay with seeing you a little crazy." He chuckled and kissed her again, giving another quiet moan before he began to stand up, holding her in his arms until he could set her on her feet. The deck where they'd met wasn't full Earth-norm gravity, but from the ease with which he picked her up, it was still obvious Orion was stronger than his lean form let on. "Window from here to Three is faster anyway, this time of the morning. I also got you some things that are waiting back at my place. I hope you'll like them."

"You got me something? You were that confident?" She was definitely surprised by that, but flattered too, since she was glad that he felt she was worth gambling on after only reading information about her. "That's very kind of you. Thank you."

"Don't thank me yet. It's still possible you'll hate it." He stepped back from her just enough for her dress to fall back into place from where he'd gotten her all askew on the couch, but then leaned down to kiss her again, just because he wanted to. His arms were loose around her as he tipped her head back to capture her mouth, kissing her a few times gently afterward when he pulled away with a smile.

Without saying anything else, he looked off to one side at the panel where she had given her authentication for him to come in for the Introduction. He placed his hand on the scanning plate, leaving room for hers beside it. "Certifying Introduction complete and accepted. One-month contract was also accepted. Enthusiastically. Orion Al-Jabbar." The

'Enthusiastically' bit wasn't something the computer would require or understand, but it was something Orion wanted as part of the official record anyway.

She smiled at his enthusiastic acceptance, and placed her hand next to his on the panel. "Mercury Finnegan, one month contract accepted. Computer, please also notify my parents." Usually only employers were notified, but she wanted her parents to know just in case it was difficult to get ahold of them. "I feel . . . so spontaneous. I never do anything this quickly. Certainly not with a relative stranger."

"Oh, I do all kinds of things quickly. But I didn't come here this morning thinking this would be one of them." He reached down and swept her up into his arms with ease, checking briefly to make sure her dress wasn't hiked up so far that she'd be giving the rest of the station a show on their way back up to the docks.

He hit the button to open the outer door and glanced behind him to watch the luggage carriers exit the unit behind him, drawing his paltry duffel bag and a much more professional-looking luggage case of hers with her own belongings. It was protocol to bring an overnight bag. Just in case. The machines would keep up until they got to the pod, that was all that mattered. "I really thought I was gonna come here, we'd chat, maybe meet later for drinks, see how things went, then I was going to be very responsible and very meticulous and sleep on it before making any kind of decision. Honest I was."

"Are you sure that's not what you want? We can stay here and sleep on it." She didn't want him to change his mind about her so soon, even though they had only agreed to a month-long contract. It was also very strange to be carried through the halls, but it made her feel dainty and ladylike. "You must be very strong to carry me like a feather." She wasn't too heavy, but she was nearly six feet tall, after all.

"Oh, right, I probably should have included that in my disclaimer. I'm prone to showing off from time to time. Usually gets me in trouble." He shrugged, but loved the feel of her against him too much to feel bad about showing off. "And no, I don't want to go somewhere and sleep on it. I'm good just like this."

"You're not in trouble with me." She smiled again and she kissed his cheek once as he carried her. After one kiss on the cheek, though, she felt as though she should continue the spontaneity, and she leaned in to kiss along his neck. Mercury truly didn't know what she was doing, only what she *wanted* to do, and that was incredibly intoxicating. There were other people walking through the hallways, matched or not, and they all turned to look at the giant man carrying the redhead.

"You taste good." She said softly into his ear, but from her tone he could tell that she wasn't attempting to be sexy. She actually sounded surprised, as if she never expected that the taste of kissing someone's skin could actually taste good.

He grinned at the matter-of-fact tone, and turned his face so he could return the next kiss she gave him, still walking toward the lift at the end of the corridor without looking. "So do you." His voice had a slightly different thrum to it as he said so, something more hungry than factual.

"It probably has something to do with diet." She considered the cause, then she realized his tone afterward, and it shook her out of her critical thinking. "How long does it take to get to Three from here?"

His eyes turned upward to think on that, and though she could see calculations and schematics running behind his eyes as he did his analysis, he didn't miss a step or falter as he carried her. They were in the lift with the luggage-carriers parked next to them by the time he answered, flicking the button for the dock level with the hand around the small of her back. "If I'm right about our positioning right now, I can probably swing it in about four and a half hours. Might actually be a little less, depending on orbital corrections. Between four and six, though, at the outside."

"That's not too bad." She said with a slight nod. "I don't

handle flight very well, it makes me queasy. But I did bring medication with me, so you don't have to worry."

That got a full laugh from him for the first time, and she could feel from how close she was against him exactly how it bunched the muscles in his abdomen as the sound resonated in the rising lift. "Anyone who says machines don't have a sense of humor needs to hear that. The pilot matched with a woman who gets queasy while flying." He kissed her again, still chuckling, but didn't put her down or let her get any farther from him. "I'll try and keep it a smooth ride, for your sake. And keep your mind off flying while we're in transit."

"I'm sure we have a lot to talk about to keep us distracted. Flying out here I was nervous on top of everything else, and that didn't help at all." They noticed an influx of people when they got off the lift, and the shift in gravity made her hold tighter to him as he kept her in his arms. "There are a lot of people around here. I wonder if that is normal."

They stepped off the lift at the edge of the dock, where the station's rotation had them almost weightless. The influx of people was coming up from the stairwells of the arm they had just ridden the lift through, and it gave Orion pause as he looked them over. They were dressed like technicians, carrying tools and protective gear, but they didn't move like technicians. Techs off-duty always looked loose, relaxed, glad to be finished with their work or grumpy about the prospect of more to come. These people looked singularly focused, and they weren't speaking to each other. Some were carrying bags over their shoulders, a few were carrying a large case between them, guiding it through the near-zero gravity space carefully.

"Maybe there was some kind of mechanical trouble that put them all in a bad mood." He floated up toward the registration desk of the dock with their luggage following in precisely calculated jumps, to remain as close to them as possible.

"I don't think I want to know what kind of technical failure could cause that kind of distress." She kept ahold of Orion and suddenly felt an urgency to get on their pod and get away to the privacy of his home. "I don't know enough about this station to know if I should be worried, but I feel worried."

"You and me both." It was the first time she had seen him look serious, and it brought out the depth of his dark eyes as he glanced around the area to take in everything he could about what was happening. The technicians weren't speaking to anybody else, headed for a corridor that would take them to their ship docked outside. Maybe their work was finished and they were just leaving for the day. He hoped that was true.

"In any event," he attempted to restore some playfulness to his voice as they approached the registration desk, "I think in the interest of time, we can forgo getting into jumpsuits for the flight. They're not regulation in the pods anyway. Sound alright with you?"

Mercury looked down at her dress, then looked up into Orion's eyes again. "If it's not regulation, I suppose that's alright." Just by that statement alone he could tell that she wasn't much of a rule breaker, but if he said it was alright, then she would take his word for it. "I should get the nausea medication out of my bag before you store it, though."

He nodded and gave her another kiss before he released her to get to her bag while he made arrangements with Registration. They recognized him by his identification and were fairly subservient to him when he made his requests, though he still spoke with them amiably enough, rather than the kind of condescending officer that he could have been to them by virtue of his rank. He took their luggage off the carriers once she was done with her bag, and headed with her off to a pockmarked section of the dock that had dozens of small pods attached to its surface for individual use.

He hadn't been kidding when he said it was a cramped fit. A third person could have fit inside the pod they were taking, but not comfortably. Instead of seats, there were three backboards with harnesses attached to them, one for the pilot and two for passengers, all facing out toward the pod's exterior with just a few centimeters between their bodies and the outer shell of glass and steel. Orion didn't actually fit comfortably in the harness at first, but she could tell that the way he had to slouch and bend his knees between the board and the glass was something he had long since gotten accustomed to, with his height.

He helped her get secured first, making sure all the webbing and straps were secured across her tightly before he started work on his own. "Good news is, you don't have to stay in harness the entire time. And the third board will collapse once we're at momentum. Just a little cozy for breakaway and docking."

Mercury nodded as she looked down at the harness and webbing, and she was grateful she had quickly taken the nausea medication, since she had a feeling she would need it in the small pod. The shuttle she had taken to meet him was much bigger, and she hadn't seen as much of the outside as she could at the moment. She reached up and ran her hand along his arm as he finished helping her get fastened. "I'm really glad you know what you're doing."

"I do." He promised quietly, turning to kiss along her palm as he finished with her. He was rough with the straps and the webbing, but clearly he knew he had to be in order to make sure she was secure, and wasn't afraid of breaking her in the process. Once he did have her settled, he leaned in to kiss her, though he had to do so from the side, since his own body didn't fit between hers and the glass. "How do you feel, alright? Anything else need a little more attention?" His hands were moving over her netting in ways she could tell were purposefully naughty, judging by the smile on his face.

She laughed and shook her head. Her burning arousal had settled at a simmer as soon as they had gotten onto the pod, especially after her concern with seeing all the busy technicians and her impending nausea. Mercury looked at his hand as he ran it over the netting, which really didn't make it any more scandalous than the fact that all the netting and harness had already hiked her dress nearly up to her underwear. Perhaps that was why people wore jumpsuits. "I feel alright. Thank you for your concern."

"You're welcome." He smiled and moved to pull the hatch shut manually so that the pod could go through its automated process to seal itself off from the dock. Harnessing himself fully took very little time, with his hands much more practiced at seeing to himself than seeing to others. "Whew, alright, here we go."

He brought the controls to life, the glass windows of the pod turning immediately to technical specifications and guidance assists that Orion could apparently make some sense of as his eyes darted around the interior. "Port control, this is pod Al-Jabbar 017, disengaging clamps. Field is checked, unlike the asshole who almost ran me over on my way in this morning . . . pressure is good, charge is full, passage is clear and wheels are up." The locking clamps holding the pod to the station began clicking themselves off right beneath Mercury's feet, and she could see the airlock closing to push them farther away, giving them a gentle shove away from the station in the process.

Al-Jabbar 017, you're clear for departure. Fly sa . . . the transmission cut off with some kind of interference, then went dead the next moment.

Orion just gave the console a confused look. "Huh. Well, 'have a nice day' to you too, pal." Orion made a few final adjustments to set the thrust away from the station, but just as Mercury felt the last of the docking clamps release beneath her, light exploded along the side of the station right in front of her eyes, and their pod was sent hurtling outward with tremendous, soundless force.

Everything was a blur. Mercury couldn't even think to be afraid as their pod went tumbling through space. She knew by the various curses flying out of Orion's mouth that they weren't flying by his control. She didn't know if their pod was damaged or what was happening, but she couldn't feel any rushing air or crushing vacuum, so the pod must have still been intact. They spun and wobbled and Orion continued to try and gain control, but all she could see once she had focused on the view in front of them was fire, debris, and one of the arms of the station . . .

Five arms of the station continued to spin beneath/beside/above them, but where the sixth had been, fire was billowing out into space through a field of shattered metal. The arm itself had been blown fully clear of the station at a break near the hub of the docks. Suddenly the initial shock wore off and she felt sick as she watched the whole scene unfurl. "Oh god . . . the arm . . ."

Orion was still struggling madly to get any kind of control over the pod, but he had them at least oriented in a stable plane within moments, the two of them watching helplessly as shrapnel tore through space. The pod was equipped with systems to target and destroy small pieces of debris before making impact, so as to maintain the structural integrity of the glass and steel, and the small burners at either end of the pod were busy as Orion and Mercury watched, keeping bits and pieces of the explosion at bay. He also had the presence of mind to turn on visual recording for the exterior, to capture as many images of what they were seeing as possible.

They were the only ship free and clear in close proximity to the Station, at least on their side, but Orion could see a larger shuttle moving away in the distance, already thousands of meters between it and Station Nine. "I guess now we know why those techs were in such a hurry." He said quietly.

Rotational inertia had kept the broken arm moving to fling it away from the hub of the station, but there had been obvious damage to the end of one of the adjacent arms as well, where the two arms had collided. Nine was off its axis of rotation from the impact and the explosion, and Orion could only imagine the havoc that was going on inside with the sudden shift in artificial rotation-generated gravity. Water was pouring out from a hundred broken lines, and people . . . there were people floating in the vacuum of space, killed instantly in the nothingness and frozen in postures of panic. Orion felt guilty for thinking of them as the lucky ones. Those on the falling arm would die a much more horrible death.

"It's already at terminal." He tried to be analytical about what they were seeing. Calm under pressure. It was a requirement of his job, even if calm often came with a lot of swearing. "Even with the auxiliary rotational thrusters on the far end of the arm, there's no way the arm can maneuver itself to regain orbit after something like that, even if someone could pay enough attention to try, with it in free-fall like that. It doesn't have the power or the maneuvering capabilities. It'll go atmospheric at that angle in a matter of minutes. And I don't see any ships in the area capable of trying to boost it back into stable orbit."

"So we just have to sit here and watch them die?!" Mercury was also usually quite calm under pressure but that was when she could do something about it; times when someone's life was beneath her fingertips, not when something was completely out of her control. They were already looking at dead bodies, but not only that, they were looking at thousands of people who were moments away from their end in Earth's atmosphere. Mercury felt sick imagining how they were feeling, those who were still alive in the disconnected piece and watching the view of Earth get inescapably closer.

Mercury had difficulty breathing as she watched, but her mind was also trying to figure out what happened. "There wasn't an alert. There wasn't any warning, no evacuation protocols sounded." They had *just* vacated that arm. They had barely made it off. Everyone, except the techs, had been calm. They were just going about their lives, and now they were facing certain death. If she and Orion hadn't hit it off, if they hadn't rushed through their meeting and been eager to get back to Three . . .

"That would have been us." She finally said as if she had just realized that he was still there next to her. "Minutes later, if we had been delayed . . ."

"Even for a few seconds. I know." He had obviously been thinking the same exact thing, but he didn't say anything else for a long while. Instead he just reached around the corner between their two seats to take her hand. It was as close as he could get to her, given the situation, but he wanted her to feel he was there.

"Any kind of structural failure would have generated warnings weeks before it actually failed. The public and loud kind. That was an explosion around the entire junction of the arm itself. There's no system that passes through that space that could have been responsible for that just by failure. They're better designed than that."

She could see him still glancing away at some of the controls, but she could also feel him getting frustrated as he watched. "This pod doesn't have . . . I've got nothing. I can't override the arm's systems from here because I don't have clearance to their central controls, and physically, there's no way anything I could do here would make a difference. It would just put us in the debris field and take us down with the rest of the arm." Even as he talked about the futility of it, he was still flipping through different reports, trying to get a fix on anything that could have been saved, but the arm was in pieces, all of the pieces beginning to arc down toward the Earth.

Mercury didn't even have enough knowledge of Earth to know where the pieces would approximately land, or what kind of impact that would have on the people down below. Sometimes she was amazed that anyone would want to continue to live on the planet's surface, knowing that they would die young, die slowly and painfully, and live lives that would have little influence simply because they were so short. Regardless, she didn't think their lives were meaningless, and she hoped the death toll wouldn't rise exponentially because of the pieces of the station potentially landing on a heavily populated area.

"So this was on purpose. Those people we saw, do you think they stole those uniforms? Do you think this is something that is going to get worse, some kind of rebellion against the Consortium or something?"

Orion was quiet as he considered that, but he didn't let go of her hand. "This is Nine. It's the Eleusis Initiative's headquarters." By his tone, it was obvious he doubted the correlation was a coincidence. "I'm going to drift us for a minute and do some more scans, see if there's anything I can pick up that would be helpful. Then I'm going to get us the hell out of here and over to Three as fast as possible. If there was more to come, I doubt they would've taken off like they did in that shuttle, but I don't want to be around to find out."

"As it is, they are going to want to question us." She knew authorities would want answers about why they were departing an arm that was destroyed only moments later. "I'm just glad we're not dead." Mercury said softly as she held onto his hand. "If I believed much in signs or omens, that's quite a sign. You saved my life."

"I'm not much for signs or omens myself, but I have to agree." The scans he had initiated chimed completion, and he sighed as he saved them, transmitting them back to his personal storage quickly before he started to work on their flight path from there. "If I had been matched with anybody else in creation, that hypothetical person and I would both be dead right now. I could just as easily say you saved my life, just by being you."

Mercury gripped his hand tighter. "Let's just get away from here. I can't watch any more of this. I'm a doctor, I can't just watch senseless death and not feel sick."

"On our way." He certainly wasn't going to blame her for that, and he squeezed her hand just to let her know it was alright.

He worked quickly, even just with one hand, and soon the thrust from the pod was pushing them at a steady acceleration away from the station and the destruction behind them, keeping it mostly out of her field of view, in favor of the moon far in the distance and the stars beyond that. The nose of the pod was pointed almost directly at the sun along their path of orbit to get to Three, but the glass darkened automatically to protect them, leaving them in a shaded, darker world, pressed into the backboards at just slightly greater than Earth-norm gravity while they accelerated.

Mercury was left on the side of the pod facing the stars, while Orion faced the Earth, looking down at the fragments of the station that were already beginning to turn into lights burning up in the atmosphere.

His mind was already doing the math on the rotation of the planet against the trajectory of the fragments, entering at a shallow enough orbit that they wouldn't entirely burn up on entry. Nine orbited along with most of the major stations, west to east around the Earth's midsection. They had been coming up over the Pacific Ocean at the time of departure, but they had moved in the meantime to pass over the District of California and the western districts of North America. The pieces of the ship would come down in the plains. Sparsely inhabited, as far as Orion was aware. That was some comfort, at least.

His eyes followed the path he knew the fragments would take, and he wondered who would be under the pieces when they crashed to Earth. Whoever it was, he hoped they saw it coming and had the good sense to get the hell out of the way.

5

Anna hoped for a better day when she woke to the sound of soft knocking on her door. She couldn't think straight through the fog of waking, and she certainly wasn't thinking about the fact that she'd slept in her bra and underwear instead of actually digging for clean clothes the night before. She hadn't wanted to bother, she had just fallen into the bed and gone straight to sleep.

When she opened the door, she was yawning and attempting to tame her hair, but she wasn't blind to the shirtless Logan standing in front of her. *Holy shit!* That was better than any coffee for a wake-up call.

"Uh, hi . . . I, um . . ." She wanted to run her hands across his abs *so* badly. No, hands weren't enough. "I forgot to set an alarm. I'm sorry."

"No worries. We're not on a schedule. Wheat'll still be out there whenever we get to it." He seemed more than a little taken aback when she got to the door in her underwear, but he wasn't complaining. He looked her over a few times before he managed to get his eyes back up to hers. "Your, um, your clothes are washed, unless you'd rather stay in your underwear for the day." He held her folded clothes out to her in one hand, the other still braced on the door frame.

"Sleep alright?"

"Yeah, I slept alright. Your house is a lot quieter than mine, though. The bed's a lot bigger too." She took her clothes with a nervous smile. "Thanks."

"Larissa has plenty of clothes if you need to borrow any of hers. The girl's one vice, online shopping." He rolled his eyes and stepped back from the door to let her get situated. "I packed up some breakfast for us, I'm gonna take it up the tower with some drinks for the day. I'll see you whenever you get up there."

Anna nodded, then looked him over thoroughly, drinking in the sight of him shirtless. He seemed completely unaffected. Usually her breasts could garner at least a *little* attention. "I'll be right out once I get dressed."

He looked her over again and shrugged with an attempt at a smile. "Do or don't. It's gonna be just us and the pigeons up there for the day. Nobody that needs impressing or the wearing of a bra if you're not feeling it."

She just laughed. "Well, alright then, Bickford. If I'm going bare chested, so are you."

He stepped back and looked down at himself in nothing but jeans and boots, and shrugged. "Looks like I'm one step ahead, then." He winked and turned around to head back down the hallway. "See you up there, bra or not."

The wink made her roll her eyes and turn back into the room to get dressed. It wasn't very nice of him to get her started and then *wink* at her. That was mean. It was always like this with them, the flirting, but they were always just friends. Nothing more.

The watchtower for the Bickford property was on a hill a few hundred meters from the mansion. The simple structure climbed nearly two hundred meters straight into the air, with bare metal stairs and a rudimentary lift to carry people to the top. The platform was covered above, but otherwise open to the air, giving an unobstructed view of the expansive Bickford farm for several kilometers in every direction. There was even a small restroom enclosed to one side that rendered bathroom breaks to the ground unnecessary on long days of monitoring the harvesters.

By the time she got up there, Logan had all the harvesters lined up around the base of the tower, finalizing grids for them to cover the entire farm. Much as he tried, though, he was incredibly slow at it. He was better at building the contraptions than driving them. He was still bare-chested and there was an entire cooler sitting between the two lounge chairs near the controls.

"You said something about breakfast, right? Your abs can be distracting." She went to the cooler first without looking at him again, since she was now feeling more embarrassed about him seeing her in her underwear than anything else. It wasn't like she'd been trying to seduce him, even if she wanted to. Not that he was seduce-able by her. Nor was she his type, if Melanie had been any indication. They also had years of history as just friends. "There better be something good in the cooler to make up for it."

"I got a variety, and I got your favorites. Even the non-alcoholic ones." He looked back at her and pointed to the smaller cooler beside the big one, which had freshly made eggs, bacon and waffles in it, with all the needful fixings and a few sets of flatware on the side. "Help yourself, we're gonna be here a while."

Anna plated some food for him before she got herself a plate and a beer, regardless of the hour. She sat down next to his seat to get a couple bites in before she started helping him. "Sorry about this morning. I was still pretty out of it. Still am, a little."

"Nothing to be sorry about." He smiled over at her and thanked her for the plate, grabbing a bite here and there between working on the layouts for the harvesters. "Normally the only other company in the house is whichever one of Liam's girlfriends he feels like having over every night for dinner, so I'm a little out of practice with other houseguests. I should've called up first on the com or something, given you some warning." He shrugged, clearly not all that sorry about it. "Last night was nice to sit around and have a decent meal with people I actually like for a change."

Dinner the night before had been a lot of fun, as they had spent most of it making fun of Liam and the various stupid situations he got himself into. Logan had only left to go to bed with the greatest reluctance, and even then, he had stood just inside his door for the worse part of half an hour contemplating whether to go to sleep or go find Anna.

She smiled over at him and ate a few more bites before she jumped in to help, since she didn't need to let him do all the work with mapping the harvesters. "Well, I always figured between you and Liam, you'll fill the house with kids eventually. That'll make for a full table of people you hopefully like. That's still possible."

Anna wanted him to have hope for his future, even though she knew he didn't like to think about the future most of the time. "My dad tells me it's possible for me too, but he also doesn't know I've been accepted to go to Eleusis, so I'm sure he'd say something else if I told him that information."

"Well, Eleusis could still be full of kids for you one of these days. I'm fairly sure I saw something like that on the brochure." He got the few harvesters in motion that he had finished programming, glad to have the harvest finally, really under way, and even more glad to see that they didn't completely shut down with the first few meters of harvested grain they took in.

"News this morning was talking about the reports they've gotten on folks who've admitted to being accepted. They only got data on a few dozen, but they're almost all young. Some even Emily's age. So they're definitely planning to give us time to do some multiplying and replenishing."

A single mention of 'us' and all Anna could think about was 'multiplying and replenishing' with Logan, which wasn't going to help her get through a long day next to him. She nearly choked on her sip of beer and tried to cover it up with a cough. "Well, no one has knocked me up yet."

He was quiet after that, both because he wasn't sure how to answer it and because the one answer that did come to mind wasn't one he knew anyone wanted to hear. There were worse things in life than being incapable of getting pregnant. Like getting pregnant repeatedly only to miscarry the baby every single time before twelve weeks.

Over, and over, and over again.

"If you decide to go, I'm sure as soon as you walk in the door, they'll go over you with some kind of scan and tell you everything you never wanted to know about what's going on with every system in your body. I doubt they're gonna be taking anyone along who's not a potential parent. Wouldn't make sense in a new world like that."

"I know. I didn't figure they would actually accept me if all that blood work up front didn't tell them what they needed to know. It's just weird, you know? I mean, it's not like I've been trying real hard, but there have been plenty of chances for it to happen. Maybe I wasn't meant to be with any of those guys anyway. My dad's never liked a single one I've been with."

"For the record, neither have I." He cracked his own beer and took a sip, while it was still cold. "Some have been worse to watch than others. It wasn't so bad when you actually seemed halfway happy with them. But lately . . . that hasn't seemed to happen as much."

Anna gave all her attention to the beer. "I don't want any of them. Not permanently. I'm not interested in any of them and I'm tired of pretending like I should be, just for the sake of procreation. It's almost too bad. I fucking love sex, but with the wrong person it's a gamble every time."

"True enough. I swear, I sat at home and seethed that whole month after you told me you slept with Warren at that party he threw at his place. As your best friend, I can't say I've ever particularly looked forward to going to your wedding, but I did *not* want to go watch you walk down the aisle to be Warren's lucky number *seventh* wife."

He didn't bother hiding his disgust at the thought of the man, but it was a commonly-held opinion. Warren was the second-wealthiest man in the district, behind Logan himself, but the differences between the two men were vast. Warren partied regularly and made no secret out of the fact that any woman who got pregnant with his child was welcome to move into his mansion and be one of his wives. Even if the life he provided was comfortable, he was a notorious asshole to every such woman who came along, and never bothered to be much of a father to the children he sired on them.

"Well, he's attractive, and once I get drunk enough, I don't discriminate. He has a decent penis, I was surprised." She laughed even though she knew he didn't want to know about Warren's penis. "I'm a freak and you know it. My curiosity gets the best of me. If I sleep around and I'm known for it, guys don't get as freaked out about my experimental nature. They certainly don't complain when my experience comes in handy."

"Yeah, I know, I've met you." He took a long sip of his beer, suddenly wishing it was something stronger for that particular conversation. He settled back in his chair to enjoy the rest of his breakfast and hide the fact that his jeans were suddenly a size too tight.

"But I've never thought your curiosity has *gotten* the best of you. Your curiosity *is* the best of you. Sexually, all I know is secondhand, obviously, but just in everything, you're always up in the world's face asking questions. Pissed off our teachers, sure, but you get shit done." He shrugged with another sip. "You also get every man for a hundred kilometers excited as soon as you step into a room, on account of what you spent all of our last year in school learning how to do, by reputation, better than any other woman who's ever lived."

That made her laugh loudly, since that was a larger reputation than she realized she had created for herself. "Ever lived? That might be an exaggeration." Anna wasn't as active as she had once been in her sex life, but she was certain she could please any man who was interested if she wanted to. "That was a crazy year. Too bad you were already taken, huh?"

She attempted to make it sound as teasing as she could, but the whole reason she had jumped into her sex adventure was because Logan had started seriously dating Melanie. One drunk night he told her that he thought Melanie was 'the one' and instead of getting depressed about never having her best friend, she decided to fully jump into lots of sex. Thanks to medical marvels that had eradicated nearly all sexually transmitted diseases, she had come out of it physically unscathed. Emotionally? Not so much.

"It really is. Just too bad." He laughed along with her, since that was all they'd ever done, joke about the other person's experience and move on with life. "And I doubt it's an exaggeration. If you were ever to find out some other woman was better than you in anything, you'd be all over her to pry out trade secrets. I can't imagine sex would be any different."

"Well, I wouldn't be all over her. Tried that a few times, didn't work for me. But you are right, I would want to know her secrets." Anna looked over at him, hesitating, then went back to work. "Can I ask you something you probably don't want to answer?"

"I'm more scared that you asked if you could ask instead of just asking." He took another bite from his plate and got back up to stand at the console with her, since it was easier to hear her when he was close by. The harvesters were effective, but they were also incredibly loud, even at two hundred meters in the air. "But yeah, sure, go ahead."

"Do you think you'll get married again someday?" She looked over at him and certainly didn't move away when he moved closer. "I know it's only been a little more than a year. I just mean eventually."

From the look on his face, she was right, it wasn't a question he wanted to answer. He kept working as he thought about it, but eventually just leaned on the console. "I don't know. There was . . ." he hesitated, which wasn't like Logan. He wasn't one to stall a conversation, didn't get flustered, didn't stutter. The fact that any subject could make that otherwise was a testament to just how difficult it was for him to talk about it.

"When we were going to Doc Weber, after every . . . time . . . she ran every kind of test she could think of. Started trying to crack vampire jokes about how much blood she took from us to send it off to this lab or that lab across the planet. It came back . . . after the fifth loss, just a month before the sixth, that there was some kind of undefined factor in my genes that, when combined with hers, was creating fetuses that would force an immune response. And once they knew what they were looking for, they could tell the response had gotten stronger in each blood sample they had taken from her. They told us that since there was no genetic therapy for it, not even a name for it, and it wasn't caught early on, there was no way she would ever carry a child to term. Not mine or anyone else's."

It was more about his late wife than he had ever said to anyone, as far as Anna knew, since Melanie's suicide, and it was an explanation that underscored everything about the way her best friend had been living his life for the past year. "So I really don't know. What I want hasn't changed. Probably never will. But I'm not going to put someone else through that. Liam just decided he's going to whore himself around as much as possible and if anyone he sleeps with miscarries even once, he's never gonna get near them again, just keep going until he finds one that sticks. I'm . . . not going to do that."

Anna reached out and ran her hand down his bare arm. She wanted to comfort him, but she also just wanted to touch him, even if it was selfish of her in his vulnerable moment. "I wished so many times that I could have helped you when I could tell you were struggling, even though I didn't know everything. And I can't imagine what Melanie went through. I just wish she would have realized that even without babies, she was with a man worth sticking around for. That she was still loved."

Anna knew if she had been the one to actually capture Logan, she never would have let him go. Anna thought at times that she was broken since she hadn't ever been pregnant, but marrying someone like Logan would have made her happy. Children or not. Children weren't everything, even if they were a priority for most. Humankind on Earth needed lots of procreation, after all, but *Anna* didn't need it.

He nodded without looking at her or moving away from her touch. "She spent . . . a lot of her time wishing for the world to be different. Even asked me what I thought about going to space once, turning Orbital. I didn't really think through why she was asking the question when I gave her my answer. Stupid of me." Time since Melanie's death had given him lots and lots of opportunity to think back on every single mistake he'd ever made in his relationship with her, and dwell on each one until each misstep was a possible cause of the catastrophe that had eventually come to pass.

"She just . . . I don't know. I feel like I had to accept the way things are after Mom and Dad died, and I just kept moving from there. But some people never do. Some people can't. It's just not in their programming, because it's not supposed to be. The world isn't supposed to be like this, half a life to live and half of what's left over spent worrying about how short it is."

"I know. It makes me angry to think about all the life we should be living. It's part of the reason why I want to go to Eleusis. Maybe my family can be saved from dying so young." She hoped that her family would be able to join her on Eleusis eventually. Anna didn't let go of his arm, and she wanted to move closer to him, though she just remained content with touching his arm at the moment. "I just want to see you happy again."

He managed to give a quiet smile and move his arm to

put it around her shoulders, holding her in against him in a friendly embrace as they both looked out over the control screens at the massive machines humming away below. "Happy is just as broad a range as any other feeling, I think. There's lots of different kinds. Right now, happy is thirty-four harvester machines that are actually doing their job, good weather, good breakfast, good beer, and good company. Hopefully a good harvest too, in . . . fourteen hours and seventeen minutes, if all goes well." He was impressed that the work was going to be done that quickly, but he had been working to tweak the machines all summer to improve their efficiency, after all.

"Fourteen hours, huh? That's a long time to be shirtless." She teased as she attempted to poke his side, but she couldn't do it easily with his arm around her, so she just ended up running her hand down his skin. "Are you going to get cold? I know I would be in trouble if I went fourteen hours without a shirt."

"If you go fourteen hours without a shirt, you're not gonna be in trouble. You'll *be* trouble yourself." He shook his head. "I'm alright, though. I didn't see the point if I was just gonna be hanging out up here all day watching the machines and watching the stations go by." He nodded up to the sky where one was just cresting the horizon, barely visible in the distance as little more than a speck. Once right overhead, they looked like far-distant snowflakes about the size of one of his fingernails when stretched out at arm's length, but so far in the distance it just looked like a shimmering white and silver dot coming up over the world.

Anna didn't pull away from his embrace as she looked up at the station above them, since she liked being pressed into his side and feeling his arm around her shoulders. "I still don't know what to do about Eleusis. I applied because I wanted to get away." She didn't say that it was to get away from him, especially because she didn't *actually* want that. Certainly not right now. "If I do go, would you consider coming with me? It wouldn't be so daunting with someone

I know. Someone I care about."

"No, it wouldn't be." He looked down at her under his arm and moved his hand up over her shoulder, just to hold her in close. "I'd rather be there with you than anyone else. Certainly over a bunch of strangers from around the world. And I feel like I could make a difference up there. Help build something new, get the place ready so people don't have to be dying for half their lives anymore."

"There's a meeting, I'm sure you remember, in St. Louis. It's supposed to be a discussion-forum type thing before we're due to report." Anna was trying to focus on Eleusis instead of the way his hand felt on her shoulder, but it wasn't working. He hadn't allowed her to be close to him in a long time. "Do you want to go with me?"

"That's a good idea. I was gonna blow it off completely, but it'd be good to know a few more details before we decide to sign on to this thing or not." He knew he should let go of her, but she was making no move to get away from him. Keeping her close felt too good to just let the moment end. "If you think you can go nine hours with me in a car without killing me. Might be harder than you think."

"Nine hours in a car? The last time I . . ." Yeah, he didn't need to know how she usually handled road trips with men. "I can handle it, I think. You're my best friend." She needed that reminder more than he did, she was sure.

He turned his back on the controls, the fields, the noisy harvesters below, the sky, and the station that was quickly making its way across the cloudless field of blue. His arm fell from around her shoulders, but the way he was standing, his arm was still braced on the controls near her waist. He wanted to reach out and hold her against him, but he wasn't sure what would happen if he took that kind of step. It could make things weird between them forever. But then again, what he was about to say also had that possibility, and he didn't let that stop him from saying it.

"I've heard from different articles that they've got a program up there in orbit that takes people and matches them with whoever seems most appropriate. Not just randomly, either, but some really deep in-depth cyber-dating predictive modeling shit. Has something like a ninety-two percent success rate of producing marriages of longer than ten years. It wasn't in the brochure, but I imagine as scientific as they're trying to be about Eleusis, they'd match us both off to some stranger as soon as we get up there. I have to say, I'm not looking forward to that part."

Anna looked up into his eyes after he turned toward her, and she wanted to step into him and hold herself against him. What would it be like to be the one on the receiving end of Logan's romantic attention? "I don't know how I feel about that, but I think I'd rather choose to be with someone than to be paired up by some algorithm." Anna did reach out to touch his hand with her fingers. "I don't care about some stupid program. I care about being with someone who matters to me."

"I think I'd prefer that too." He said without allowing himself to think about it, though he froze completely afterward. What was happening? Was she actually interested in him? She'd been beating him up since they were in elementary school and he'd been giving her shit for her taste in boyfriends since she picked up the very first one.

There were reasons why he had kept his distance from her, reasons why they had just remained friends for so long. He didn't want to ruin what they had, the friendship that had been so important to them both. But if he said anything else, did anything at all, then there was a chance they would do exactly that.

Even frozen as the rest of him was, though, he moved his hand to take hers.

That was an innocent thing, right? Friends could touch each other that way and not worry about it later.

Right?

"I . . . think it would be . . ." he gripped her hand tighter, looking for the right word, but he was cut off mid-sentence by both their phones going off at the same time across the platform, chiming out a shrill claxon that broke his concentration completely and had him looking away from her to see what the hell was going on.

All it said across the front of either device was EMERGENCY, with no other details specified. "What the hell kind of emergency could be happening? It's calm as a cave out here, can't be any kind of tornado warning."

Anna wanted the warning to be some kind of malfunction. She didn't want to lose the moment, but it was already lost. She moved away from him to look out over the fields for anything out of the ordinary, but it looked calm and peaceful around them.

Until she looked up.

Anna had to squint, but there was definitely something going on in the sky. "What is that?"

Logan had checked his phone to see if there were any more details to be had, but he looked up when she said something. As he approached the edge of the platform with her, his eyes got steadily wider as the fireball in the sky got larger and larger.

He could see the station that had been coming overhead just beyond it, incredibly small at such a distance, but visibly spinning in ways that the stations were absolutely not supposed to spin. And not only was it spinning, one of its six arms was missing.

"That's incoming." He had been watching the fireball in confusion, wondering why it was nothing more than a growing sphere of light in the sky when normally meteors formed trails of fire behind them. A few seconds told him the reason it was getting larger and not longer was because it was coming straight for them. "Holy shit, that's incoming!" He gave a shout as a delayed reaction, and grabbed Anna by her arms and pulled her away from the edge.

He had barely enough time to throw her to the floor and cover her body with his own before they saw and felt the impact. The tower shook beneath them as if a giant had kicked it.

Through the screened bottom half of the deck beneath the control panels, they could both see pillars of fire assaulting the ground in furious falls kilometers away to the west as they huddled against the floor. Some pieces of debris fell faster than others, and the fires on the ground were too far away to interfere with the sight of an entire station arm cutting down in a firestorm toward the plains. It hit like a giant dagger before cracking apart under the shattering force of the impact, and fell in a thousand pieces to the ground as if in slow motion.

Only when they had seen the entire arm beginning to break apart and the hail of broken pieces turned to a light drizzle of devastation did the sound and full force of the impact finally reach them through the air. It assaulted the tower like a hundred sonic booms, hitting the morning stillness like a sledgehammer to the face. It left their ears ringing and set the tower swaying dangerously, but Logan held Anna in a vice grip through it all.

There was nothing for Anna to do but hold onto Logan. If a piece of debris came at them, there was nothing they could do to protect themselves from something that had fallen from space, and certainly nothing could stop something the size of a station arm. She couldn't even hear him saying her name at first, but eventually through the ringing in her ears, she opened her eyes to look up at him.

By some miracle, they were uninjured, and most of whatever had fallen was kilometers away, but the pieces were so large that they were certainly visible from a distance.

"What the fuck?!?" Anna hissed. If there had been some kind of station malfunction, they should have been warned, for fuck's sake. "What was that?!? A whole fucking arm?" God, had there been people on that arm?

"That's what it looked like." He was still looking back and forth between her and the sky, but it didn't look like there were any other large pieces still coming down, just flashes of light in the upper atmosphere as bits of dust and debris were vaporized on their way down.

He pulled away from her just enough to help her to her feet and stood there looking out at the devastation in the distance for a while, completely dumbfounded. "We need to get moving. If that came down where it looks like it did, that's over the Reeves farm. Are you okay?"

He was still looking her over frantically and still looking back out at all the fires as well as his own equipment. Some of the harvesters had actually been shoved off track by the impact, but it looked like they were working on self-correcting down below. They weren't his primary concern. Anna was.

"I'm alright. You were my body armor." She patted him on the arm, but when they were both up on wobbly legs, she could see the damage. "The fires. They could rip through everything! We need to check on the Reeves and get people out here to get the fires under control!" Shock had stopped her from panicking immediately but she had never been the type to let panic linger for long.

He didn't trust the lift after the tower had been shaken, so he immediately ran to the stairs and raced down them quickly once he was steady, barely touching each landing on the way down, Anna right behind him. It was a short jog back to the house and the massive auxiliary garage off to one side, but luckily Logan's truck was parked close to the front with the keys still inside. There were emergency supplies already stowed in the bed of it for general use around the district.

As soon as he got the truck started and Anna was in the seat next to him, he pulled her across the seat to sit in the middle beside him, unwilling to let her get even a few feet away from him. He didn't comment on the move, didn't make a big deal out of it, he just got the truck moving as quickly as possible before he grabbed his phone. He tried calling Larissa or Liam, but lines were jammed. "Probably fried cell service in the whole area when it came down.

Damn it."

"I can't get through either." Her phone was giving her all sorts of warnings, but otherwise she couldn't get it to make a single phone call. "Ben and Liam will take care of everyone else." Hopefully they were alright enough to do that, since it didn't look like any debris had gotten as far as the homesteads. "Do you think there were people on that? There had to be, right?" Her stomach twisted as she thought about all the people that could be dead. "Could anyone even survive that?"

Logan shook his head with obvious grief in his eyes. "Not a chance. Not moving that fast with that much debris through the whole mess. That was an entire arm of a station. There had to be thousands of people on it when it came down. Unless they evacuated it beforehand and did the demolition on purpose, in which case, they need to work on their fucking landings. Bring it down in the Pacific or something, it's an easier target." He didn't sound like he thought it was intentional, though, and he only drove angrier once he was out on an open stretch of road.

"We would have gotten warning about a demolition. And most of those they jettison off pieces at a time and then dispose of the pieces. A whole arm? That's unlikely. It must have been some sort of accident." She looked up toward the sky again, then linked her arm through Logan's, and he could feel her trembling. "I hope everyone is okay. Our families. The Reeves."

He moved to hold her hand as he drove, his eyes scanning the sky and the sides of the road to make sure things were clear. There were two places where debris had shattered part of the road and he had to take the truck around it, but most of the damage seemed to be off the main stretch between his estate and the Reeves.

The Reeves farm was a smaller farm when it came to crops, but they had massive amounts of pastureland set aside for cattle, some of which Logan saw stampeding in panic as they got closer. There was an entire herd of horses that had apparently broken free of their paddocks and rushed onto the road just ahead of Logan's truck in time for him to stop and let them pass. Cows weren't far behind, rushing away in every direction to get away from the devastation.

The Reeves' home was nowhere near the monstrosity Logan's was, but it was still a large estate house, or it had been, minutes before. Half the house had been immediately destroyed on impact with a massive shard of metal and twisted glass, and some of the other half was still on fire. The main crater of impact from the bulk of the arm itself was visible just a few hundred meters away from the house. The landscape was dotted with fire and choked with dust. Smoke was beginning to cover everything, and Logan cursed as he saw an entire bevy of cars and trucks parked in front of the house.

"Of all days to have a fucking party . . ." He pulled up near the side of the house that wasn't burning, and left the engine running as he jumped out and grabbed a crowbar and fire extinguisher from the bed of the truck. "Check the back of the house! There has to be somebody!" The fires were incredibly loud around them, and his ears were still ringing from the impact as it was.

Anna jumped into motion, but she had no idea what she would be able to do with a wildfire and such massive debris that someone would need a crane to remove. She ran around to the back of the house as quickly as she could, but she couldn't hear much over the roar of the fire.

"Can anyone hear me? Hello?!?" She ran wherever the roaring flames weren't, and didn't even hear screams. She couldn't get very close to the house, but she could see part of the arm, and tiny compartments pockmarked along it. It looked like residential units, some kind of orbital apartment complex. There was smoke coming off the arm, glass everywhere, but she had to look closer.

The arm itself was every bit as sterile and lifeless as she might have expected from a space station, and as a result, the fires burning along it were contained to broken air ducts and sparse furniture that had caught fire on entry. Instead of fires, though, there were masses of death everywhere she looked, telling the story of the arm's final, terrifying moments.

There were huddled groups of what had once been living people crushed up against the bulkheads of the broken corridors, turned to little more than gelatinous masses of burst skin and shattered bone on impact. Some others had apparently had the foresight to web themselves into restraints within their chambers or small craft, but the safety webbing hadn't been anywhere near enough to help, let alone save them.

A few of the bodies she found were intact, but either the people's necks had been snapped or some other piece of shrapnel had broken free and killed them on contact. One woman Anna couldn't look at for long had secured herself perfectly, but the metal against her back was still glowing bright orange from the heat of atmospheric entry. What remained of the woman was still on fire.

The closest thing to a survivor she found was a man webbed into what looked like a tiny escape pod with two other unoccupied boards, surrounded by mostly-intact glass and steel. The board had failed in the landing, and had cracked behind him, crushing the man's spine in the process to leave him broken beneath a single massive fracture in the glass. On the man's chest, falling halfway out of the jumpsuit he was wearing, was a handheld tablet with one corner cracked by debris. The screen was still on and flickering with an image of the man's face, living and screaming, over and over again. He seemed to have been recording just as things were coming to an end.

Anna had to look away several times, and she had thrown up more than once at the sights in front of her as she wandered through looking for survivors. She stared at the man who had probably suffered the least horrific death, though the entire sight was one horror after another. Tears ran down her cheeks at the sight of the poor man playing over and over on the tablet, and she couldn't help but say something. Maybe . . . "Sir? Sir?" He didn't stir, but she moved closer anyway.

In her shock and distress over the entire scene, she slipped and fell forward toward the dead man. At first she screamed, both in fear and pain, since something had sliced her arm open in the fall, but the pain wasn't as bad as coming face to face with the man who had died. She retched several times before she scrambled to get away and get free, and the tablet caught her eye again. Maybe it would give them answers about what had happened. There had to be some kind of answer, didn't there? She grabbed at the tablet several times before she managed to grab it, but it was made even more difficult by all the slippery blood pouring out of her arm.

Anna held it to her chest as she stumbled out of the pod, twisting her ankle in the process and eventually ending up on her knees on the ground where the tablet skittered out of her hands again. She closed her eyes as she tried to get her bearings. She had never seen so much death, mutilation, destruction, and death was a daily occurrence for life on Earth.

A few minutes passed with her getting her head back on straight, but she was shaken out of her thoughts by an explosion nearby on the main part of the arm, throwing more debris into the air. Someone was calling her name at what seemed like an incredible distance through the flames, but it seemed like a very long time before the person actually reached her.

Logan looked like a different person from the last time she'd seen him just a few minutes before, his shirtless torso covered in blackened marks that could have been soot or burns. It was difficult to tell through the smoke and haze of the fires. "Come on, we've got to get to Doc Weber's! I got Kevin and a few of the others out, they're in the truck."

Anna agreed, though she was dazed as she attempted to

get up, and she became even more dizzy once she was standing. She barely had a chance to look down at her injury to see that her arm was flayed open the entire length of her forearm and still bleeding before her vision started to get blurry. "I don't know what I cut my arm on . . ."

Logan was already ripping at a scrap of fabric he brought with him from the front side of the house to wrap her arm tightly. If he didn't, she was likely to lose too much blood and pass out, or worse.

"Looks like the glass." He said as he picked a few shards off her arm before he finished wrapping it up. He looked down at what she'd found and saw the tablet give a final sputter of the man's face on the screen just before it switched off completely. He grabbed the tablet and put it into her hands before he scooped her up in his arms and started jogging back toward the front of the house. She could feel he was favoring one leg, but he didn't falter as he ran.

There was one other able-bodied man out in front of the house, a young man no more than Cory's age, sitting in the bed of Logan's truck trying to hold pressure on two of his family members at once, one of them an older sister, the other a cousin, if Anna remembered correctly. Their mother was bandaged up about as well as Anna herself was, lying unconscious but otherwise apparently whole. Logan took Anna to the front seat and shoved the tablet beneath it before racing around to his side to get the truck in gear.

Anna's vision remained blurry on the way to Doc Weber's, since the doctor's home wasn't exactly close, and her arm continued to bleed. The ringing in her ears was still a constant annoyance, since it made hearing Logan more difficult on top of feeling weak and dizzy. "There were so many people. Half of them . . . just . . . goo. It was worse than any horror movie I've ever seen."

"I saw." Logan managed to say, putting the pedal down to the floor every time he had an open stretch of road, while trying to take even the gentlest curves slower so as not to aggravate the injured he was transporting. His truck was no ambulance, but it had to suffice. "I don't know how something like this happens. A failure on that kind of scale makes no sense. Those stations have been flying for hundreds of years, replaced bit by bit to make them new all over again. I've never heard of anything like this in all that time. Not even close."

"Then it had to be an attack." Which was also unheard of, but to Anna it was more likely than the kind of technological failure it would take for such a catastrophe to happen. Humans were capable of such senselessness and violence. Technology was more careful and precise. "I don't know what that means, or why anyone would attack that station . . ." She held her uninjured hand to one of her ringing ears. "I wish I'd never seen it. That's going to give me nightmares for the rest of my life."

Logan got to a long stretch of straight road and put out his hand to take hers, careful to avoid any of the damage that had been done to her arm. "I wish we hadn't either. All I care about right now is getting you to Doc Weber and getting you fixed up."

Anna looked down at his hand holding hers and her eyes filled with tears again. Anna wasn't often a crier. This day was different. She could have died. Logan could have died. They could have died in the tower, he could have died running into the burning house. Some other part of the arm could have exploded and killed them both.

Then what?

Then they would have been an almost, a sad, pathetic almost, and nothing else to show for their lives but loneliness and pain. That was what.

"Promise you'll stay with me? You could have died. I don't know what I would do without you, Logan." She found herself saying through the ringing in her ears. She didn't want to leave his side.

"You're not getting out of my sight." He promised with another squeeze of her hand, though he couldn't take his eyes off the road as he drove. They were eating up countryside in a hurry, but it was still a long way to the Webers, and there were lives to be saved in the back of the truck.

6

When she woke up, it was in a place she'd seen more times in her youth than she wanted to remember. Doc Weber's house and the clinic she operated were in the middle of the only thing in their district that could be called a town, though it was home to just under three hundred people. It mostly consisted of the shipping depot and market where products were imported and exported out to more major traffic routes. The clinic took up a small, oft-rebuilt wing of what had once been a full hospital, back when the town had been a full city.

Anna opened her eyes to a broad, open room that echoed with other people's footsteps. She was lying in a bed with the railing raised on both sides to keep her from rolling off, next to the windows where she could look out at the sun beginning to set. From the way she'd been laid out on the bed, she could see the Reeves family across from her, or what was left of it. Mrs. Reeves was still unconscious, as was her daughter in the bed beside her, with her brother sitting and looking back and forth nervously at them both. The cousin was nowhere to be seen.

Next to her bed, away from the windows, Logan was sitting in a chair with a blanket draped around his shoulders, working away at a message on his phone. It was obvious from the look of him and the scent of smoke still hanging in the air that he hadn't washed or been tended to since the rescue, if he even needed such attention.

Her own ankle was set in a tight brace that was keeping pressure on it to take the swelling down, and her arm had been wrapped in a clear bandage after cleaning. Beneath it, she could see the spray Dr. Weber had used to bind her arm back together and regrow the skin. It was only a patch until her own body took hold, but she knew from previous scrapes and cuts that she would be back to a normal arm within a day or two.

"Hey." Her voice crackled as she spoke to Logan next to her, and she tried to sit up slowly, but she was feeling lightheaded and her mouth felt dry. The taste in her mouth was rancid, probably from all the times she'd thrown up. "Logan."

He looked up immediately when she said his name, and she could see not only soot but a few burns on his face that had been only hastily treated. Still, he moved quickly, and got to the side of the bed to take her good hand. "Nice of you to wake up. Doc said she thought it would be later on tonight before you decided to join us. How's the arm?"

"It feels pretty numb." She glanced down at it again but she scooted aside so that he could sit more on the bed with her instead of on the edge. "I feel numb. About everything. How are they?" Anna nodded toward the Reeves family, but she didn't think he would have good news.

"Those three are gonna be alright. She's gonna keep them here for smoke inhalation and some more treatments for their burns. Kendra caught the worst of it, and Kevin's still freaking out about her, no matter how much the doc says she'll be fine. Their mom took some hits to the head, but Doc said the scans come through clear, just a matter of waiting for her to wake up. Their cousin is in surgery. Cathy. Been there for most of the afternoon."

He nodded across the room at the boy sitting with his

sister, and actually smiled as he shook his head. "Crazy idiot saw a fireball coming straight for his house and his first instinct was to start taping every damn thing. He got most of everything on video, including you and me showing up to the house. He was taping from the cellar where he ran when things started blowing up, but then kept recording from his house once he got out."

"He better hide it. Authorities will come through soon enough, I'm sure, and they'll want to confiscate anything that might have information. That's how they deal with problems." Anna curled into Logan's side as soon as he was on the bed with her, and she closed her eyes, pretending the tears that came were from the pain and not from the reminder that she could have lost Logan. "Are we staying here?"

"No. She said as soon as you were awake, we could go. Though she made me promise to let her give me a once-over before I left." He put the blanket around her along with his arm to run it along her back, heaving a sigh of relief that she was awake and talking.

"Cory was apparently messing around with one of the horses and got his collarbone broken when they spooked at the boom earlier. He's fine, don't worry. Sierra was down that way already, so she stopped in and took care of him. I told your dad I would take care of you up here and get you back to my place to rest for the night before we go the rest of the way back to your place in a couple days. They were all asking about you."

"I'm an idiot for getting myself all banged up. I just . . . I couldn't do anything to get into the house from the back, it was all on fire. I thought I should at least check and see if anyone had survived the crash, even though I knew it was nearly impossible. I had to see. I had to make sure there wasn't someone I could . . ." She sighed and wiped at her tears with her good hand. "Now all I can think about is all the wasted life, and I thought about how meaningless my . . . I don't . . . I don't want to be meaningless."

Without allowing himself the time for any hesitation, he leaned down and rested his forehead against hers, his grip on her back tightening as he moved in close to her. "You could never be meaningless, Anna." He stayed like that with his eyes closed, then pulled away enough to kiss her cheek, resting his face there as if he was either hesitating or thinking. He slowly pulled away, sighing as he looked down at her. "I'm gonna go see if she's out of surgery so we can get going, alright? Decent sleep in a decent bed is as good an antidote for anything as I've ever heard of."

Anna was still crying quietly as she agreed, but she didn't look at him after he pulled away. She couldn't. Not even Eleusis was worth it if Logan wasn't with her. She needed Logan, but she didn't know what would happen if she told him the truth. Anna could see clear as day that he wasn't ready to be with anyone, and she knew it was possible he would never actually want to marry again, much less marry her. What she didn't know was how much longer she could go without telling him the truth. After all that had happened, she knew she needed to. Sooner rather than later.

True to his word, Logan didn't leave the large room with all the care beds in it, but the Reeves' cousin never returned either. Doc Weber came back a few minutes after Anna woke up and broke the news to Kevin that his cousin hadn't made it through surgery. The next half hour was spent with the doctor fussing over Logan and his many injuries, most of them burns, before he finally managed to argue her into releasing him to take Anna home.

Logan did look much improved by the time he got back to her, though he had bandages around part of his ribs and one low on his left cheek against his jawline where the burns had been most severe. He helped her up out of the bed and held onto her hands to make sure she could walk for a while. Anna managed to clean up a little too, and she felt a little more herself with some soap and toothpaste before he held her hand as they went down to the truck.

Afterward, as before, he didn't seem satisfied just having

her there with him. She needed to be under his arm at all times and tight against him so that he would know she was alright. "Word already got out somehow that we were the first ones on the scene." He said quietly, and only once they were in motion. "Some guy came by Doc Weber's wanting to talk to us a few hours ago. She told him we were both still unconscious from smoke inhalation. She didn't recognize him."

"I knew someone would come. It doesn't matter." She looked down at his leg instead of up at his face, since her insides were twisted into knots. "Obviously we don't know anything."

"We do know one thing." He said just as quietly, rubbing at her shoulder as he sighed. "While you were asleep, I watched some of the headlines. That arm broke off of Station Nine. Orbital headquarters of the Eleusis Initiative. There was no report on whether the people who died were part of the Initiative or not, but still, it's . . . unnerving."

"Do they think it was someone attacking the Initiative? All those people died because of that?" She knew there wasn't an actual answer to her questions, but she had to ask it out loud. Especially if they were still going to consider being a part of it.

He shook his head. "Officially, they're still claiming it was a catastrophic technical failure. But they're naturally running a full investigation to determine the truth of the matter. Some outlets are theorizing about protesters attacking after the acceptance letters went out the other day, all kinds of things are floating around. And any combination of it could be true, honestly. I have no idea."

"I don't even know if I can think about Eleusis right now. It seems so unimportant. Unreal, even." She closed her eyes and memorized the feeling of being close to Logan, since if the truth actually did bubble up and spew out of her mouth, she wanted to remember what it was like when he still wanted her to be close to him. "Maybe that's the pain medication. I don't know."

"Well, if it is, I'm glad it's working." His tone attempted to be light, but failed, and he rubbed her shoulder again as they drove into the evening. "You can go on and sleep if it's still making you drowsy. I'll carry you in once we get to the house."

"I don't want to miss any more." She said softly as she slowly opened her eyes to finally look up at him. "What if you die tomorrow and this is the last thing I have to remember of us together, sitting next to you?"

"I've got no interest in dying. Certainly not tomorrow." He said without looking back at her.

A few kilometers later, he found a spot that had once upon a time been a house and the driveway that led up to it. The ruins of the place had long since caved in and been reclaimed by nature, but the first part of the driveway was intact enough to let him park.

He brought the truck to a stop and paused with his hand on the gear shift, having some kind of conversation with himself before he turned slowly to face Anna. "And no, if I was going to die tomorrow, I wouldn't want your last memory of me to be just sitting here driving home."

The stillness of the world, the absolute emptiness of the planet on which they lived, seemed even deeper, surrounded by endless fields long since grown to seed, bounded on two sides by a two-lane road that might as well have stretched into eternity in both directions.

They were utterly alone, and their world began and ended with each other.

In the stillness, he reached up to caress the side of her face in a gesture that would never come from just a friend.

Nor would the look he was giving her as he held her close.

"The last thing I would want you to remember would be this."

The silence of the world seemed to explode into motion as soon as the words were out of his lips, and his lips claimed hers in a deep kiss that rendered all her other senses absolutely irrelevant.

Anna was so shocked that she could feel Logan's lips on hers that it took her too long to respond, but just as he started to pull his lips away, she put her good hand on the back of his head and pulled him back to her so that she could kiss him back. Her heart was racing in her chest, but she didn't want him to think for one moment that he'd made a mistake or that she didn't want what was happening. She wanted it more than anything.

He had been expecting her to be shocked, even angry about the kiss, before he had decided he cared more about honesty than he did about fear. She could feel his own shock when she started kissing him back, along with a renewed urgency about the touch that made him turn completely into her and put an arm across her body to hold her against him.

Whimpers escaped her chest under the kiss under the pressure that had been building in her heart for years. She wanted every kiss, every touch, so badly that she didn't want them to end, even if it meant another one began.

Anna felt like she couldn't breathe when he pulled away from her lips, even though he didn't go far.

What did it mean?

Did he really care for her as more than a friend, or did he pity her?

Was she that transparent about her feelings for him?

"I've wanted that for so long, Logan." She finally admitted in a whisper. "Years and years, I've wanted it. You, I've wanted you."

That revelation was nothing he had ever expected to hear from Anna, and all he could do in response was kiss her again, one hand moving gently up her ribs to feel her close to him in the silence of the world around them.

"I've wanted you like this since I was old enough to know how." He admitted quietly, reaching up to caress the side of her face just because he could. "It always seemed like you were right around the corner from what you wanted with the men you were with. I didn't want to interfere in that." He shook his head, yelling at himself for a hundred wrong decisions that were beyond changing. "And here I thought you'd be pissed at me."

"I chased after all of those men looking for something I knew I couldn't find. I only applied to Eleusis because it was too hard for me to watch you with . . ." She shook her head and kissed him again. "It doesn't matter. I'm not mad."

He rested his hand against her neck near her shoulder, and gave her another heated kiss before he turned back to the steering wheel and threw the truck back into gear. "We need to get home." Were there possibilities waiting behind the fact that he had simply called it home instead of *his* home? She didn't know. The kisses had left more questions than answers, but Anna was excited, for once, about what she might still not know.

The rest of the ride was quiet for all sorts of reasons, but Anna didn't once move from Logan's side. Despite his own leg injury, he helped her out of the truck when they got home, but she stood and looked at his house as if catching her breath would also collect her thoughts. "Liam and Larissa are going to have a million questions and just as many curses for you, I think." She wasn't ready for his siblings to shatter whatever had started between them, especially if it would lead him to regret kissing her in the first place. "I don't have to stay. I can ask Ben to come get me."

"I told them back at the hospital not to wait up for us. And you're insane if you think I'm letting you go anywhere right now." He didn't go toward the front door of the house, oddly enough. Instead, he picked her up and headed along the side of the massive house, past windows removed from the ground and multiple cellar doors leading down to the lower level of the home.

He stopped eventually near the back corner of the house where she knew his suite was located, and set her down next to what appeared to be a blank piece of wall. He took his keys from his pocket and slid one into a crack in the exterior, to reveal a door set into the siding. It opened a small room where Logan had to key in the same kind of code he had to use at the main entrance to the house, but the door inside opened onto the short hallway that separated his bedroom from his bathroom and faced his closet.

He shut everything tightly behind them once they were inside, and smiled over at her without apologizing for the secret. "I found it one day when I was twelve. Scott knew about it, the old groundskeeper we used to have. He helped me get the locks changed and everything updated. Larissa and Liam don't even know I have it, but it comes in handy sometimes."

She was shocked herself, really, since she didn't think there was much that could surprise her about Logan anymore. He was proving her wrong in multiple ways. "I wish I had a secret entrance to my house. It would have meant not getting caught by my dad so often." She kept her one good arm wrapped around him but the other hung at her side. "I think before I can pass out again, I need a shower." She squeezed his shoulder gently. "You too."

He had no argument with that, given the state he was in. He helped her walk into his bathroom and started the water to let it heat up. His shower had no curtain to it, since it was just a walk-in portion of the bathroom, oversized to the point of absurdity. There were half a dozen different showerheads pointing down in different directions, but he only activated one before he turned back to face Anna where she had stopped against the outer wall to lean against the tile.

He put a hand on either side of her waist as he looked down at her in the dark. They both cast doubled shadows, one from the nightlight above the sink and one from the streetlamps that lit the long curve of the house's driveway. "You need some help?"

Anna actually trembled as he offered, fantasy getting too close to reality.

Was it now reality?

Anna found herself nodding, since speech seemed to be

lost on her. All her life she'd been called opinionated and loud, but there she was, speechless. It seemed to be a night fit for the impossible.

He nodded back, as if to acknowledge the insanity of what was happening between them, but his lips against hers afterward were warmer than the steam beginning to dampen the air. His massive hands found her waist and took their time moving to the clasp of her jeans. Undoing each was like stripping away a level of the world they had lived in up until that morning.

When the clasp and zipper were undone, he left them hanging on her hips and moved to pull her shirt off instead, taking his time pulling it up over her head. Once it was clear of her arms, he threw it aside on the bathroom floor without even glancing to see where it went, and smoothed her hair back away from her face with calloused fingers.

He'd seen her in her bra and underwear more times than he wanted to admit he had counted, but the last time he had seen her naked, they had been little more than children together. They weren't anymore.

Anna watched him as carefully as she could in the darkness, watching to see what his expressions would reveal about what he was feeling. He had always been a difficult man to read, but she hoped all the desire she thought the shadows showed in his face was real.

He had already been shirtless when they went rushing out to the Reeves farm, but with her uninjured hand, she loosened his belt and the button to his own much-abused pants. She was still shaking, but she wasn't hesitating or stopping.

"Is this real?" She whispered in the dark.

He actually chuckled, the sound ringing through the tiles from the deep thrum of his voice. "I was just asking myself the same question." He put his arms around her waist to hold her against him in a deep kiss, but then reached up to unclasp her bra and nearly tore it off her shoulders, looking her in the eyes the entire time. When he held her close against him afterward, things felt much, much more real, her bare breasts against his chest and his hands grasping her waist. He kissed down along the inner slope of her breasts as he ensured that her jeans followed, peeling them down her legs to the floor for her to leave him down on one knee in front of her.

It looked like he was either worshiping her or about to propose, and Anna could barely breathe at either prospect. She stepped out of her underwear last, and she gripped his face with both of her hands. "Maybe this seems too fast, but I feel like I've waited an eternity for this. It's been a long time since I allowed myself to hope you would ever want anything like this."

"Never underestimate what I'm capable of wanting." The words were a low growl as he stood up slowly, his body the most solid thing in the world against her own. He made sure her hair was back over her shoulders and then stepped back to look at her, taking in the sight of her one piece at a time, his hands lingering on her bare waist.

"I'm of a mind right now not to ask too many questions. You . . ." he shook his head and definitely growled that time, raising his hands to explore her gently with his fingertips, calluses brushing lightly over the sides of her breasts. "I've always thought you were beautiful, Anna. I have a good imagination, and I've put it to work picturing this kind of dream for a long time. But you're better. So much better."

Anna actually blushed, but she hoped he wouldn't notice in the near-darkness. She hadn't thought there was anything about sex that could make her blush anymore, but Logan was different. Logan was her dream. "God, your hands." She said with a moan as his calloused fingers explored her sensitive skin. Amazingly, though, Anna stepped back out of his embrace so they could get closer to the water. "I want to clean you up."

He didn't push her to stay when she stepped away, he just pushed down his pants and kicked them to one side of the bathroom along with her own, leaving him and the wounds of the day completely bare to her in the near-darkness. On his way to follow her deeper into the shower, he pressed a button to turn on all the other showerheads, each of them flowing into life one by one. It created a cocoon of water in the broad shower stall, hitting them both from all sides.

"I like my showers hot. Not sure if you knew that." His deep voice cut through the chaos of the water as he joined her, smiling as his hands found her again. "There may not be many things we don't know about each other, but I'm really, *really* looking forward to making those few things into exactly zero things."

"I hope so. I know you know what kind of reputation I have, but with you . . . You're the only one I want, Logan." She grabbed a bar of soap and lathered up her hands before she ran them gingerly across his skin so that she didn't hurt him or herself. Burns didn't go well with hot water, but she knew he had been treated, so he was probably numb in those places. "I love the way you feel."

The soot and grit from the day took some work for both of them to get it off, but Logan took the soap from her when she was done with it, and he worked on her as she did with him.

He tended to her arm first, removing the provisional bandage that had been there so the sprayed bandage would cure up correctly. With that gone, her arm looked perfectly new again, even though he knew it was false skin and it would take some time for her own to grow into it and regain sensation. The rest of her he could reach was undamaged, but bloody, and he took care to lather all of her until the day had been washed away.

"You . . . god, this is still unreal." He turned her around beneath the hot water and put both his arms around her, one over her waist and one weighted heavily over her chest to hold her. His grip was like stone, fastening her back against him so he could lean down and kiss her neck in a lingering caress.

She closed her eyes again as he held her back against him. "You're not joking. I never thought I would feel your cock against my skin. I also didn't realize the rumors about your size were true."

He moved as if to illustrate the point she had made, but he let go of her so she could turn back around, his hands slipping over her soapy skin in the process. "Someday you'll have to tell me where you heard those rumors. At some point, I had more women throwing themselves at me out of curiosity than gold-digging. It was a nice change for a while, but it got old." The rumors were not, however, exaggerated, as Anna could see and feel for herself. He and his twin were pushing six and a half feet tall and built thick throughout their frames. Apparently the same build applied to their genitalia. "There's all kinds of rumors out in the world. What I'm interested in is what I find out about you myself. Directly."

"We have time, don't we? I don't want to rush, I want to savor you. I want both of us to be better." She ran her hand along the length of him anyway, because she couldn't resist the opportunity once it was in front of her. She'd never had the chance before. "It's going to be a tight fit."

"I'm not in a hurry." He said with a low moan and a tighter grip along her waist. She could feel him instantly get harder in her hand, and from the way he was responding, it was clear he hadn't touched a woman in a long time. "Though I could be persuaded to be in a hurry if you keep on like that." He kissed her again with a grin, and reached behind him to grab some shampoo for her hair, since that had gotten some blood and dirt in it as well from the crash.

"I couldn't resist." Anna responded breathily, since the harder he got, the more she ached for him. "I have to touch you. I need to."

He moved behind her to wash her hair, and though his thick fingers were rougher than she was accustomed to being with herself, he was thorough. He made certain to miss nothing, massaging along her scalp and down to the back of her neck as he worked under the jets. His hands ran down over the rest of her as the shampoo was rinsed away, exploring her with the same kind of need, his caresses punctuated by sighs and groans as she moved under his hands.

"I need . . ." he started to say, but was still too distracted with his exploration of her, "I need to know you don't plan on going anywhere. At least for tomorrow."

"Unless you tell me to go, I'm not going to leave, Logan." She said firmly, since she wanted nothing more than to stay with him for the rest of her life. Shortened life or not, every second would be worth it with Logan. "I would spend every moment with you if I could."

Logan actually gave a deeper laugh at that, and leaned down to give her a kiss, even though both their faces were streaming wet from the shower. "I can't imagine a world where I would ever tell you to be anywhere but right next to me, Anna. Not under any circumstances. Especially naked circumstances."

She kissed him again and continued to run her hands over his face several times. "Even to sleep? The only time we ever slept near each other was with a group. And not naked."

"More's the pity." He reached up to wring out her hair for her with strong but gentle fingers. He stepped back and took her good hand to spin her around, ostensibly to make sure she had gotten clean from head to toe. "If you want to go ask Larissa for some pajamas, be my guest. Otherwise, it's either naked or one of my shirts for you. No point in getting a pair of my boxers, they'd fall right off you. Actually, on second thought, go ahead, grab a pair of those too."

Anna laughed softly, which felt almost foreign after the day they'd had. She stepped up to hug him anyway before he could wrap her up with a towel and separate them with a piece of cloth. "I'll take one of your shirts, but I won't wear anything underneath. I don't want Liam or Larissa to know we're here."

He rubbed her down once she was under the towel, though it was just another excuse for him to put his hands all over her. He grabbed a towel for himself once she was wrapped up, but he just toweled off the water from the shower and hung it back up rather than walk around in it. Clearly the man was comfortable walking around naked in his own suite.

"They'll know we're here in the morning." He promised quietly, walking beside her down the broad hall to his walk-in closet to find her a shirt. "This place echoes, no matter how hard I work to soundproof it."

When he tossed her a shirt, she brought it up to her face and took a deep breath. It smelled overwhelmingly of Logan's excellent scent, and she finally pulled it over her head after the sniff. "This is a grown up version of getting to wear the letterman's jacket I always wanted to steal."

"Back corner, if you're ever in the mood." He pointed to the far corner of the rack where the jacket had obviously been hanging ever since the last days of class. He took the towel from her once she had the shirt over her head, and threw it unceremoniously on the floor before smacking her ass with a nod toward the far side of the bedroom. "Come on. It's been a hell of a long day, and I've been waiting about seven years to get you into bed. Move that ass."

"Really? Seven years?" She grabbed his hand and walked with him to his bed where she fell into it as quickly as she could without hurting her arm further. The shirt hiked up her thighs almost all the way to her waist before she scooted back toward his pillows. "I love how everything smells like you."

His bed was a king set squarely against the far side of the room from the door, but otherwise, the room was simple, and sparsely furnished. It was a different room than the one they'd played in as children, before his parents had died. It was also different from the one he'd had for most of his teenage years, since he had shared that one with Melanie. His things had been moved into the room, but there were still boxes in corners and one of his lamps was set on the pile instead of a table. The bed had grey sheets and no comforter on it, just an assortment of blankets that were strewn whichever way he had left them last.

He stopped at the foot of his bed to look down at her in it before he went to join her, grabbing one of the blankets in the process. He pulled it up over them both and laid down next to her, grabbing the lone pillow and settled it under both their heads.

As soon as he was laying there next to her, she curled into him as if she had done it a thousand times. Anna turned onto her side and kissed his neck gently. "I love you, Logan." She whispered against his skin, but the words felt so right that she didn't even feel scared. It wasn't rushed, it was just right. Years and years of loving him and she felt like she finally had the freedom to say it.

It had been a long time since he'd had someone sleeping in the bed next to him, but he turned toward her so she could be pressed entirely against him, one of his arms around her shoulders and the other free to run over her side. "I love you too, Anna. It's gonna take me a long time to say just how much, but I plan to take that time."

Anna pressed her face into his bare chest and closed her eyes so she could savor every second, but she felt extremely tired. "Don't go anywhere, okay? I'm falling asleep, but I don't want to wake up alone."

"If you do, it'll be because I'm either taking a leak or stealing breakfast for us from my own kitchen. Either way, I'll be back as quick as I can be." His hands cemented the promise, wandering over her back and her side to lull her to sleep, even as the bottom half of their bodies wound around each other, bare and still warm from the heat of the shower. "I hope you have sweet dreams. And I hope you take them out on me."

7

Having grown up on some of the smaller stations, the approach to Three was overwhelming to Mercury. The three largest stations, those built first and most often expanded, were the backbone of the Orbital Consortium, but they were also worlds unto themselves as a consequence of housing so many people.

Lesser stations were built as massive wheels, with a central anchoring hub and arms moving out like spokes to provide the room for habitation. The first three stations, on the other hand, had been built more like enormous cylindrical columns. It was as if two dozen copies of Station Nine had been welded together at the dock-hub, arms and decks jutting kilometers out into space. Small ships constantly buzzed around it, and large freighters were coming and going from the several open docking areas along its length. Lights and signs of life sprung from every piece of the station, shining in the otherwise-perfect darkness of the night sky out of sight of the sun.

"Home sweet home." Orion chuckled as they flew along the entire length of the station, a city of living technology so large it was easy to forget they were even in space.

"Wow." Mercury was in awe of the station's sheer size,

but she was still incredibly sedated after everything they had witnessed only hours before. "I thought Seven was big. This is monstrous."

"You've never been to the Big Three before?" He thought that was fairly surprising, given her level of education and the fact that her father was a government official. "You think this is big, you should see Prime. That place is like a whole planet to itself. But yeah, Three has kind of a lot going on."

"When I was very little I visited Two, but I don't remember much about it." She shrugged. "My dad didn't take me to all his official events, he liked to keep as much of my privacy as possible. And usually I was busy with my own studies." She took in the sight with a sigh. "It will be good to get inside, take a bath and relax. I have a headache from the stress and nerves. I'll have to request a small dose of medication to alleviate it."

"I've got some aspirin back in my unit you can have, if that works for you." He reached back to squeeze her hand again, since they'd been forced to strap back in for deceleration and approach. "There's some things you have to ask for here, still restricted by the system, but mostly it's a matter of finding somebody who has what you want and then finding out what kind of price they want for it. Works out pretty well for us, though I know we get a lot of shit for it from the other stations."

They were on their final approach, sloping down toward the end of the station that was pointed north, looking down on Earth below. Traffic of smaller vessels was much heavier the closer they got to the docks, but Orion seemed perfectly at home navigating between them to get to the section of the dock reserved for pods. It looked like there were thousands of them all in one place, clustered on outcroppings from the dock for storage and accessibility. Finding a place to lock in was easy, and he hadn't radioed in to the dock authority to do it, aside from a verification of his clearance to land. Clearly they did things differently on the Edge.

Once they were locked and he had verified their security, he unbuckled himself and turned to help her out of her harness. "Doing alright?"

"I've felt better." She admitted honestly and sighed in relief as soon as he helped her out of the harnesses again. "So you don't have to run everything through the system to get what you need? Food? Medication and supplies? Hygiene products?"

"The easy stuff we still mostly run through the computer." He replied with a shrug as he finished unharnessing her, then worked with the hatch to get them out of the pod they'd been in for the past four hours. They'd been talking nearly the whole time, about anything they could think of to keep their minds off what they had witnessed.

"Basic rations, residential supplies, necessities like that, sure, go through the computer. But if you've got your eye on something that's not strictly necessary to your survival, there's always a way to find it. Just have to know the right people." He got the hatch open to the docking corridor outside, and actually breathed a slight sigh of relief once they were out in it and he could stretch to his full height again. "Any guesses how much time they give us to ourselves before somebody comes to take our statement?"

Mercury didn't even get a chance to respond, as they barely got into a hallway leading away from the dock before they were waylaid by officials. She frowned. "I knew it wouldn't be too long. This, however, is quite punctual. I'm sure they'll want to get our statements separately. We're suspects until we aren't, unfortunately."

"Fun. I've never been a suspect for something before." He tried to keep things as light-hearted as possible between them the entire way back from Nine, but it had been difficult at times. He squeezed her hand as they approached the officials, both of them silent as the dark uniforms with the body armor and sidearms of typical law enforcement met up with them. Orion wondered if their glare came standard issue too. "Don't let them keep you too long. I'll see you afterward."

Mercury agreed with a nod, then gave his hand a parting squeeze before she let go and looked at the officials expectantly, though she wasn't the type to be lighthearted like Orion. "Officers. I assume you want to speak to me about what I saw while leaving station Nine." Mercury had no cause to lie or to be in any way antagonistic to the officers who were doing a job as they were commanded. "Where would you like to question me?"

"Law station is two corridors over." The man in the lead took her luggage and handed it off to a subordinate so it could be searched and inventoried. He and three of those accompanying him formed a ring around Mercury to escort her down the corridor, while Orion was taken the other direction.

Station Three was a far cry from Seven. The bulkheads clearly weren't cleaned as often, the glass on the doors was faded and cloudy, and the doors sometimes squealed in protest when they were opened. The noise was the strangest aspect of the entire thing, a dull roar that made itself a backdrop to every other sense. The law station where they stopped was filled with officers reviewing reports or goofing off with their own conversations in a far corner. The table in the interrogation room had been dented in a previous altercation, and the chair she sat in was uneven on the floor due to one of the legs being bent.

A far, *far* cry from Seven.

The officer who handed off her bag was the only one who remained in the room with her. There were no windows or even an observation port aside from the single light in the ceiling and cameras in opposing corners. "Since you've come along willingly, Doctor, you have the right to begin interrogation with a formal statement. Please comment on what you witnessed of the cataclysmic structural failure that took place four hours ago on Station

Nine."

Mercury folded her hands properly in her lap since she had a tendency to fidget, and keeping them folded would keep them still. She didn't want to appear nervous. She had nothing to hide.

"I went to Nine to meet with my match, Orion Al-Jabbar. My scans on the station can corroborate my location with my story, since I needed mapping assistance to find the meeting room. I waited in the room, and nothing seemed out of the ordinary." She knew she was telling him more than he asked to know, but she felt it was necessary to give him the entire rundown.

"Orion and I hit it off nicely and decided to take the time to get to know each other further. When we left the room on our way to the dock, I noticed that it seemed busier than usual hallway traffic. There were a lot of technicians in a hurry as we walked out, more than I would hope or expect to see."

"How do you know they were technicians? Did you know some of them personally?" The man seemed incredibly at ease on the other side of the table from her, leaning against the far wall.

"Do I know technicians from Station Nine? You're making a joke, right?" She replied with an extremely confused expression. "They were wearing technician uniforms, so I assumed they were technicians. My friends are doctors from Station Seven, officer. I spend my time elbow-deep in placenta, not fraternizing with technicians from an entirely different station."

"I rarely make jokes." He said without otherwise responding to her incredulity. "You and Lieutenant Al-Jabbar left the station in quite a hurry afterward. Did the technicians make you nervous for some reason?"

"Yes, they seemed nervous and rushed, which was concerning, but most of our hurry was due to how interested we were in spending some private time together. Lieutenant Al-Jabbar is a very attractive man, and I've never found myself as interested in physical intimacy as I was at our meeting." She again saw no reason not to be honest about her reasoning. Clearly it didn't matter to her to tell people that Orion made her aroused.

The man looked her up and down with his own incredulity at that statement, and actually laughed once, though he kept watching her and slowly realized she was being serious. "Convenient that you two were so turned on you got out of that dock just ten seconds before the whole place blew."

"Convenient? Normally I think people say it's luck. I don't believe in luck. It just happens that we were leaving ten seconds before we would have died. It's coincidence, and nothing more. I have nothing to hide from you, officer, so you can assume all that you want, you can search all you want, but you'll find nothing in my personal correspondence, my relationships, my home, or anything else that will tie me to the atrocity that I witnessed earlier today. I'm a doctor. I save lives whenever I can, not end them."

The man was clearly enjoying how defensive she was getting so quickly. "Current estimates hold that five thousand, three hundred and ninety-four people died as a result of the failure earlier. If it does come out that you or the lieutenant were involved, that will be quite a lot of endings to answer for." He went toward the door, giving no indication that she was welcome to leave. "Sit tight, Doctor. My superiors may have more questions for you based on your testimony."

They made her sit in the room for an hour without any kind of further information, but eventually she was brushed out of the law station with a warning not to leave Three without registering herself by the port authority. Her luggage had obviously been thoroughly violated, but it appeared otherwise intact. The third person she asked finally relented and took her to another separate law station several decks away, where Orion had apparently been taken to be questioned in the presence of his superior officer.

She was still organizing her things after they had been torn through when Orion made an appearance. Some of her clothes were literally torn as she went through them, though she had no idea what purpose that served except she figured the officers wanted to show her how serious they were about being rough.

Mercury didn't feel particularly frightened. Her innocence was obvious and it would keep her safe, even if people didn't act like they believed she was innocent. She closed her suitcase when he stepped up to her, then gave him a weak smile. "Apparently the officers here have an issue with my wardrobe."

Orion shook his head as he looked down at her suitcase, and picked it up for her. They were at only a third of Earth-norm gravity, so it wasn't as if any of it was heavy. "Officers here love thinking they're heroes and tough guys. Tend to act more like thugs with guns." Obviously he had been released as well, though, so there was nothing for them to hold him on. "I might have to file charges on them myself. Ripping your clothes is my job, not theirs."

"I'm sure they didn't believe me, though I'm also certain if they do all the digging they threatened to do, they're going to be very bored. I rarely leave the hospital to even go home, let alone plan some elaborate scheme to murder thousands of people." She reached out for Orion's arm and held onto him before they started to move away. "I'm glad to see you again. It's nice to see someone I recognize. Even if we just met earlier today, I feel like we've already gone through a lot together."

"Could be you feel that way because we have." He gave her a weak smile, and squeezed her arm against him as they walked down the corridor. Once they were out of sight of the law station, he stopped against a wall that had once had some kind of poster plastered to it and ripped down badly. He pressed her against it and kissed her gently, just as glad to be back with her as she was to be back with him. "You were talking earlier about getting a bath and relaxing. How about we get to that?"

"Is your home far?" She asked as she attempted to recover from his kiss, since it had set her heart racing.

"Hop, skip, and a jump." He smiled and kissed her again before pulling away to pull her with him down the corridor. "Military quarters are kept near the docks, especially pilots. My room is at about .4 gravity. I hope that doesn't bother you too much." Most people who lived in space had gotten accustomed long since to the fluctuations in gravity that were a reality of their lives, but some people were still more sensitive to them than others. "It has a killer view, though."

"I was trained to handle changes in gravity, so I think I will be okay." She felt like his kisses were affecting her more and more, and she had to wonder if the shared experience of the horror on station Nine had made her feel closer to him. "All I care about is spending time with you right now. Unless they intend to send me home."

"Nobody's sending you anywhere without me." He told her with a grin and a squeeze of her hand, before he turned his attention back to the hallway to lead the way.

Not only was Station Three itself very different from her experience, but the people who lived there were incredibly different from most of those she had served and worked with her entire life. People weren't in uniform, for one thing. Anyone in Station Seven or Nine could have been identified by the uniform they were wearing and the position inscribed on it. Some of those in Three had that to define them, but most of them were dressed casually, sometimes even scandalously. The docks were surrounded on all sides by bars and clubs, with people flowing in and out steadily as she and Orion made their way through.

A few times, as they walked, Orion actually picked her up to carry her past a broken section of corridor. Once, in not-quite-zero gravity, he grabbed their luggage in one hand and grabbed her in the other, then took a running jump that carried them over an entire open shopping plaza that opened beneath them. There were no guideposts, no directional columns to catch people in mid-air, and it was a testament to Orion's own kinetic awareness that they actually landed at the other corridor entrance more than a hundred meters away.

He was still laughing as he carried her around another corner and hopped down several flights of steps to a much more cozy-looking corridor that was obviously made up of residences. "Is your heart back in your chest yet?" He asked as he set her on her feet so he could have a hand free to key the door. They had returned to almost half of normal gravity, but it had been an interesting ride to get there. "I did warn you that there was jumping involved."

"I don't think the warning was sufficient." She looked at him with a glare that was as playful as she could manage, though she definitely felt like her heart was in her throat. "I've never seen things in such disrepair like that. Why would your station allow that? That's a hazard."

"Structure over cosmetics." He said with a teasing smile, then pushed open the door to his unit to let her go in first, to get a look around at the incredible luxury that he did *not* live in.

The entry was small, as was standard for residential units in order to enable security measures in a crisis. Past that, she saw in quick succession the main room off to one side, and a small kitchen area to the other with a tiny two-chair table folded up against the wall to make more room. A hallway beyond went only a few steps back to a bathroom and a bedroom. The main room was taken up with a single incredibly-long couch that was bolted to the floor and wall, but he hadn't been kidding about the view.

One full side of his living room was open to what looked like bare space at first glance, the Earth barely starting to come into view with the rotation of the station along the bottom of the window. They were out on the end of the entire station, with a completely unobstructed look out at the universe, which was a rare enough thing on a station like

Seven, let alone a monster like Three.

In one corner of the room, adding hilarity to the majestic image of the world below them, there was a floor-to-ceiling cage, with two incredibly excited animals jumping up and down in the bars and making noise at their appearance. The ferrets were clearly well-accustomed to lower gravity, since they were leaping from the ceiling to the floor with ease to show their excitement. It made Orion laugh behind her.

On the floor in front of the couch, between Mercury and the far corner with the ferrets, was a low coffee table, holding a deep red vase of water, with a dozen blood-red roses in full bloom. There was a box on the coffee table in front of the flowers that was easily nicer than anything else in the room, since it clearly contained some kind of jewelry and had been polished accordingly.

She looked at the animals and then over to the flowers, since both were equally shocking in her eyes. The flowers were a safer bet to touch, though, so she walked slowly toward them and reached out and ran her fingertips against the silky petals. "These must have cost you a fortune. I've only ever seen real roses once, and they were from my father to my mother. They're incredible."

"I'm glad you like them." He set their luggage down just past the entry with a smile. He closed and locked the door behind them, setting his handprint on the door and affirming they were not to be disturbed for any but emergency reasons. "The box is for you too."

"But how did you get them, and so quickly? You didn't know we would like each other so much, did you?" She looked back at him but she didn't reach out to grab the box. "I didn't get any gifts for you. I feel bad."

He just smiled, and walked up to her to run a hand over her waist. "You're in my house. I get the gifts. You receive them. My rules." He chuckled and kissed her again. "I told you. On Three, if you know the right people, you can get whatever you have in mind. I didn't know you at all, so I thought flowers would be a fairly safe bet. And, I might not have known we were going to like each other this much, but I did go into this wanting you to know that I'm in this all the way. That includes the privilege of getting you expensive presents when possible."

Mercury actually blushed and she kissed him back several times before she gave any sort of reply. "You're so very different than the life I am accustomed to. It confuses and excites me at the same time."

"I think I'm comfortable with that." He grinned against her lips, and kissed her slowly, returning to the moments they had shared hours before on Nine, except for the fact that they were upright. On their feet, Mercury had to tilt her head back completely in order to kiss him, and it left the rest of her vulnerable to him, wandering hands and all, roaming over her to spread the fire his lips had started. "You're nothing like I'm used to either. I imagine I'll have my share of confused when it comes to things between us, but right now, I'm gonna go with excitement."

She gasped between kisses whenever his hands wandered to places that had seen very little action, and soon enough her cheeks were burning. Mercury kissed him back the best she knew how, though she had little experience to know if she was a good kisser or not. It was crazy, but the longer he kissed her and touched her, the further away her mind wandered from reality. After the terrible things they had witnessed that day, it was a good thing. "I can't think when you're touching me. It's so strange."

"I read an interesting essay on that topic the other day." His kisses moved down her jawline to her neck, his hands roaming over her hips to press her against him. "It talked about how new sensations short-circuit the brain, confuse your neurons too much for the old faithful pathways to work properly because they're too busy making new ones. So if someone's doing something to you that's never been done before . . ." his hand ran over the skirt of her dress to play between her thighs on its way up over her waist. "It just means your brain is busy. Which is the way I think I plan to keep you."

Her face burned some more, but the spot between her legs he teased became more needy and achy by the minute. "I've had sex. I've been touched." Just apparently not by the right man. Greg and Eddie never produced this kind of reaction in her. It was incredible. "You read medical journals?"

"Why, don't you?" He teased with a grin. "I don't normally have company like you on long flights between stations. I read a lot of things." He leaned down to kiss along her collarbone, then came back up holding the small box from the table in his hand between them. "The second part of your 'welcome-to-my-home' present. I would say it's the second half, but now that I've known you for about six hours, I know I've got another good one for you later."

Mercury laughed softly and eventually reached out to take the gift from him. "This is all very kind. Thank you." She hadn't even opened the gift, but she already felt overwhelmed.

When she opened it, there was an artfully worked pendant inside, made mostly out of silver, but edged in burnished metal and a few gemstones that made it look like fire frozen in place. It was on such a thin fiber it would be invisible against her skin, and on the reverse, it had the symbol for the planet Mercury worked into the metal. "I realize it's a little on the nose, but I figured it would go with your hair."

She ran her fingertips over it slowly and smiled as she stared at it. "It is so beautiful, thank you." Mercury had a few pieces of jewelry, but it wasn't practical to wear them as a doctor, so she kept them stored away in a small box her mother gave her. She held it back out to him, then turned around and pulled up her hair. Mercury was still wearing her green dress, so she knew the pendant would sit nicely against her chest. "Will you put it on me?"

He undid the small clasp and settled it in place on her skin before he adjusted the clasp for her at the back of her neck. For a big man, his fingers had no difficulty working nimbly at the tiny catches, and he reached over her shoulder to settle it in place just above the cleavage her dress was showing.

Once it was on, he started stepping backward away from the table with his hands on her waist, walking her backward with him as far as the corner past the living room. The bathroom was on the other side of the wall, and the light inside turned on as soon as it saw motion. There wasn't much space to stand or do anything else with the sink and the toilet taking up most of the available space, but the tub itself was actually square and fairly large. All of it was pristinely clean, since he had obviously prepared for her potential arrival.

The mirror directly above the sink in front of her showed the image of her with the necklace on, and gave her the first glimpse of what she and Orion looked like together. He stood behind her smiling, with a hand on her waist and his uniform every bit as crisp as her dress was soft.

Mercury looked at their reflection and she smiled brighter, since they looked good together and happy, even though they had only been together less than a day. "We should take a photo."

"We should." He leaned down to kiss the side of her neck before he turned away enough to go pick up his communicator. He set it by the mirror and stepped away to pull her back against him tightly. It took several pictures of them as they stood there smiling, and he leaned down to kiss her cheek for one of them before it finished. "I wonder how many people take match pictures on the first day."

Instead of looking at his communicator afterward, she continued to look at them in the mirror. "We look good together. You look good. Amazing, actually." Somehow he was more and more attractive, and it put some downright dirty thoughts into her mind. That hadn't ever happened before either.

"You're one to talk." One of his arms rested across her

chest, and his thumb reached up along the neckline of her dress to tuck itself inside, running in a slow caress down the slope of her breasts. "You're beautiful, Mercury. And in the interests of full disclosure, I have to tell you, I feel a very strong urge to finish off your tour of my unit and show you the bedroom."

Mercury shivered as he touched any part of her breasts, and she wanted him to do more than tease her. She turned around slowly so she could face him, since she wanted to look directly into his eyes. "That would be alright with me."

He stepped back out of the bathroom, tugging her with him by the hand. It was only a few steps around a corner to his bedroom, since the entire place was designed to be compact, after all. The bedroom had the same view of space and Earth the living room had, but it was completely unobstructed, open floor to ceiling without interruption or decoration, allowing for a view of the Earth below that lit up his entire room.

The bed took up all of the remaining space, massive as it was.

There were shelves high up on the walls that stored his clothes and a few other possessions, and a row of books that was secured to the wall with bars. A standing closet bracketed to the wall held all of his uniforms behind a plastic seal.

The bed itself was nothing more than a plain black sheet with a few blankets folded neatly off to one side and tethered with a thin strip of fabric so they wouldn't float away in times of lower gravity. A long pillow ran the length of the headboard and came close to stretching the entire distance from one wall to the window.

Designs of flight paths and a live map of Earth relative to the station's current position adorned his walls, along with a long, strange-looking tube of tightly-packed wire that it took her a moment to realize stretched all the way to the cage in the front room.

He saw her eyes trace it back through the open doorway

of his room and chuckled. "Don't worry, it's shut off. I usually let them run, but I decided they'd be better off in their living room while I was away for the day."

Mercury sat down at the edge of his bed, though he hadn't given her permission to do so. She hoped he wouldn't mind. "I can't believe they let you have any pets at all. The only animals they allow on Seven are for medical research. How did you get permission?"

"They were actually management's idea." He smiled as he told the story, and went to one side of his room to take off his boots and leave them with the rest of his uniform materials. "About twenty years ago, there was a mix-up at a research lab a few partitions over. Few hundred mice got loose. They rounded up most of them, but what they didn't know was that they got into the greenhouses. Bunch of food, no real means of control, within two years there was a massive population explosion. Huge. Still a problem that's not completely gone in some parts of the station. Kinda hard to be sure."

He finished with his boots, then went back over to Mercury, but he didn't sit down on the bed with her. Instead, he knelt on the floor in front of her and started sliding off the heels she'd worn to meet him, slowly, without looking away from her eyes.

"Somebody had the bright idea to bring up a limited number of ferrets from Earthside, tag them so they could be tracked, and let them loose to deal with the problem. Made sure to track them so they wouldn't have kids without anyone knowing about it, tagged the kids, kept on with the process. When the problem went away, a bunch of people got to adopt the leftover ferrets as pets, myself included."

She was mesmerized by his storytelling since she enjoyed listening to him talk. That hadn't happened with Greg either. Mercury only looked away from him when he stopped talking, glancing in the general direction of the ferrets. "You're not going to let them loose without warning me, are you?"

That made him laugh as he tossed her second heel aside, running his hands up over her calves once they were bare. "They don't bite. And they mostly play with each other, not with anyone else in the room. But yes, I'll tell you before I let them out."

Mercury raised an eyebrow, since she didn't believe they would leave her alone if they were given the chance to investigate freely. "Aren't ferrets curious creatures that like to get into trouble?" Apparently she'd read up on the animals somewhere.

"Well, yes, but they're also closed in a fairly small residential unit. The amount of trouble they can get into is pretty limited." He shrugged and stood up again, going to work on some of the fastenings of the coat of his uniform. "One thing to know, if you're walking around in a skirt or a dress while they're out loose, that . . . that will end in trouble." He chuckled at that warning, since it had obviously been something he had seen before. "They tend to get a little more friendly when that happens."

"Something they learned from their owner, I'm guessing." She laughed and stepped up to him after that, then reached out slowly once he was halfway through unfastening. "Can I help?"

His fingers stopped working as soon as she offered, and he held his hands up as if to surrender. "I'm all yours."

Mercury wanted a chance to explore him, but she moved slowly as she finished taking off the coat. When he was actually barechested, it was difficult to breathe. It wasn't as though she hadn't seen a man's chest before, she was a doctor. But Orion . . . he was a different kind of man. Instead of touching him immediately, she took the pieces of his uniform and placed them over the back of a chair so they wouldn't get dirty or ruined.

He stayed by the edge of the bed, watching her the whole time. When she turned back to face him, he lifted his arms so she could get a good look at him, and even turned around for good measure.

On his right shoulder, he had a flaring kind of tattoo. It was all in black, but the symbol was one she had seen during their walk to his unit, painted on various walls like some kind of graffiti. On either side of his ribs there were phrases in Arabic calligraphy designed to flow with his abs, which might as well have been chiseled from stone. On his back, the only visible tattoo was a pair of hands pressed together in prayer. Other than the tattoos, he had no marks or scars except a few small patches low on his left side that looked like badly-healed gunshot wounds.

He held her eyes as she looked him over, since it was the first time she'd gotten a proper look at him, after all. "Not sure if you're into tattoos or not."

"If they're on your body, I like them." She smiled at him and moved close to him again so she could explore his ink with her fingers. Mercury ran her fingers over them slowly, memorizing them and him. "You're the most attractive man I've ever seen."

"Apparently the program is really, really good at guessing physical attraction." He certainly didn't mind her exploration, and stepped in to kiss her and encourage her to explore further. "You're easily the most beautiful woman I've ever laid eyes on. If somebody were to sit me down and tell me to design the perfect woman, I would not have been able to do this good a job." He ran his hands up her sides to accentuate everything about her that he was talking about, and each kiss lingered longer than the last.

"Didn't you say you dated models?" Mercury didn't think she could be the perfect woman against models. She had more curves than models did. Mercury didn't have any problems with her body, but she didn't consider hers to be particularly perfect. Her hands trailed to his waist where she dared to tug at his belt, but then she decided things should only be fair. If he was shirtless, then she should at least get down to her underclothes. She reached back for her zipper and started tugging it down the best she could on her own. "I don't look like a model."

"Thank god for that." He said with an earnest smile, turning her around to take over taking off her dress. His fingers moved even more slowly than hers had on the zipper, but it was clear from the caress that followed down her back that he was taking his time with her.

"They live their whole lives making sure they can fit into size zero clothes. Fine for fashion, people can do what they want, but it's . . . not fine for everything else. You . . ." he actually moaned quietly once her dress was unzipped far enough for him to push it forward over her shoulders, his hands following over bare skin as he freed her from it. He tossed it with the rest of his uniform, but he didn't take his eyes off her. Had she not looked at herself in a mirror? All of her? "You . . . I mean, seriously. My god, you're incredible."

Mercury wasn't wearing a bra, since the dress was cut deep and had parts of the back left open. She turned around slowly to expose more of herself to him. His expression as he looked her over fanned the newfound heat inside her. "You look at me as though you want to devour me, and I want to let you. That look drives me crazy."

"Get used to it." His hands moved to her waist, provoking completely different sensations moving over bare skin rather than the fabric of her dress. "You're gonna be seeing it on my face a lot. Like every single time I look at you." The kiss that followed was hungry, and only got hungrier as he held her tightly against him, her breasts moved roughly against his rock-hard chest.

Mercury had plenty for him to hold onto, and when he finally moved a thumb over one of her nipples, the moan that escaped her lips was uncontrolled. It was like he had lit a match with one touch, and she wanted more. Her skin was a creamy white, her nipples hard, pink and just as needy for him as the rest of her. "I don't know very much." She reminded him between kisses. "But I want you to teach me."

He couldn't imagine having the kind of sexual history that she described herself as having, but he had no problem working with curiosity as a starting point. "You want me to teach you something, then lesson one starts right here." He kissed her again and took her hand, guiding it to his groin, where she could feel for herself the effect she was having on him. "This is yours, along with the rest of me. You do with it as you please, and you come and get whatever you want from me. I'm not gonna be shy with you, and there's no reason for you to be shy with me."

"I'm confident in what I know. When I'm learning something new, it takes time for me to acquire confidence about it." Mercury admitted, though she didn't let go of him right away. She was in front of him in her underwear, but she stripped him down to nothing quickly and eagerly, and tentatively touched his growing cock. "I know I want you."

She could feel his hips shudder against her as she stroked him, and the rest of his touches became more heated as they wandered over her body. When she let go to move her hand along his hip, he reached down and picked her up by the waist, tossing her onto his bed in a tumble before he grinned and followed.

He kissed her roughly until she settled in place beneath him, but he didn't stop there. His lips moved down over her jaw to her collarbone, stopping to give attention to her incredible, full breasts as he continued down over her body. When he got to the underwear, he peeled it down over her thighs, following every caress, every gesture, with his lips.

Mercury wasn't expecting him to kiss any further down than her waist, and while she'd heard of such things, she hadn't exactly let a man put his face near her genitalia before. "Are you sure you want to . . ." She was all sorts of aroused by the back and forth game they had been playing, and the thought of him getting so close was . . .

His lips moved along her inner thigh as he pulled her underwear free, and he chuckled at the question before he started working his way back up her body. "Oh, I'm sure I want to, but maybe not just yet. I think that might break you for life." He kissed his way up between her breasts and stopped to find exactly where she liked to be kissed on her neck before he returned to her lips.

"I'm gonna take a leap and guess that neither of your other lovers managed to make you come when you were with them." He said between kisses, moving himself between her legs to let his weight rest against her in the low gravity.

"They're both doctors. Just because we know how bodies work doesn't mean they always know what to do." She replied as he continued to tease her neck, which was driving her crazy. "Anyway, you don't have to worry about that. I know how to take care of myself."

He rose up sharply on his hands and gave her a look that was half-surprised and half-amused. "Knowing how to take care of yourself is one thing. Knowing what it's like to be taken care of is something else." He kissed her again deeply, writhing against her until she could feel the tip of him pressing against her core.

Mercury actually whimpered when the tip of him teased her, her hips reacting on their own to rock up against his. His teasing had her so slick that she had no fear of handling even a man of his size. "Don't tease me." She met his eyes, her breaths coming quickly as she held onto him by the shoulders. "I want to feel you inside of me, Orion." That was definitely a first for her.

He nodded as he kissed her again, spreading his knees between hers to open her legs even wider for him. "No teasing." He said breathlessly, then reached down between their bodies to guide himself into her, watching her eyes the whole time. He took his time, since he knew how difficult he was to handle from past experience, but he wasn't in a hurry with her, and he loved the way he made her writhe beneath him.

Mercury moaned loudly as he slowly slid into her, and she gripped his dark sheets beneath her so tightly that her knuckles turned white. "Oh, god . . ." She wrapped her legs around him as he sank himself deeper. He felt so . . . good.

He was beyond everything she'd ever felt, everything she had thought she would ever feel. His size made it possible for him to hit every sensitive spot inside of her she had never even known she had.

Every time she thought she had all of him, there was more to be had, and he rolled with her on the bed to make things interesting for her in the lower gravity. He moved in bed the same way he moved everywhere else she had seen him, with an easy fluidity to his motions and an intensity of focus when it came to watching and listening to her pleasure. His kisses never stopped as he worked inside her, letting her get accustomed to him a little at a time. Finally, she could feel his hips pressing hard against hers, and his arms wrapped beneath her shoulders to tie her up completely in him.

He moaned loudly against her ear, obviously not shy about letting her know how she made him feel. "Holy fuck, you feel amazing." He managed to gasp between the moans that even small movements brought from them both.

She shuddered in pleasure from both the feeling of him entirely inside of her and from hearing him growl into her ear. There was something incredible about hearing how much pleasure she was giving him, being taken by him, being . . . possessed by him. Thankfully, the eradication of nearly all STDs and standard birth control protocols for all citizens in orbit made for more pleasurable sex without the weight of worries. "You . . . actually fit." She replied with another moan, because she couldn't help but move, and every movement sent electric pleasure through her body.

He gave a shuddering laugh, but it was overridden quickly by how incredible she felt beneath him, and he couldn't help rocking slowly inside her. It didn't take much at their kind of angle to feel incredible, so he didn't push things too wild too fast. Especially with her lack of experience.

"That's a first." He managed to say against her lips, every motion on his part hungrier for her the longer he stayed inside her. "No woman . . . ever . . ." he devolved into moans after that, his hands wandering up over her chest and teasing each nipple as they kindled the fire between them ever hotter.

Soon enough, slow movements were more torture than pleasure, and Mercury wanted more. She gripped her hands against his back, her fingers digging slowly into his skin as she picked up the pace. Mercury was learning quickly and eagerly the things that made Orion moan loudest and what seemed to please him the most, and she repeated them often with every twist of her hips. She could feel the tension inside of her building with each stroke, and it amazed her. Could it be possible for her to achieve orgasm while having sex with Orion? She'd achieved it on her own a few times, but it wasn't a regular occurrence. It certainly hadn't happened before during sex. With him, she might actually find enjoyment.

Orion had had more than enough lovers to know exactly what a woman's body wanted and needed, and at Mercury's encouragement, he was more than happy to comply. He pushed himself up away from her with his fists bunched in the sheets, and drove himself into her with longer, harder strokes, growling himself at how amazing it felt to be able to take her completely. His own orgasm wouldn't be too far away if he kept up his pace. It had been a long time since he'd been with anyone and he certainly hadn't anticipated things going so incredibly well with Mercury, but he didn't care. All he cared about was driving her wild.

It had been over a year since she had slept with Greg, and half that since her last orgasm, so it didn't take much longer for Mercury to reach what her body was craving. His exploring hands helped, keeping her on edge as he drove into her. As her orgasm broke over her, her moans turned louder and more desperate, since nothing she had ever achieved on her own had ever felt *that* good. Her fingers were scouring down his back, but she didn't know what was going on with her body other than extreme bliss. "Orion . .

." She repeated his name a few times, worshiping him each time.

She felt him reach his own orgasm while her legs were still shuddering, and she could feel every muscle in her temporary husband's body go taut all at once against her. He gasped through his release, and laid himself against her heavily, moaning her name against her shoulder and neck as he kissed every part of her he could reach. Some part of her mind latched onto the soft shadow he cast over her of the light from the Earth in the window, eclipsing the world for her with his long, lean body, but pure physical sensation quickly overruled all such abstractions.

Once his lips reached hers again, Mercury kissed him feverishly. Her breathing was heavy and her chest was heaving with each breath, but she clearly enjoyed every moment. It had been quick, but enjoyable nonetheless. "That . . . was . . ." She muttered between kisses, with her arms still wrapped around him. She didn't want to let him go.

He still couldn't talk for a while himself, but eventually his kisses calmed, even if they didn't cool in the slightest. "Little better . . . than your other . . . experiments, I hope?" He pressed his hips into hers one more time as if to punctuate his point.

Mercury groaned in pleasure as she held on to him. She could tell that her body was going to be sore, but it was worth it. "I didn't know . . . sex could be like this."

"Hell yes it can." He moved his hands over her side as if to take in the feel of her entire body, memorizing her part by part. "Can be and will be, so long as I'm the one you're having it with. I'll make sure of that."

"Mmmm. That might be dangerous." She rested her head back against his pillows and took a few deep breaths to try and calm herself. "I always wondered why people made such a big deal out of sex. Now I have an idea."

"You don't know the half of it yet. But you will." He finally moved to slide out of her, groaning the entire time, since they were both still incredibly sensitive and there was a lot of him to move. He went to lie on his back next to her, stretching out on his bed with his feet hanging off the edge, even with his head up by the wall. "God, that was something new. Phew." He reached up and put an arm around her back, moving her to lie back against his chest so he could continue caressing her as they talked.

Mercury rested there against his chest with her red hair splayed out against his skin, some strands sticking to the sides of her face. "Is it strange that an experience like that makes me want to understand you even more? It makes me want to know you. I know not everyone can feel the kind of intimacy we just had."

"I think everyone can, but not everyone does." He reached up with one hand to comb her hair over his chest, leaving caresses along her neck and cheek as he brushed it aside so he could see her clearly laid out against him.

"You've gotta make a choice to be as into another person as I'm into you right now. Matching helps with that, I'm sure, but matched or not, there comes a point where you've gotta look at another person and decide you're gonna give that person everything you've got. That you're not gonna hold back. Sometimes that ends well and sometimes that ends really, really badly. But if you've got two people with no holds barred like that . . ." he reached up to caress along her neck, his fingertips whispering over the rest of her bared torso freely. "Well, some good things can happen, I'm guessing."

"I'm interested in a successful match, not a fling or just a good time. I want to make this work, and I think it can. Unless you have some dark secrets lurking around." She kissed his hand as it ran back up over her cheek, then nipped at his fingertips playfully. She was completely bare except for the necklace he had given her, and she found it made her feel sexy.

Had she ever truly felt sexy before? Had she ever wanted to? Not like this.

"I've got secrets, but I hope you don't think they're too dark for you. I don't think they will be." He promised, leaning up to kiss her cheek. He chuckled afterward without explaining why, and turned her over on the bed to lay her out on her stomach on the sheets. "In fact, I've got one secret I'd like to share with you right now." He kissed the back of her shoulder, then got up and rolled her back over, with a playful hand over her eyes. "Close 'em. I'll be right back."

"I really don't do well with surprises, but I'm choosing to trust you." She said with a slight smile as she laid back on the pillows. She felt like she needed a shower, but the thought of getting under a hot stream of water with Orion only made her start to feel needy all over again. "You better not have a ferret behind your back. That would kill my libido."

That made him laugh, and she felt him kneel on the bed beside her and set something down on the bedside table. "No, no ferret. I promised I would warn you first." He ran a hand up over her chest to her lips, separating them with his thumb. "You can trust me. Open your mouth."

She wasn't expecting him to ask her to open her mouth, and while the first thing she thought of was something she didn't think she was ready for, her mouth wasn't anywhere near his genitalia. At least she didn't think it was. After a few heartbeats' hesitation, she parted her lips as he had asked.

She heard a slight crinkling, but then the next moment, he placed something small into her mouth. The taste seemed to hit her entire body all at once, and only got better once she bit down, the luscious chocolate joined by soft caramel inside it.

The sound she made was similar to the ones he'd heard her make on his bed, and she savored the taste for as long as it would linger before she opened her eyes. "Chocolate? How did you get chocolate?" She didn't know what else she had tasted along with the chocolate, but it was simply decadent.

"Welcome to Three." He said with a grin, leaning down to kiss the remnant of the chocolate off her lips. "We get pretty much everything here."

"You weren't kidding." She said as she kissed him again, with even more heat behind it. There was instinctive guilt associated with eating chocolate, but it tasted too good to pay attention to the guilt. "May I have one more?"

"You can have the whole bag if you want it." He reached back and took another one out of the bag to pop it in her mouth, this time caressing along her jawline as she enjoyed it. "I like the way you moan, so any chance I get to get that out of you, I'm gonna take."

Mercury blushed at his comment, but she didn't think he could see it in the mostly-dark room. "No one has commented on it before. Am I too loud?"

"That's not possible. The louder you get, the better a job I know I'm doing." He handed her a few more pieces, then laid down on the bed beside her to enjoy watching her eat them. "No reason for you to hold back on anything with me, Mercury. You wanna scream, you scream. And I'll love every second."

She savored the chocolates, but put a few back for later. She wanted to take her time with them. And with her provisional husband. "Out of curiosity," She kissed him again through the chocolate on her lips as her hands wandered down his body. "Is it possible to wear you out on sex?"

"I don't know." He said playfully, squirming a little under her exploration. "Why don't you try, and we'll find out together, in the name of scientific curiosity?"

"I don't think I'm physically prepared for that, though I previously thought I was in good physical condition." She moaned again as his hands wandered over her still-sensitive skin. "I feel like a starved woman in front of a buffet. You make me feel so much . . . need."

Orion smiled at her curiosity, and pulled her into a gentle kiss, his fingertips caressing her cheek to deepen and soften the gesture. "I've got what you need. Come and get it."

8

When Anna woke, she was momentarily confused about where she was and who she was lying on top of. When she rubbed at her eyes and left sleep farther behind, she remembered she was in Logan's house, in Logan's bed, wearing Logan's shirt, on Logan himself.

Anna sat up enough to look down at him, then reached out to touch his cheek. It was as warm as the rest of him. Just as real. He was real. Everything she remembered had really happened.

He didn't wake up at her touch, but she did feel one of his hands tighten on the shirt she was wearing. It seemed that he'd been holding onto her the entire time they'd slept, and wasn't willing to let go of her even in sleep. His chest rose and fell steadily, covered in coarse brown hair she had been laying on, his mouth slightly parted. He snored, but not loudly enough to be grating. There was a mark of tears that had run down his cheek overnight, flowing down onto the rough hair covering his cheeks and chin like hard-grit sandpaper. She had taken most of the blanket with her, but the rest of him was completely still beneath what was left covering him.

Anna traced the trail of tears lightly with her fingertip

before she leaned down and kissed his lips lightly. She didn't want to wake him, but she couldn't help but kiss and touch him. He was real. It wasn't a dream. What had he cried about, though? Was he upset that she was there, or did he feel guilty about having her there with him? They hadn't done anything too destructive or damning yet, kissing and touching. Not that she could ever forget what he looked like naked. But they hadn't had sex. If he wasn't ready for that, she could respect that.

He began to stir at her kisses, but if anything, he held more tightly to the shirt to pull her in close against him. "Morning, Beautiful." His voice was gravelly, his eyes not quite open yet. "You sleep alright?"

Was he aware that it was her, Anna, or was he too asleep? Did he think he was with someone else? She didn't know what she would do if he called her Mel while his eyes were closed.

"Morning." She said softly, running her thumb along his bottom lip. "I thought I was dreaming. But you're really here. I'm really in your bed."

"And my shirt." He smiled, bunching up the shirt in his hand again before he started running his hands over her again. He opened his eyes a crack, and didn't seem surprised to see her there. "I woke up earlier and went to grab sustenance. I'm sorry if I woke you up." He motioned off to one side of the bed where there were some granola bars and bottles of water sitting on the table next to them. "You seemed like you were having a good dream. I tried not to bother you."

"I dreamed about you. It wasn't the first time." Anna was relieved that he didn't seem surprised to see her, and began to relax. She reached out and traced where she could tell tears had fallen. "Are you alright? What happened?"

His smile dimmed at the fact that she had noticed his tears, and he shook his head. "Always happens in my sleep. Don't worry about it." He managed to smile up at her and turned his head to kiss her fingertips. "I asked Doc about it once, she said it would go away eventually."

"Do you have nightmares?" Clearly she wasn't judging him, but she could feel her anxiety on his behalf coming back in full force to invade the moment.

"None that I usually remember when I wake up." He reassured her, and pulled her into another warm kiss. "Certainly none that matter when I wake up to something like this."

Anna kissed him back and sighed as the kisses broke. "I wondered when you realized that I was here with you if you would think that I was . . . someone else."

He shook his head, and looked her up and down in the shirt she was wearing. "I know who you are, Anna. I might've only just started getting a feel for you being this close about ten hours ago, but I've got a good taste for it. And there's nobody else I'd rather wake up to."

She wasn't convinced that there was *no one* else that he would rather wake up to, since she knew if he could bring Melanie back to life, he would. "There is no one I would rather wake up to either. I've wanted to be with you for so long." Anna kissed him gently. "I felt guilty about how much I wanted you after she was gone. I still do. I couldn't be here with you if she was here, and it makes me feel guilty because I don't want to be anywhere else but here with you."

"I don't want you anywhere else either." He assured her, still running his hands over her as if to reassure himself that she was really there. "The past is what it is. No sense feeling guilty about wanting something in the present just because of the shitty past that got you there." He looked into her eyes and moved to push her beautiful brown hair off to one side so he could get a clear look at her. "For a long while, I thought there *was* no life I wanted to live. But that was a lie. There *is* a life I want to live, and it involves a whole lot more of waking up to you mostly-naked on top of me."

Anna moved to straddle his waist, which put all of her bare parts against his bare waist. She was naked underneath his shirt, exactly as she wanted to be. Anna leaned down again to kiss him heatedly, feeling wonderfully refreshed after a night's sleep. "I love you, Logan." She remembered telling him the night before, but she wanted to say it again. She wanted to say it as often as she could. "I have loved you for so long, and I want to be with you for the rest of my life. You mean everything to me." Anna kissed him harder and gripped his shoulders with her small hands since she didn't want to let him go.

Logan took a few deep breaths under the kisses that followed, but his arms closed around her back to bind her against him in a vice of muscle and long-burning need. "I love you too, Anna. I want that too." For his entire young adult life, he had wanted that, and there had been reason after reason that kept it from being a possibility. The reasons didn't matter. The past didn't matter. Only the fact that she was there with him, and that she wanted to be for the rest of their lives. "What are you doing next weekend?"

That confused her, since it seemed like it was out of left field for him to ask. "Um, I don't have any plans . . ." She was mostly naked on top of him and he was asking about next weekend?

"Good. Now you do. You're marrying me next Saturday." He kissed her casually and pulled the shirt she was wearing up over her waist so he could put his hands on her bare waist and move upward from there.

Anna was stunned at the declaration but then she smiled and kissed him roughly. "Really? Just like that, Bickford?" She laughed and grabbed his shirt on her and pulled it the rest of the way off her body. "I'm keeping the shirt, too."

"Keep whatever you want. Shirt, bed, house, all of it." He reached up to take her breasts in both hands roughly. Between the feeling of her against him and the sight of her on top of him, she could feel him getting hard beneath her.

She groaned as he took her breasts in his hands, since it felt absolutely amazing. Anna slid her backside closer to his groin so she could tease him with her bare ass. "I want to keep the shirt and *you*. And your cock." She had a dirty mouth, but she'd never used it on Logan. Not the way she had always wanted to.

"Absolutely keep that." He moaned at the way she moved, and he knew from the single movement that none of the rumors that had passed around about her sexual expertise were exaggerated. He had never doubted them in the first place, but it was something else entirely to feel it for himself.

Something switched in Anna as soon as she regained her confidence. It was as if her doubts and fears had dissipated in the single declaration they would be married in a week. Anna reached back to run her hand along his quickly hardening cock, but then she decided to quickly flip herself around on top of him and give it more personal attention with her mouth.

He gasped as soon as she went after him, and groaned loudly with his hand moving over her back to her backside. He couldn't stop groaning as she took him. "Good . . . god . . ."

Anna was so happy she was finally able to take one of her fantasies and run with it that she went crazy on him. Anna knew how to do all sorts of things with her tongue, and her hands knew just how to touch him. When his groans got louder, she slowed her pace and pulled her mouth off him with a pornographic pop of her mouth. "You taste even better than I've fantasized."

"Holy shit . . ." he was still panting as she turned to look up at him. He immediately wanted her to get back to what she was doing, but he couldn't stop touching her at the same time. "You . . . I . . . my brain already doesn't work. God help me when I get the rest of you." He hauled her close and attacked her neck with his lips, pulling her in close because he couldn't tolerate the idea of having her anywhere else.

"I would finish you off, but I want more than that. I want to feel you finish inside me." Anna moaned as he teased her neck, since she liked what he was doing. She didn't even hesitate to position herself over him. She was in her element, and there was no way she was going to waste a single moment of having Logan in it with her. She slowly lowered herself down over his deliciously hard cock, and felt like she was going to explode with the feeling of a dream come true as he slid into her.

He put his hands on her waist to feel her take him, and she certainly hadn't been kidding. It was a tight fit, but she took him with more confidence than any other woman ever had. "God, you're one to talk. Do your worst, baby. I want it all."

Anna cried out in pleasure as soon as he was completely inside of her. She waited for her body to adjust to the size of him, then started rocking desperately. Apparently all her dreaming about him had her more than ready for the opportunity to get on top of him. She was wet, needy, and it had been too long since she had last been with a man. Logan was the epitome of them all. "I don't know if you can handle my worst, babe." He was calling her baby now? She really was in one of her fantasies.

He wasn't shy about letting her know how much he loved what she was doing on top of him, and he wasn't backing down from her either. "No, you don't know." He grabbed her waist and thrust up into her hard. He had fantasized about her every which way a man could have a woman, but he didn't have a preference about which way to have her first. All he cared about was being with her. "But you'll fucking learn. I want it all."

As soon as he grabbed her waist and fought fire with fire, it turned her on even more and she was not quiet about how she felt or how much she enjoyed what they were doing. "I'm . . . all yours, Logan." She tilted her head back, but her hips kept up pace with him and his roughness. "Mrs. Bickford. God, that sounds amazing . . ."

He knew from past experience that she wasn't gentle and hated being treated gently by anyone, so he wasn't shy about slamming himself into her as roughly as she inspired him to be. He vaguely remembered her talking about how long it had been since she'd had sex and how much she missed it, and it only made him redouble his efforts.

He rocked her against him and encouraged her to dig in and take whatever she wanted from him, watching her face twist in pleasure the entire time. "I want to see you come for me, Mrs. Bickford." He sat up on the bed and gripped her ass in his hands as she rode him, slapping her ass to add to the shock with a tiny bit of violence to their lovemaking. Logan was not a gentle man. Not by a long shot.

Clearly she enjoyed the ass-slapping as much as she enjoyed the rest of it, since her moans and groans only got louder and more enthusiastic. Anna wanted to see him come as much as he wanted to see her break, and she knew it wouldn't be long for her. She wanted Logan for so long, and now she was there with him, riding him, the realization of it was amazing. She wanted to talk, since she enjoyed some dirty talk, but she couldn't even force her lips to form the words. "Mmmm . . . Logan . . ."

He growled as she said his name, and rocked his hips in time with hers, shaking the entire bed they were on with the violence of both their movements. A thousand fantasies were shooting through his mind, each of them featuring Anna's face twisted in pleasure exactly the way it was above him, but he wanted her to know she had him, every way she wanted him. "You're going to . . . make me . . ." he growled again as he leaned down to leave harsh kisses on the slopes of her breasts wherever his lips could reach, closing her in tightly against him so that her movements were that much more intense as she rode him.

"Good. I want . . . I want . . ." She moaned, just before her orgasm shot through her body like a drug. Anna was always loud in everything she did, but it felt so good she wanted to scream. "Fuck! Oh, god!" She somehow managed to keep her hips moving for his sake, but the rest of her was twisted up in an aching knot of pleasure. Logan and his cock were better than she could have imagined, and she wanted more. So much more.

With her screaming and shuddering on top of him, it didn't take her much longer to get his climax out of him, and the stories about how good she was truly sank in as she writhed slowly against him afterward, stroking him with her body to make sure she got everything he could give. The prolonged orgasm was one of the best he'd ever had in his life. He was reduced to a gasping, moaning mess as he collapsed back onto the pillow behind him, dragging her down with him to keep her pressed against his chest.

He couldn't talk for a long time as he rested there, but his hands continued to work over her back and sides. "Good fucking god. You could kill a guy with that thing. And the guy would die the happiest guy on Earth."

"I . . . could kill someone . . . with my pussy?" She laughed and kissed every part of his chest she could reach. Anna still felt electric with energy from their lovemaking, and she loved it. It was rare that she felt emotional about sex, but with Logan, the whole world was changing. Her whole world, anyway. "I don't want to kill you. I want you to be the most satisfied man on this planet."

"Only if you take the other half of that tiara." He moved his hips slightly against hers to highlight the way they were still connected, and rocked his rough hands over her ass. "In case I spend the rest of the day without enough blood supply to my brain to actually say so, I need to tell you right now that you're fucking amazing. You know about most of the women I've been with and you know I've had more than my share. You're on your own planet compared to any three of them together. The best I've ever had and I have not even *begun* to have you."

Anna grinned and kissed his lips gently but firmly, since she wanted to enjoy the afterglow a little bit longer. Everything felt so magical and perfect, she didn't want to let go of it. "The only man I ever really wanted to please is you. All my experimentation, all of my 'adventures', it was so I would know, if I ever got the chance to be with you, every way possible to make you happy." She kissed him again and rested her hands against the sides of his face. "I love you." She repeated, but she felt like she couldn't tell him enough. "We're going to get all kinds of hell from our families, but I love you, Logan."

"Most of the hell I'm going to get from my family is for not going after you as soon as we were old enough to get married." He looked into her eyes as she said it, and he completely believed her. He'd never had any reason or desire to distrust Anna, and he certainly wasn't going to start because the nature of their relationship had changed.

"I've loved you since I was twelve. Maybe eleven, but twelve was the year I admitted it to myself." His hands massaged over her entire body as she stretched out on top of him, still reaching up to caress over her breasts casually as they spoke, keeping the spark between them lit by small strokes and teasing brushes against the most sensitive parts of her. "And Larissa and Liam have known about it pretty much the entire time. Only reason Liam never went after you. He knew I'd have gelded him for trying."

She wrinkled her nose as she thought about Liam coming after her, and though the men looked similar, (they were twins, after all) there was nothing about Liam that would have enticed her to be anything but a friend. Even friendship with Liam was difficult for her sometimes, since Liam annoyed her. "I never would have slept with Liam. I've wanted you for too long, and sleeping with Liam would have never done any good. I probably would have lost you as a friend, and our friendship was helping me to survive not having you as anything else." Anna kissed him several more times. "Since you were eleven, huh? I didn't even have tits when I was eleven."

"I love you for more than your tits, thank you very much." He finally withdrew from her, but he didn't move away, relaxing on the bed beneath her with his hands still wandering. "It was around the time when Quentyn and Veronica Stearns got married, threw that massive party out by the Waste. It was the first time I'd really been out anywhere in public since my parents' accident, and I was just happy to be invited somewhere. I danced with you four times, I think, and I just . . . you're my best friend. And I wanted to keep you with me. All the time. That part hasn't changed."

Anna rested her head on his chest and smiled as she remembered the party and the dancing and wanting to keep him with her, too. She was silent a while before responding. "So we're a bit late. So what? We have each other now, and unless you were joking, we're getting married next weekend."

"Yeah. I would totally joke about something like that." He gave her a sarcastic glare and flipped her onto her back, kissing his way down from her lips to her shoulder and farther still to trace rough kisses over her breasts. "You're mine, and I'm gonna make sure the world knows it as soon as possible. I only said next weekend because I don't think I'm gonna be able to convince myself to leave this room anytime before then."

Anna smirked at him and writhed under his kisses, but her smirk faded slightly as she thought back to what they had seen and experienced only the day before. "We still have a harvest to take care of. Reality is still waiting for us."

"I checked the report when I went to get granola bars. Machines took longer than they should have, but it finished up around two o'clock this morning." His kisses continued, and he moved back up to look down in her eyes as his free hand wandered. "Liam can see to the rest of the process. Though he's gonna have to get creative. The warehouse is overflowing." He smiled, since it had clearly been an excellent year for the harvest.

"He's probably cursing us both right now." She moaned again until he touched a spot on her hip which made her squirm. "Hey, hey. I'm ticklish there."

"What, here?" He poked her there again, and then again a few times to set her squirming on the bed.

"Logan!" She was squirming wildly as he attacked her several more times, and soon she was scrambling to get away. "Sto-ho-hop!"

He started cackling as he pursued her mercilessly, tickling her into a frenzy against the sheets and pulling her back into him by her hips when she tried to get away. He tackled her face-down on the sheets and pinned her beneath his bulk. He knew she was anything but weak, but he was stronger. "You really shouldn't have told me that." He pressed the attack until she was gasping for breath between laughs. He loved hearing her laugh too much to show mercy.

Her backside was squirming and wiggling against him as he kept her pinned, but she was still struggling to breathe. Anna had tears running down her cheeks, and her stomach hurt from laughing. "Mercy! Please! I'll do anything!"

That did get him to stop, but when he did, he just changed the nature of his attack and began kissing over her shoulder, his hand moving up to grip her breasts as he pressed himself against her from behind. She could feel him, amazingly, already starting to get hard again, even though it had only been a few minutes since she'd gotten off him the first time. "Anything, huh?"

"Anything." She promised, especially when he grabbed at her like that. It was so sexy. He was so sexy. "Your cock seems excited by that idea. How is that possible? Are you inhuman?"

"I've been called worse." He didn't move away from her, and only pressed himself against her more tightly when her ass began to retaliate. "Fastest refractory I've ever timed for myself was three minutes and twelve seconds. So if you ever want a break from me once I get going, you're gonna need to get some distance."

"You *would* time your penis." She said with a laugh that melted into a moan. "I don't want a break from you, I want to have you so many times we both physically cannot do it again." Anna whimpered as he teased her by running the tip of his cock along her backside and then along her core. "I may well leave this room with so much of you that my ovaries can't help but give us multiple babies at once." She had fantasized about so much, including a quaint (sex-filled) life with Logan, complete with a brood they couldn't keep up with. Even if they had no children, though, she would be happy with Logan.

That made Logan laugh, but he trailed off into a moan just as she had. "Joke about it now, but in a few months when you get the word from Doc that we've got five kids inbound, you're not gonna be laughing about it." He laid against her to pin her to the bed, and reached between her waist and the mattress to tease her clit directly with a skillful, callused finger. "Laughing or not, though, I'm still gonna do my best to make it happen."

"Mmmm . . ." She moaned as he teased her clit, since that was no laughing matter. "Fuck, babe. You . . . yoooo-hoo-hoo . . . know what you're . . . doing." She had slept with men all along the spectrum of knowledge regarding a woman's anatomy, but most of them still didn't know what the hell they were doing. Those like Logan, who knew what to do . . . that was the best.

"*You* are what I'm doing." He said as he stroked her, his hips still moving against her backside to start driving himself into her slowly. She had gone crazy on him first, but he didn't want her to think that he was going to lie back and make her do all the work in their new relationship. He had always been a hard worker, and he planned to go to work on her as often as possible.

✳ ✳ ✳ ✳ ✳

By the time several hours had passed and they had showered (once together, once apart to actually get clean) they decided to emerge from his room. They could hear people talking when they walked toward one of the kitchens, though the rest of the house had been quiet. Larissa, Liam, and Brianne were sitting at the table eating dinner. Anna's stomach growled, which caused Brianne to look up.

"Well, well, well, look who finally emerged from their sex marathon! We heard the last one, sounded like a winner. Good job, Logan!" Brianne smirked as she clapped, since she'd been trying to get Liam to hook Logan up with someone for a few months. Logan desperately needed to get laid.

Liam was smiling as Brianne clapped, even if he didn't join in the applause himself. That felt like it would have been too weird for comfort. "Is there an actual threshold for 'marathon' when it comes to sex?" He took a sip of the beer by his dish and winked at the most recent acquisition to his girlfriend collection. "What is it, just over twenty-six miles for an actual marathon? So I'd say you'd have to have sex at least that many times for it to be a marathon. Plus maybe some mutual head to finish off the spare change. That'd be a workout, even for the best of us."

"I think my brain is too busy drowning in endorphins to count anything." Anna went to sit down, since she had already been a member of the family even before recent developments with Logan. She reached out for a plate and then looked back at Logan as she set the plate down in his spot. "We got pretty close, though I admit I lost count. Right, babe?"

"Oh, come on." Larissa said with her eyes covered by her hand. "I'm not going to be able to sit at this table if you guys are going to talk like this the whole time. Some of us are just trying to eat, please?"

Brianne giggled as she looked over at Liam. Larissa didn't know the half of it. Brianne had given Liam a blowjob in the kitchen, been fucked right on the table in front of them. She was an adventurous and curious lover, to say the least. "You could throw in your own stories if it'll make you feel better."

"No, no, she couldn't." Both Liam and Logan said nearly at the same time, sharing a laugh with each other afterward as they shook their heads. It was Liam who actually commented, though, while Logan filled up his plate along with Anna. "So far as I know, she doesn't have any stories, and if she does, I don't want to know about them. Nor would the guys involved in said stories want me to know about them, since they'd soon wake up and find themselves without genitalia."

Larissa turned a bright red and turned her eyes to her food once she removed her hand from covering her eyes. "That's my problem. No one wants to chase after the younger sister of the Bickford boys." She muttered as she forced herself to take a bite from her plate. "At this rate I'm going to end up alone on this farm because you jerks scared everyone away."

"I actually want to talk to you about that later." Logan chimed in through half a mouthful of food, reaching out to rest a hand on his sister's arm to reassure her before he looked over at Anna. "No, I haven't had a chance to talk to her yet. Been a little preoccupied."

Anna leaned in and gave him a kiss on the cheek. Brianne replied to Anna's kiss with an 'awww' across the table, and Anna sat back down before Larissa could reply. "We have news, actually." She looked at Logan again with a smile. "We're going to get married next weekend."

Brianne choked on her drink and then stared at Anna and then Logan. "Wait, what? Next weekend?" She looked at Liam in shock, since Liam was the twin with three girlfriends and prior to now, Logan had been single. "How did he beat you to it? Just . . . how?"

Liam looked just as shocked, but he turned defensive quickly. "Hey, in my defense, Logan's been hot for her way longer than I've been hot for anybody currently in my life. Besides, it's not about who's beating anybody to anything. Right?"

"It's a little bit about that." Logan hit back from the other side of the table with a smile at Brianne. "But if you want, you can partly blame me instead of that guy. I'm the one who's supposed to be arranging matches for the two of you. No way am I leaving that idiot to his own devices."

"Hey, my *devices* work just fine!" Liam shot a kick at Logan under the table that Logan easily dodged.

"Good luck trying to pick one of us." Brianne laughed and took another bite from her plate, looking at Logan with the full force of her considerable talent for sarcasm. "Even he can't make a choice and he knows us a lot better than you do. He hasn't said, but I think he's playing a new version of Russian Roulette to make the decision for him." She smirked and grabbed her glass of wine. "But it's okay. I like his version."

Liam had the decency to look the tiniest bit found-out at that, but he still didn't look guilty about it, exactly. All three of his present girlfriends knew that he wasn't being exclusive with them, so it wasn't like he was trying to be sneaky or making them promises of exclusivity without keeping them.

"Liam," Logan asked once he was finished with the bite of meatloaf in his mouth, "dear brother, are you in a hurry to get married?"

Liam gave his brother a look of both anger and terror at the same time, as all three women in the room turned their gaze on him at once. "I wouldn't call it a hurry, but I'm not opposed to the idea."

Logan rolled his eyes. "You need to run for public fucking office someday. That was a politician's answer if I ever heard one." He chuckled and put an arm around Anna's back before turning his look over to Larissa. His expression when looking at his sister was a good deal more serious, but there were a lot of reasons for that. He could beat the shit out of Liam one moment and know the man still had his back the next.

Larissa he needed to take care of. He had needed to be her caretaker ever since she was seven years old and his responsibility. Never mind the fact that he had only been ten at the time. "What about you, Sis? If I were to hand you the right guy, would you be in a hurry to get married?"

"Hand me the right guy?" Larissa looked at her brother curiously. "I'd like to get married, yes. If I thought the man was acceptable." She glanced over at Liam and when Liam gave her a shrug to indicate he had no idea what Logan was talking about, she looked back at Logan. "We haven't gotten a chance yet to yell at you for being an idiot, running off to the Reeves' without help. Don't try to butter me up."

"It's pretty good butter, I think." Logan took a sip of the beer he'd gotten from the fridge with a shrug. "But, you know, if you'd rather yell at me than talk about the possibility of marital bliss, then fine. Yell away."

Larissa glared at him in silence. "Are you being serious? Did you really arrange something? Or are you just trying to tease me? When did you even have time?"

"I haven't arranged anything yet. You know I wouldn't do that without talking to you first." He looked hurt that she apparently hadn't thought so, but then he continued. "So far it's just an idea, but the guy is on board to give it a try if you are." He let her stew about it a while, then nodded over at Anna. "I'd like you to think about Anna's brother. He . . ."

Larissa had heard rumors that Ben was looking for a second wife, and while she didn't want to be a second wife, she would consider it if Logan was asking her to. She didn't look excited at the idea, though. "So it's true? Ben wants a second wife?"

"No, no, different brother." He shook his head, and caught Liam looking confused out of the corner of his eye. "What do you think of Cory?"

"Cory?" Obviously Larissa hadn't even considered Cory, since she thought that Cory would never consider her. "I thought he was pursuing someone else? Some girl across the world?"

"That was unreasonable in the first place, and it didn't work out." Anna said gently in response on her brother's behalf. "Cory already said he's interested, because he knows you're smart and beautiful. His words, not mine. Also mine, but also his."

Larissa was incredibly quiet after that, and it was several minutes before she responded. In a world like theirs, a marriage proposition before pregnancy was not frequent. And most women didn't take long to consider their options. Time was on no one's side. "What do you think, Logan? Liam?"

Liam looked at Logan, but Logan nodded at him to speak first, since Logan had been the one to suggest it in the first place. "I don't know. Seems like a nice enough guy, I just worry about him having a spine to him. Seems like he does whatever Ben yells at him to do. I don't think I've ever seen him put up a fight."

He turned and looked at Brianne and narrowed his eyes slightly, tightening his arm around her shoulders. "You're closer to his age and I saw you chatting with him at the last party we were at all together, I think. You haven't slept with him before, have you?" It was clear there wouldn't be any judgment to come from any answer she would give, only curiosity on Liam's part, since they were talking about his sister's welfare, after all.

Brianne shook her head. "Cory isn't my type. But he has more of a spine than you think. He just has to feel passionate about something first." She opened her mouth to say something else but she looked over at Anna first, considered it, and apparently decided to say it anyway. "I've heard he's a virgin, actually. I think someone said he was waiting for that girl, the one across the world. Didn't want the chance of knocking up and getting stuck with anyone else."

Liam wrinkled his nose and turned back to look at Larissa, since she was the one who would be dealing with the consequences of that fact, if it were true. "You really want to break a guy in? We're slow learners, as a general rule."

"It's not like I would know the difference." Larissa admitted softly. "I told you, no one wants to take the chance to cause trouble with me. They want to keep their genitalia." She turned her glare to Liam but then looked at Logan.

"If you think it will be a good match, then I'll do it." She knew Cory was a good man, hardworking and kind, and the

Prince family was obviously a good family and close with theirs. Cory was cute too, in a boy-next-door kind of way. She wasn't going to wait around for another chance, because she might never find someone better at this rate. It took long enough for Logan to mention anyone at all in the first place. The world was a barren place, and the pickings for partners or friends got slimmer every generation. "He's a good man. That's all I care about."

"I'm not going to set a wedding date or talk about going to find rings until you two decide it's what you want." Logan said gently, since it was a serious matter, and he wanted Larissa to know how seriously he took her well-being.

"I do think it would be a good match, though, from what I know about Cory. In the next couple weeks, I'm hoping we can get the Prince harvest finished and stored away. Anna's gonna stay with me in the wing I've already got to myself, Liam and his harem will stay in the northwest, and we'll talk to Cory about coming up here so you two can take the middle southwest wing, with the overlook." It was a big house, and much more of it was empty and unused than was even furnished at any given time. It took some planning and usually a good deal of work to open or close any part of the house, for visitors or moves or other reasons.

Larissa nodded and looked at her plate again. "Anna? Do you think . . . Could I have Cory's communicator contact?"

Anna smiled, since she figured that Larissa would want to talk to Cory sooner rather than later. "Of course, Larissa. I'm sure he would be glad to hear from you."

"I'll start working on cleaning the southwest wing." Larissa said after that, then looked at Logan again. "And we'll need a large order from St. Louis for your wedding. Our food stores aren't right for a party. The stores of alcohol either."

"We're running out of alcohol?" Liam had a sudden note of panic in his voice.

"Calm your tits, Liam. We'll be fine." Logan rolled his eyes before looking back at Larissa. "Whatever you think we'll need, especially planning for . . . six to eight people from now on, instead of three or four. You can use my account. I've got plenty of surplus left from the first part of the year, just leave me enough for my usual fourth quarter. Should be more than enough for an order to St. Louis."

"I can take the truck out there this weekend." Liam offered with a look at Brianne. "You're free on Saturday, right?"

"For you? Always, baby." Brianne grinned and finished off her glass of wine. "Weddings are so much fun! I'm excited." One of her hands snaked under the table and gripped his thigh. Brianne was head over heels for Liam in such a short time, and she was actually glad he was willing to consider her even though he already had two girlfriends. She didn't care about the other girls, and actually, she knew Rachel and liked her. As long as she got to spend time with Liam, she was happy.

"Actually, I think Anna and I will take this trip." Logan said quietly, rubbing at Anna's shoulder to share their own secret as to why they would need to go to St. Louis. "We've got a lot to catch up on. And now that you've started with the harvest processing, I wouldn't want to interrupt your flow."

"Yeah, well, my flow is pretty annoyed with your flow right this second." Liam glared, but he nodded. "I'll take care of it. Margo's got a couple little brothers who are always looking for some work, I'll grab those two for a few days. You're better at negotiating than I am anyway. I'll have a final count of harvest for you by the time you leave to go to St. Louis, so you can go see the brokers and see what kind of magic trick you can pull off this year. Looks like it's gonna be roughly a metric fuck-ton, though. I've never seen productivity this high."

"Hopefully it'll be that good for us too." Anna wondered about her family's farm, but she realized after that when she said 'us' she should be thinking of her new family. Her and Logan. "I mean, my family. My dad is getting worse, so we'll need extra funds to pay for his care." She put a hand on top of Logan's hand on her shoulder. "Do you think we can drive over there? They'll want to make sure I'm still alive. A phone call is only so convincing."

"Yeah, we can head down there tonight." He said immediately, leaning over to give her a quick kiss between bites of mashed potatoes. They had both been starving after the day they'd had, but it was an excellent kind of starvation and exhaustion. "How sturdy is your bed? Still that old twin with the squeaky frame?" He grinned as he said so, and took another sip of his beer as he saw Liam and Larissa roll their eyes at him in unison out of the corner of his eye.

"Yeah, still that old thing. I don't think it can handle you and your bulk. Or how rough you are." Anna added with a grin as Brianne giggled and Larissa let out a noise of disgust.

"I'm leaving now." Larissa got up from her chair and went to take her plate to the sink. "And I'm going to message Cory. This kind of talk is making me queasy."

"Not for long, it's not." Liam joined in on the laughter, and raised his beer to Larissa with a grin. "Give it a couple months of this supposed 'work ethic' Cory's got, and you'll feel differently."

Larissa turned red again and tossed a piece of ice from her water at Liam. "Shut up. You're making it sound so dirty!" She glared at Liam again. "I'm beginning to wonder if you think about anything other than sex."

Liam sighed in contented amusement, not buckling at all under his sister's criticisms. "Kids are so cute. They still think there's something important in the world besides sex." He shook his head and finished off his beer as everyone else in the room laughed and Larissa beat a hasty exit.

9

It was late by the time they reached the Prince farm, but she could see from the house lights that everyone was still awake except for the little girls. Anna hesitated to get out of the car, though, when she saw a car she didn't recognize. There was an Eleusis insignia on the side of the car, and her stomach dropped. Did someone show up to talk to her? She hadn't even told her family yet. "Who the fuck is that?"

Logan's look turned dark when he saw the car. "I guess they want an answer to the acceptance in person." He sighed and looked over at her, clearly worried about the repercussions of someone from Eleusis coming through to speak to her family without her present.

"That's not what the email said! You saw it!" She suddenly scrambled to get out of the car, because she was sure her family would be angry. More than angry. Furious. The news should have come from her, not some stranger. When Anna ran into the house and saw half her family sitting around the kitchen table, she was confused when she saw relief on their faces. "Dad? Ben?"

"Anna. Come on in, baby girl, have a seat. Mr. Bickford." Her father was in his usual seat at the head of the table, leaned back with his old, worn hands resting on the older, even more worn arms of the chair. Ben and Susan were off in a far corner of the room, leaning against part of the countertop. Cory and Danny were sitting to either side of their father as if to guard him, and the strangers were sitting across the long table from their father.

"This is Mr. Emmanuel Garcia and Ms. Orisa . . . Kalu?" He hesitated a long time on the woman's name, but he got a nod from her, so he must have pronounced it at least somewhat correctly. "They actually just arrived, you have good timing. They'd like to ask some questions about the crash, since the two of you were first on the scene afterward and the Reeves are in no position to comment on things right now."

It took a lot of effort for Joseph to get through the entire speech without coughing, but she could tell he was trying his best not to show any signs of sickness or weakness in front of the strangers, for all the good it did.

Anna felt relief of her own when she heard that all they wanted to do was ask her some questions. As long as they didn't mention her acceptance, she didn't care what they asked her. "There isn't much to talk about. We didn't see much since we had to rush the Reeves to Doc Weber." She went and sat down anyway, but only as long as Logan stayed beside her. "What, um, what does the crash have to do with Eleusis?" She gestured toward the insignia on their uniforms and looked up into their faces.

They were both clearly confused by her confusion, but the man cleared his throat and began anyway. "The arm that suffered structural failure was a piece of Station Nine, which is home to the Eleusis Initiative's headquarters. The majority of those who were in it when it fell were civilians assigned to other projects, but there were a few labs and offices on the arm with data specific to the Initiative. It's been a difficult few days, for everyone."

The man had significant signs of strain on his face, but he was controlling his emotions as well as he could for the meeting. "Our people arrived at the crash site a few hours after it came down, but by then most of the wreckage had fallen in on itself and been destroyed in the fires. We had hoped that if there was any possibility of survivors, you two would have been the ones to see it."

"I'm sorry, I didn't know." She said quickly before she glanced over at Logan and back again at the strangers. "When I tried to see if anyone was alive, I cut my arm pretty bad and twisted my ankle. I lost a lot of blood, so I was out of it for a while. I don't pay much attention to the news anyway." She looked down at her mostly-healed arm and her voice lowered almost instinctively. "I didn't see anyone alive. What I saw was . . . the worst thing I've ever seen. Things from nightmares. I didn't know people could die like that."

Logan took her hand and eyed both of the investigators coldly. "She's right, it was hell. Or the closest thing to it I've ever seen. Looked like the arm came right down on one end and got itself pulverized through a few hundred meters of decks, like somebody crushing a mile-long beer can. There was a lot of debris around, bits and pieces of the station that had broken up on the way down, and a few pods with people in them. I don't know if they were ships or meant for some kind of compacted sleeping compartments. The people I saw in them were mostly puddles of goo and broken bone. So no, I don't think it's likely that there were any survivors."

Anna shuddered when she remembered what she saw and then shook her head. "We didn't see anything that would have made us think that the arm was connected to Eleusis. Just a lot of dead people and busted-up space station."

"So you didn't see anything suspicious? There was a lot of equipment that has gone unaccounted for, but we know that it was likely all destroyed. We want to make sure everything that can be recovered, will be." Ms. Kalu spoke up, but she looked just as tired and stressed as her partner. "We were hoping you would have some good news for us. This can set back our hopes of getting to Eleusis soon." She gave them a knowing look, but she didn't say anything else.

Logan jumped in and shook his head in vehemence before Anna had a chance to. "We went there with a pickup truck and some emergency supplies, and left with a truck full of wounded and dying. I didn't show up with some kind of intent to commit technological espionage while my neighbor's house was on fire."

"Can you give us a description of who else lives close to the crash site who might not have had your particular kind of charitable intentions?"

"Sure, let me run down the list of my neighbors who I think would look in the sky, see a space station crash, and immediately think about how they can turn a profit off it." His glare turned even colder. "Clearly you're not from around here. We're good people."

"Of course, Mr. Bickford. Please understand, we're here to investigate everything we can. It's still unclear what caused the accident, exactly, though it has been called a tragic structural failure. Just in case, though, we want to make sure that we cover all avenues." Ms. Kalu gave Logan a polite smile. "We want station Nine to be a safe place for all those involved with Eleusis. Especially when we have a new group of people joining the Initiative soon."

Anna didn't like the woman's smile, since it revealed too much, and clearly the woman knew Anna hadn't told her family about her acceptance. It was like the woman enjoyed knowing she could hurt Anna by revealing the news before she was ready. It was more than a little unsettling. "Look, we told you what we saw and what we know. It was brief and it was horrifying. You'd be better off moving on to your next location."

"I understand." Garcia pushed himself up from his seat. "We're very sorry for what you witnessed the other day, and the terror it must have put you through. Ms. Kalu and I were in our offices in St. Louis at the time, and the impact registered on seismometers even there. I can't imagine what it must have been like to be so close to such a tragedy."

He reached into a folder he'd been carrying and pulled out an embossed card with their names and the logo of the Eleusis Initiative on it, together with a plethora of contact options. "Please reach out if anything comes to mind or if there's anything at all we can do for you. We'll be in the area for the next few days working with our crews at the crash site and visiting with others in the vicinity, before heading back to St. Louis this weekend."

Anna felt a chill run down her spine as she thought about seeing the pair when she and Logan went to St. Louis, but they would figure that out later. "We'll let you know if there's anything more, but don't count on it."

Garcia nodded without breaking eye contact, and shook her hand and Logan's before stepping back toward the door. "Thank you also for the tea and for your time, Mr. Prince." They waved at Anna's father on their way out, but nobody in the kitchen said a word or even breathed audibly until the car had backed away from the house and was on its way back to the main road.

"No way those two are here just to ask questions." Danny said to break the silence, standing by the window to watch the lights disappear in the distance. Danny was a nice kid most of the time, but he took more after Ben than Anna, and he had a mean and suspicious streak a mile wide when he got properly riled up. He turned around to look back at Logan and Anna, a tiny bit of suspicion on his face. "They really thought you had something of theirs. Otherwise they don't look like the type that would come this far out of their way to ask questions."

Anna looked over at Logan as well but she shrugged when she looked back at her brother. She did have something of theirs, but she wondered if even Logan would remember she had taken it. Now that two people had come to question her about it, she was certain that it was probably valuable in one way or another. Since she wasn't completely sure what to think about the Eleusis Initiative, she wasn't going to hand it over quickly. Maybe not even at all. Not until she felt like she had more answers. "I'm not sure what they think could be left after a crash like that."

"We saw the pictures." Cory said as he came up and gave Anna a one-armed hug, gingerly, without asking much permission. He hadn't been wearing his sling during the visit from the Eleusis officials, but he held his arm against his chest to make sure he didn't put himself through too much more pain. "I'm glad you're okay. We felt it all the way down here, so I can't imagine what it must've been like right next door to it."

"Logan was my shield." She smiled quietly at Logan and looked over Cory in concern. "Are you alright? You can't be all banged up when Larissa comes calling."

"Doc told me I'd be fine in a few days. She knows it's harvest time, so she gave me the good stuff. It hurts like a cranky bitch, but I can already feel it healing. It's weird." Cory had never broken anything before, unlike Anna and Ben and most of the rest of the family, and it was his first experience with some of Doc Weber's more potent solutions.

"Won't be the last time you need some of it, I'm sure." Anna hugged Cory tighter and looked back at the rest of the family. "I'm glad you're all still awake, even though I'm not happy about the reason. I didn't expect to see Eleusis officials when we got here."

"Neither did we. Half of us were already on our way to bed." Ben said with a suspicious look back and forth between her and Logan. "They hadn't been here long when you got in. They were mostly asking questions about you. Finding ways not to answer them was getting interesting."

"I'll worry about them if they come around again." Anna said with a dismissive wave. "We have news for you all, Logan and I." She actually smiled in spite of how angry she still was about the Initiative officials sniffing around her home.

Her father stood on the far end of the table and raised an eyebrow at them both, looking back and forth between them in confusion. "Do you?"

Anna didn't know if Logan had intended to ask her father for permission, but she didn't have the patience to wait. She wanted to tell everyone. She smiled even brighter as she looked around. "Logan and I are getting married next weekend."

Stunned silence fell on the room for a solid ten seconds after that announcement, as Cory and Ben and Susan and Danny looked back and forth at each other and at the two of them in shock. Their father broke the silence of the room by launching into a brief coughing fit, steadying himself on the table as he worked it out of his lungs and looked back up at the two of them. "I'm sorry, I'm going to need to hear that one more time."

Her first reaction was to rush to her father to make sure he was alright, and once she was close enough to put her hand on his arm, she finally repeated herself. "I said I'm getting married. To Logan. Next weekend."

He managed to stand up mostly on his own, and he looked back and forth between the two of them with a smile that he couldn't hide. He put an arm around Anna's shoulders to hold her close, and playfully glared over at Logan. "Well what if I don't think he's good enough for you?"

"I'd say you're a good judge of character." Logan agreed with a smile from across the room.

Anna rolled her eyes, but she kissed her father's cheek. "Even if he wasn't, though he is, I'd still want to marry him. I love him." She looked over at Logan as she said it, since she never wanted to pass up a chance to let him know.

"And even if she didn't want to, I'd have to steal her and take her back by force." Logan said with a matter-of-fact shrug. "Just the way it's gotta be. But I love her too, Mr. Prince." Everyone in the room knew Logan, had known him for either their entire lives or since Logan himself was an infant. If he said something, he meant it. "Took us a while to get out of our own way to figure it out, both of us, but there's nothing like the sky quite literally caving in on you to make you say everything that's on your mind, no matter how crazy it sounds. I love her, and I hope to have your blessing on it."

Joseph didn't want to make either of them suffer through waiting for his approval after everything else they'd been through in the last few days. "She makes her own choices, so if you're it, then god bless and god help you. Treat her half as well as your old man did your mother and I'll have nothing sour to say about it."

Anna squeezed her father's arm gently and she kissed his cheek again. "I bet you thought you'd never get rid of me, huh?" She laughed softly before her smile faded slightly. It was more and more likely by the time she actually got around to having a baby that he wouldn't be alive to see it. At the very least, though, he would be able to see her get married.

"I'd be a fool if I thought I was actually getting rid of you. You'll only be an hour away, and that's with your driving. Cory over here can make it in half that." Joseph nudged Cory with one elbow and fell into more of a coughing fit, but like the first one, it didn't last long. "So long as Liam doesn't have any illusions about having Emily or Gwen shipped off to your house in a few years, I think I can handle sending two of my children up to your place."

Cory chuckled and shook his head. "Just trading girls, really. Bickford for a Prince, Prince for a Bickford." He laughed and went to hug Anna again. "Congratulations, Sis. I'm happy for you."

"Thank you." She hugged Cory carefully, but she held onto him for longer than she normally would have. "It's a good trade. You'll be happy with Larissa."

"That's not the part I'm worried about so much as I'm worried about her being happy with me." Cory replied sheepishly, looking over at Logan.

"Good. Stay worried about that." Logan said with a grin that could have been taken as either encouragement or a warning, it was hard to say. "You stay worried about that, and she'll be happy with you. I'm not concerned."

Anna stepped away from Cory and turned her attention to Ben, who had remained quiet the whole time. She walked over to him and pulled him away from Susan for a hug, one that she didn't let go of right away. "I was planning to tell you about the Cory and Larissa thing before the sky crashed in. I'm glad everyone is more or less alright."

"It's alright. I get it." He held onto her tightly, grateful for what she'd done without needing to say so. "Next time something goes completely to hell, though, at least make an effort to keep your distance? They've been showing Kevin's phone footage non-stop on the news, and I've seen you look a whole lot more graceful than you did trying to break in and do CPR on a corpse."

"Phone footage? What have they been showing everyone on the news?" She looked concerned about that, especially because she had no idea about any of it. "I've been a little distracted."

"Yeah, no one in this room wants to hear about your distractions. Sorry." Cory said with a grin, but he was already picking up a tablet on the other side of the room.

The video clip streamed on the wall of their kitchen, in vivid color and clear definition, even if Kevin's hands were obviously still shaking. The video started with the arm coming down as a shining fireball in the sky, Kevin attempting to run back toward the house with the rest of his family while still holding focus on the fireball. When it crashed, the video cut out for a moment as Kevin was thrown back from the force. Kevin obviously made it out alive, but most of the rest of his family wasn't so lucky.

He kept the video feed going as he rushed from one of them to the other after emerging from the cellar, but it was a helter-skelter piece of footage at best, with blood and panic everywhere. Mostly it was a soundtrack of Kevin's screams.

Cory fast-forwarded through most of the clip to get to

Logan and Anna's arrival, with Kevin having gotten into the half of the house that wasn't on fire in search of any other phone that would still make calls. He saw them arrive, taped Anna going around to the back of the house to look through the carnage and the fallen pods, but Kevin had gotten trapped in the upper room by the fire. He watched Anna through the window, unable to even scream for help because he had shredded his voice long before that. He saw her get to the pod, saw the glass give way and slice her arm, heard her throwing up as she tried to wake up the occupant, but then Logan burst through a flaming door and picked Kevin up to carry him down to safety.

The footage continued, but it was focused on Kevin's family, since he was in complete hysterics, thinking that everyone was going to die except him. He kept muttering that he was going to be alone. Eventually his muttering was covered up by the sound of the wind whipping the back of the truck as Logan drove away at breakneck speeds. Kevin got a few more final shots of Anna and Logan in the front seat, Anna with her head on Logan's shoulder, before the video feed died completely with the phone's battery life.

"You guys are heroes already over pretty much the whole world." Cory said when it was over. "There's already petitions to get you guys medals or some kind of decorations. They even had Director Vance on yesterday, talking about how terrible a tragedy it was for all the families of those aboard the arm, and praising you two for jumping right in to try and help even if there was nothing that could have been done."

Anna felt like she was thrown back into a nightmare as she watched the footage, and she couldn't respond for a few minutes as she stood there next to Ben. It hadn't felt real, even though she knew it was. It wasn't some horror movie that she had tried to block out in her mind, it was real. No wonder the Eleusis officials came sniffing if they saw her in one of the pods, but she would deal with it later. "Logan is the hero. He saved lives." She said softly but loud enough for everyone to hear. Anna hadn't done anything, and she knew it. "We should get some sleep. It's late."

Her brothers and Susan seemed to take that dismissal at face-value, and each of them gave her a hug before they headed off to their own rooms in the basement. Only she and her father had rooms upstairs, so he walked with her and Logan up to the landing and held to the railing on his way back toward his own room.

"If I had known you were bringing company, I could've switched out one of the old queen beds we've got in storage. That and also spent some time soundproofing the attic." His voice was weak as he tried not to give in to another coughing fit, but he was still smiling.

"Don't worry. We're going to go straight to sleep. It's been a long day." She didn't know if that was true or not, but she didn't want her father to have to think that he was going to hear her having sex with Logan. "Did you get more medication from Doc Weber?"

"I'm fully stocked for now, don't worry about me." He looked and sounded ancient as he said so, though, even though his body was still that of a man in his early forties. He and her mother had gotten married young, which was the only reason they'd been able to have seven children together. But young as he was, Anna was twenty-one, and that made him an old man, by Earth's standards. "We'll talk more in the morning. You get some rest."

Anna didn't move until she watched her father disappear into his room. She could hear him coughing, but that wasn't anything new, and it wasn't going to end. She looked over at Logan, who had remained quiet behind her. "I hate watching him get worse."

He put a sympathetic hand on her shoulder as they headed into her room and shut the door behind them, his face solemn as he thought about her father. "My parents were their executors for a while." He took off his boots and set them by the door. "They told me and Liam about it because they wanted to make sure we understood how things worked. You and Ben were too young still to do things, but your mom and dad had my parents as backup in case anything happened to them. It's just who your father is. He looks out for people. It's hard not to be able to look out for him the same way."

She nodded again and slowly took off her shoes as well before she went to her closet and pulled out a deflated air mattress. It was bigger than her bed and she usually reserved it for camping, but there was no way she and Logan would fit in her bed without breaking the thing. Her bedroom wasn't large, so the mattress took up a good portion of the floor when it was spread out. Once it was inflated, Anna pulled blankets off her bed and her pillows and tossed them onto the mattress before she looked back at Logan. "This is the best I've got." Her family was bigger and their house was smaller, so it made for some tight spaces. Anna started taking off the rest of her clothes as she watched Logan carefully. "We have to be quiet."

He smiled slightly, since the mood had clearly been a somber one. "Easier said than done." As he stripped down as well, Anna could see the burn marks on his torso clearer than they had been the day before, healing with the assisting material Doc put in place. He didn't act like he was in pain as he got onto the air mattress, though, and he shifted to bounce her as she joined him, smiling the whole time. There was no way he was ever going to be in a bad mood if he was in bed with Anna. "Whose room is right below this one? Danny?"

"Mhm. Danny and Cory's. We knocked down that wall last year so that they could have one giant room instead of two small ones. They've been bunking it up so that they can have their own little bachelor pad on the other side with games and stuff. Though I imagine Cory will keep it now and Danny will come up here to my room. Depending on how things go between Cory and Larissa." She snuggled close to him as soon as she could, touching his burns lightly. "I almost got sick all over again, watching that footage."

"The house looked worse than it was. Kevin just wasn't in his right mind. The stairs were still intact, he could've gotten down on his own." He wasn't comfortable being thought of as a hero, that much was obvious. He put one arm around her shoulders and ran his other hand up over her waist, careful of her arm still healing though even a day had improved her wound immensely. "At the time, I considered telling you to stay in the truck, but I figured you would've told me to go to hell, so I didn't try."

"I wouldn't have said that, but I would not have stayed in the truck." She turned into him even more and kissed along his cheek and jawline. Anna took a deep breath of his scent and moved to kiss his lips gently. "We're getting married next weekend." Anna didn't want to think about the fact they nearly died. She wanted to think about being Logan's wife.

"Yes we are." He returned the kiss, moving his huge hands over her back to warm her up in the slight chill that lingered beneath the blankets. Every little move got a squeak from the air mattress, but that was a price he was more than willing to pay. "You know what that means, of course." He said teasingly with a kiss to her jawline. "It means you're gonna have to put up with Liam *forever.*" He whispered the last word with as much sarcasm as he could muster, even if sarcasm wasn't usually his strong point.

Anna actually laughed but she followed it with a groan. "Do you really want me to think about Liam when I'm naked? Doesn't he have enough women fawning over him?"

"He does. He really does." He shook his head and kissed her some more, his hands roaming over her without trying to start anything. It was still too new that she was there, his to have and hold. His hands treated her like a shiny new toy he couldn't bear to put down.

"I wonder about what's going to happen with him if we do go. To Eleusis." He kept his voice so low that nothing beyond the air mattress could have heard him, but he didn't care about much in the world beyond the confines of the air mattress at the moment. "I'm not too worried about the estate itself, so long as Larissa and Cory hit it off, which I think they will. She's smarter than either of us, so she can manage the business perfectly well on her own. Not to mention she's not half bad with the machines either, in a pinch."

"I just worry if we leave, Liam will turn his wing into his private harem and some gold-digger will come along and fuck him until he agrees to turn over half. You know him. I like the girls he's already got, but he's clearly not shy about picking up more when the mood strikes him. Which is always."

"You like the ones he has? As in, all three?" That actually made her laugh again, though it certainly wasn't unheard of for a man to take more than one wife. Her own sister-in-law was trying to make it happen for her brother. "At the rate he's going, he'll knock one of them up before anyone else comes along to get tangled in that mess. Or maybe he'll have a good week and get 'em all at once and then he'll have a house full of girlfriends and babies. He's gonna need the help anyway. If we do go to Eleusis."

That got Logan thinking, apparently, and he settled on his side on the mattress, which produced its own set of squeaks and creaks. "That would keep him in line, for sure. If he was actually locked down to those three. Rachel is the most level-headed of the bunch, Brianne is . . . kind of a freak, as far as I can tell, and Margo . . . well, Margo seems to actually care about him more than the other two, but that makes sense, they've been together the longest. Between the three of them, they might actually be able to keep him in line."

"Are you actually considering it?" She couldn't believe that, and it made her laugh out loud again. "Talk about one hell of a wedding night. What makes you think they would even agree to that? Or that he would?"

"I have no idea if they would or not. Any of them. Certainly not Margo, I don't think." He shook his head. "I don't know, I just worry about the guy if I'm not going to be around. He's a good man, underneath all of it, but he's definitely used to me running things. If I'm gone, that'd be him, and he'd need to do a lot of growing up in a damn hurry."

She kissed along the side of his neck and smiled as she kissed down to his shoulder. "I think you should see if the girls will do it and if they agree, talk to your brother last. I would love to see his reaction to that."

Logan couldn't help but laugh at that proposition, even though he had to admit it sounded cruel and unusual when he thought about Liam's usual whimsical nature. "God, he'd be in such a bind." He chuckled against her shoulder and kissed over her skin a few times, taking in the taste of her and the warmth of her beside him. "Let's you and me figure out what we're doing about Eleusis first. Then if we decide to go, I'll see what his girls think about the arrangement. We've got enough to worry about right now without that."

Anna focused on kissing him all over before she slung a leg over his waist. "Whatever we're doing, we're doing it together."

"Damn right we are." One hand moved down to her backside to press her in against him, since lying there next to her naked was more than enough to get his body's attention. He moved slowly, though, which was a first for them, and his kisses were long and lingering as her body pressed against his. "You're not getting away from me. Now or ever."

10

Mercury wasn't sold on the idea of going to a club, but Orion promised her it would be a good time and a perfect way to get out for the evening to enjoy Three. She took a long time to get ready, but it was worth it when she came out in a silver dress that went to her knees, hugging her curves in all the right places. Her hair was down again in shocking red waves, and she was wearing heels, celebrating the fact that she could, when standing next to Orion. "Are you absolutely sure that we should go to this club? I rarely drink alcohol."

He wasn't in uniform, and it was the first time she'd seen him dressed in anything but military attire or pajamas, during the one night when they had decided they needed to wear something in order to get any sleep at all.

Not that it had worked.

His dark grey pants were long and loose above his boots, and only accented how incomprehensibly tall the man was. The black shirt he wore was unbuttoned most of the way down his chest, but didn't quite show his dog tags. It was enough, however, to show the fractal tattoo on his shoulder, which she had learned was the insignia for his unit when he'd come through flight school, with which he was still associated. The only other adornment he wore was a mesh band around one forearm that functioned as his communicator.

He stood by the door and made no secret of checking her out thoroughly. "You know, I *was* sure we should go until you walked out looking *this* good." He pulled her into a kiss, his hands settling on her lower back to hold her against him. "But yes, I'm sure we should go. This might be the last day off we get for a while."

Mercury put her arms around his neck to pull herself up into a kiss, arching herself against him as she agreed. "We'd better go, then. Before I change your mind."

When they got close to the right district, Mercury could feel music through the soles of her heels. The open corridors were a warren of humanity, with impromptu stalls set up in every corner selling alcohol, drugs, all the way to a clothing store set back from the rest with spinning racks of scandalous outfits.

The population presented the full range of modesty, from Mercury's comparatively conservative dress all the way to women in nothing but the bare minimum of coverings. Some men wore little more than boxer shorts. The rhythm of the place and the sound of the buzz through the hallway, peppered with laughter and spiced with shouting from high-spirited groups, was a different kind of world than she'd ever seen tolerated on Seven.

Most people nearby ignored them as they made their way through the corridor. Some stared at Orion's height before minding their own business. They passed the open front of a tattoo parlor where a topless woman was mid-tattoo. The man tattooing the woman's cleavage raised a hand to wave at Orion, though, which he returned, before squeezing Mercury's hand. "You alright?"

It was clear she was out of her element. Mercury and Orion had tried several different things behind closed doors to broaden her sexual experience, but she was nowhere near comfortable showing anything off in public. "The people here are much more . . . free with their bodies."

"We tend to be." He laughed and put his arm around her shoulders instead of just holding her hand, trying to let her know she was safe as she took in the sights. "There's a whole arm toward the south side that's a nudist colony, actually. Interesting place to visit. Not a place I think I'm ever going back to by choice. That was a weird day."

Mercury held tighter to his arm, since she felt a sting of jealousy slice through her at the thought of a whole group of people ogling Orion. "I'm glad you're not going back. I don't want to share."

"Good. I don't either." He held her tighter, enjoying her possessiveness. "So that means no running back and getting your chest tattooed tonight. I know you're heartbroken. Try to work through it."

She winced at the thought. "I don't think I'll ever do that. I don't want anyone looking at me without my clothes on except you."

He stopped them outside the club in the short line waiting to get in, and pulled her in with both arms around her waist. "Any kind of tattoo on you would be ornamentation on perfection. Completely unnecessary."

Mercury knew she might someday grow accustomed to Orion's compliments, but for the time being, she blushed a deep scarlet and pressed herself against him in a kiss. She never felt so sexy in her life, so desired by someone that she, surprisingly, wanted to be desired by.

"Hey, pal, you coming in or what?" A rough voice said from behind them, coming from the bouncer who was larger than Orion, but not as tall even as Mercury.

Orion hadn't realized they had finally moved to the front of the line. "Oh, yeah. Sorry. I was distracted. Don't even try and blame me." He scanned his communicator to pay the cover for the club, and the burly man passed them inside.

"Nothing like last time, got it?" The man was glaring at Orion as if he'd been personally offended. "You're on notice."

"Relax. Last time was a perfectly legitimate misunderstanding. Won't happen again." Orion seemed supremely confident as he stepped through, pulling Mercury along with him into the even-darker space of the massive club.

Her face was still burning from all of the thoughts he had put into her head, but her confusion won out over her arousal. "Last time?"

"One of my exes told her boyfriend she was cheating on him with me, to avoid telling him who she was really cheating on him with. Guy saw me here, blindsided me. Pretty good fight, but I ended up getting kicked out. Last year sometime." He shrugged it away, since he clearly didn't think it had been a big deal. "Like I said, I've been single for a long while. Shouldn't be anything else hanging around that needs dealing with. If there is, I promise I'll warn you when I see it."

"Alright. I believe you." She kissed his cheek but took a deep breath before she steeled herself to look around the place.

The club was arranged in tiers, with the DJ booth resting on the highest apex of the cone. Steel grating rose in thin layers above them, all filled with bodies. Clearly it was a popular spot for people to get away. The second tier, where he took her, also contained the bar, illuminated brilliantly in the otherwise-dim interior.

The highlight of the party seemed to be people jumping from one tier down to the next and crowd-surfing in the lower gravity, to general cheers and raised glasses. The music was loud and dirty, with lyrics that no one could readily understand, but which didn't seem to matter. People tried to pull her away to dance the same as they tried to pull away Orion, but he politely shook his head and kept moving, never letting go of her hand.

He found a two-seater couch that was unoccupied and claimed it for them, then pulled away to head for the bar and fetch them some drinks. All around her, people were laughing and dancing right up against the couches that lined the outer edge of the room, some with more dignity than others.

She watched Orion as he went to the bar, even though everything in the club seemed to demand her attention at once. She felt the increasingly-familiar but still shocking stab of jealousy when she saw a mostly-exposed blonde sidle up to Orion while he waited, but all Mercury could do was shift in her seat for a better view. From the look on Orion's face, the blonde was someone he knew, but his eyes didn't linger on her for long. Everything about the woman's body language was making an offer she clearly hoped Orion wouldn't refuse, but it appeared he turned her down, since the blonde did eventually walk away, leaving Orion alone.

Just as Orion was turning back to the bar, Mercury felt someone take Orion's place on the couch with a comfortable sigh. "This place gets pretty crazy, huh?" The newcomer said in what she recognized as a vaguely Spanish accent. The man was cause for a double-take in the same way that she'd needed a moment to take in Orion's appearance on first sight, though for slightly different reasons.

Even sitting down, she could tell the man was nearly Orion's height. Where Orion was built lean, though, the man beside her was a truly massive human being, well-muscled and built like the rugby players her parents had watched when she was a child. His physique was on open display, as he was wearing only a thin white singlet for a shirt. It hugged his abs and chest and left the huge bulk of his arms exposed for her examination. His eyes were dark, and in the dim lighting of the club, it was hard to tell if he had an obvious nationality to him at all. Where Orion was clean-shaven, the man beside her kept a short mustache and goatee, though his head was shaved. He had an open smile to go with his impossibly-deep voice, and seemed right at home as he leaned back into the couch cushions. "I'd ask if you come here often, but if you did, I'd remember you."

Mercury gave the man a polite smile, though she was vaguely aware that he was probably trying to be more than polite. If she didn't return his advances, she assumed he would understand that she wasn't interested. "You're right, I don't come here often. This is my first time. My name is Mercury, I'm here with my Match. What's your name?"

The man's grin didn't seem deterred by the revelation that she was there with her match, and he offered a massive hand to take hers. "Carlos Espinoza. Pleased to meet you, Mercury." When she gave him her hand, he actually kissed the back of it, and crossed one tan boot over his knee to get comfortable. "I feel like your name comes with a moral imperative toward a pick-up line. Maybe something about how completely appropriate it is that you're the hottest woman in here and named for the hottest planet. It sounded terrible even in my head, but I can't just not say so when it's so obviously the truth."

She chuckled politely. "Thank you, that's quite a compliment. I feel I should tell you, though, statistically that is impossible. There's always someone more attractive than any one person in the room, based on the qualities each person finds attractive. To some in this room, I could be considered the least attractive."

"So you don't believe in objective measures of beauty, but you do believe in objective measures of compatibility with another person? You did say you're here with your match, right?" He looked around as if someone was going to come out of the woodwork to claim his seat, then shrugged. "Not that I see anybody about to fight me for this spot, but I believe you."

"The matching program takes a lot of things into account that can be measured by individual tastes. I didn't even know what my match looked like before I met him, or if I'd be attracted to him. I was alright with that as long as there were enough other categories where we matched well." Mercury glanced around as well, but once she got started, it was hard for her to stop talking. "I'm happy with my match, actually. I'm not looking for anything or anyone else. He went to get drinks."

"Of course he did." The man sipped his beer and laughed, but it was hard to tell whether he was laughing at some private joke or at something she'd said. "So what do you do, hotness? When you're not getting drinks with your new match, of course."

That question actually made Mercury relax. Her job was safe. She could talk about that. "I'm a doctor from Seven."

"Are you? Well, that explains the posture and the general kind of reserved thing you've got going on. Plus I think your skirt is longer than anyone else's in here. That's a compliment." He reassured her with a charming grin. "I work in security. I used to bounce for this place, actually, a while back, but I got a steadier job a while ago, private contractor. Being a doctor would take more finesse and restraint than I think I'm cut out for."

"That aspect might be difficult since you are a large man, but not impossible. If you want to learn." Mercury looked away again, more nervous the longer Orion was away. Had he left her for the blonde after all?

"Well, you know, if I had the right person to teach me, maybe." He smiled at her again, but then Orion finally appeared, carrying a shot and a drink in each hand. It should have looked difficult, but his long fingers made it look easy. The look he gave Carl was dark as he handed Mercury her two glasses. "This guy bothering you?"

"Not particularly." She immediately jumped up to get close to Orion. It wasn't because of Carl that she was so eager to see him, she was just glad he hadn't run off with someone else. Mercury was aware of the fact that she could be annoying or difficult. "We were discussing Carl's possibilities as a doctor." She looked up at Orion again. "I was wondering where you were."

"Bartenders always cater to anything in a skirt before they pour for a fellow prick. I'm sorry about the wait." He put an arm around her easily with a smile, but then glared past her to nod at Carl. "This guy thinks he can be a doctor? You're stupid enough to keep pushing your luck with a matched woman, what makes you think you'd have the brain cells to be a doctor?"

"Same thing that made me push my luck." Carl said as he got up, leaving his beer on the table as he stepped up to Orion's challenge. Her earlier estimate had been correct. Carl was shorter than Orion, but it somehow didn't seem that way when the two men were standing and staring each other down. It was a difference of only a few centimeters between giants, and Carl was a behemoth of a man compared to Orion, with easily a hundred pounds on him, mostly muscle. "I've got a very high opinion of myself. And my luck."

Mercury looked back and forth between them. "If you think you're going to fight for my hand or something, you two will be sorely disappointed. I decide for myself, thank you very much."

They both looked over at her with a smile at that comment, but Carl eventually looked away at Orion and stepped back to retrieve his beer. "I like her, man. I had my doubts the other day when you were talking over her profile, but seeing is believing. I approve."

"Yeah, I think I'll hang onto her." Orion said with a chuckle, then moved to sit in the seat Mercury had gotten out of, pulling her down into his lap as he laid a hand on Carl's shoulder. Obviously they weren't headed for a fight. "In case this asshole didn't actually introduce himself, Mercury, this is Carl Espinoza. Rent-a-cop extraordinaire. And my best friend for the past twelve years or so."

"He did say his name and that he was security." She looked over at Carl from where she sat primly in Orion's lap. "He must have left out the part where he knew you."

Carl gave a shrug that was only mildly apologetic. "What can I say? I'm this guy's one and only line of defense against himself, most of the time. Had to make sure he wouldn't need it where you're concerned."

"Your faith in my ability to make my own life choices is appreciated, pal." Orion glared and reached past Mercury for his drink, but kept one arm around her waist, his hand moving over her side and her back idly as they sat there.

"Whose idea was it for you to get matched in the first place, huh?" Carl shot back with his own glare, then lifted his beer in a toast to Mercury. "You put him under a lie detector and ask him that, then send me a thank-you card afterward. You're welcome."

"Well, thank you, then." Mercury said with a polite smile, then grabbed her drink and sipped at it slowly. "Are you interested in being matched if you pushed Orion to do so?"

"Oh, my application is already in the works." He finished off his beer and tossed the empty bottle at a trash can twenty feet away, barely over the heads of the people in the crowd. When he hit it dead center, some people sent shouts in his direction, but others applauded, and he bowed in the couch to those who were clapping. "Then a few days ago when we all got our acceptance for Eleusis, it asked me for permission to recalibrate my results based on all participating personnel."

"Smaller pool, but I hope it works out for you." Mercury said kindly as she leaned into Orion. "I'm glad Orion and I were both accepted."

"She was worried she was gonna lose you to your dick's poor judgment." Carl chuckled next to his friend and scooted farther away to give Mercury room to adjust however she saw fit against Orion. Mercury wasn't actually his type, but he had meant what he said about her being a gorgeous woman. It was best that he keep his distance. "Who snagged you up there? Jaz? I thought I saw her slinking around earlier, but I wasn't sure it was her."

"Yeah, it was Jaz. Seemed to be out thirsty for the night. Not too happy with me when I told her I was taken." Orion shrugged off any mention of the girl with a kiss to the back of Mercury's shoulder. He was taken, and happy to be so.

"Well, knowing her, she's interested in making you jealous right about now." Carl rubbed his hands together and got up from the couch, stepping clear over the low table in front of them to get back out toward the dancing. "And who better to help out with that than your best friend, right?"

Orion rolled his eyes. "You're a twisted fucker, you know that?"

"I do. But it still means a lot to hear you say it." Carl clasped a hand over his heart to treasure the compliment, then turned his grin on Mercury. "It was nice to meet you, Doctor. I'll see you again soon, I'm sure. Take good care of my brother."

Mercury was quiet after Carl left, then she turned on Orion's lap so she could face him. It turned more into a straddle, but since she wasn't doing it to intentionally entice him, she hardly noticed. "I was worried you went off with someone else. I'm sorry I doubted you."

"I've got history. Nothing to be sorry about. But nothing to be worried about either. I'm not going anywhere." He smiled and reached over to the table to grab her shot. "Mercury, this is Tequila. Tequila, meet Mercury. Oh look, Tequila has a twin!"

Why had she never laughed so much before in her life? Had she lived around unfunny people, or was there something about Orion? She didn't have enough data yet to draw a conclusion, but as she tried new drinks and new dance moves in the packed club, she became more and more convinced that fun was a symptom of being around Orion. Laughter was a rule of his existence, and if he had his way, no one would ever live without it.

The dancing of the evening gave them more opportunities for the ongoing inquisition they had been conducting on each other since they met. Insatiable curiosity seemed to be one of many insatiable aspects they had in common.

"You are quite the anomaly." Mercury said at one point,

in the middle of the dance floor. "Did your parents decide your genetics? Or do these tall genes run in your family?" She leaned in and kissed his cheek lightly as they made their way back to an open couch. "We would have some very tall children together."

"I don't think our genes leave us much choice." He reached up a hand to caress her cheek, and he could feel a slight flush to them both from the heat of the club and the alcohol. So much for an Irish predisposition toward strong liquor.

"My brother wasn't modified, but they did me when I came along, and they did Khadi a few years later when she came around. The way they tell it, they went in to see the geneticist, went through the usual options, and they were told the only way to get the results they wanted was for us to end up freakishly tall. So here I am, free of fatal congenitals and still growing about three centimeters a year."

Mercury laughed only loud enough for him to hear her, and glanced down before she kissed him again. "It's not that odd. Some men, rarely, continue to grow until age twenty-five."

He had to shift on account of the way she kept squirming against him. "Only you could be giggly *and* informative at the same time."

"I'm mostly concerned about being informative." She moved her kisses to his lips, but when she could feel he was getting hard again, she heard someone clear their throat loudly behind her, followed by a low, rich, feminine voice.

"Yup, that's my brother. Mauling someone in a club, no regard for the public gag reflex."

Mercury was taken aback by the statuesque woman who had spoken. There was a dark tawny cast to her skin, crowned with dark hair and Orion's dark eyes. The woman was lean, but she knew how to dress to accentuate what she had. "Oh, hello. You must be Khadi?"

Orion sighed as he leaned back into the couch again to

glare up at his sister. "She must be. She's the only person I know who's capable of killing a buzz *that* fast." He cocked his head to one side at Khadi and motioned to the couch cushion next to him. "I didn't have a chance to get a drink for you yet. I thought you said you'd be late?"

She gave a dramatic sigh before she sat down. "I thought Drake would come with me, but then we got into another fight and I told him to go fuck himself and came alone. He makes me crazy."

"No crazier than you drive him." He shook his head at his sister's constant fighting with her match. "Should I even ask what you're fighting about this time, or is it just another prelude to make-up sex?"

"He wants us to move to a different station after what happened on Nine and with you leaving. He thinks there are 'shady characters' everywhere here." She growled and leaned her head back. "My career is here. I don't want to leave. Whatever. I'll dance with some 'shady characters' and show him."

"Only thing that's gonna show him is that you can dance, and the only thing it's gonna show you is that everybody is more shady than Drake." Orion chuckled at the thought of his sister's match. He was probably a little too good a man for Khadi, but he wasn't much for pragmatism. It wasn't the first time he'd gotten nervous about the possible safety of Three.

Mercury kept quiet during their entire exchange, not wanting to interject her opinion when she had barely met the woman. From the conversation that followed, Mercury discovered that Drake wanted to move with Khadi to a data processing station with only a few hundred people on it and no night life. Khadi was obviously less than enthusiastic about the idea.

Eventually Mercury decided to say something. "You know, studies show that a relationship is much more likely to succeed if a couple learns how to have effective discussion and to make compromises. Maybe you could convince him to find another station that would allow you to work or commute but isn't as large as this one?"

Orion had to grin at the look on Khadi's face as she slowly realized that Mercury was not only being serious, but earnestly helpful. "Khadijah, meet Mercury." He ran his hands over Mercury's back to reassure her. "She knows things."

"Sounds like she does." Khadi said as she stared at her brother's match. "Do, uh . . . do you study relationships a lot?"

"Only in the last year, after I decided to take the matching program into consideration. I wanted to make sure that I was adequately prepared for a relationship."

"Uh huh." Khadi wasn't sure that relationships were anything anyone could prepare for, but she had to give it to the redhead for trying. "I think I'm going to get a strong drink from the bar. That seems like good relationship therapy to me. Do you want to come with me, Orion?"

"Yeah, sure." He scooted over to deposit Mercury back on the couch with a heated kiss that ended with the tiniest growl to tide her over until he got back. "Finish that beer, you'll feel better. I'll be back with better."

"Alright. I'll be here." Mercury looked disappointed that he was leaving again, but she wasn't going to complain. Watching Orion with his sister made Mercury smile. He was so obviously concerned for her, and she for him, judging by the many looks she shot back at the couch where Mercury was sitting.

It wasn't until they got further away before she said anything, but Khadi looked at her brother curiously. "She seems . . . interesting. Not your type. At all."

"I know, isn't it great?!?" Orion realized that he was probably more excited than he should be, but he'd had a few drinks, and tended to get more wound up when that was the case. "She's nothing like the rest of them. And I mean nothing. Not at all. It's amazing."

Mercury watched the two of them for what felt like an

eternity as they waited for their drinks. The time passed even more slowly on account of another man who had taken Khadi's seat and was chatting her up even though she had no interest. She just wanted Orion to come back. More than that, she wanted to go back to his unit where they could spend time together and not worry about anyone else.

"That sounds interesting." Mercury replied distractedly to the stranger, though the man's explanation and conjecture about what happened with Station Nine didn't sound interesting at all.

"So I think, hey, it's about to be the end, what's it matter?" The man was drunk, and the two friends with him even more so. "Any minute now, we're gonna find out the Conshitium," the word never failed to get a chuckle from one of his cronies, "has one of us planned for next. Just start dropping arms off the stations like petals off a flower. Flower just like you."

He reached out to run his fingers over the side of her dress, again to the laughter of his cronies. "It's all gonna come down. Can't go nowhere to get around it, can't go back to the ground because we'll fuckin' die of the virus in a year down there . . . doesn't seem like there's much point in things, you know?" He looked her up and down, and his hand rested along her leg as he turned more into her. "Well, there's a point in some things, I guess."

She tried to move away without causing a scene. "Sure, there's always a point in some things. But I really don't think that the Consortium wants to kill us all." Mercury cleared her throat and grabbed her beer again as she attempted to use it as a barrier between them. "It, um, it was nice meeting you, Mister . . ."

"Randall." Instead of allowing her beer blockade, he took it from her and set it aside on the table. "And you're not done meeting me yet, Red, so how could you know how nice it's gonna be?" His hand returned to her leg, and he had his other hand braced on the back of the couch behind her shoulder. "You should come back with me and the boys.

Got a pad up in the dockworkers' quarters that's better than this place. You'd like it. I know they'd like you."

Mercury shook her head and tried to pull away, but the couch didn't give her much room to move. "No, thank you. My match should be back any minute, and I have no interest in spending time with anyone else."

"Oh, you know that's not true." He pushed up the hem of her dress, his fingers moving up her thigh as he leaned in against her. "Matched woman always wants to get out and see what she's missing in the rest of the world. Just because a computer put you with one man doesn't mean you shouldn't give others a chance." His two friends were still laughing at everything he said and did, and the two of them moved in closer to form a kind of screen to keep her on the couch and keep out prying eyes.

"Stop touching me." She shoved his hand off of her thigh. "I told you I'm not interested in you, and I'm tired of being polite when you won't get the hint. Get away from me."

"No need to be like that about it." He wasn't bigger than she was, but his hands were rough and he was clearly strong for his size. He shoved her dress up farther by force, his free hand grabbing her shoulder to press her against the couch where he wanted her. "Fine woman like you probably thinks you taste too sweet for the likes of me, and maybe that's the case, but we're gonna find out the hard way now."

He managed to lean in and leave a sloppy kiss along the inner curve of her neckline, still groping at her with one clumsy hand, before Mercury saw the two men in front of her start into an argument with something beyond them, barely visible in the ever-shifting lights.

A breath later, she saw someone's elbow fly as both friends tried to stand up and were shoved aside for their trouble. One man kept trying to fight, and Orion took his head and bashed it into his knee to send him crumpling to the ground, before he set his sights on the man with his hands all over her.

Getting the man away from her was more a blur than anything else, but people scattered quickly once there was a brawl going. Mercury had a clear view of the beating Orion gave the man afterward. His two companions tried to get up and rejoin the fight several times, but Orion sent one's head through the coffee table and the other went flying into a set of metal stairs a few feet beyond that. Orion saved most of his focus for her main assailant, yelling at him the entire time as he dismantled the man with military efficiency.

Mercury was too stunned to move, still in shock at how foreign everything was around her. The place was nowhere she would have gone on her own, the people were not people she would have associated with, and the behavior was nothing she had encountered, since no man had ever touched her without her permission. She had certainly never seen a brawl like the one in front of her, even though she had seen medical patients a few times who had been on the wrong end of one.

"What did you think? You could put your hands on whoever you wanted?" Orion ducked a few punches from the drunk easily before he stepped back to make the man swing himself stupid in the low gravity. "You think the word 'no' doesn't apply to you? Wrong fucking move, jackass!" The man was clearly no slouch in a fight under normal circumstances, but he was no match for Orion.

Orion actually stood and allowed himself to be punched not just once, but twice, before he retaliated with a set of punches that sounded like they had cracked a rib at least, if not broken the man's sternum outright. "If a woman wants you, she'll tell you. If any woman has standards low enough for you, I'd be fucking shocked, but . . . oh, you want a reminder too?" Orion got suckerpunched in the kidney by one of the friends, but he spun the man around, took a fistfull of his shirt and the back of his belt, then hauled him in the air and threw him at the crowd nearby.

People parted quickly to allow the man to fall on his own, rolling a few times until he was moaning in pain. The second friend wisely got up and ran off, but Randall was still trying to get to Orion, unwilling to be made to look like a fool.

Orion caught one punch in his fist and squeezed until it looked like the man was going to pass out, then pulled him in to wrap one of his massive hands around the man's throat. His fingers sought purposefully up along the sides of the man's thick neck until he found what he was looking for, and he squeezed more tightly, cutting off the man's blood supply rather than his oxygen.

"Go to sleep. You'll wake up in a law cell on charges of sexual assault. Enjoy prison." The man continued to struggle, but the way Orion was holding him, his feet were up off the ground and it didn't take long for him to sputter and go limp. Orion dropped him on the tile floor like a sack of dead fish, and left him to finally go check on Mercury.

Mercury was up to get to Orion as quickly as she could when he came near, and she held tightly to him. The shock had worn off, and she was glad to see that he was more or less unscathed after defending her from not one, but three men who wanted to see her hurt. "Thank you." She said softly before she looked up at him. "I thought he would stop, or go away, I didn't think he would . . . do that."

Orion nodded quietly, and put an arm around her tightly as he scanned the crowd, his eyes challenging anybody else to try anything. Instead of any other takers, though, it was Carl who appeared, with Jaz not far behind, the two of them having obviously witnessed the fight from a distance.

"Man, you didn't leave me *any*? Really? Dick move, man. Dick move." Carl looked incredibly disappointed as he got a good look at the assailants.

"Feel free to take a second round on them. They deserve it. And call it in for me, will ya? There's eyewitnesses aplenty and surveillance to boot. These fuckers need to do time."

"Already called it on my way down here. I'll get them bagged and handed over." Carl glared over at Orion and kicked Randall as he began to try and get up. "Stay the fuck down, asshole. You've done enough. Get friendly with that floor for a while, see if it likes you back."

Mercury looked up at Orion again as his sister appeared behind him, finally making it through the crowd.

"Go on, get her out of here." Khadi sounded legitimately angry that she hadn't gotten there in time for the fight, but she was physically shooing Orion and Mercury toward the exit. "I'll stay here with Carl and make sure everything gets sorted. I'll call you later, alright?"

"Thanks, Khadi." He stopped long enough to give Khadijah a kiss on her cheek, though he didn't let go of Mercury at all in the process. Once they were away, he saw her press the sharp point of her stiletto heel into Randall's throat to keep him where he was on the ground, and he shook his head.

Woe to any man who threatened Khadijah Al-Jabbar. Anyone Orion didn't murder first, Khadi would put through a meat grinder.

It seemed colder outside the club after the heat of the interior, and Orion could feel Mercury shiver once under his arm. "I'm sorry." He didn't know what to say or how to begin, but it seemed like the best place to start. "Normally pricks like that get weeded out, but some always crop up. I shouldn't have left you alone in there."

Mercury certainly didn't blame Orion for someone else's behavior, but she did feel hurt that he would leave her in an unknown place. "I thought he would leave me alone." Her voice was weak, since nothing she could say would change what had just happened. "I should be able to defend myself, shouldn't I?"

Orion shook his head. "There were three of them. There's only so much a person can do if the rest of the world has different ideas. You shouldn't have had to defend yourself in the first place." He guided her back through the halls a while in silence, eventually picking her up to carry her back across a few broken stairwells. "I'm glad things are better where you're from. That people are more . . . civilized, the way you tell it. If they've got even half your class, they're twice as good as this place."

She hung onto him until he got to a better section of the corridor and put her down, but she still looked at the floor. "I can do just about anything with a scalpel, but I can't defend myself for fifteen minutes." She looked down at his hand holding hers and sighed. "Are we going back to your unit? I don't think I want to go anywhere else."

"That's where I was headed." He squeezed her hand to reassure her, and swung their hands between them. "You're not weak. And you don't need to start carrying around a scalpel wherever you go. I don't think that would work out well. I'm the one who should be sorry. I enjoyed that back there more than I probably should. The beating up part, not the part before that."

"Are you alright?" It was only after they managed to get some distance before she realized that he might be hurt after going up against three men at once.

He let go of her hand long enough to shake his hand out. His knuckles were bruised, but the blood on his hands was from the men he'd beaten, not from him. "It's been through worse, don't worry about it. I can't even feel it yet."

"I can look at it when we get back to your unit." She glanced down at his hand as he let go of hers, but it made her nervous not to be holding onto him. Was that who she was? Weak? Vulnerable? Who she had allowed herself to become in her sheltered life on Seven?

Mercury didn't say anything else until they got back to his unit and she could get a better look at his hand. "If we agree to a permanent relationship, it's good to know you'll protect me." She washed the back of his hands and examined a few scratches over his knuckles, but there was no damage that would need stitches.

"Of course I will." He said quickly as she looked him over, giving her a confused look. "Did you doubt that would be the case when you decided to be matched? Thought you'd get a husband who would stand back and let something like that happen to you?"

"No, I . . . don't think anyone I would've chosen for myself would've been able to handle himself back there in a situation like that." She ran her fingertips gently across his knuckles and kissed the top of his hand gingerly. "The men I know from Seven are academics, not fighters."

Orion hadn't thought about it in quite those terms. "I like to read as much as the next guy, but some situations need something stronger than paper. Unfortunately." He caressed along her cheek once she kissed his hand, and pulled her up into a gentle kiss.

Mercury returned the kiss gratefully, holding his face afterward. "Is it alright if we just cuddle? Or watch a video or something? I don't . . . everything that happened tonight makes me feel a little dirty. Not in a good way."

"Yeah, of course." He kissed her one more time and put some distance between them, holding her hands to help her back up to a sitting position. "My video feed is probably about ten clicks long. I normally watch when I'm out on long flights. Obviously I've been distracted." He smiled at her and squeezed her hand before he let it go, getting up from the couch to head for the bedroom. "Videos require pajamas and popcorn. Both of which happen to be available, coincidentally."

"Only a little bit of popcorn." She said with determination, but she followed him to the bedroom so she could change into pajamas as well. "If I let myself go, you might not want to be matched to me anymore. I have to watch myself."

"If you're watching yourself, then you can see what I see. Which is someone I cannot imagine ever not wanting to be matched to." He pulled a loose set of shorts over his hips and a thin t-shirt over his head to cover his dog tags.

Mercury smiled and watched him before she walked over to the small unit where he stored his clothes. "Can I borrow one of yours to wear to bed, then?"

He smiled, and poked his chin at the drawers. "What's

mine is happy to be yours. Grab anything you like." He headed out of the room to let her change in peace, and she heard popcorn popping shortly after.

Mercury took her time undressing, eventually deciding on underwear and a worn t-shirt of Orion's as pajamas. It was a dark t-shirt with a band logo over the front of it, and since he was so much taller than she was, it looked like a cocktail dress on her. When she came out, she gathered her hair into a sloppy red bun on the top of her head before she went to sit down on the couch and wait for him. "Where did you get this shirt? It looks like you like to wear it a lot."

He smiled at her from the kitchen where he was waiting for the popcorn. "You have good taste in shirts. That was a concert I went to back when I was seventeen. Few weeks before my eighteenth birthday." His tone had started out light, but mentioning his eighteenth birthday chased the smile away from his face. "Band was Lunar Power. Great show. My brother took me."

"Maybe I can listen to some of their music sometime?" Mercury watched him quietly after that until the popcorn was finished. "Is it a bad memory?"

"No, no, the concert was great. It was a good show, Khadi was there, Ahmed, Misha, it was a good time." He took the popcorn out when it was ready and gingerly emptied it into a bowl. "It's a good memory, but it was also the last time I saw him alive. He died in a debris-field accident three weeks later."

"I'm sorry." She looked down at the shirt again afterward, wondering if she should wear it at all if it was something he cherished. "I can go change. I read in your file that your brother had died, but it didn't say how."

"No, keep it on. It's a favorite for a reason." He gave her a reassuring smile as he crossed the room, and pulled her into a brief kiss to let her know he was serious. He settled into the corner of his couch and pulled her against him to relax.

"It was four years ago, I've had plenty of time to process.

You don't have to worry about upsetting me by talking about it. He was a pilot too, flying a hop from Prime out to one of the lunar orbitals. On the way back, there was a bunch of shrapnel from an explosion. The orbit had decayed as he was coming back inside Earth orbitals. Wasn't on anyone's radar, nobody could have seen it coming. Nobody's fault. I've seen the telemetry. Ship got shredded in a matter of seconds. No survivors."

"Being a pilot is a dangerous job. I've seen a lot of injuries from it, people who were seriously injured or permanently crippled. I hope nothing like that ever happens to you." She curled into his side and kissed his cheek gently. "I like you more and more every day, Orion. I want things to last between us."

"I want that too." His hand moved lazily up and down her back as she settled against him, and he closed his eyes to rest his forehead against her hair. He put his arms around her to hold her tight as she tucked her head under his chin, treasuring the warmth and softness of her against him.

"I'll protect you from everything I can." He promised, kissing her hair as his hands moved over the worn t-shirt to warm her. "I like you, Mercury." He said quietly, the tone of his voice making it seem as though there should have been a different word in place of 'like' when he said it. "Just wanted you to know that."

"I *like* you too." She emphasized it as he had, since she hadn't missed the change in his tone. Mercury ran her hands up and down his muscled arms as they were wrapped around her. "I can't imagine that changing, except to get better."

11

"Well, that's it, it's on the record now." Logan couldn't stop grinning. "My criminal record. 'Driving while distracted by a blowjob'. Official criminal record. I've never looked forward to paying a ticket more in my life."

Anna laughed as he held her at his side, and she reached down to run her hand up and down his thigh. "It's your fault, you were all over the road. I mean, can't you pay attention while my lips are all over you?" She smirked and kissed his neck as well. "I don't think you should have to pay that ticket. He interrupted before you were finished and ruined all the work I put into it."

"That's alright, you made up lost ground in a hurry." Logan leaned to one side to kiss the side of her head, since he couldn't take his eyes off the road. There was actually traffic on the road for once. That was a rarity for them.

It was strange, for both of them, to be in a place with so many people. Even in St. Louis, though, empty space still dominated the landscape, and it was painfully obvious that the city had once been home to hundreds of thousands of people, whereas it now held only thousands. Still, thousands were enough to take the edge off the feeling of constant loneliness that Logan had come to expect from the world, and it was almost nice to have other people around, even if they were strangers. The hotel had been packed, but that hadn't stopped him and Anna from making the most of the brief window in their room, with a promise of resuming exactly where they left off later that night.

Eleusis vehicles were obvious off to one side of the orientation site, which had once been a university. Most of the campus was still deeply under the reclaimed control of Mother Nature and degraded by Father Time. A few of the buildings had been restored, and there was a wide field that had been converted into a landing area for shuttlecraft. An Eleusis Initiative ship rested close beside the parking lot, long and narrow and severe.

It was the closest Logan had ever been to a functional spacecraft, and he made no secret of gawking over it as he got out of the truck. "So. This is what takes us to heaven. Little less angelic than I envisioned."

"I'd hardly call it heaven. Heaven is between the sheets with you." She added without even looking at him, since she was also staring at the shuttle. "I almost want to run up and touch it, just to make sure it's real, you know? I mean, we see stuff up in the sky, but it doesn't seem real until it's close like this."

"It's dirtier than I thought it would be." He got up close to her and put an arm around her shoulders casually as they inspected it together. "From re-entry burns, I'm guessing, but still. So much for everything out in space being polished and sterile."

"Polished and sterile is clean and boring." Anna's fingers itched at her side, but she focused on holding Logan's arm to keep herself from running to touch something that had touched outer space. "I'll take something with a few dirty miles on it any day. That's how you know it works."

They were greeted by the friendly, smiling faces of Eleusis officials when they walked into the building, which was more off-putting than endearing. Instead of going around meeting new people, Anna held tightly to Logan's hand and went to find a seat. They sat down close to a full-figured woman who was off by herself, but her scowl made it obvious that she wasn't interested in making friends.

The auditorium was easily five times larger than it needed to be to hold those already in the room. There was a selection of food set out on descending tables going down one walkway between seating sections, but Logan didn't feel hungry. More Eleusis officials in clean suits and ruthlessly-efficient expressions stood around at the front of the room, obviously going over last-minute notes for the presentation between themselves.

The whole thing made Logan feel like he was about to attend the worst middle school play in history. "They seem pretty easygoing for people who just had a station break in half on them a week ago."

"And isn't that just the most unsettling part of it all. Considering the station was home of the project itself." Anna kept herself close to Logan, refusing to let go of his arm. "No one looks happy to be here except the officials. Are we all that skeptical?"

"I think we've all heard too much about things that sound too good to be true." He continued scanning the room along with her, but she was right, most of the others present weren't even talking to each other, they were all eating and sitting off by themselves to listen.

In scanning the room, he eventually stopped and did a double-take, his eyes widening. "Holy shit." He whispered, nodding past her toward a door. "Sierra Weber, four o'clock. And she's got Gary Cowell with her."

"Doc's daughter?" She looked over where he pointed Sierra out, and sure enough, their beloved doctor's daughter was standing by the door with a man who looked a few years older than her. "I didn't know she was seeing anyone, did you?" Anna leaned into Logan's side to hide the fact that she was staring. Sierra hung on the man's arm like he was the only thing in the world that mattered. Anna knew the feeling. "It's so cute. She either adores him, or she's adopted him like the brother she'll never get. I wouldn't put my money on the brother thing."

"No, I hadn't heard anything about it." He glanced back over his shoulder and shook his head. "She's Larissa's age. And I used to play holo-games with that guy. That's too weird."

Anna kissed the corner of his lips. "If they love each other, nothing else matters, as far as I'm concerned. I know that's how I feel about you." She reached for his hand and held it firmly as the officials started talking at the front of the room.

"Good evening, friends." A familiar face with a distinctly Spanish accent said at the front of the room, hands clasped in front of himself politely as he smiled at the room. "My name is Emmanuel Garcia. I am a recruiting manager for the Eleusis Initiative, and I've been looking over the information for everyone in this room for pretty much the past year straight, so if I know your name without you introducing yourself, that is why. That's my job."

"So the past year has been about me getting to know you, and tonight is about you getting to know the Initiative." His smile was broad and friendly, and he paced along the front edge of the presentation space, eyes moving from one small clump of people to the next in the far-too-large space. Obviously they hadn't had the turnout they'd expected.

"We're going to begin tonight with a quick overview of what we anticipate for the following sequence of events, should you decide to join us on this endeavor. After that, we'll talk about the role the First Wave, that's all of you, will play in the colonization of the new world, followed by a presentation on what we already know about Eleusis, which is something that is growing every single day. Then we'll leave most of the evening for you to mix among yourselves, get some refreshments, and ask questions. I'll introduce my staff later as questions come up and as we move through the presentation. How does that sound to everyone?"

Logan scoffed beside Anna. "It sounds like you're about

to record an infomercial, not talk about saving our species." He said it under his breath, but the fact that he spoke at all still got a glance from Garcia before his eyes moved on through the crowd.

"No one is going to be listening to all of that when we've got a million questions on our minds." The curvy woman by herself behind Anna and Logan spoke up when no one else would. The woman's appearance wasn't immediately remarkable: tall, brown hair and eyes, a fair complexion and ample figure. She didn't let that stop her from speaking her mind.

"We've all read the material. Talked to recruiters. Went through the extensive application process. We know that shit already. How about you tell us what happened with the station that came crashing down and why we should even listen to your little slideshow after that?"

The man's amiable attitude evaporated, but he didn't seem irritated by her interruption. Instead he turned to her with a sad expression. "I lost friends and colleagues I've been working with for nearly a decade in that accident. As for what happened to cause it, investigations over the past week have shown that it was a combination of factors that led to the failure." He ticked them off on his fingers as he spoke.

"The regulation systems that help manage the balance of rotation were under maintenance earlier in the day, and therefore there was no even distribution of weight between arms, which can eventually lead to orbital decay. Part of the arm's anchoring to the central hub of the station had already been scheduled for removal and replacement due to being twenty years old and approaching the end of its life-cycle. When the system tried to counterbalance the rotational anomalies, the strain on the arm became too great. After the first failure, the rest was a domino effect that tore out even the newer couplings under the strain. It was the single largest disaster in the history of space exploration, and all the greatest minds of the Consortium have been digging through the recorded data non-stop since it happened."

"So you're saying that there is absolutely no evidence that this was an attack? No evidence that someone might be targeting the Initiative and its people, in order to halt the colonization of Eleusis?" The woman was not deterred or placated by the barrage of technicalities. "How long have those stations been up in that sky, and how far has technology come since the very first station? This has never happened before, and I can't be the only one to believe it's suspicious that it happened now. It just so happened to kill thousands of people working on the Eleusis project. That this happened right before a new wave of people are planning to go up. I want to believe this is the future of humanity, but I'm not about to go up to die sooner than I would have died down here anyway." The woman crossed her arms over her ample chest and stared the man down, clearly not about to take his first answer without more explanation.

Garcia acknowledged her questions, and looked around to acknowledge the rest of the mutterings that were floating around the room. "I'm glad you've brought up these concerns. Let me first answer your question by saying that no, there is no evidence that this failure was the result of sabotage or assault by anti-Eleusis organizations. You've all heard of the different terrorist organizations of recent years. The Earth First movement, the One Sky Alliance, a few others. Some of them have attempted to take credit for what happened on Nine, but there was no evidence that any of them were involved. It's also worth being aware that while several offices of the Eleusis Initiative were housed on Arm Four, the main headquarters of the Initiative are housed on Arm One, along with all of our most sensitive information and prototypes for the transportation that will take us to our destination."

He shrugged as if that by itself would explain, but continued anyway. "If I'm a terrorist, that's the arm I'm targeting, not the offices for structural development, habitation research, and hundreds of other people who are working in Orbital rotation maintenance, asteroid belt reconnaissance, solar flare investigations and a hundred other things that have nothing to do with Eleusis. The headquarters of the First Wave, which is what you'd be a part of, will be in Arm Two of Station Nine. Because of what happened to Arm Four, your arm is going to be cleared of all non-Eleusis personnel, and heavily secured. Crews are already working to perform maintenance inspections of all relevant pieces of the station in order to ensure that nothing like what happened last week ever happens again. To anyone. The work we're doing is too important to allow anything less."

The woman didn't look entirely convinced but she didn't say anything else from where she sat. Anna watched until their eyes met, then looked back at the officials. Clearly they were waiting for more questions, but none came.

A small, Kenyan woman came forward and decided to speak after her colleague. "If there aren't any more immediate questions, let us proceed with the meeting as outlined." Her accent was thick, but understandable as she spoke. "My name is Orisa Kalu, and I'll begin with the overview of events." She brought up a screen with a flick of her hand, then scrolled through it with her fingertips in the air.

The dates and expectations she rattled through went so quickly. Anna was sure she would need to copy someone else's notes later. Just as the woman was picking up speed to talk about the possibility of someday returning from Eleusis, a voice spoke up to interrupt her.

"About that." The speaker was clearly polite enough to actually rise and identify himself rather than remaining seated as the first had done. "Kazuo Tanaka, from here in St. Louis. We've been hearing for a while now about how we're supposed to be getting from here to Eleusis in a matter of years instead of generations, like most people who've passed a basic physics class would expect. Now you're telling us that we're expecting a one-year flight time from Orbit to Eleusis? One year? How is that possible, exactly?"

The man was a rarity in the post-Crisis world, with distinctly Japanese features that neither Logan nor Anna had seen in person in their entire lives. His speech even retained a slight Japanese accent, though his English was perfect. He and a woman who was potentially his sister were focused intently on the speaker, well-dressed, and just as thoroughly confused and worried as everyone else in the room.

"Transportation has vastly improved in the decades that we've been working on getting humanity to Eleusis. In the last few years, our teams have been able to create ships that can travel faster than anyone thought possible, and the discovery has been monumental. It gives us great hope that after the initial settlement, we'll be able to help those on Earth who need it the most, and we'll be able to help them quickly." Officer Kalu smiled at the young man brightly. "I'm not involved with transportation, so I'm not able to break down the science for you, Mr. Tanaka, but I assure you that it is possible."

"At some point, we're all gonna want to talk to the people who *are* involved with transportation. That kind of speed isn't impressive, it's impossible." Kazuo said bitterly, but then sat down anyway, to let the officers continue their presentation.

"Once a colony is established, will preference be given for the families of First Wave members on these fantasy ships?" Logan piped up without standing, watching the officers' reactions for any sign of duplicity. They seemed to believe what they were saying so far, which was actually surprising to him. He had expected a bunch of thieves and shady dealers. Instead, he felt like he was looking at true believers.

"Yes!" Kalu nodded at Logan with a sincere expression on her face. "The project owes a lot to those who are willing to volunteer to be the first on a new planet, the first to establish human life on Eleusis. As part of the reward, your families will be able to join you before anyone else. We want you and your families to build Eleusis with us, and we have no intention of keeping you apart for longer than necessary. We understand your sacrifices, and we appreciate those of you willing to make them."

That promise seemed to shut up part of the room, at least, and seeing silence, Emmanuel stepped in to continue their presentation. "Those sacrifices are going to involve a lot of hard work. The plan for all of you, as the First Wave, is to go up to Station Nine, spend around nine months in training and development, and then depart for Eleusis. The trip will take fifty-six weeks, and you'll be the first human presence on the planet. We've already been sending probes and supply ships and just about everything else we can think of, so we can get as clear a view of the place as possible before anybody arrives."

"Today is October 8th, 2376. According to timetables as they're presently written, you'll all be celebrating touchdown on Eleusis right around August 24th, 2378, a little over a year and a half from now."

That didn't get many reactions either, since it was a level of detail that most of those in the audience hadn't been expecting. "If all progresses well with setup on Eleusis itself, the Second Wave will arrive two years after that, then two years after that, and so on until we can ramp up transport, hopefully around the fifth or sixth wave, taking more people, on larger transports. But that's all in the future and it'll all probably change as progress is made, could be faster intervals, could be slower. What's important right now is you. All of you, and what you can bring to this Initiative."

Anna looked over at Logan as he watched the officials and thought about what kind of future they could have together on Eleusis, all the years they could have that they wouldn't be able to have on Earth. She looked down at their joined hands and decided to speak up as well. "When we applied for Eleusis, the application stated that we would be automatically entered into your Matching Program. What if we don't need or want that?"

"I'm glad you asked about that." Garcia said with a slightly more serious expression on his face, pointing at Anna and Logan but looking around at the rest of those in attendance. "Because this is something that I know is going to be a deal-breaker for some of you, even though it doesn't have to be. Under normal circumstances, by which I mean single, unmarried, voluntary, age-of-majority circumstances, our matching program examines a full range of factors that have been developed over centuries to make for the best possible match between individuals. Currently, sixty-four percent of all marriages that take place in orbit are the result of the matching program, and as much as sixteen percent of those on the ground, by recent estimates. That is a huge number of people, and a lot of data that's been collected over time to refine the process. I've been matched for seven years, and I'm grateful for it every day. My wife maybe a little less so, but you'll have to ask her." He gave them a charming smile before he moved on.

"The Initiative has not and will not set in place any rules that prescribe who you may or may not be with, romantically, sexually, socially, anything. That's anathema to any ideas of freedom. What *will* happen, however, is that when you all arrive on Station Nine, your profiles will be entered into the matching system, with slightly different parameters than it would use under more normal circumstances." He paused to take a drink of water from a bottle he had nearby, and stepped forward to the edge of the stage to explain more fully.

"For Eleusis, the system has been programmed primarily to examine genetic compatibility, with a focus on diversification of profiles among potential offspring. As a part of a colony, you will all be encouraged, though hopefully little encouragement will be required," he smiled, as if it were an inside joke he was sharing with all of them, "to be fruitful and multiply, as it were. The match program defines the partners with whom that fruitfulness will be best achieved, while also factoring in elements like personality compatibility, social outlooks, personality strengths, weaknesses, etc. That will be a part of our lives once we arrive on Eleusis, and in preparation for that, it will be a part of life in the Initiative once training begins."

Anna didn't care what the matching system said about genetic diversity, she didn't want to multiply with anyone else other than Logan and that was that. It could spit out whatever information it wanted, she didn't care.

She leaned in and kissed Logan's cheek as soon as she heard other people talking about the explanation they'd been given. She whispered into his ear afterward. "They're not going to have much use for me, since if I'm not already knocked up, I soon will be."

"You sound pretty sure of that." He said back to her with a grin. "Little determined, are you?"

"He said they won't set any rules or prescribe who we will be with. I've already picked you. And I'm going to fuck you silly, if that's what it takes." She continued to whisper into his ear, then nipped at his earlobe afterward with a smirk. "So yes, you can say I'm determined."

"I like you determined." He chuckled and turned to kiss her, ignoring most of a question that someone toward the back of the room had asked until Garcia began to answer it.

"Yes, all of you will go through a rigorous health screening between here and liftoff. Not only will you be treated for any mundane diseases you may be carrying with you, but you'll also be put through treatments to eradicate any traces of the Crisis Virus from your systems. Those treatments will have to continue through the first month of your time on the station by way of daily treatments, but it can be cured, and you will not suffer the effects. We will *not* be taking the Crisis to Eleusis."

He spoke with conviction, getting approving expressions from most of the other officers behind him. "We are going to create a world free from the Crisis. Free from the past that we've burned into this planet. It will be as good as we are capable of making it. And you are all very, very capable. That's why you're here."

Growing up on Earth, knowing that the Crisis Virus was in every molecule of the planet, in the air, in the water, in every plant and animal, in every human being, was a dread that everyone had to learn to live with sooner or later. In Orbit, with systems of control, quarantine, intensive medications, it was possible to eliminate it from an individual, from a controlled population. It was that possibility that had driven humanity into orbit in the first place, in the early years following the Crisis itself.

But with Earth itself as the problem, the virus was too widespread to ever have any hope of eliminating it. "I wish they would fix Earth too." Anna spoke softly to Logan. "Or at least try. Though I know it's already too late for some people." Too late for her father, certainly.

"Maybe someday." Logan said quietly, the same thoughts running through his own mind. "When they've evacuated everyone off Earth and moved them to Eleusis, then maybe they can be sure this whole place has been wiped clean of the virus, and start bringing people back here. That's the only way I can think it'll be destroyed completely."

"They don't care about Earth. They just picked another planet." She shook her head but held tightly to his arm as a few more questions were asked, then they were allowed to break for drinks and snacks. "Let's get something to eat. I'm starving."

Most of the prospective Initiates went off in small groups to talk amongst themselves, which meant no one was talking to the woman who'd come by herself. She was left alone through most of her plate of food, but when she was nearly finished, a voice interrupted her halfway through a bite of one of the rolls that turned stale due to the length of the presentation.

"So." The voice was a pleasant baritone, slightly on the high side, but not so high as to take away the masculine thrum of it in the row behind her. "What percentage of this crowd do you think actually bought the bullshit answer he tried to sell for your question about the explosion?"

The woman didn't even turn around when the voice spoke, since it didn't matter who it was, she'd give them the same answer. "At least half of them wanted to hear someone tell them it was just an accident. People always buy the bullshit they want to hear." She put the roll down on the paper plate and tossed it all in the trash bin. She didn't like to eat around other people, since she figured she got enough judgment about her appearance without people telling her the carbohydrates in bread wouldn't do her any favors.

She finally looked over at whoever had decided to speak to her, and she raised an eyebrow in her assessment before she said anything else. "Why, what do you think?"

"I think you have one of the better noses for bullshit in the room. I always appreciate that in a person." He stayed where he was so that she could get a good look at him, hair falling partly in his face. He had a wiry build and sharp, focused brown eyes that seemed to take in nothing but her. He leaned forward and put a hand out to take hers, trying to hold eye contact so that she wouldn't get distracted and start asking questions about the scars on his hand. "Gordon White, pleased to meet you."

She didn't even look down at his hand as she put hers in his, but her scowl didn't dissipate. "Jessica Rogers. Jess. Though I have a feeling you already knew that." Jess shook his hand firmly before she pulled her hand back. "That look in your eyes tells me you know more than you're willing to say."

"Like I said, one of the better bullshit detectors in the room." He sat back in his seat and looked her over without trying in any way to make it look as though he wasn't. "I know your name and I've seen bits and pieces of your profile, but I know better than to think something like that tells the full story about a person. I wouldn't have expected somebody from the Great Lakes district to have your kind of attitude, either. It's refreshing. Did you pick it up somewhere, or does it come naturally?"

"This is all natural, baby." She said with the same biting sarcasm he would expect from the kind of comment he gave her. "It gets worse as I get older, according to my dying mother. Last month she told me I'll die alone and I am the reason all of my siblings moved away. Cancer makes her so pleasant." There was a flicker of pain in her eyes she tried to hide by looking down into her drink. "So, were you looking for a bullshit detector, or is there another reason why you decided to come say hello? Don't tell me that you're some bleeding heart that felt bad for the woman sitting alone."

"I don't befriend people out of pity. Which is convenient, since I don't actually feel pity for people often. The only time my heart bleeds is when someone is cutting into it. I always get cranky when that happens." He shook his head and moved forward again to lean on the back of the seat beside her. "And you're not going to die alone. Didn't you hear the officer? Your perfect match awaits you in orbit."

"Uh huh." She clearly didn't seem convinced about that either. "Considering the small pool of people that have been collected for this project, I highly doubt it will be a perfect match. Maybe genetically, considering that's what they care about. They don't care if I like someone as long as they get me up there." She looked up at the ceiling as though she could see through it. "I'm still deciding whether I care or not if I turn into one of their pets. I mean, the end result is a one-way ticket to Eleusis, after all."

"Well, the ticket won't quite be one-way. At least, not if certain individuals have anything to say about it." Gordon shrugged as he looked her over, smiling at her crisis of decision. "And being aware that someone wants a pet is the first step in avoiding a leash. Obedience doesn't strike me as your primary virtue."

"Never did get that obedience thing down." Jess finally turned her attention back to Gordon and took her time examining him before she said anything else. "So if you don't befriend people out of pity, then why do you? I don't have anything to offer you."

"I've always believed that friends are their own reward. I don't make many, but that's mostly because I think the majority of people are complete morons with no sense of what's actually going on more than ten feet from their faces. And what is that supposed to mean, exactly, that you have nothing to offer?"

"Exactly what it means." She said plainly, since she wasn't looking for pity. "I live on a farm with a large vineyard and my mother. Other than lots of Earth money that will mean nothing up in the sky, I don't have anything to offer you. I don't have information or connections."

"That's a virtue in itself. It's a precious thing sometimes in this world to come without any strings attached. So few of us do." He chuckled and held her eyes, clearly unafraid of being thought to stare too long when he thought someone was worth staring at. "Plus, if you're rich and you own vineyards, maybe what you have to offer is some really good wine to bring along to orbit. The liquor they produce up there isn't bad, but they're shit with wine."

Jess looked confused at that comment, since she didn't realize she was talking to someone who had already been up in space. Usually people didn't come back once they went up. "I'm not sure the trip wouldn't affect the flavor, and I've always been careful with the flavor." She didn't know why he was looking her over so intensely, but she tried to ignore it. "You've been up there already? Why are you here then?"

"Easy." He glanced around as a precaution to make sure no one was close by listening, but they were being ignored, for the time being. "I didn't make the trip up there in the first place by choice, for one thing, and I'm here because Eleusis is the best opportunity humanity has ever had. I don't intend to let it get fucked up by people who think they know what they're doing and clearly don't."

"You don't intend to let it?" She leaned in closer to him,

since he seemed to be intent on being secretive. "Who are you, that you think you can control something like that?"

He leaned in the same as she did, until he was just a few inches away from her. "Who am I? Wonderful question. If you figure it out, please let me know. I've been wondering for years." He grinned with a tiny spark of malevolence, and moved one hand in closer between them to rest on her shoulder.

"For right now, I'm the guy who likes you, Jess Rogers. Who wants to be friends. Who wants to make sure Eleusis is a place for everyone on the planet, not the chosen few the Consortium deems worthy to enjoy it. I'm also the guy who happens to share your general distaste for bullshit, as well as your hope for better things to come."

Jess looked at his hand as soon as he put it on her shoulder, but she left it there until he was done talking, then plucked it off. "Maybe we can be friends. I'm not sure I trust you any more than I trust them, but you make a good speech. A little idealistic, maybe." She let go of his hand and leaned back. "Besides, you barely know me. You can't possibly like me. Even the people that know me don't like me very much."

"Don't tell me what I can and can't do." He said sharply, but still with a grin, as he pushed himself to his feet. "I'll like you if I want to like you, and there's not much you can do about it." He moved down the row behind her to leave, the conversation clearly over.

On his way by, he left a brief caress on the back of her neck that could have been an accident, but from the rest of his nature, probably wasn't. Especially with the grin he gave her afterward. "I'll see you on launch day. If not before."

Jess didn't know why he would continue to touch her or how he would possibly see her again before launch, if she even chose to go in the first place. He didn't know where she lived. Did he? She watched him go and shook her head as she looked away. He was trouble, she could already tell. Whatever he was planning would be trouble too, but like everything else, she would have to decide if it was worth it.

12

The second time Orion and Mercury shared a pod was significantly less terrifying than the first. Leaving Station Three had gone without a hitch, and they had again been permitted the use of a small service pod to get from Three back to Nine, where their Eleusis briefing was scheduled. They had seldom left his unit in the time since the unfortunate incident at the club, which was fine by Orion.

They were still over an hour out from Station Nine, on course, with no warnings on their instruments, and they had abandoned their flight jumpsuits more than an hour before.

There appeared to be nothing in front of Mercury but empty space and stars through the clear glass of the pod. There was nothing behind her but a control panel and Orion, his knees tucked up against the back of hers, his arms wrapped around her shoulders and her waist to hold her back against him. It felt like he was keeping her from falling into the abyss that filled most of the universe.

On the night-side of Earth beneath them, small veins of gold could be seen where humanity persisted on the ground, but otherwise their bodies were lit only by the instrument display, the moon, and the stars.

"This is the best view the moon's had in a while, I'm

betting." He said with a kiss to the back of her shoulder as the pod rotated to face the distant crescent, lifting his arm off her for good measure to leave the entirety of her exposed to the moon before he took hold of her again. "Hopefully no kids up there on the lunar stations with a telescope trying to check out dots flying orbital patterns. This is not a kid-friendly show."

Mercury laughed and kissed his arm so he would keep it in place against her, since she liked the way he held onto her, the way it seemed like he wanted the world to know that she belonged to him. She left her lips pressed against his skin for a long time before she said anything. "Do you think it is premature to want to get married?" They hadn't spoken in depth about marriage, only that they would see how they felt after a month of being together. Even so, Mercury didn't want to wait.

"I hope not, since I'd really like to talk about it." He chuckled against her back and continued his kisses along her neck and shoulder. "I feel like there's still a lot that we don't know about each other, but every time I try to tell myself that, I realize I'm more excited to learn more about you than I'm afraid of anything I wouldn't like hearing."

"Is there anything I wouldn't want to know that you're keeping from me? You seem like an honest and forthright man." She reached to run her hand along his side. "I know being matched isn't a perfect science, and there are a lot of things that go into a marriage. But I also know this is better than I could have hoped, and I don't want to go looking for anyone else. I'd rather plunge into the unknown variables of marriage with you. I don't see a reason not to. Even if it were to fail, I don't think I would regret trying in the first place."

"I don't think I would either. As a connoisseur of failed relationships, believe me, I've thought about it." Their bodies were connected along their entire length, braced in place only by Orion's feet tucked into restraints along the foot of the pod's backboards. It left the opportunity in zero gravity for him to move against her however he saw fit, to keep the fact of their connection alive in their bodies' awareness of each other. It had been a truly delicious flight, and one that he looked forward to repeating as often as possible.

"All I know is that we're gonna be asked to make a lot of sacrifices for Eleusis. That idea doesn't bother me right now, but I realize that's because for most of my life, I've been in it for me and nobody else. Sacrificing time with you is gonna be hard. It's still something I'm willing to do, since I still believe the new world is gonna be worth it, but it's still gonna be hard."

"But we'll do it together." She groaned from his movement, since she couldn't stop enjoying herself whenever he gave her the chance. "We'll explore and enjoy the new world together. And make beautiful babies. You know, eventually."

"Eventually." Babies were one thing that they had only spoken about briefly, since it had been obvious they both wanted children, but they weren't in any hurry about it. "The Initiative might want faster movement on that than we were really thinking about. But If we've still got at least a year of flight time, I don't know if they'll want the variable of having babies aboard or not. I wouldn't, but I'm not gonna be the one at the helm."

Mercury wasn't thrilled about having a baby so soon, since even a year sounded like it was too soon for her. "I want more time with you before adding a variable like children to the equation." She leaned her head back against his chest and took a deep breath. "What do you think this meeting will be about? I'm so curious I can't stand it."

"I assume it'll be mostly things we already know. But I doubt everyone is as well-informed as we are. Some people might take a little more work to bring up to speed." His hands wandered freely over every exposed inch of her whenever any inch of her was exposed to begin with. That moment was no exception, his long fingers leaving heated caresses all over her pale skin, still flushed from their recent exertion. "I'm also hoping we'll get some recent data on Eleusis and maybe some revelations about the flight path, but that's just me."

"I would love to get any data they could give me about what to expect from training and from Eleusis. Not that I think we'll get much." She shivered in enjoyment as his fingers traced over her skin. "You know, I've wondered if I would get past the novelty of how aroused I get being around you and being with you. I wondered if it would wear off once I'd had more than my fill of satisfying sex. I'm glad it seems I don't have a limit and I haven't gotten bored. Your touch still affects me the same as it did the first time."

"I'm always glad to hear that." He admitted with another kiss to her shoulder, his hand moving to cup her breast completely, warming her skin before she had a chance to realize she was cold. "When we first met and you told me how limited your previous experience was, I was worried that we'd get into things and you wouldn't really have much of an appetite for it. Imagine my surprise when we went seven rounds that second day and finally fell asleep from exhaustion." He chuckled at the memory, only a few days old but already funny. "I've got no problem with you being insatiable. Just gives me more reason to work on satisfying you."

"If *you* were surprised, imagine how I felt." Her breast responded to his touch, her nipple peaked beneath his warm hand, both from the cold and the stimulation. "You know so much. And you feel so good. It's incredible."

"I hope it only gets better. For both of us. You're incredible." He hugged her back against him tightly, which pulled a moan from both of them. "I hope to keep surprising you in the future. Even after a week, I still haven't shown you *all* of my tricks. Have to save some good ones for later." His hands moved down over her thighs, inching them apart to emphasize how exposed she was to him and to the moon. "I hope if you find out there's something you want or that you're curious about, you'll tell me. I do take requests."

"Mmm." She replied at first as his hands moved over her thighs. "There are a lot of things I'm curious about, I'm sure, I just don't know all the things to be curious about. I intend to study more about sexual behaviors once we get back to Seven." She moaned again once his fingers teased her. "Particularly, I want to study first about oral sex."

"Giving or receiving?" He asked with a smile, pressing the conversation as always even while he was intent on teasing her. It had begun by him being impressed by how long she could maintain proper conversation, and had turned into a habit between them to talk things through as they were about to devour each other.

Mercury writhed against him as he teased, but she still attempted to focus on the conversation. "Both. I want to learn about how to give it more, though, I think. It's important to me that I know what to do. You already know so much about how a woman works. It's not fair to you that I don't know as much."

"You don't need to question whether I'm satisfied or not." His caresses over the rest of her body turned heavier as she writhed against him, and he loved how free things had become between them. Sex in zero gravity was very different from sex in a weighted environment, but he felt like he could take his time more in weightlessness. Things seemed much more sensual when all the body had to do was feel instead of focusing on how to hold itself up. "You know plenty about how I work and what I like. Especially since what I like is as much of you as I can get."

"Mmmm." She enjoyed the feeling of his body against hers and his caresses over her skin. "Is it . . ." she started to say, before a jolt of pleasure interrupted her thought with a whimper. "Is it different for you, being with me compared to the other women you've been with? Other than my body being more accommodating. Certainly every woman must bring something different to the experience."

"It is different, but it's hard to quantify how." She could easily feel him getting hard again against her as he continued to tease at her while he spoke, his free hand closing over her breasts to press her against him as he grinned at her moans.

"It feels less like you want something from me but more like you want something *with* me. Which is a big difference I had never really understood before. And it's just . . . it's still amazing to me and it's still going to take a lot of getting used to the fact that you just don't play games. Every woman plays games. With what they want, what they *think* they want, what they think *you* think they want, and how they go about getting it. It gets tedious. And you are anything but tedious."

"I'm glad you don't think I'm tedious." Mercury closed her eyes and got lost in his touch on her breasts. "I've never seen much purpose in playing games. Nor do I think I really understand how, honestly. Facts matter more than games. Twisting any kind of truth just to attempt to achieve an end seems like wasted time." She moaned louder as one of his fingers circled one of her nipples. "That feels wonderful. Please don't stop."

It was more specific than anything else he'd gotten from her previously, and he had no trouble obeying precisely, bringing her nipples more to attention. "I love winding you up. I can't think of many things I've enjoyed more in my entire life than seeing you when you're finally so horny you just turn and attack me. I love it."

Mercury tried to laugh, but the way he was touching her wasn't funny in the least. It felt so good, especially when he found different ways to trace lines and patterns along her sensitive nipples. "Why . . . why is that so special?"

In answer, one of his hands continued the caress she had requested on her breasts, while the other moved down over her waist to explore between her legs, further complicating the teasing. "I might not have known you for very long yet, but I do know you. In the rest of the world, the rest of your life, you're as contained and controlled as anyone I've ever met. But if I can get you to go wild with me, break that control, maybe have you screaming about multiple orgasms, all those times . . . I cherish those times. Just because I know how hard it is to get them out of you. That makes them more than worth it."

Mercury could only groan in response as she felt tense and needy, but it didn't stop her from trying to speak. "You care . . . about me? Cherish . . ." she replied with a pant. "You said cherish."

"Damn right I did. And damn right I do." He didn't let up on his torment of her as he said so, kissing up along the back of her neck as he turned her inside out.

Mercury was unable to speak coherently after seeing stars on top of stars, until an alert went off to signal final approach and she knew that she shouldn't remain naked much longer. "I love spending all this time with you, Orion. Not only for physical reasons. I look forward to the life we'll make together."

He spun her around in the pod to face him, hooking his legs with hers to give them leverage against each other to stay close, and kissed her thoroughly before he reached over to start helping her pull her jumpsuit into place. "You and me both. I look forward to coming home to you. I don't look forward to leaving you all the time to go fly, but that's the nature of both our lives. I just know I'm going to really look forward to coming home as long as you're my home."

"I want to be your home." She kissed his lips several more times and wiggled to get her suit back into place properly. It was strange to wear a jumpsuit after being used to other types of clothing, but she didn't mind it. Mercury reached up and ran her fingers along his cheeks afterward. "You're so gorgeous. I am going to write an excellent review about my matching experience." Mercury smiled against his lips afterward and laughed.

Her laugh made him smile, as it always did, and he shrugged his way into his own jumpsuit, in which he was fairly comfortable, even though he would always be more comfortable when naked with Mercury. "Oh fuck yes. That program is getting a five-star review from me, that's for damn sure. My matching experience . . ." he chuckled and leaned in to kiss her neck above the collar of the jumpsuit, groaning slightly at the taste of her and the warmth of her in his arms. "I am very much enjoying the experience of my match."

He kissed back up to her lips, the look on his face more serious as he looked her in the eye. "I want to marry you, Mercury. Before we go into the Initiative, before we get locked away and blast off to the other side of the galaxy, before anything else, I want to be yours, and I want you to be mine." They had talked about marriage slantwise earlier, but never in any kind of firmly committed way. That had quickly become insufficient for Orion. "You're easily one of the best things that's ever happened to me, and I have a bad habit of letting good things turn into regrets that I let go or couldn't hold onto. I want to hold onto you, make you laugh, make you scream as often as possible, and overall, make you happy." He moved down in the cramped space of the pod so that it looked like he was kneeling against the base, his hands sliding down over her sides and her legs until he was looking up at her with his face at her waist, grinning broadly. "What do you think? Sound like fun?"

His smile and his playfulness was infectious, and she nodded as he ran his hands over her sides and legs, since she wanted to marry him too. She knew it was fast, faster than she ever imagined possible, considering her original doubts. Now she knew how wrong she was, and for the first time, she was happy to be wrong. They still had a lot to learn about each other, but she wanted to learn it as his wife. There couldn't possibly be anyone out there that was a better match for her, and even if there was, she didn't care to find him. "It sounds amazing. I would love to be your wife, Orion."

His grin actually expanded, though it was hard to see how that was possible, and he slowly kissed his way back up her body before he got back to her lips, pressing her against the glass exterior of the pod to stay wrapped up in her a while longer. "I ordered your ring before we left Three." He said between kisses, his hands resting on her backside to keep her pressed into him. "It should be ready by the wedding. I had to get it from a contractor on Prime to get what I wanted for you."

"You were that confident, were you?" She wasn't offended by the fact that he had proceeded without asking her first, in fact, she was glad he was so confident in their relationship. "When will our wedding be?"

"Well, entry date for the Initiative is 11.15, which gives us another week for the remainder of our Introduction, and two weeks after that to get back to work and get everyone coordinated to attend. I figure we can have it 11.12 and have the weekend to ourselves before the Initiative begins that Monday." Clearly he thought things through, if he had already run those kinds of dates, and he shrugged through his playful smile. "You went to sleep early the other night and I had a bout of insomnia. I was awake for a while thinking of this stuff before I attacked you in your sleep."

Mercury continued kissing him after he broke down all of the dates and explained it all to her, partially because she couldn't stop, but also because she appreciated he had planned it all out and knew all of the answers to her questions immediately. She appreciated his take-charge attitude. It was refreshing to her. "That sounds great. Perfectly planned out."

She looked past him briefly at the station as they got closer to it, but seeing it again left a flutter in her stomach and a taste of remembered panic in her mouth. She hated that the accident and the interrogation afterward had somewhat soured her excitement for being part of the Eleusis project. "I hope this place has settled down. I'm nervous about being here."

"I have strongly mixed feelings myself." He tried to keep his tone light-hearted as he spun her around and started strapping her in, kissing her afterward with a grin to make it feel a tiny bit kinky. They hadn't tried anything with restraints or anything quite that creative yet, but they had only been together barely over a week, after all. "On the one hand, it's where we almost died and things exploded and a lot of other terrible things happened. On the other hand, it's where I met my wife. So you know. Give and take."

Hearing Orion call her his wife brought Mercury's smile back to her lips, and she squeezed his hand afterward before he moved away from her seat. "Your wife. I really do like the sound of that. However, I'd like to keep my last name. My family line stops with me, and I don't want to change things up with my patients and my current research. I hope that doesn't offend you."

"No, not at all. Al-Jabbar is kind of a mouthful. I get it." He gave her a reassuring smile before he pulled away out of her line of sight, and she could hear him working through the various controls to get their landing sequence under way. "You've got a lot that you've accomplished under Finnegan. I wouldn't want to take that away from your family."

"You wouldn't be taking it away. I just want to keep it. I've worked hard to develop my identity." She smiled at him even as he worked, just because he had that effect on her. Frequently. "When my colleagues meet you, they'll be stunned. I'm sure they're expecting someone who doesn't smile quite as often as you do. I'm not known for being funny or clever or really even spending time with people who are."

"What are you talking about? You're the cleverest person I know." He had to stop responding as he maneuvered them around a few larger ships that were working on departing from the docks, but he managed to talk through his distraction. "And I'm really not that funny. But I'm glad you think I am. I doubt your friends will think I'm funny, though. Mostly people just tend to complain about how much their neck hurts trying to talk to me or make jokes about giants walking the Earth . . ."

He stopped as they drifted farther away from the dock, so as to avoid hitting another ship that was leaving, and both their eyes were drawn to the gaping maw of destruction that was the scar left over from the breaking of Arm Four. There were still maintenance ships anchored all over the area, tethered technicians working on null-atmosphere welds across the gap of the scar.

By appearances, they were patching over the breach rather than trying to build on it with the intention of constructing a new arm in the future, but Orion imagined that was a temporary measure. Still, it was unsettling to see.

Orion let out a low whistle at the extent of the damage. "This . . . wait, that's not right."

Mercury was too stunned by the sight and the cold feeling that settled in her body at seeing it up close to register his voice at first. She finally looked away, though, confused by what he said. "What? What's not right?"

Orion hit a few pieces of the display, and highlighted parts of the structure while they drifted there, the station spinning slowly in front of them as they waited for their turn to dock. The main supports of the vast structure lit up as they would have on a schematic of the station, to show her where the arm had been anchored to the dock in the first place.

"All the exterior junctions, yeah, clearly all those were blown to hell. You can see all the jagged breaks where the explosions were, all the way around the arm. Those were clearly blown up. And those would hold the arm on by themselves, they're designed as triple failsafes. Outer ring, inner core, secondary core. But you see the inner and the secondary there . . . they're exposed, but the crew isn't working on them, because they've got no jagged edges. They're clean breaks. Which means those structures were cut. Cleanly. *Before* the explosion."

Mercury's stomach twisted as she thought about what he was saying about the structure. "They did say that they were working on the arm before the accident happened. Perhaps they cut them so that they could be fixed? And they just . . . they thought that the arm could handle more than it could, and then the outer layer broke?"

Orion felt his own stomach twist knots, but Mercury watched him shake his head in the reflection of the glass. "When they work on structural repairs like this, protocol is that they work on half of a ring at a time. So if you've got three full rings, two of which are completely severed, that's . . . either the worst breach of protocol I've ever heard of combined with the worst kind of coincidence, or it's . . . not." It was clear from his tone what he thought, but he moved the pod away from the site quickly once the path to the pod-dock was clear.

Mercury was silent until they were nearly docked, and she found her voice again. "So if it was on purpose, then there has to be a reason why they've announced a lie. Clearly we're not the only ones who can look at that and see what you saw, and we're not the only ones who can understand what that means. So if they're publicly lying, then either they know what happened, or they still don't know and they're trying to keep an investigation a secret while lying to keep the public from going into a frenzy over it."

"That pretty much sums up the available options." He agreed in a dour tone, running his fingers through the display to remove the traces of the operations he had performed in analyzing the breach scar. He didn't need other people walking in behind him and seeing the evidence of his own investigation. "And I'm not sure I'm a fan of any of those options. Either way, they're lying, but one way they're incompetent and the other way they're . . . well, I don't want to think about the other way."

"I don't either." She whispered, clearly distressed. "I simply cannot believe they would keep it from us unless it was for our own good not to know." Mercury didn't agree with withholding information, but she wasn't in a leadership position and she needed to focus on what she was good at. Being a doctor. Not being a politician. "I have faith in the

Consortium. They've given me so much."

"They've given us both everything we have." He agreed as he settled into the dock with a mild shock to the entire pod as they locked in place. The landing arms pulled them down into the pod socket on the side of the dock, and the darkness of space was replaced with the low-level lighting of the pod dock interior corridor. "I hope you're right."

"I hope I am too." Mercury didn't move immediately, but when she finally did, her hands were still calm and sure in their movements as she slowly unbuckled herself from the several harnesses surrounding her. She refused to make assumptions; she needed facts. She always needed facts. "Maybe they'll have more to say about the accident at the meeting."

He was unhooked from his own restraints before she was, and he helped her with the last few restraints by her feet before he floated out with her into the corridor. He paused at the control panel for the pod before moving on, and even with the serious tone of their conversation, he couldn't help the grin that spread across his face. He typed in a recommendation for the pod to be thoroughly cleaned and sterilized before it was put back into circulation for general use.

People got motion sick and threw up in pods all the time. Typing in that there was a need to clean for possible bodily fluids wouldn't be outside the realm of normal maintenance.

* * * * *

When they arrived at the meeting, the room was already mostly full, but there were people still greeting them at the door. Mercury smiled at the grinning official, and she reached her hand out to shake his. "Hello, Sir. Mercury Finnegan checking in. I'm excited to be here."

When he answered, it was with a thick Australian accent and a firm handshake to go along with his smile. "Dr. Finnegan, of course. We're very glad to have you. Welcome.

I'm Stephen Kaplan, one of the operations overseers for the prep phase." He looked up at Orion afterward and offered his hand. "And that must make you Lieutenant Al-Jabbar. *As-salaam alaikum.*"

"*Wa-alaikum as-salaam.*" Orion returned as he took the man's hand. "Looks like we're a little late to the party."

"Nah, right on time. You and your lovely lady are reserved right up front, section for military personnel. Names on the chairs. Fall in and we'll get started in a minute." He gave them both a smile as they walked away, but Mercury noticed him looking her over as she turned to walk down the aisle with Orion. She realized, as she saw it, that she'd gotten such looks from a large number of men before in her life, though she'd never paid much mind until she received many of exactly the same kind of appraising look from Orion.

Mercury didn't say anything as they walked through the aisles to get to their seats, but as soon as she was sitting down next to Orion, she took his hand. She didn't care about looks, but she didn't want anyone to think she was interested in anyone except Orion. "I never really noticed the . . . attention . . . before. Not from most people, anyway. But you must be used to the attention."

"Hm? Oh, yeah, I got used to the freak looks years ago. Plus the top three questions everybody always asks me. How do you spell Al-Jabbar, how's the weather up there, and how tall are you exactly. Like everybody in the world has this inborn right to a measuring tape where other people's dimensions are concerned."

"I'm surprised they don't ask your measurements elsewhere. That's much more interesting than your height." She gave him a teasing smile and kissed his cheek. "Have you ever heard of that man before? Kaplan?"

He shook his head. "I think I saw his name on the roster I glanced over before, but I've never worked with him. He's pretty high in seniority with the Initiative, but he's a groundling, which is weird. That's all I know about him.

Why? Is he the one that was checking you out?" He put an arm around her shoulders and turned around to glare, feeling immediately protective.

Mercury moved the armrest between them out of the way and she pressed herself into his side. "I didn't say that." Even though Kaplan *had* checked her out, she didn't want Orion to feel jealous or possessive. He didn't have anything to worry about.

He gave her a sarcastic look and glared back at Kaplan before turning his attention back to the front of the room. The place was filling up quickly, and everyone fell into their places as the time to start approached.

"I see Carl made it." He pointed across the aisle at the other pseudo-giant in the room, but Carl was busy talking to a group of other men who looked like they were capable of violence, all of them laughing and watching the stage as if one of the officials of the Initiative was the butt of a joke and too far away to hear about it.

"I don't think your friend would miss this. He's still waiting for his match, though he seemed like he had an easy time finding a woman when we were at that club." She held tightly to Orion's side as the officials finished speaking to each other and moved to their own seats on the stage. "We're the lucky ones who don't have to worry about that anymore."

"Lucky is a word I've applied to myself about every minute and a half for the past week straight." He smiled and turned to kiss the side of her head, his fingers leaving a caress along her neck.

The man who stepped up to the front of the raised stage above the rest of the crowd was tall without being towering. He had black hair that was going silver at his ears and a black goatee with silver highlights that stood out in stark contrast to his dark complexion. "Good afternoon." He said in a deep voice with a thick Nigerian accent. "Thank you all for being here today, and for your willingness to be a part of this Initiative. My name is Hugo Vance. I'm the founder and general director of this Initiative."

There was a round of applause after his introduction, and Mercury was no less enthusiastic than anyone else about meeting an important person to the project and to be in the audience. She had waited her entire life for Eleusis, worked tirelessly, and being in the same room with the director of the Initiative brought her closer to her goal. It was right in front of her, and she had an amazing man to share it with.

"Thank you." Vance gave the room a smile once the applause began to die down. "Before my colleagues begin their presentations, please allow me to say a few words about the state of this project and the world that we have envisioned." He headed for the front of the stage, reaching up once to adjust the microphone that was unobtrusively perched over his ear to make sure it was comfortably in place as he addressed the crowd.

With a gesture, a holographic image took shape in the air behind him, light coalescing one beam at a time to show a world that was much greener and much more mountainous than Earth, with much smaller ocean masses between its continents.

"There is a reason why this planet was named Eleusis when it was first surveyed." Vance began as he watched everyone in the room look over the image behind him. "After her winter in the Underworld, Persephone would return to the surface to be reunited with her mother, to bring the return of the growing season. Her return to the surface meant that the dark times were over, that a time of plenty, of growth, was at hand. The place where she emerged from darkness to announce such a change was Eleusis. So too shall it be for us."

He smiled at the brief indulgence in the poetic, nodding his confidence out to the assembled crowd before continuing with the facts of their endeavor. "It has 167% the landmass of Earth, and more than three times the immediately arable land. Early scans have shown that the soil is compatible with most staple Earth crops, and many of the indigenous trees have been shown to produce wood that is every bit as suitable for construction as those found on Earth, in addition to providing chemical compounds not found naturally on our home planet. Less is known, as of yet, about local fauna, but satellite research is ongoing. What we do find encouraging is that none of our probes have been eaten by a dinosaur in the course of exploration or hijacked by aliens. At least not yet." Vance said with a grin.

Mercury laughed and shook her head as she imagined what problems they would face if they ran into dinosaurs. "That's good to hear, right?" She whispered with a smirk at Orion. "At least we won't die by dinosaur."

"You know, I'm actually a little disappointed. I was looking forward to having a pet dinosaur. You know, like a horse, keep him in a stable, take him out and run laps once in a while? Make a saddle, the whole thing." He shook his head. "Maybe that's too many cartoons as a kid talking, I don't know. Still, makes me a little sad on the inside."

"Main landing site will be here." Vance turned around and expanded a spot on a continent in the southern hemisphere with a broad temperate zone between a range of mountains and its eastern coast, near the mouth of a river. "The main settlement has been tentatively named Firsthaven, or the First Cornerstone, and supplies have already been sent along with the probes we have been launching as frequently as possible over the past five years, including tools and basic equipment."

"From Firsthaven, colonies will expand up and down the coast and up the main channel of this river into the mountains to allow for constant contact. The region's resources and situation make it ideal for habitation, and the part of the ocean adjacent to it is most favorable for water landings due to the planet's weather patterns, making it an ideal landing site."

"This is the part of the world you will be calling home a little over two years from now. It's the part of the world you will cultivate and set in order for those who will follow you, and those after them and those after them and so on. I want you all to get a good, close look at it, think about what your life is going to be here. This will be your home."

Mercury definitely took a good look, because she loved getting any information she could about Eleusis. She was fantasizing about where her house and her clinic would be when she heard someone speak up from the back of the room. Mercury glanced back after the woman started to speak, clearly out of turn, but apparently her question just couldn't wait.

"I've heard rumors that you're bringing mudpuppies up here. To train them to go to Eleusis also. Is it true? Are you going to bring a batch of diseased up here and send them off with us to Eleusis? If you are, that's asking for trouble. They'll just ruin the new planet too."

The woman was dressed in a jumpsuit similar to Mercury's, so Mercury wondered if the woman was a pilot also. She winced at the derogatory term used for Earthlings, but she remained quiet. Lots of people had hateful things to say about the people that lived on Earth, but Mercury didn't waste much of her time thinking about them other than during her CV research. She had her own life to focus on, not someone else's life down below.

Instead of Vance stepping up to give a response, the man who'd greeted them at the door stepped up from the back of the stage with his hand raised slightly. "Hello there. Molly, right? Molly Ashford? Yeah, I thought I recognized you from your file. Well, Ms. Ashford, speaking as a mudpuppy who grew into a full-sized dog, I can tell you that yes, we'll be bringing Earth-born up into the Initiative to go with us to Eleusis. Any of you who are concerned about contamination, don't worry, they'll be undergoing full treatment once they get here and be cleared of the Crisis Virus, same as I was when I got here as a little tyke."

"After that, they'll be working alongside you, under your command, maybe even commanding you. Especially since, if I remember correctly, Ms. Ashford, your area of expertise is in resource allocation and operations oversight. That's my area of expertise, so you're already set to be under a mudpuppy from day one. I suggest you get used to it." He smiled at the woman, then at the rest of the crowd, a few of whom had laughed.

"Earth-born have skills we're going to need living on an actual planet instead of up here where we have one hand on the thermostat and the other on the latest fashion magazine all the time. They can do things you haven't even thought of yet, and we know the answers to questions they've never thought to ask. We'll need both on Eleusis. That's how we thrive."

Mercury was quiet as she listened to that explanation, since she didn't know how she felt about sharing her Eleusis experience with Earthborn people. Not that their contagion was a long-term concern; the current regimen of treatments for the virus was effective and fast-acting. Only a month of daily treatments would eradicate the virus and reverse most of the damage it had caused in their bodies, if the damage wasn't extensive enough. In young people, the damage was almost always reversible.

Eventually Mercury raised her hand, even though she didn't know how the meeting was supposed to go; if they were supposed to listen or if they were allowed to ask questions and provide input. She didn't wait for permission to speak. "Is the current report date for training still accurate? I noticed when we arrived at the station today there were still a lot of repairs in progress after the accident. Will that delay us?"

Vance was the one to answer that, as he approached the side of the stage close to her. "At the moment, the Arm Four conduits are being sealed. Replacing the arm has been designated as an eventuality, but not an immediate priority. The Initiative is currently in the process of outfitting Arm Two as your intended center for training, and yes, your timetable is still accurate. What we *have* altered, in light of recent events, is the fact that you will be alone in Arm Two for the training process, to allow the Initiative to entirely take over the maintenance tasks for that arm and allow us complete autonomy within that sector. We have also chosen to expedite the training program in order to achieve a launch date of 6.14.77."

"Expedite the training. Wow." She settled back into Orion's side. "I apologize for the secondary interruption, Director. I'm sure you have an outline of what you wish to discuss."

He smiled at Mercury and nodded, clearly approving her apology. "Not necessary, Doctor. I'm happy to answer any and all questions in due course." He turned back to the rest of those present and returned to the side of the stage so that the hologram of Eleusis was clearly visible.

"The following presentation and all the relevant pieces of research that have been conducted so far will be made available to each of you directly after this meeting is over, for your own review and consideration. As of your acceptance, you are a part of this team, and you will be expected to contribute as you are able in your own areas of research. For now, allow me to introduce Dr. Maria Santos, the lead medical director of the Initiative. She has some items to review with you regarding issues of public health and social arrangements to be maintained throughout the training and colonization process."

A smaller, dark-haired woman with dark, sharp eyes walked forward and smiled at the receptive crowd. "I'm so happy to see all of you here today. I had concerns that we would lose some of the brightest initiates we have because of the accident. This proves that you all have an awareness of risk, and that you know Eleusis is worth that risk." Her smile flashed around the room before she continued.

"First and foremost, before you leave, we'd like to conduct a biometric screening. Everyone had one during the application process, but you all know that data needs to be updated consistently to provide accurate analysis. During the screening, we'll remove or reverse any reproductive blocks or birth control measures." The crowd didn't remain quiet after that, but they weren't loud and raucous either. It was obvious that everyone was surprised to hear something like that, at least so soon.

"You'll all be matched on the first day, and since we know that all of you will be a part of the First Wave, procreation is one of the biggest priorities. Extensive medical facilities will not be established on Eleusis until after you arrive, so I'm sure the women in the room would appreciate taking babies with them instead of giving birth in less than ideal situations."

It was Orion's turn to jump in with a question, but he wasn't the only one to raise his hand, and another man on the other side of the room was chosen to voice his question before Orion could. The man was of fairly average height and build, and wore glasses, marking him as an initiate from one of the less sophisticated Stations that didn't have standardized eyesight correction. Even with the glasses, though, the man was still attractive, with aquiline features and short, dark hair. The woman next to him leaned into him the same way Mercury did with Orion, placing them obviously together.

"It was our understanding during the application process that matching would be optional, for those who were single at the time of entry. What about those who are already matched or married or otherwise more focused on the work to be done on Eleusis other than procreation?"

"As I said, one of the top priorities for any colonial enterprise is procreation, but it won't prevent you from being able to focus on the work you will do on and for Eleusis. Everyone has their own responsibilities, and childcare is something that will be assigned to certain people who are best suited to care for children." She heard more people talking in response, but she continued anyway.

"As for those of you currently matched or married to someone else who has been accepted into the program, you do not need to be concerned. Your marriages and matches will not be dissolved. What may happen, however, is that you may be asked to contribute to the genetic diversity of Eleusis with someone who is not your match or your spouse. I don't think I need to remind you all why genetic diversity is important." The common memory of those who lived in orbit was usually confined to the events of their own station, but everyone knew about an isolationist station in the early days of space colonization. Within only a few generations, the inbreeding among them had become so extreme that eventually the station had to be disbanded and destroyed.

Orion's hand slowly came down, since he'd had the same question in mind and she had answered it, even if he clearly wasn't fond of the answer. He thought over what was said, then leaned down to add to the buzz of conversation by speaking low against Mercury's ear. "Personally, I'm not sure how you get more genetically diverse than an Egyptian-Arab and an Irishwoman. We should be alright."

Mercury responded with a kiss. "A contribution of sperm does not mean that anything will happen to our relationship. Those collection procedures are simple enough, if they really want to use your 'genetic diversity' with someone else, or with me." Mercury kissed him harder. "Anyway, if they remove the reproduction barriers and we enjoy each other as thoroughly as we have been, I don't think anyone else will have the time to 'contribute' to me before your sperm snatches up one of my eggs."

"That's gonna be incredibly weird. I've had my preventative in since I was twelve." He shook his head and looked down at himself as if he could see it through his clothes. "Gonna be very, very strange to be without it."

Mercury completely agreed. "Mine has been in since I was fourteen, after I had my first menstruation. It's been a very long time." She looked up into his eyes as soon as he lifted his gaze. "That makes you feel a bit *dangerous*, knowing that you could impregnate me. That usually requires government permission."

Orion grinned as the buzz in the room began to settle down, those who wanted to express an opinion to their neighbors having already done so, and all eyes turned back to the front of the room for whatever additional revelations may be forthcoming. "I'm comfortable with being a little dangerous. But only a little." The glint in his eyes was wicked as he leaned down to kiss her again, but the officers on the stage started talking again, so he turned his attention back to them.

Dr. Santos continued when the crowd quieted down, still pleasant and smiling as ever. "Another item that we needed to discuss as a priority matter- we need a group of volunteers to go with us down to Earth to retrieve the Earth-born Initiates, so that you may all enter your training at the same time. We came to the conclusion that it would be best to have volunteers from this initiate group so that you have a chance to meet each other and interact. We'll need pilots, crews, and medical personnel so they can all be examined and receive their initial treatment before leaving Earth. Also, travel into space is often very difficult for people leaving Earth, so illness will need to be seen to as they make their ascent."

She looked around the room. "Please consider volunteering, but I won't take a count now. Those of you interested can approach me after the meeting is over and I will make the proper arrangements for you."

Orion turned to Mercury again and met her eyes as he shrugged. "I've never been down, have you?"

She shook her head, but she hadn't originally intended to volunteer her services. She had her own patients that still needed her, even though she knew that once the project was in full swing, she would never see her patients again. "Do you want to go down?"

"Might be the last chance you or I ever get to see Earth up close and actually walk under the sky." He shrugged again as he thought it over. "Seems like a shame to go off to another planet without ever actually setting foot on our own."

"You're right." She nodded and gripped his hand. "Walk under the sky. You are much more romantic than I know how to be."

"Wait until we're cleaning out my unit and you run across my stash of early adolescent love poetry. It's horrendous, but what it lacks in quality, it makes up for in quantity." He chuckled, but looked back at the stage, since the officers were continuing to answer questions.

"No," Vance was saying, "you'll receive your initial assignments when the Initiative meets for the first time as a full body on Arm Two, as well as your matching assignments. From there, the full body will proceed with identifying training needs, finalizing the details of colonization planning, and establishing internal organizational structure. One word on this," he turned to look specifically at the military section of the room. "Those of you who are members of our military, you will retain the ranks you currently hold within Consortium Aviation, but in addition, you will be the military arm of the Eleusis colonization initiative. As such, new ranks and new command structures will be determined. You will be expected to take on greater responsibilities within this structure as you are found fit. Be advised."

"Ooooh." Orion said with a chuckle beside her. "Admiral Al-Jabbar. Has kind of a ring to it, don't you think, baby?"

"Is that what you want me to call you now?" She teased, though she knew how hard he had worked to obtain his current rank and she knew he wouldn't stop working hard. "Admiral?"

"Only if I earn it. Even then, I think I still want you screaming out Orion in the bedroom. It'd feel like I'm abusing my authority to fuck a subordinate." He chuckled and kissed the side of her head. "Maybe scream it out a *few* times. Could be fun."

"I'll try to keep that in mind." Mercury laughed softly

and turned her attention back to the stage, but it seemed like everyone was focused on questions instead of listening to a planned speech.

The barrage of questions was instructive, but frustrating when questions were repeated or restated in slightly different ways until finally the Initiative leaders shut them down. Everyone was released with the promise of a meal provided, which turned out to be sumptuous and plentiful enough that the room fell nearly silent as people fell to their food.

Orion had a better view of the crowd on account of his height than nearly anyone else, but he kept one arm around Mercury's shoulders as they picked their way along the line with the food. Having access to so much, and so openly, was incredibly strange to him. The message, however, was clear. Life on Eleusis promised to be plentiful, once things were up and running. There was no reason to limit things if they could be grown on a farm next door.

"I'm looking around for the rest of the medical personnel, but I don't see anybody who looks like your friend you told me about. Just that one short guy with a pediatric designation."

Mercury shook her head. "I got a message from Greg last night. He wasn't accepted." The thought made her sad for her friend, since she knew how much Eleusis had meant to him. It meant a lot to most people she knew. "I told him I was sorry to hear it, but that things were going well with you and I. I think . . ." She had long since realized that she wasn't the best at reading other people's intentions, but Greg hadn't been subtle about his opinions where she was concerned. "I think he was trying to suggest that I could stay here in orbit with him, if things between you and I weren't going well. I'm sure he was disappointed to find out that they are."

Orion returned the kiss and licked his lips afterward, enjoying the tang of the fruit they'd enjoyed. "I can see him feeling bent out of shape about it. It's always rough to have a friendship get destroyed like that. On the other hand, I sympathize. Have to give the guy credit for having the good taste to know an amazing thing when he sees it. I can't be mad at him for pursuing you, only for doing it if you flat out told him not to. What did he say when you told him you were gonna get matched in the first place?"

"The same. He hoped it wouldn't work out. And to be honest, I didn't think it would." She lifted her hand and traced his jaw lightly. "I thought that you and I were too different, based on the data. And I've always believed that I would be better off marrying another doctor."

"So you could go to work and bring babies into the world all day long, then go home and talk dirty to each other about randomized controlled trials and birthing statistics by demographic cohorts?" He chuckled and leaned down to kiss her heatedly, wanting to make sure he brought her back completely to being focused on him in the wake of discussing her doctor-friend. "I'm completely on board and supportive of you doing everything to be the amazing doctor I know you are, and I don't mind feeling lost when you start really getting into an explanation. I'm just glad to be a distraction."

Mercury kissed him again, but she took her time in quiet thought before she met his eyes and spoke again. "I'm beginning to think that even though my life's work is being a doctor, maybe it was narrow-minded of me to think something else or someone else couldn't be equally as important to me."

"Really? What was it that expanded your thinking, do you think? Was it . . ." he leaned in to whisper against her ear through her hair, with his arm around her shoulders, "that first time in the shower when I had your legs shaking so hard you couldn't stand up for about fifteen minutes? Or was it after that?"

Mercury blushed and turned her face toward his so no one could see her cheeks go crimson. "Orion." She tried to sound threatening, but there was nothing behind it. "I'm not marrying you for your sexual prowess, thank you very much. That's not what is equally important to me. You are."

Orion still gave a single low laugh, and reached up to caress the blush on her cheeks before he moved to kiss the blush once with a strangely chaste touch, considering the image that had put the heat in her cheeks. "Just wanted you to know that I'm glad your thinking has expanded a bit, that's all. I'm very much looking forward to you being the center of my universe."

She shook her head. "You're trouble, Orion Al-Jabbar. You shouldn't talk about such things while we're here. That's not fair."

"If you wanted fair, baby, you should've asked the matching program for a judge. Fair I am not. But even if I play dirty, just remember how much you like it when I play." He kissed closer to her neck, but then slid down into his seat as the officers tapped their microphones to get everyone to settle in to resume the presentation.

The rest of the meeting went smoothly, and everyone seemed to feel positive, though Mercury felt uneasy. She was quiet as they walked through hallways to get to their temporary unit after it was over, and only once they were truly alone again did she say anything at all. "What do you think?" She ran her fingers through her hair to distract herself. "They didn't say anything else about the accident, and . . . it makes me worried."

"I was really surprised nobody asked much." He sat near the door to take off his boots, but he was still glancing up at her as he took them off. "I thought somebody would, but I guess everyone collectively knows better. I think that aspect of it worries me even more, even if I also have to admit that I'm part of the problem, since I didn't ask either."

Instead of taking off her own shoes, Mercury actually knelt down next to Orion to help him unlace his boots, since helping him made her feel better than doing nothing at all. "Do you still think we should be a part of this? To go to Earth too?" She wasn't looking at him at first, but then she looked up to look into his eyes. "I felt so happy when I got my acceptance. I don't like feeling uncertain about it."

"Neither do I." He was surprised when she stepped in to do something like helping him with his shoes, but he let her do it, and remained sitting when she was finished to pull her into a brief kiss as she knelt between his knees. "Right now, here's how I see what's going on. We know there's more to what's happened than they're telling us, which means there's almost certainly more to Eleusis and the rest of the Initiative than they're going to clue us into by choice."

When she was finished with his boots, he turned the tables on her and began undoing her jumpsuit for her. "So we've got two choices. Stick with the opportunity we've got, or walk away from it. Walking away means we won't be involved with whatever happens and we'll have to stand back and watch as things unfold, however they're gonna go down. Sticking with it means being a part of it and having the chance to maybe help things as they happen."

"A big part of me wants to say we'll just step away, go back to Seven. I can fly jumper carriers the rest of our lives. I'd be happy with that, it's not a bad life. But I'm not known for choosing the sideline when there's a chance to be in the middle of things. That usually gets me in trouble, but it at least puts me in a place to be in the right kind of trouble when the time comes. Plus, I know how much this opportunity means to you too. You've been working for it just as long as I have. If there's a chance that it can be what we both wanted it to be, I think that's worth taking. But I want to hear what you think about it."

He could see the wheels turning behind her eyes but she didn't say anything until she shrugged out of her jumpsuit and sat down on his lap. "I still want to do it. I still believe that even if we aren't being told everything, there has to be a good reason for it. Even if I wish they would tell us." Mercury kissed him gently again before she pressed her forehead to his. "I want to go to Eleusis, and I want to go with you."

"I'm less optimistic about why we aren't being told everything." He sighed, but nodded against her forehead as he put his arms around her waist. "Alright, then. We'll fly through the black with these crazy bastards and do what we can to be a part of a new world. And we'll handle it together." The kiss they shared was deep and warm, sealing the decision they had made, but it was sedated, almost solemn, the kind of kiss that closed one door and opened another, filled with possibilities rather than certainties.

13

Anna was again in Logan's house, off in a quiet wing attempting to get ready. All she had actually accomplished, though, was staring at herself in the full-length mirror and thinking about all the things that were about to change.

They had told their families about their acceptance to Eleusis. No one was happy about the idea that they might be leaving. Anna and Logan told their families that they hadn't yet made a decision, even though she felt as though they were still leaning toward getting on the ship and going, no matter the risks. The promise of a new world with a brighter future for everyone she loved was too much to ignore.

Anna glanced over at the simple, white, summer dress hanging up nearby, knowing that even though she'd asked for privacy, her younger sisters, Larissa, and Liam's girlfriends would all descend upon her soon to help her get ready. The thought of all the attention and the makeup made her want to lock every door around her, but she wouldn't deny them the chance to enjoy themselves. Weddings were a cause for celebration, and everyone deserved to enjoy them, not just the bride and groom.

Instead of grabbing a brush and getting started with her

hair, she grabbed a robe and tugged it on quickly before sneaking out of the room. She tiptoed through the house to get to Logan's room, since she desperately wanted to see him. All day she'd been forced to deal with wedding prep, and all day he'd been pulled in a different direction. She just wanted to see him before she had to share him with the rest of the world all over again.

When she found his designated room, knocked lightly on the door, listening closely. "Logan?"

She felt rather than heard his heavy footsteps as he got to the door, but it eventually opened a crack. "Are you as interested in some bad luck as I am right now?" She could tell from Logan's voice that he was smiling, and there was no other sound in his room. It seemed he dismissed everyone he'd been dealing with the same as she had, for the time being.

"I think it's only bad luck if you see me in my dress, and considering I'm only wearing a robe, I don't think it counts." She whispered through the crack in the door. "Let me in, please? I really want to see you."

"I'll take it." He opened the door wider to let her in, keeping his voice down even though they were the only people in the wing. Everyone else was outside getting bossed around by Larissa, Liam, Ben, and Susan.

Logan was still in his boxers, but he'd obviously showered recently, since his hair was still damp and the scent of his soap still lingered. "You doing alright?"

Anna looked him up and down openly, groaning at the sight of him in his boxers. "Feeling a little better now, thanks." She gave him a weak smile before she stepped up to him and reached out to run her hand over his bare chest. "We should have just eloped in St. Louis. This is all too much for me."

"I think you're right. I've never been a big fan of being the center of attention." He pulled her in to hold her against his chest, sighing at how much better a place the world was when he had her close. "I think all three of Liam's girlfriends are trying to out-wedding-decorate each other so as to get the guy to buy a clue. And if I see Larissa and Cory shoot each other one more meaningful glance, I'm going to gouge my eyes out. I realize I don't have much room to talk, being the one who arranged it, but she's still my little sister."

That made Anna smile. "They're so cute together, though! I feel like quite the matchmaker. I can't believe I didn't see it sooner. I know he's still a bit heartbroken over the other girl from across the world, but I don't think that'll last much longer. Your sister is so pretty and kind, and she cooks better than anyone I know." She hugged Logan tightly and sighed against his skin. "Are you nervous?"

"About being your husband?" He shook his head against her hair. "Nah, you don't scare me. Am I nervous about standing in front of a hundred people and then jumping on a shuttle next weekend to leave this planet possibly forever? Yeah, some of the nervous from those things is definitely hanging around."

Her smile faded and she held him even tighter. "I think they're still hoping we'll say we're not going. But I still think we should." She stepped back to look up at him, then grabbed his face and pulled him in for a rough kiss. "I'm nervous about standing up in front of everyone too. But I can't wait to see a ring on your finger that means you belong to me."

"You don't need the ring on my finger to know that." His hands nearly closed completely around her waist as he pressed her against him. "I woke up this morning missing you. Then I walked out and saw everybody working on setting up chairs in the hall and getting decorations started and I couldn't help feeling like this is both our wedding and our way of saying goodbye."

"It is. But it's not goodbye forever. I refuse to believe I won't ever see them again." She paused and tried not to wince at the pain of the thought that she couldn't refuse the idea for everyone. "Except maybe my father."

Logan nodded against her forehead. "I'm glad he'll be

here, though. He told me the other night when we were down there that it was all he wanted. Seeing you and Ben married and happy. He knew if he could get the two of you that far, you'd take care of the rest of your brothers and sisters between you. Which is what you've been doing."

"Except now I'm going to leave, and it will be all up to Ben. He'll have to take care of the rest of them *and* my dad. That's not fair." She knew Ben could handle it, he'd been the 'oldest' child all along. He was organized and bossy, and though Anna was plenty bossy, she wasn't like Ben. "I want him to worry less and now he'll have to worry more. But if we get to Eleusis, if we can get everyone there . . . he'll get to live a long life with Susan and his children."

"That's the plan." Logan agreed, since it wasn't fair to Ben just like it wasn't fair to Liam or Larissa. No matter the benefits he wanted to tell himself he was trying to arrange for his family, it still felt like abandonment. It felt like they had both decided separately that Eleusis was for them, in spite of the uncertainties and the shady dealings. But Logan couldn't bring himself to second-guess his own choice. There was too much to gain. "I'm going to talk to Liam's girlfriends during the reception, see what they think on the subject. If I can talk the three of them into it, then I'm sure Liam will go along. He can arrange Cory and Larissa's marriage once we're upstairs."

"They won't need much arranging. Any of them, I think." Anna pulled Logan into another kiss. "I wouldn't be able to go at all without you. I applied to get away from all the history . . . but I can't. I won't. Certainly not now. I need you too much." She let her hands slide down his sides to the waist of his boxers. "Definitely *need* you."

He didn't stop her, but his own hands didn't move from the waist of her robe where it was tied in place. "If I'm not mistaken, this is the longest we've gone without each other in almost two weeks." He moved to press her back against the door of his bedroom with another kiss. "I definitely woke up missing you last night. More than once."

Anna kissed him several more times, since she didn't want to stop kissing him or touching him ever again. She was thoroughly addicted and she knew it was going to become a problem. The best kind of problem. "More than once, huh?" She asked with a smirk. "Did you do anything about it?"

"Not the same. You're worth waiting for." His kisses got more heated, but clearly he was trying very hard to control himself. "And *need* goes both ways. I hope you got some decent sleep last night. You won't be getting much later."

She pouted as he held himself back. "I don't want to wait until later, I'm already mostly undressed as it is." Anna teased him by pressing into him and opening her robe just enough to give him a peek. "Do we really need to wait? We're not exactly virgins, here."

"Mmm." He growled as she opened up her robe, and leaned down to kiss along the inner curve of her breasts. She could feel through his flimsy boxers that he was already more than ready for her, not that it ever took long in her presence for her to have that kind of effect on him. "No, we are not." He forgot how to even think straight as soon as he was touching her, but the intercom in his room clicked on as his lips began to go lower.

"Hey Logan, Anna's not in her room." Liam's voice sounded more amused than worried, even over an intercom. "You think maybe she broke and ran? Can't say I'd blame her."

Anna let out a strangled growl when Logan's lips left her skin, and soon as he moved to touch the intercom, she smacked his hand and planted his hand back on her breast. She then touched the button on the intercom herself. "Logan's busy right now. Harass him later, Liam."

Liam broke out laughing at that over the intercom. "Yup, I probably should've guessed that. Make it quick, there's decorating to do and you two are getting married in three hours."

"Quick? Well, that ruins the fun." Anna said to Liam

before she pulled her finger away from the intercom and pulled Logan into another heated kiss. "Three hours, huh?" She kissed him again as her hand slid downward, since she wasn't about to leave him high and dry after she'd tempted him. "That still seems so far away, but so close at the same time."

"No time is enough for me, when it comes to you." He pulled her robe open some more as she took hold of him, and one of his rough hands moved down to part her legs under the kisses that reached a fevered intensity between them. It was clear he wasn't even going to move back into the bedroom or away from the door. He wanted her too much to be patient about anything.

Some time later, they were a puddle on the floor next to the door, tangled up together and panting heavily. They heard another warning crackle of noise through the intercom, but they had both ignored it in favor of each other. They were the bride and groom, after all. She was on top of him, mostly, running her fingers through his still-damp and sweaty hair. "I take it back, I definitely like it fast and rough too. God . . ."

"You know," he said breathlessly, his hands moving over her sides slowly as he tried to recover from having his brains fucked out by his future wife, "I'm starting to get the impression that you just like sex. All kinds, any kinds, all times, any time. There's a word for that. It's called fucking amazing."

Anna laughed between breaths, which sent shocks through her still-sensitive body, but she enjoyed that too. "I thought you were going to call me a nymphomaniac. But I'll take 'fucking amazing'. That doesn't have a negative connotation to it." She kissed his lips roughly as her hands continued to wander. "It's not true, though. I'd gone months without sex before you and I got together the first time. I don't think a real nympho can do that."

"I don't think so either. You're not psychotic, just an enthusiast. I'm very comfortable with enthusiasm." He rolled onto his back to relax on the floor, which had never felt more inviting in his life. "If that does end up developing later, though, you should know I'll be glad to be your addiction as well as your husband."

"I don't know if you could survive it." She teased as she poked his side afterward, perfectly content to stay right where she was for the rest of her life. "I don't know if I could survive it either, but it would be sure fun to try." As she leaned into another kiss, they heard another voice over the intercom, this time feminine.

"Logan! Two hours until the ceremony! Kick Anna out and get yourself ready!" Larissa could be surprisingly bossy when she wanted to be. "I mean it!"

Logan rolled his eyes. "You'd better get going. She sounds like she means business. You want to use my shower real quick first?"

Anna went back to pouting as she kissed Logan for the hundredth time. "Really? You're more afraid of your sister than you are of your fiancee? This isn't right." She slowly extracted herself from being on top of Logan and groaned as soon as they were untangled. "I like this better than parading down an aisle in a dress."

"You and me both." He got up slowly after her, but couldn't convince himself to get up off the floor. He sat against the wall with his arms around his knees, watching her get up and walk across the room. "This is the last time, though." He said with a hopeful shrug up at her. "One and only time you and me are gonna do this. Might as well get it right." He grinned up at her and winked.

She couldn't help but smile after he winked at her, then she rolled her eyes dramatically before she walked the rest of the way to the bathroom. "Our honeymoon is no-clothes-allowed! Just sayin'!" It was the last thing she said before she rushed the rest of the way into the bathroom so she didn't turn back around to attack him again. Larissa was right. Anna needed to get ready and she needed to march down the aisle for everyone to see, if for no other reason than to make her father happy and to say 'I do' to Logan in front of the whole wide world.

Even when they switched places in the shower to let Anna get back to her own room, Logan had a hard time keeping his hands off her, but he managed to let her go with nothing more than a few heated kisses. When he was alone in his room again, all he could do was wander around to look over everything. The side of the closet he would shortly be cleaning out to make room for Anna's things. The side of the bed that had been hers for weeks already and would be hers until they left for space. The half of his life that was currently his, but wouldn't be for much longer.

He should have felt stranger about that. He should have felt more anxiety about sharing his life with someone else when the last person he had shared his life with had ended her own life rather than continue to share it with him. But it was Anna. He couldn't convince himself to regret wanting his best friend to share his life. He couldn't bring himself to look back or second-guess his decision. He wanted her there with him. It was that simple. Earth, Space, Eleusis, there was nowhere he wouldn't want to be right beside her in everything he did.

When he finally emerged from his room, he was wearing a white button-down shirt, a silk tie, and an actual pair of dress slacks over his boots. A vest to match the pants completed the outfit, not quite a tux, not quite a suit, but certainly the nicest thing he had ever worn by choice in his life. He encountered Larissa halfway between his room and the main gathering hall of the house, apparently on her way to retrieve him, and he just smiled. "I'm coming, I'm coming. How is everything in there?"

His sister smiled brightly and wiped at her eyes to make sure there were no more tears. Thank goodness for waterproof makeup. "She's beautiful. I think you're going to be blown away." Larissa looked her brother over and stepped up to make sure that he was straightened up and ready to go. "How are you feeling?"

"I'm good." He reassured her with a smile, rolling down his sleeves to button the cuffs in place. "I'm sorry, did you want me to be nervous so you could give me a pep talk? I can still listen to one of those, I don't mind."

"I would be nervous." She admitted as she turned her attention to her own dress. All of the bridesmaids were in royal blue dresses, but each woman had picked her own design, and Larissa hoped that Cory would enjoy seeing her in hers. It was relatively conservative, but the back of her dress was open and she couldn't help but imagine what it would feel like to have his hands touch her bare skin when they danced. Even in a short time of really getting to know each other, Larissa liked Cory a lot already. "I get nervous just imagining it."

Logan put an arm around her shoulders as they headed back toward the hall. It was a massive house, and they had a long way to go. "You've spent a pretty good chunk of time with him now, what with getting the supply ordering done, helping finish off the harvest down there at the Princes' and all that. You haven't said much about what you think of him."

Larissa chewed on her bottom lip as she thought about what she wanted to say to her brother. "He's a gentleman, which I don't always expect anymore." She and Cory *had* spent a lot of time together, privately, and while they were definitely learning to explore each other, it was slow. "He's pensive and smart. He even wrote me a couple of poems, and they're just beautiful. I . . ."

She held her breath for a moment and then sighed sharply. "I feel like he's out of my league, Logan." Larissa wasn't the most beautiful girl by the standards she had set for herself. She was smart, one of the top in her class, but she was quiet and reserved and it was hard for her to share how she really felt about things. She loved to cook, but Cory didn't need a cook. He needed a good wife.

"Out of your league? What are you talking about?" He hooked his arm more forcefully around her shoulders to hold her in close, with an incredulous look on his face. "If the Premier of North and South America had a son, and that son happened to be your age, he wouldn't be out of your league. No one is out of your league."

Larissa rolled her eyes. "You're my brother. You don't know . . . you think of me differently than someone else who would be interested in me thinks of me. I know I'm pretty, but I'm plain. And I don't have a reputation like Anna, so I don't really know what I have to offer Cory. He doesn't want a nerdy cook, does he?"

Logan rolled his eyes. "I know I approached putting you with Cory a little bit like just a practicality measure. You're roughly the same age, the Princes have always been good friends to us and we to them, our parents were close, it makes sense on the surface of it to honor those relationships. But I didn't arrange for you and Cory because it was a business meeting. If you spend time with each other and you like each other, then that's what matters. More than all the rest ever will."

"From what Anna says, he's crazy about you. Especially if he's writing you poetry and shit already. If you like him too, and feel like you could love him someday, that's the best I think any of us can ask for in this world. Don't worry about what kind of . . . fucking *resumé* you think he's looking for. Whatever it is he wants, either you already are or you're more than capable of being. Same goes for him when it comes to what you want."

"It wasn't love poetry." Larissa said as they continued through the house. "I like him a lot." She said quickly, even though she didn't look at her brother when she said it. "But he still has feelings for someone else. I went online and found her picture, she looks like a model from Orbit. No wonder he was so hung up on her." She had wondered at first how she and Cory hadn't spent any time getting to know each other before, but as soon as she found out about the girl that he had originally wanted to marry, she quickly figured out why. Cory had been wrapped up with someone else and secluded because of it.

That didn't make Logan feel good about Cory's current attentions, but he hoped the guy wasn't stupid enough to try and actually continue to pursue some girl who had obviously left him behind in the dust. "Have you talked to him about it? About her?"

"Only once, just to know who she was and how he felt about her. He said that she had someone else and he wasn't interested in talking about her or about it." She shrugged and went back to chewing on her bottom lip. "I know that we don't live in an area where there are a lot of options, but I don't want him to be with me just because he wants *someone*. Is that too selfish?"

"No, that's not selfish at all. That's the way it should be." He rubbed his hand over her shoulder as they turned the last corner near the hall, and sighed as he looked down at her. "Well, figure out which way it is, then. If this girl is leaving for Eleusis, I'm sure Anna's set to give her a strong kick in the ladyballs as soon as she sees her, just for stringing along her brother like that."

"Today isn't about me anyway. It's about you. You and Anna don't need to worry about the rest of us, we'll be alright." Even if Cory didn't want her, Logan would never know, since he was probably leaving. She wasn't going to make him think about her problems by talking things to death. There was no sense in making him worry about it now. "Come on, it's time for you to get married."

Anna, on the other side of Logan's expansive house, was left alone in her white dress while Susan brought her family back to see her before the whole world did. Cory was the first to show up, and she nearly leapt out of her chair in order to get to him and hug him. Her hair was braided in a delicate fishtail that fell off to the side and over one shoulder, and her sisters had demanded that she put tiny white flowers in it, so there they were.

Her dress was short and low cut, with a lacy, sheer band in the middle around her waist, held up by thin white straps.

It was classy and yet she knew Logan would be happy to see her in it when she walked out. It showed plenty of her cleavage and tanned legs. She hadn't wanted very much makeup, but her eyes were still lined black and there was a light pink sheen to her lips. "Cory!" She was jittery, but she was always happy to see Cory.

Clearly their father had gotten all of her brothers into some of their better clothes for the occasion, and Cory was in a crisply-ironed shirt and tie with a pin in it that she recognized as a piece of their family's inheritance. Ben was the only one who had gone so far as to put on a vest, and she recognized the cufflinks he had in his sleeves as part of the same collection. Their family wasn't anywhere near as wealthy as the Bickfords, and their farm was a great deal smaller, but it had been theirs for generations, and that much family came with precious things every once in a while.

Cory hugged her tightly before standing back to give her an approving smile. "You look great, Sis. You feel like you're about to puke yet, or does that come like, just a few minutes before go-time?"

"Trying not to puke, thank you very much. That would make for a terrible kiss after the exchange of vows." She winced at the idea, but then she started pacing around the room, each step a click from her heels. "I should have just eloped. This is too much." She put her hands on her hips as she took a few deep breaths. "I hate crowds. Especially crowds of people that will contain at least fifteen men I've slept with, if not more."

"I counted nine. But that's just what I know of." Ben said from closer to the door, prompting scandalized giggles from Emily, confused looks from Ginny, and a smack on the arm from Susan, all of which only managed to produce a teasing grin from Ben and a shrug. "Sorry. Probably not helpful."

"No, not helpful at all, thanks." Anna turned and looked as the rest of her family came into the room, then went up and hugged Ben even though he wasn't helping ease her nervousness. "Did you feel this nervous?"

"Our wedding was a lot smaller and less fancy than this, so no, not really." He hugged her tightly, then stepped back to let Susan step in as well, plucking at his wife's dress once with an explanatory grin on his face. "There were maybe forty people in the room and Susan was pretty far into her maternity wardrobe, so I figured I had things pretty well locked down by that point."

Susan just smiled at Ben and gave him a kiss on the cheek after he plucked at her dress. She did her share of scolding him, but she loved him too much not to look at him adoringly. "I'll have to get those back out soon. Good thing you never seemed to mind."

Anna raised an eyebrow and looked between Susan and Ben. "Really? You guys . . . really?" Susan had been so concerned about not getting pregnant again quickly after their first, and Anna was immediately over the moon for them if they had managed to do it again. It meant that maybe Susan would let up on the second-wife thing, and Anna knew Ben would be happy about that.

"Looks that way." He leaned back against a covered chair with Susan leaning against him, his arms loosely around her waist. "We haven't been up to Doc Weber for the workup and official word yet, but sticks tend not to lie when they've been peed on. We just found out a few days ago, we're gonna talk to Doc later tonight."

"Wow. Congratulations!" Anna smiled and watched her brother and Susan together, since it oddly seemed to comfort her, even though she was supposed to be focusing on her own wedding. It was one more thing that gave her hope for the future, and one less thing for her to worry about with Ben and Susan. Anna looked over at Cory after that, though, with a smirk. "Are you next? What's the deal with you and Larissa?"

Cory rolled his eyes. "Don't rush me. I barely started spending time with her." He was smiling, though, and he shrugged with his hands in his pockets. "Honestly, she's out of my league. I don't know how you deal with the whole Bickford thing. I know we're the ones with the Prince last name, but they're the ones who seem like royalty. Except Liam, but Liam's just . . . yeah. He's Liam. But Larissa and Logan both, you could put them in a palace on the other side of the world and they wouldn't be worried about fucking up the flatware. It's not a bad thing, it's just . . . she's just different. But pretty great, even with the differences."

"Well, I'm glad it's working out so far. Don't let her slip through your fingers, you'll regret it." She gave him a look of warning before she finally turned her attention to her father, who entered the room last. Liam's girlfriends were helping her father, and Rachel smiled at her when she walked into the room with him.

"Your father is very particular about making sure everything is just right. He also wanted to go talk to Logan before the ceremony started, but we made sure he didn't miss you." Rachel stepped back, since Anna's father wasn't an absolute invalid, letting him approach.

"Dad." Anna said with a smile as she went up to him and hugged him tightly. "You better not have been trying to scare Logan off. I swear I'll be a good wife."

"I know you will. Never doubted it. But every husband should have a little fear in him when he marries a man's daughter. Not too much, but a little." Joseph smiled and pulled her into a hug, speaking softly so as not to aggravate his cough and thereby worry everyone in attendance.

Every time she'd been around him in the preceding months, she could feel he was slowly getting weaker, changing from the man she'd known to work on the farm from sunrise until sunset into someone whose endurance simply couldn't measure up to the not-so-distant past. But in spite of the fatigue in his eyes and the growing weakness in his disposition, he was still her father. Still watching out for everyone in the family so long as he was able. "You look beautiful, Anna. I'm happy for you."

"I'm so nervous." She admitted softly as she held onto her father even after the hug. "I love him, I want to be with him, but I'm scared of such a big change. I've never been anyone's wife before."

Joseph pulled back enough to look his daughter in the eye, and laid a hand carefully along her neck, making sure not to disturb her hair or her makeup. "Is there anything you wouldn't do for the guy?"

Anna didn't hesitate as she shook her head, since even though he'd married someone else before her, she'd stuck by as his best friend whenever he needed her. It nearly drove her to Eleusis without him, but there still wasn't anything she would not do for Logan. He meant the world to her. "No, I'd do anything for him."

"Then I wouldn't worry about being somebody's wife. Just be his. There's nothing he wouldn't do for you either. That's as far as anyone needs to be worried about when it comes to the way two people choose to go through the world. Any world." He had promised that he would try to be supportive of her going off to join the Eleusis Initiative, but she could see that there was no little strain in him when he made reference to it. It wasn't going to be easy for any of her family members to watch her go, especially when there was no guarantee of her ever coming back.

"Now, time to finish getting ready." He reached into the pocket of the suit coat he was wearing and pulled out a long, small jewelry box that still had some dust clinging to the velvet exterior. She had known the box since she was a little girl, especially since most of the time it had sat closed on her mother's dresser. The woman hadn't had occasion to wear the contents very often as the family grew, and as far as Anna knew, the box had been closed in the same place on the dresser ever since her mother had died.

Anna's mouth suddenly felt dry as she looked at the box, and her eyes stung as she thought about her mother. It had been years since her mother died, but some days were still harder than others. Her wedding day was one of the harder days. When she had her first baby, she knew it would reopen the same wound that grief left behind. Some things the world took from everyone, and parents living long enough to see all their children married was more of a rarity with every passing year.

"Daddy . . ." There weren't many pieces left of her mother, and she couldn't bear to take another one away from her father. Rarely did she feel reduced to a little girl again, a daddy's girl, but she did in that moment, and she wanted to protect him as much as he wanted to protect her.

"Go on." He took her hand and placed the box in it for her. "Your mother was a very particular and very precise woman. She knew exactly what she was doing no matter what she was about, and that includes exactly how to spoil our children. This has always been yours. I was just under very specific and insistent instructions to find the right time to give it to you."

He didn't talk about their mother often, but when he did, he always smiled. From what Anna remembered, he and her mother had made a very happy life for themselves on that farm for the short life they had managed to live together. "So if you don't take it, you're gonna make her mad, and I speak from experience when I say that's a bad idea."

Anna was suddenly grateful for waterproof makeup, even though she normally didn't care for makeup at all. She wiped at a few tears as she opened the small box, which creaked softly in protest at being closed for so long. She couldn't breathe as she looked at the contents and ran a finger over it.

"I miss her so much." She said just above a whisper. Anna remembered her mother telling her to take care of the family and her father for her, and she didn't think about those last few days of her mother's life unless something forced her to. Her chest ached, but she still managed a smile.

"So do I." Joseph agreed, then lifted the necklace out of the box for her and unclasped it to place it around her neck. Their family, the Prince family, didn't have much, but her mother had actually brought the necklace with her from her own home, far to the northeast in the Quebec district, and had worn it on her own wedding day. The Brasseaux family hadn't been particularly wealthy themselves, but several generations back, they had been, and the necklace was one of the last living pieces to prove it. The entire length was woven platinum in a delicate chain, picked out with flecks of diamond set at regular intervals. The centerpiece of the chain that settled into place against Anna's chest was a brilliant flourish of diamonds in swirling arms like an inverted fleur-de-lis, with a final weighted teardrop diamond hanging from the lowest point. It was a necklace fit for a princess, beautiful and intricate without crossing the line into extravagance or gaudiness.

Anna cried some more as she looked down at the necklace, but she wiped her tears eventually when her younger sisters came up for a closer look. "Mom was so beautiful. Prettier than I am, too." Anna always believed that, even though most people who knew her mother said that she looked almost like her mother's twin, except that she had her father's eyes.

Her brothers were left shaking their heads, but it was Danny who actually said it out loud, since he was young enough either not to know better or not care as much as he should. "You look just like her. Especially with your hair braided up like that." He smiled, but then looked over at their father. Danny gave a quick sigh of relief when their father agreed.

"It suits you, Princess." Joseph mostly-whispered, still trying to favor his voice to keep from coughing. He closed the jewelry box and handed it over to Emily, who was constantly looking for some way to help with things, then turned back to Rachel, who was still by the door to make sure they found their way back to the hall for the ceremony. "I think that about does it. Ginny, go run and grab the flowers, you remember where you left them?"

Ginny had to pause to think, but then she bolted out of

the room to get the flowers, since it had been her job to watch over them. Anna smiled as her youngest sister ran out, then she moved to walk beside her father. She looped her arm through his and gave him a kiss on the cheek, glad he could still walk her down the aisle, even though she knew it would mean that he would need to be in a chair the rest of the day to recover. He had insisted, though, and she wasn't going to deny him something he wanted if he really pushed it.

"You're going to make sure I don't fall, right? I wouldn't be surprised if there were at least a dozen women who put traps down the aisle as revenge because I seduced their husbands before they did."

"Nobody's putting down traps. And if anything, you're going to be the one catching me if I trip. Though those heels do look pretty dangerous." He looked down at her as they started down the hall, the rest of her family going ahead of them at Rachel's direction.

"Clearly I had nothing to do with the selection of my footwear. The dress I had a little bit of say in." She smiled and walked quietly with her family until they got to a hallway just outside the hall. Her family scattered to take their seats, Ginny handed her the bouquet, and then it was just her and her father waiting for their cue. As soon as she got a nod from another of Liam's girlfriends, Margo, they started walking.

When Logan came into sight, Anna couldn't see anyone else, and she clung to her father's arm so something could keep her moving. He looked incredible, and in that moment, one of her fondest dreams was reality in front of her eyes.

Logan had spent the last half hour standing up at the front of the hall with Liam, looking over everyone who came for the wedding, saying goodbye internally to each one of them in turn. The Webers were there, including Sierra's boyfriend Gary, which made him smile. Kevin Reeves had come as well, even after what his family had endured. Everyone Logan had ever gone to school with seemed to all be there, along with those of their teachers who were close enough, Quentyn and Veronica and all the others he employed from time to time on odd jobs around the estate, very nearly everyone he had known his entire life within a three-hundred-mile radius.

He had been happy that so many people cared to attend until he looked over the crowd and realized there were only about four hundred people, and he could not think of a single one more he would have invited. It was one more reminder to him of how empty the world was, and had oddly been one more piece of encouragement that the decision to go to Eleusis was the right one to make, for the sake of the entire world.

When Anna appeared, all such thoughts evacuated his brain to make room for the vision of her walking toward him. He smiled at the playfulness of her dress, since it suited her perfectly, but it was her eyes that he focused on the whole way up the aisle. He still couldn't believe what they were doing, where they were standing, what was happening. It felt too much like a dream to be real.

There was no way Anna was really going to marry him. That was just a fantasy. There was no way his life was really going to become the thing he had always wanted it to be. That wasn't the way the world worked. People didn't get what they wanted, people got what they could eke out for themselves and decided to be happy with that. Dreams didn't come true.

Yet there she was, walking toward him, proving every shred of common sense completely wrong.

By the time her feet stopped moving, Anna was almost close enough to reach out and touch Logan. She felt like she needed to, to prove she wasn't dreaming. She kissed her father's cheek when he let go of her arm, and Ben came up to make sure that their father made it back to his seat. As soon as she actually felt Logan's firm grip on her hands, she felt like crying all over again. "This is actually real." She whispered incredulously as she stared into his eyes.

Logan just smiled. "Stop reading my mind. It's a mess in there." He held onto her hand as if he was making sure to keep her from running away, and didn't even look away from her when the officiator began speaking. Logan hardly understood a word, and he actually thought to himself that it was a good thing somebody in the audience was getting everything on film. He would need to go back and watch it again later to remember anything at all about what was said. All that mattered was Anna there beside him and the grip of her hand in his.

Anna barely registered when the officiator asked her to say her vows, and while she hadn't prepared anything, she knew that she wanted to say *something*. She had to say something so that Logan would always know how much the moment meant to her.

"I've wanted to be your wife for as long as I can remember." She eventually said, even though she was aware that the rest of the crowd knew their history, and knew she wasn't his first wife. That didn't matter to her. All that mattered was that she was his. "Ben can attest to this, but I used to practice writing your last name in my notebooks, and everyone here knows I'm not usually that sentimental." That got the crowd laughing, but she still didn't look away. "This really is a dream come true for me, Logan. We've spent so much of our lives being partners in everything, especially trouble, but this is something new for us. Something amazing. I love you so much, Logan Bickford, and I will always love you."

His grip on her hand tightened, and a few giggles and awws drifted out of the audience. "This life, this world isn't really known for granting wishes. I can't say anybody ever expects to get most of what they want. But right now, right here, you're the only wish I care about coming true. I'm not going to waste that, and I'm never gonna look back from that. I'm yours, Anna. You might have been scribbling my name in notebooks, but everything I am has got your name on it. I love you, and that's for always."

The officiator gave them the traditional vows afterward, and after a couple of 'I do's and a declaration that felt too long, the words finally came out of his mouth. Man and wife. Mr. and Mrs. Logan Bickford.

Anna felt like jumping up in joy, but she didn't have time before Logan's strong arms hauled her to him and he was kissing the breath out of her lungs. Anna wrapped her arms around his neck and probably ruined all of her flowers in the process, but she couldn't bring herself to care. All she cared about was the feeling of his lips on hers and the realization that she was now Anna Bickford. She was Logan's wife.

There was applause and cheering from the crowd as Logan picked Anna up off her feet in the kiss, but he eventually put her down, a few protesting petals from her bouquet falling on the ground between them as she regained her balance. "Hey there, Wife." He said in a low voice that only she could hear, completely ignoring everyone else in the world.

Anna giggled against his lips and stole another kiss before she replied. "Hey there, Husband." She pressed her forehead to his. As the crowd continued to applaud, she moved her lips closer to his ear. "I so want to get out of here with you, Mr. Bickford."

"You and me both." He groaned against her ear before he leaned back, still holding onto her by her waist. "Dancing first, and mingling. Then we let the rest of these people party as long as they like while we get on with our own."

Anna nodded and walked with Logan down the aisle before everyone else, making their way across the expansive front lawn to where a bonfire was set to be lit along with tables upon tables of food and alcohol. As they walked across the grass, mostly alone with people trailing behind them, she looked down at the beautiful ring that he had planted on her finger. She'd had no ring until the ceremony, but she was mesmerized by what was on her finger. "This is so beautiful, Logan. I . . . it steals my breath away. Not quite like you do, but close."

That made him smile, since he hadn't been sure whether she would like the ring or not. It was more fragile-looking and elegant than Anna tended to style herself most of the time, but he had wanted to get her something that would be uniquely hers. It was a single band, since they'd only been engaged for two weeks, but the platinum was worked in almost an organic pattern, a single marquis cut diamond as the centerpiece with many more smaller flecks dotting the rest of the ring.

"I'm glad you like it. When it came in, Liam and Larissa spent most of an hour telling me how much of an idiot I was for getting you something sharp enough to cut me when you inevitably punch me for saying something stupid."

"I'll learn to punch with my other hand." She replied with a smirk and pulled him into another kiss as they got closer to the reception area. If there hadn't been a path laid out through the grass, she was certain she would have kicked off her heels already. Or requested that he carry her, which she knew he could do. Easily. "You should also know," She looked back at the crowd. "I'm not wearing any underwear, so don't get too crazy with the dancing. I have a lot of exes back there."

That had him grinning all over again, and he squeezed her hand before he twirled her once, which made her dress fan out, though not so much that she would be flashing anyone. "I'll keep that in mind. I would say I could go for the garter later, but . . ." he looked down to check her out, "I'm pretty sure that's not part of the deal."

Just the idea of him going down underneath her dress to pull a garter off with his teeth gave her chills. "I should have picked a longer dress."

"No you shouldn't. I wouldn't change a thing." They finally got to what was obviously the head table, and he stopped with her to let some of the other guests make their way into the gathering area and get comfortable. He ran a hand up over her shoulder to brush his thumb against her necklace with a quiet smile. "Your mom's?"

Anna nodded as she looked down at the gorgeous necklace again, and it felt, for a moment, as if her mother really was there with her. Anna hadn't been raised a religious person, but she did hope that her mom was out there somewhere in some kind of afterlife, waiting for all of them to be with her again. Anna's eyes prickled with tears, but none fell this time. "It's beautiful, isn't it? Just like she was."

"It is, and so are you." He didn't want to make her cry, so he didn't dwell on it, instead he leaned down to kiss her as people began coming up to congratulate them. They had to be social, if only for a little while, but Logan was going to make sure it took as little of their night as possible.

14

Logan and Anna didn't have to move much during the reception to talk to their guests. Anna took random moments to sit on Logan's lap to torture him, they smiled, were pleasant, danced, ate like royalty, and shoved cake in each other's faces. It was one of the most perfect days of Anna's life.

Once it was dark they were able to sit by themselves a while, and Anna moved back to sitting on Logan's lap. The crowd had dwindled but it was still a loud group of people having a great time, and Anna sighed her contentment from Logan's lap. "I still can't believe this day. It's been incredible."

"Yeah it has. The first of many." He clicked his glass against hers, even though neither of them had alcohol in them. Many of those in attendance had gotten in deep with the open bar, and Logan didn't mind. The fire was going hot and everybody seemed right at home, exactly the way he wanted it.

For the most part, things had been fairly sedated for the two of them, talking with everyone they almost never got to see and weren't likely to see again, though neither of them had mentioned their Eleusis acceptance to anyone outside of family. Logan looked off at the other side of the bonfire where his brother was currently dancing with Rachel, and sighed, putting his arms back around Anna's waist.

"I need to go see if I can take care of business with Liam's girls. Are you okay here for a bit?" Most of her exes had left as soon as it was polite to do so, and those who remained certainly didn't scare Logan, but most of her family had also left half an hour before when their father couldn't stay around any longer. Cory and Ben were the only ones left.

Anna nodded and slid off of his lap slowly. "I'll go steal more dances with Ben and Cory. Don't take too long, alright? I've waited long enough for you, Husband."

"We'll ditch this place right after, I promise." He gave her a lingering kiss as he stood up, then ran his eyes over the crowd until he found the person he was looking for.

Liam was still focused on his dance with Rachel at the moment, so when Logan got up to his first target, she was sitting by herself on her phone instead of paying attention to anyone or anything else.

"Hey, Margo." He said from the other side of the table, then glanced at the house. "I'm gonna run back into the house and grab a few more bottles of wine, the table looks like it's running out. Care to come along? I'd like to talk to you about something."

Margo raised her eyebrow as she looked up at the groom, then shrugged and stood up, quietly following Logan before she glanced back at Liam still dancing with Rachel. Margo watched Liam a moment before she turned her attention back to Logan as they walked.

"You know, for being nearly identical, you and your brother are quite different." Margo was Liam's longest-running girlfriend of the three, and it showed in the way that she looked at him with Rachel. She clearly loved the man. All three of his girlfriends were quite different in appearance, and she'd been teased that she was part of Liam's 'collection', but she didn't care that often. She was the most average-looking of his girlfriends, with dark brown hair and an average body shape and weight, but she never left him with any complaints. The only thing that was truly remarkable about her appearance was her dark blue eyes, and even in the night Logan could see her emotions in them. She cared about Liam, and she wanted him to be happy, even though she wished that it was a one-woman show. Margo knew she had no hold on Liam, though, since she hadn't managed to get pregnant.

"Thank god for that." He teased as they headed toward the house, passing the outermost of the people who were still hanging around and enjoying the cool night. "I think we would've driven each other more than a little crazy by now if we had both been born with my tendency to be overly serious most of the time. There's only so much of that a person can take. Any fun our parents had in their genes, they shared it between Liam and Larissa."

"He's more serious than you give him credit for. Maybe not around you, but it's there." Margo didn't look back again, though anytime she wasn't with Liam, she wanted to be with him. She was more serious than Liam was, certainly, but she had a lot of fun with him. He was definitely playful and wild, but he was also smart, caring, and considerate. Most of the time. "He told me that you're going to Eleusis, and that probably makes you worried, leaving him and Larissa behind. But he can handle it."

"I know he can. Especially with Larissa around to help keep him in line." He grinned at that thought, since Larissa wasn't what anyone would consider bossy, but she certainly had her moments where Liam was concerned. She might have been shy with the rest of the world, but not with the two of them. "There are things that would make me feel better about leaving him, though. I think Larissa and Cory are doing pretty well together, especially given how much they've been stuck to each other all night tonight, so I don't really worry about her. But I do worry about Liam."

"Don't worry about him. I'll make sure he's alright, make

sure he's fed when he needs to be. That's the main thing to worry about. If there isn't food around for him, he'll go straight to beer. I'll take care of him." Margo gave Logan a reassuring smile. "I've been with him for two years now."

"I know, that's why I'm coming to you first." He said with a smile that was quickly fading, since it wasn't really a conversation he had been looking forward to. They were approaching the house, but they were the only people in sight, and that had been by his own design. In case she started screaming at him.

Logan had never completely been able to get a fix on Margo when it came to knowing what to expect from her, so he didn't want to take any chances. "I like you, Margo, and I know how much you love Liam. I've never once had a problem with you or the way you take care of my brother. But I need to be the serious brother here for a minute." He opened the door to the house and started heading toward their wine cellar, following a trail that lots of people setting up for the party had obviously been following that day from the trail through the dust in the house.

"I want to leave Liam in the best possible kind of situation when Anna and I go up to join the Initiative. And the best situation not just for him, but for this estate. You already know we've got about seven hundred cousins and second-cousins and ninety-seventh cousins twice removed who would love nothing more than to try and press some kind of inheritance claim on this place, especially if I'm going to be on another planet."

Margo looked down at her feet as soon as he said that, since her mind went immediately to the fact that she hadn't given Liam a child and she'd been with him for a couple of years. "Are you going to ask me to leave him alone to give him a chance to make a baby with someone else?"

"I'm serious, not a complete asshole." He said with a slightly reproving glare at her, but he knew that wasn't entirely outside the realm of possibility for their world. He'd heard of people being set aside for a lot less than infertility.

"I would never tell somebody who loves Liam as much as I know you do not to be with him. I know you'll take care of him when I won't be around to, and that's a comfort." They finally got down into the wine cellar itself, and Logan sighed as he leaned back against the wall, since there was no subtle way to get to the point.

"He's been with you the longest, but he's been with all three of you back and forth for long enough that it's looking like it'll be a while before he has any kids. Otherwise I imagine he'd have had them by now. What I'm suggesting doesn't have to do so much with having children as it does handling this place and taking care of Liam. I'm going to talk to all three of you tonight, and what I want to know is if you'll consider marrying him, without knowing whether or when you'll have any kids, without any other guarantees except that you know what kind of man he is and you know he loves you. All three of you."

Margo was thrown for a loop when he said that he wanted to ask if she would consider marrying Liam, since there wasn't a day that went by that she didn't hope he would ask her. But the loop turned a twist in her stomach when he said 'all three'. "You want him to marry all three of us? What if he doesn't want to marry all three of us? How do you know he even wants to get married? He hasn't even touched on the subject more than five times in my entire relationship with him, and I only know because I've been hoping for over a year now that he would ask me."

"I'm going to talk to him last. If all three of you are on board, I'll be able to convince him into it." He didn't smile when he said it, since he didn't expect it to be a smooth conversation.

"He doesn't want to get married, or at least he didn't the last time I talked to him about it. At the very outside, if he and the three of you stay here on Earth, you'll be like Joseph tonight for Anna. Time isn't on anyone's side with the virus. Liam doesn't want to get married because he feels like he has to choose between the three of you, and you know Liam well enough to know that making up his mind on anything has never been his greatest strength. Man can't even decide what brand of beer he prefers, for crying out loud. So when it comes to this, this is me taking eldest privilege into my own hands."

Margo looked around and grabbed a bottle of wine that was one of her favorites, then looked down at it as she shook her head, since she was going to need a drink after this conversation. "*If* he wants to marry me, then I'll do it." She said softly and she still didn't look up at Logan. "I already hate sharing him with anyone else, but I hate the idea of losing him more. But if he's just dating them because he's trying to push me out, then I don't want to be involved."

"He's not." Logan said quietly, sifting through the bottles with his head low and obvious guilt on his face. "He picked up Rachel right after Melanie died." Logan said without looking over at her. "He never told me why, but it didn't have anything to do with you. You two had been together a year and everyone knew things were going really well. Melanie liked you a lot, by the way, in case you ever wondered. It was hard to tell with her, sometimes."

He moved past that quickly, since there was a lot behind that statement that he didn't really want to think about on his wedding day. "Anyway, he never told me why, but whenever I mentioned it to him, he would always start talking about somebody who'd had a kid recently somewhere else, one of his friends or the damn Carters and their fucking twelve kids I think now or something."

"I think he got with Rachel because he started getting nervous about being able to get somebody pregnant. It didn't look like I was going to end up providing anybody to take over the estate, so he thought he had to start taking more chances. Then a few months ago, after being with Rachel for most of a year, Brianne comes along." He finally looked back over at Margo briefly and shook his head. "He's not trying to push you out. He loves you. All three of you, I'm pretty sure, but he's been with you the longest, like you said. It's just more complicated than that."

Margo finally lifted her blue eyes and looked at Logan briefly before she looked down at the wine again. "I don't know why it hasn't happened. I worked extra jobs to pay Doc Weber to send off for testing so that she could give me more information. Nobody knows, I didn't tell Liam I did it. But Doc said I'm fine, that I should be able to have babies. She tried to tell me that there are a lot of things that could prevent it from happening, but I don't have to be a genius to know that the less time he spends with me, the less likely it is to happen." Margo rubbed the dust off the label on the bottle meticulously as she avoided looking up at Logan again. "You don't need to hear my troubles. Anyway. I love Liam. I want to be his wife. If this is what he wants, then it's what I want too."

Logan nodded, since he hadn't expected her, or any of them, to be happy about the arrangement on the face of it, though he hoped they would be happy eventually. All he could do was try to make sure they all had the opportunity to get to that point. "Thank you." He eventually said, picking up a few bottles and tucking them into one arm to carry them back out to the party. "In case I don't get the chance to say it between now and another planet, thank you for loving my brother." He tried to manage a quiet smile, then headed for the steps leading back up into the rest of the house and back out toward the party.

Margo stayed behind, even though he had asked her to help bring out more wine. She went looking for something to pull out the cork, and once the wine was open, she didn't even wait for it to breathe before she took several long swigs. She should have felt happy at the idea of marrying Liam, and she wanted to. It wasn't as though she was being shackled to someone she hated, she loved Liam. She adored him. But it wasn't the situation she had hoped to find herself in, and it hurt to know that her only chance of being Liam's wife was to be one of three.

Tears slid down her face as she sat down on the cold

ground in her dress and drank more wine. She felt defeated and angry, but only at herself. Somehow she had failed at doing what she should be able to do, and this was the price she had to pay for it.

Logan wasn't angry that Margo had decided to stay behind, and he could only imagine, from what he knew of the woman, how she must have been feeling. He wasn't too happy himself about what he felt he had to do, but that didn't stop him from feeling as though he had to do it. He wished he could have had the conversation with Margo that he knew she had wanted to have in the first place, but that wasn't the world they lived in. Not yet, anyway.

When he got back, the dance that Liam had been sharing with Rachel was obviously done, and as he approached, Liam was actually standing and talking with both Rachel and Brianne, laughing at something Rachel had said between sips of his drink. Before Logan could get very close, Liam headed back off toward the dance floor, taking Brianne with him into the pulsing music. The song was nothing whatsoever like the one he'd been dancing with Rachel to earlier, but Logan couldn't find it in himself to be surprised by that.

"Hey Rachel, have we got a corkscrew around here somewhere?" He asked as he approached the drinks table, where there were plenty of mostly-empty bottles of wine, but not a corkscrew in sight that he could see.

The tiny, but busty, darker-skinned woman smiled up at Logan and nodded, though she looked around furiously to try and find one. "You could have asked one of us to go get more wine, silly. You're the groom. What are you doing looking around for corkscrews?" She laughed and spotted one several tables away.

He waited behind the refreshment table for her to get back, and took the moment to look around for Anna, who was sitting to one side of the fire talking with Larissa and Cory. That made him grin all by itself, since she was working every bit as hard as anyone else to make sure the two of them stayed together. It was every bit as important as what he was doing with Liam's girlfriends, and he hoped it would be more pleasant, for Anna's sake.

"Hey, thanks. I think I've lost about a hundred of these in my life. Probably means I drink too much." He worked the corkscrew into one of the bottles and popped it easily, then set it aside on ice to breathe for the next thirsty person to come along. "And I'm allowed to play host, it is my house, after all. I promise very soon to resume doing nothing whatsoever I'd consider work."

Rachel's mouth turned up into a smirk and she shook her head as she stood there next to Logan. There was no pain or longing in her dark eyes as there had been in Margo's blue ones. She pushed back some of her hair that was sticking on the back of her neck after dancing with Liam. "Good. That's how it should be on your wedding night. Heck, every night that you can get with your spouse should be more play than work."

"I think if that's the case for anyone, that's the sign of a truly happy life." Logan had to grin and raise a bottle in her direction at that, as if he was about to toast with the whole thing all at once. "I'd like to talk to you about something along those lines, actually, if you don't mind."

"Along what lines, sex? I don't think I have advice for you on that subject, and honestly, you wouldn't want it from me. I think that might reveal more about your brother than you'd care to know." Rachel laughed and poured herself a drink before she looked back out at Liam. He and Brianne were certainly getting down and dirty on the dance floor, which wasn't Rachel's style, at least not in public. She could definitely get into things behind closed doors with Liam, but she wasn't interested in sharing that knowledge with the rest of the world. "Anyway, I think Anna knows what she's doing. Or so I've heard."

"No, not along the lines of sex. I'm pretty well covered in that department." He grinned over at Anna, who still hadn't seen him come back, but it was fun to watch her with her family and his for once. "No, I actually wanted to talk to you about getting married. To Liam."

Rachel nearly choked on her drink, and she sputtered as she wiped at what little she had spit out, glad that she'd chosen a dark-colored dress. "Excuse me? Shouldn't *he* be asking that question?" She definitely wasn't looking at Liam anymore. Rachel held her hand out in Liam's direction, but Liam was clearly too distracted to even notice it. "Does that look like a man who is interested in marriage right now?" She laughed afterward and attempted to take another drink.

Logan had to laugh as he shook his head. "No, no it doesn't. Which is why it's a good thing he's got a ten-minutes-older brother who takes a slightly longer view of things." He chuckled and poured out the remainder of a bottle that had been nearly empty for himself, since he knew he was going to need it.

Once he'd had a good sip of it, he turned back to Rachel with a sigh. Even though he was still smiling, he clearly wasn't joking. "I like you, Rachel. I was shocked half to death when Liam started up with you, since you've got more common sense than all his former girlfriends combined. He doesn't have a history of going for the smart ones, and you're definitely one of the smart ones. I'm being serious when I talk about you marrying him. I plan to talk to all three of you tonight, to see where you stand and what your thoughts are on the subject. Before Anna and I leave for the Eleusis Initiative, what I'm proposing is that you marry Liam. All three of you."

She guzzled the rest of the glass in her hand quickly before she said anything in response. "He's going to kill you once he finds out you're doing this." Rachel shook her head and laughed incredulously. "And then he'll probably thank you. But you should be prepared for the killing part first." Rachel sighed as she looked down into the now-empty glass and then back up at Logan.

"He's never going to make a decision on his own, I know that already. I've been with him for a year, and I know him well enough to know that if he's dating three women at once, he's never going to pick one." She was smiling as she shook her head, though. "And while he's pretty smart, he's going to need more people than just Larissa to help him run this place once you're gone. He mentioned that you were accepted into the Initiative, but he didn't say that you were going for sure."

"I don't think Anna and I are a hundred percent packing our bags yet, but we're certainly leaning heavily toward it. There's too much to be gained for us to risk not being a part of it." He shook his head and smiled over at Rachel. "And I can accept him wanting to kill me for doing this. But like you said, hopefully he'll come around quickly. I'd prefer not to get the shit kicked out of me on my wedding night if I can avoid it. At least not by my brother." He shrugged and tipped back his wine glass again. "Is that a yes, then?"

"I don't know that you're going to get anyone else to agree. I can't imagine that Margo would agree to something like this." Clearly she was hedging on whether or not she wanted to absolutely say yes. "I just . . . I guess I figured one of us would end up getting pregnant and that would be the end of that. I didn't consider something like this."

She refilled her glass and looked in Logan's eyes again. "Alright. Yes. I love Liam, and while this is not what I imagined would happen, being in a plural marriage wouldn't be the worst thing in the world. It's better than waiting a couple of years and being pushed onto someone else by my parents. Someone I didn't choose. And having other women around will help with managing the estate. And managing Liam." She laughed again, then reached up to tuck her hair out of her face and behind her ear. "You're still crazy for asking, though."

"Oh I'm aware of that. But I've been crazy for a while now. I think I'm starting to get good at it." He smiled down at her and took her in a brief hug, kissing her cheek afterward. "Goes without saying, but please go without saying for the time being. I've got Bri to talk to, then I'll go see about getting murdered by my twin brother for trying to ensure his happiness and well-being.”

“You should be happy he’s been drinking, then. His aim will be off.” Rachel went to a nearby table and filled up one of the untouched glasses with water from a pitcher at the center of the table, still shaking her head. “I’m gonna go give him this water and get him to eat something so he doesn’t get totally wasted. Good luck, Crazy.” She gave Logan another look of amusement and walked away, only to approach Liam and Bri who were off to the side after their scandalous dance. Logan watched as Rachel handed Liam the water and then convinced him to go with her to get food. Seemed as though every one of his girlfriends knew how to sweet-talk him in one way or another.

Logan moved in smoothly once Rachel had sidelined Liam, and nodded to Brianne to follow him back to the drinks table. He had to chuckle at the fact that the woman was still breathing heavily.

“So, that’s how they do it in New York, huh?” Margo was the only one of Liam’s current girlfriends who was actually from their district with family living close by. Rachel had come into town to work on one of the wind farms Logan operated farther west, and Brianne . . . had just kind of been passing through on her way to wherever she wanted to go. Liam and Logan met her and her family three years before at an agrarian conference in St. Louis. Her brothers back at home took over her family business after the death of her parents, and Brianne just happened to be the free spirit of the family.

“Oh, babe, if only I could truly explain how things go in New York.” Brianne laughed and ran her fingers through her strawberry-blonde hair as she grabbed a drink for herself. She didn’t even bother with the water, she went straight for the wine. Brianne was a year older than both Logan and Liam, but she certainly didn’t act like it. She had lived in the lap of luxury for most of her life, and she was wilder and far more playful than most of the women who were local.

"What are you still doing around here? God, if it were my wedding night, I would have told everyone they could stay until the booze was gone, then they needed to get the fuck out. Then I would have just up and disappeared."

"Funny you should mention that. I actually wanted to talk to you about those kinds of plans." Logan laughed, since that was his primary reaction to everything that came out of Brianne's mouth. She was loud, she was every bit as crass as Liam, and she didn't quit. He knew better than to think it was because she was just vapid. She was smart and she knew what she was doing, and that made her even more dangerous, in Logan's mind. "You ever thought seriously about marrying Liam? I know you two haven't been together that long, but you seem pretty sold on the guy."

"Thought about it? Sure. Seriously considered it? Not really. Your brother is a shitload of fun, and I love being with him, but there is no way in hell he's going to choose me over the other two. No matter how wild he tells me I am. And between you and me, if he did pick me, I'm pretty sure Margo would poison me or strangle me in my sleep."

Logan rolled his eyes. "Don't get crazy. Margo is a lot of things, but violent isn't one of them." He looked her up and down quizzically. "I haven't hung out with you enough while you're drinking to really be able to tell, are you sober enough to have a serious conversation about this? I want to make sure. Because that's what I'd like to have."

"I don't have many serious conversations, as a rule. But on a scale of one to seeing ten of you, I'm fairly sober." She took another gulp of wine and raised a rust-colored eyebrow at him. "You're really fucking serious? You really want to discuss your brother marrying me? He's a big boy. I've spent a lot of time with his penis, so I can confirm that. He can handle his own marriage arrangement."

"Can he, though?" Logan asked with a grin. "Look me in the eye and try to tell me with a straight face that you don't think he's playing sperm-donor Russian Roulette right now and hoping that fertility is gonna make his choice for him?"

"Hey, I said it first. He totally is, but that's only because we're letting him do it." She said with a shrug, since she was guilty of enabling Liam's indecisiveness. "I like being a part of his game, thank you very much. I've met very few men who fuck like he does. You can't be serious about this, though. What makes you think he wants three wives? Can you imagine the horror that man would have to go through when PMS hits?" She shook her head. "Even I'm afraid for him."

"I'm a little afraid for him, but not enough to stop me from arranging this for him." Logan continued, obviously unfazed. "He's made no secret about how much he likes you, or you about how much you like him. That being said, I'm not looking to arrange a marriage for my brother to somebody's who's only interested in fucking him. Clearly the guy's got no trouble finding that on his own. What I want to know is if you would want to be his wife, and be one of three. Help him run the estate, take care of the kids if they ever come around, keep him from completely destroying himself too many times a week, and actually step up to be with the guy even when things aren't fun. I know you haven't been with him that long, but you don't seem to me like the kind of woman who takes very long to know when she wants something and when she doesn't."

Brianne was quiet after that, since he was asking her to be serious and she really was quite terrible at it. "When someone matters to me, I stick by them. If Liam fucking wants three wives and he wants me to marry him, then I would be crazy to say no. I want an amazing ring, though. I deserve that much if I have to deal with Margo."

Logan felt like the axis of the world had shifted slightly once she agreed, but all he did was nod. "Amazing ring. I'll make sure to pass along that particular demand." He smiled and shook his head at her general attitude, then lifted his wine glass and clinked it with Brianne's. "Time to go talk to

Liam and let him know I've condemned him to holy matrimony. This should be fun."

"The other two already agreed? Are you serious?" She actually burst out laughing and drank her wine quickly afterward. "I hope you run fast. He's going to want your head on a spike."

"Don't worry, I have a plan, and I'm not as drunk as he is." Logan said with a grin, then finished his wine and walked away, leaving his glass on the table. He went to find Anna first, and pulled her up out of her seat without any explanation, only to take her place and pull her back into his lap almost commandingly, sighing as he sat down and she got comfortable. "What did I miss?"

Anna was quick to curl up into him with her bare ass on his lap, though no one else knew about that part except Logan. She kissed him several times before she responded. "Cory and Ben were telling me all sorts of stories about what they plan to do to expand the farm, I bugged Cory and Larissa for a while and told my brother to step up and propose already, and I danced with them each several times." She kissed him harder and nipped at his bottom lip. "I missed you."

"I missed you too. And unfortunately, I'm not quite finished yet." He explained reluctantly, though his hands moved over her waist and mostly-bare legs to enjoy the feeling of having her silky smooth curves against him. He kissed her with a low moan that only she could hear, then moved to whisper in her ear to make sure only she got what he was saying. "All three of them are in. If I'm being honest, a part of me thought that would never happen. But apparently it is."

Clearly Anna was surprised by that, but she kissed him again anyway before she responded. "Don't let him beat you up, okay? You promised me a naked honeymoon, and I don't want to have to tend to any broken bones."

"Every single one of you has said that to me in the last half hour. I'm beginning to take it as a vote of no confidence in my ability to kick my own brother's ass. Are you people not aware that I've been beating the shit out of this guy since we were in the womb? Come on. Give me some credit. You're my wife, you're supposed to be on my side."

"I'm on your side. And under normal circumstances I would say that you would have no problem. But you just made a triple-arrangement of marriage for your brother *behind his back*. It's not going to be pretty."

"I'll give you the highlights once it's over and done with. Just promise me that if I die, you'll make sure to mourn me properly. I expect to be able to look in on copious amounts of masturbation to my memory when I'm a ghost."

Anna smacked his shoulder and slid off of his lap. "No dying. Now go take care of business and get back here quickly. My vagina can only take so much neglect."

"Neglect." He scoffed as he stood up, one hand resting on her waist, his fingers moving over the smooth fabric of her dress to pointedly remind her that there was nothing underneath it to stop him. "Not a word you can use on me. I'll be back soon, even if it's not soon enough."

"You better be." Anna pulled him into a heated kiss and then looked him in the eye with a smirk. "I'm going to say my goodbyes. I'll wait for you in our room, alright?"

"Sounds good. Tell everybody I had to step away for a minute and that if they need anything, see Larissa. She'll handle closing up." He kissed her again, closing her dress in one fist with a moan. "Keep the dress on until I get there."

"Aren't you bossy." She smiled as he held onto her dress to keep her from getting away, then she whispered to him again. "I was hoping you could rip it off of me."

"Great minds." He chuckled as he finally let go. "Dirty minds, maybe, but still great ones." He left a caress along her side as he stepped away, still looking back at her for a while before he had to turn his attention to finding his brother.

Logan approached Liam cautiously across the trampled ground of the dance floor, and smiled when his brother greeted him with a hug. He'd clearly been drinking, but unlike Brianne, Logan knew his brother well enough to know when he was too drunk to take something seriously as opposed to buzzed and having a good time. "Hey, walk with me a minute. I want to talk to you about something."

Liam put down his beer and gave Margo a kiss goodbye to go along with a slap on the ass as he walked away, still grinning both at Logan and back over his shoulder at Margo. Apparently Margo had collected herself and returned, and Liam was none the wiser. "Yeah, man, what's going on?"

"Just walk with me someplace." Logan put an arm on his brother's shoulder as they walked, still smiling and trying desperately to think through what the hell he was going to say. "You feeling alright?"

"Yeah, I'm good. Some of that old shit we had down in the cellar is stronger than I gave it credit for, but I'm alright. I switched back to beer a while ago, so I'm set." He wasn't walking crooked or slurring his words either, which gave Logan quite a bit of hope for the conversation to come.

"The old shit is the good shit. We'll have to see about picking up more from our cousin connection out on the West Coast next time we talk to them." Logan agreed with a grin, then turned a corner on the trail to come around a rise, heading for the watchtower that served as the overlook for their estate.

"What the hell are we doing out here?" Liam asked in confusion, finally realizing that Logan had a destination in mind for their walk.

"I told you, there's something I want to talk to you about. It's right up here." Logan reassured his brother with a tap on the shoulder, then pulled away to head for the foot of the tower where the lift was waiting to take them to the top. "After you."

"You're worried about bugging the controls during your own wedding party? After the harvest is over? We're not even gonna use this shit for another year, man, what are you doing?" Liam was still walking as he spoke, though, and he stepped into the lift to wait for his brother to join him.

Logan calmly pulled the metal grating of the lift door closed between them as Liam looked around in confusion, then took a pitchfork that had been thrown down nearby and jammed it into the locking mechanism on one side, wedging it in place so that it couldn't be opened until the pitchfork was removed.

"Hey, what the fuck?!?" Liam began to shout, instinctively rushing at the bars to try and get out.

"Calm down, it's only for a minute." Logan reassured once he stood back up, looking Liam in the eye and remaining fairly close to the grate so he could talk to his brother. "I just needed to make sure you weren't gonna try and beat the shit out of me and this was the easiest way to do that."

"What am I gonna beat the shit out of you for?!?" Liam was starting to get even more frantic, but he calmed down slightly with the reassurance that he'd be let out. "Can't you just say 'hey man, don't punch me when I say this, alright?' Don't you trust me to hold my shit together for ten seconds?"

"Majority of the time, yeah, I absolutely trust you. This time it's iffy. So calm down and let's talk for a minute, alright? I want you to keep an open mind." Logan did back away once it was obvious that Liam wasn't going to go completely ballistic and try to tear his way out. Logan wasn't actually sure the metal grating would hold him for any significant length of time, but it only had to do the job until he calmed down. He didn't think that would be too much to ask.

"What am I keeping an open mind about?" Liam backed away from the bars, pacing behind them from one end of the lift to the other out of sudden nerves. "Is this something about Eleusis?"

"In a way, yeah." Logan heaved a sigh. "Larissa looks like she's pretty happy with Cory, but she's not the one who's gonna be head of the family while I'm gone. That would be you. You're the one who's gonna be in charge of the estate, running the business . . ."

"What, and you don't think I can handle that?" Liam started raising his voice again, approaching the bars like he was going to try and break through them.

"No, you can handle it fine. I was just saying I *don't* worry about that." Logan snapped forcefully enough that Liam actually stepped back and resumed his pacing. "I don't worry about you handling shit around here because you're one of maybe three people in the world who I can always, always trust to have my back, no matter what, no matter where. I know you're gonna handle it and I know you're gonna keep it together. But it's my job, as your brother, to make sure I help you do that any way I can."

"How the fuck are you gonna help me from orbit, exactly?" Liam's question was more confused than accusation, and he actually laughed afterward, shaking his head. "It's great that families of pioneers get preferential treatment when it comes to settling a planet on the other side of the galaxy, don't get me wrong, but that's gonna be years from now, and there's no guarantee me and Larissa are even gonna want to go by then. A lot can change in a few years. So I realize you're doing your best for humanity and for us, and I'm all for that. I'm proud of you for going, if I'm being honest. But you going isn't gonna do shit to help me here. You don't need to do that anymore. I can handle it as well as you can."

"Well, let's not get crazy. I do a pretty damn good job." Logan teased with a smile that Liam returned weakly, since he was still looking out for whatever was going to make him angry about the discussion. "I know you can do it. I know you'll be great. But one thing you do suck at doing is looking out for yourself in the process. That's usually what I'm here for, and it's what I'm here for now." Logan looked down at the pitchfork to make sure it was still in place, then looked back at Liam warily. "You ready to want to punch me?"

"Man, I was born ready. Just fucking spit it out already,

will ya?" Liam was starting to get angry just at the fact that he was being prepped to get angry. "What the fuck is the big fucking secret?"

"I asked all three of your girlfriends if they would marry you. All three of them, at the same time. Plural marriage straight out the gate. Right here, before Anna and I leave for Eleusis." Logan only gave Liam a moment to let the full implications of that set in, then put the final nail in the coffin. "They all said yes. Wedding is going to be the weekend before I lift off." Logan sighed, glad to finally have that off his chest. "Try not to break the bars. I won't be around to fix them, so it'd be on you."

Liam's eyes had first gone wide as his mouth dropped open, but his jaw clenched slowly and his eyes narrowed at the announcement of the wedding date. "You shady mother . . ." he attacked the bars and rattled them as he screamed unintelligibly, but he didn't quite break through them as he vented his anger at being backed into a corner, ". . . *fucker!*"

It was a long while before he stopped screaming profanities at Logan, but eventually he stood back from the bars and growled about it, pulling at his hair and swearing under his breath until he finally quieted down, eventually leaning against the side of the lift.

"You good now?" Logan finally asked from the doorway.

"Yeah, I'm good. You can take the pitchfork off. I'm not gonna punch a guy on his wedding day." Liam sounded defeated as he said so, and didn't even watch Logan remove the pitchfork or open the gate. He rolled his head to one side to look at Logan once the door was clear again. "How the fuck did you get all three of them to say yes? I mean, Brianne I get, and Rachel maybe, but Margo?"

"She'd rather share you than lose you." Logan explained with a shrug, since it had seemed like a logical choice to him at the time. "Eventually your roulette game is gonna wear out and you're gonna get one of them knocked up. For your sake, I hope you hit all three of them at the same time. But they're all into you enough to want to be your wife, even if they're not the only one. And you're rich enough not to have to worry about taking care of all of them, no matter how many miniature versions of yourself you manage to create."

Logan actually chuckled at that possibility, looking off toward their house. "You could fill that place, if I know you. And I hope you do, in the few years between now and the next time I might be able to get back here to see it."

Liam stepped out of the lift, still glaring at Logan with his hands in his pockets, possibly to keep himself from throwing punches. "I get it. You know how much I hate it when you handle me like this, or Larissa, but I get it. It's your prerogative to arrange shit like this, and eventually, I'm sure I'll probably be grateful, since it makes sense. I can never make up my fucking mind about my own shit most days. You'd just better realize, eventually you are gonna get the shit kicked out of you by me for pulling this stunt. Not tonight, I'll let you off because you've got a honeymoon to get to and I'd never do that to a guy, but eventually, you've got an ass-kicking tab that's gonna need to be paid."

"I can live with that." Logan stepped back, starting on the trail back toward the party with Liam eventually following. "I just barely talked to all of them tonight, so they know I'm talking to you about it. Go on and make your plans and announce to everybody whenever you want to. You can even tell everybody it was your idea if you want, I don't need credit for that, and it would probably make the girls feel better."

"I'll deal with it." Liam still shook his head and sighed as he walked, completely floored by the future he was walking into. "Fuck, man. Can't I just tie *you* up and leave *you* here to deal with this shit and fly off to Eleusis in your place? We're basically the same person, how would they even know?"

"Anna would know. And then she'd castrate you for trying to slip into my place." Logan said with a grin.

"True, that's true. Yeah, that would be worse." Liam agreed with a weak chuckle, still shaking his head. "Get out of here, man. Your party is just getting started. I'm gonna go back and see about straightening up this mess you've officially made of my fucking life."

"You're welcome." Logan said with an arm around his brother's shoulders. "I love you, Liam. You already know that's why I'm doing this."

"Yeah, I know. Doesn't make it any less of a mindfuck." Liam returned the hug briefly, then shoved Logan aside toward the house. "I love you too. Now fucking go. I'll see you in a few days."

Logan watched his brother return to the party, but he was too close to the house to actually see his reunion with his wives-to-be. He wanted to see what happened, but the knowledge that Anna was waiting for him was more of a draw than the drama in his brother's life that he had created. It would be up to Liam to handle what he'd been handed. If Logan was going to start bowing out of things, there was no time like the present.

He closed every door on the way into his wing, for the sake of soundproofing, and he was grinning as he stepped through the last door into his bedroom.

No, not his bedroom anymore. Officially *their* bedroom. His and Anna's.

The door was around the corner from the bed, and he didn't see her at first, since the room was dimly lit. "What, did you go to sleep already?" He asked as he stepped inside.

Anna stepped out of the bathroom at the sound of his voice, and he could see she was taking the flowers out of her hair and shaking it loose from the fancy braid woven into it. She was still in her dress, as promised, but she was barefoot. "No, I didn't go to sleep. How could I go to sleep? I was too worried about your survival and what I was going to do if you died."

"It's alright. I locked him up in the lift on the watchtower until he was done throwing a fit about it." He grinned, but he realized that part of the reason he was grinning so much was because he was relieved to have actually pulled it off. He stopped by the door to pull off his boots and toss them aside, happy about the fact that he wasn't going to be wearing clothes for a good long while. And neither would Anna. "He says he owes me an ass-kicking eventually, but if I know him, he'll be too busy dealing with his new wives to deliver it. I should be in the clear."

"I can't believe you got them to agree. You're even more charming than I give you credit for." She sauntered up to Logan as he finished taking off his boots, and she helped him unbutton his shirt and vest. "I can only imagine their responses. You must have sounded insane."

"I'm sure I did. But crazy can be a good thing once in a while." He let her do as she liked when it came to undressing him, glad to be free of the shirt and tie. "The important thing is that he's in on it and he'll deal with it. It's his problem now, and his helping of crazy to deal with."

"I'm glad you're not like your brother in your tastes." When she straightened herself up, one of the thin straps of her dress fell down off her shoulder. "I wouldn't be able to share you. It would tear me apart."

"Nothing's going to tear anybody anywhere. I'm not interested in sharing or being shared." He promised as she pushed his shirt off over his shoulders, slowly edging her back toward the bed. "I'm glad you're not like any of his girls. Liam and I share a lot of things, but we've never once had the same taste in women." He leaned down to kiss her as she got his belt free and tossed to the floor. "I want you to be you. Nobody else."

"I've never changed myself to fit what anyone wants me to be, and I don't intend to. I'm just me, and just-me wants you and loves you." Anna unbuttoned his pants as she continued to kiss him, and the tension between them built by the second. "We do make sense, but this is so much more than that."

His kisses agreed, pressing her back until her thighs brushed the edge of the bed. The cut of her dress dipped slightly between her breasts to show off her cleavage, and his hands moved up over the smooth fabric to take the cut of it in both hands. A single rip was enough to tear the dress straight down the center, all the way through the gossamer fabric covering her midriff with flimsy wisps of studded gauzy nothingness.

His hands moved quickly down over her exposed breasts and ribs to grab the fabric a second time at her waist to rip away what was left. The rip of the skirt was less straightforward, but in the end, she was left in nothing but the tatters of her dress with her naked husband pressed against the bare entirety of her, flimsy fabric barely hanging on by the single remaining strap hooked over her shoulder. "I think all your clothes should be that easy to destroy from now on. Just dress in tissue paper and make things easy for both of us."

Anna's chest rose and fell quickly as her whole body tingled with need after he had literally ripped the dress off of her. She felt so ridiculously turned on by it that she couldn't think clearly or speak, especially with his body pressed against hers. Anna would never have worn the dress again anyway, and it was worth the purchase to have him rip it off of her.

"Fuck, I want you so bad right now. That was so hot." Her skin was blazing as she dipped her shoulder down once to let the dress fall away, and she pressed her breasts against his skin. The lingering tension alone was enough to light a torch with the heat between them.

"You've got me, Mrs. Bickford." His hands moved up over her thighs to hold her around her back while the rest of him pressed her backward onto the bed. He kissed her the entire way down, allowing no space between them while the sheets hit her blazing skin like silky ice. "Anytime you want me, anywhere you like, you've got me, now and forever."

He kissed her until it felt like she was the oxygen the fire inside him needed in order to keep burning, and his arms wrapped around her shoulders as the full weight of him pressed into her. She was really his, and he was really hers.

He wondered if that would ever feel like anything but a ridiculous fantasy. Even if it never did, he would still live in it happily.

15

Mercury and Orion had only been on Seven for two days, and she could already tell Orion was not enjoying his stay nearly as much as he'd hoped. She got up before he did so she could make him breakfast, though it was strictly with healthy ingredients. She was allowed to order some meat to fry up because his allowance was larger than hers, but the rest was more of what she was used to than what he'd had on Three. Mercury whipped up some healthy omelets, filled with mostly vegetables and just a tiny bit of cheese, then put the meat on his plate and filled two small glasses with synthetic orange juice. She carried the plates on a tray back to her bedroom and set it down on a side table so she could crawl into bed and wake him up.

The return to the structured life on Seven never once bothered her.

It bothered Orion.

"Hey, sleepy." She slid into bed next to him and kissed along his neck. "Today is the big day. I made breakfast for you."

"Mmmm." He groaned low in his chest, moving a little to put an arm around her shoulders to keep her close without opening his eyes. "I thought I sensed something delicious on its way back to me." He turned into her and left his own kisses along her neck and down over the slope of her breasts before he just rested his head against her sleepily. He sniffed once, and finally got a whiff of the breakfast. "Oh, and there's food too. Even better." His words slurred against each other and against her chest, the stubble on his cheeks scratching her a little as he spoke.

Mercury giggled as his stubble scratched her skin. "Yes, I brought food. I figured we would both need it." She ran her hands over his head and scratched at the back of his neck. "You should eat it while it is still warm. I didn't know if my request for meat would be granted, but we must have burned off enough calories to get it. For you, I mean."

He opened his eyes and tilted his head back enough to look around with teasing suspicion on his face. "Are there cameras watching us eat so they'll know if we share?"

"No, but they do a bio screen on us when we sleep. Not with cameras, but with room scanners. It's how they monitor our health so we remain within ideal parameters." She glanced over at his plate and then back at him. "It's not as though anyone would punish me, certainly."

Mercury had never heard of anyone being punished for pushing back against the regulations of the station, but she had heard of people being put on very restrictive orders for ignoring regulation for an extended amount of time. "I know it sounds very controlling and cold, but it really is for our benefit. When I first started my training as a doctor, I was staying up too late every night to study and my bio screens showed poor sleep patterns with insufficient time in REM. I was informed that I had been screened consistently for poor sleep for two weeks before they prescribed me a sleeping aid. It really did help me, and I learned not to push myself so hard."

"Well, you definitely got into REM last night. You were talking in your sleep." Orion kissed along her chest one more time lazily and then pushed himself up in the bed so that he could sit up against her headboard with the sheets still draped over him. It was the closest he was willing to get when it came to actually getting up at the moment, since he was still mostly asleep. But the unit would continue getting brighter whether they got up or not, until it was impossible to sleep.

For their health, of course.

"I was talking in my sleep?" Mercury was surprised to hear that, especially because she'd never read anything in any of her personal health reports that mentioned sleep-talking. She passed his plate and utensils. "I didn't realize that I do that."

"You don't seem to normally, unless you're very, very tired and you pass out mid-conversation." He smiled back at her and bent a knee to hold the plate in place, making sure she had her own as well. "What you said didn't make much sense. We were talking through the list of your cousins when you fell asleep, so at first I thought you had just kept going with that, but then you started talking about some kind of project that was tracking immune system anomalies in relation to the Crisis Virus. That's pretty much all I caught of that. Then you said something about bears and strawberries. That's where you lost me."

"Oh." She replied with an embarrassed chuckle, then turned her attention to her plate. "Some information I requested about some research I started before I left came through yesterday. We have research librarians that dig things up for us when we don't have time to do the digging ourselves, and so I was thinking about that yesterday. Since we're going down to Earth, I was looking at data collected over the first several decades and then the most recent several decades about babies and CV. It has a very strange pattern, and I'm still trying to figure it out." She looked confused for a moment, but she took another bite before she continued.

"The data shows that instances of CV strength aren't going down, they follow almost a wavelike pattern. There will be years where the CV strains seem less invasive in the babies at birth, and then when the pattern goes down, it spikes again a few years later. The babies with less invasive strains of CV are adults that live longer, and are less sick, obviously, and then babies with deadlier strains die particularly young for an Earth lifespan." She looked over at him since she didn't know if he even cared, but it was nice to talk it out.

"And then, strangely, in the last hundred years or so, there have actually been babies tested that have no traces of CV at birth. They show up as red numbers on my data sheet, but then even stranger, they have the shortest lifespan of all. They end up dying as children. I can't make sense of it. Over time, everyone is exposed, but it's strange that mothers who have it don't always pass it on to their babies."

"That is really strange." He knew much less than she did about all of it and almost nothing about immunology, but he enjoyed watching her when she got really excited about something, and if it was something she was interested in, then he wanted to understand as much as he could of it.

"In looking at the patterns of occurrence, is there any kind of trend so far as geography goes? I heard something when I was growing up about some religious group that basically holed up I think somewhere in the Ural district east of Moscow and said they had completely cured themselves of CV. They isolated themselves, allowed no contact, and then they apparently all went crazy a few years later and the whole place turned into a bloodbath. So not a happy ending. But it made me wonder if it was possible to isolate instances geographically."

Mercury just shook her head. "The only geographical connection that I can see is that the heavier-populated areas show more distinct trends, but you would expect that from areas with a larger population." She shook her head again as she thought about the religious groups that he mentioned. "There will always be someone down there claiming that God has given them the answer and the cure. If he had, he wouldn't wait this long to do it after so many people had died."

"The fact is that there isn't a cure, so long as they stay on Earth. We can only target and eradicate the virus if someone removes themselves from Earth. And those religious groups cause more problems for themselves when they close off the world because inevitably it leads to infighting, eventually to inbreeding, which only exacerbates the problems that CV causes in the first place. It ends up attacking their neurological pathways from a very young age due to the increased concentration of CV and genetic deformities, and the occurrences of mental illness skyrocket. It's really quite sad."

"It is." He took a few more bites of his breakfast in silence, but he was still mulling over what she'd said. "What ends up killing the kids, if there's no indication of CV in their systems?"

"There's no *one* thing that ends up happening to them." She eventually put her plate aside on her large bed and moved away to grab her communicator so she could pull up the research. "Since the Consortium is so desperate for an answer, they request additional yearly testing after a child is born CV-free. Nothing too invasive, just more blood tests, a few more physical checkups."

"But as you can see, they die of different things. Some of them by pure accident, car wreck, farm accident, but most of them die of different kinds of illnesses that they should be able to fight off naturally even if they had CV. Pneumonia, Influenza, Chickenpox. The data doesn't say, but it's almost as if their immune systems don't work at all, but logically, their immune systems should be better than everyone else's. The only way I could see complete immune failure was if somehow their immune systems were suppressed, but I don't see any evidence in their workups of other diseases that would cause that either."

He shook his head, both agreeing and deferring to her expertise. "If there's no pattern, then there's no pattern. But that is a lot of dead children, which is sad enough all on its own." He shook his head and leaned his head back against the wall behind him. "You should keep at it, though. I know how much you love digging into a problem, and that's definitely the big one for this millennium."

"It's a lot of research and a lot of data. I don't know if I'll have time to do much when we start our training, but I'd like to try." She shrugged and kissed his cheek afterward. "I can't tell you how grateful I am that you are so supportive. I've been friends with lots of doctors who don't even care to hear about my research. Some doctors just like to do their jobs and go home and not worry about anything else, but not much would get done in the world if we all did that."

That brought a smile back to his face that the discussion of dead children had certainly chased away. "I feel like if you're in a job you plan to do the rest of your life, you've got a personal investment in trying to figure out how to do that job better than anybody else, and an obligation to push the boundaries a little for both yourself and the next guy. Even more true about medicine than about piloting, but I have my tricks that I've definitely developed over the years." He gave her a mischievous grin and started in on the food she'd cooked for him, perfectly as always. "And if there's one person I've ever met who's both smart enough and stubborn enough to move the needle a little on finding a cure for CV, it'd be you."

"A permanent cure, at least." There was already a process of eradication, if people were willing to come up into space like the initiates they were going to Earth to retrieve, but it could only reverse damage in those younger than thirty, and even then it wasn't a complete guarantee.

People given CV treatments who continued to live on Earth showed only a moderate increase in life expectancy, but the treatments were incredibly expensive since they had to be shipped down from space facilities to Earth. Most people on Earth couldn't afford it.

"One of two things has to happen to help Earth. We either have to pinpoint the cause, or people have to become immune. It's hard to do either one of those things. Even with decades of research."

Orion nodded, and leaned back against the wall with one arm around her as she finished her own breakfast, scratching idly at her back. "I worry about Eleusis." He admitted quietly.

"It's a chance worth taking, in case it really does work, but if the Crisis affected all of humanity, at a basic cellular level, killed everyone who couldn't tolerate it and left the rest of them just passing the same thing back and forth until it kills them, then what happens if it makes the jump to Eleusis? It'll just be Earth all over again. Same lifespans, same limitations . . . I just worry."

"The Initiative doesn't seem concerned about it because I'm sure everyone is going to be screened on the way there, but we're talking about millions of people potentially coming along to Eleusis eventually. Something is bound to get through with those kinds of chances, on a long enough timeline."

Mercury agreed completely and she nodded after he spoke his concerns. "That's why it's important to me to figure out some answers with this research. It's the only way of stopping CV from ruining Eleusis and the only way to save Earth."

Orion's fingers moved up over her back to brush her hair over her shoulder and continue their caress along her neck. "Very serious day. Start with a very serious breakfast, talk about saving the world, then make a lifetime commitment later in the afternoon." He grinned over at her as his caress continued over her shoulder and down to her side. "Pretty heavy shit, all around. But I don't mind, so long as it's all with you."

She laughed softly and curled into him after abandoning her plate of food. "I'm sorry. I shouldn't talk about such serious things today. Today is a special day." Mercury ran her fingers over his bare skin and thought about the commitment they would be making in just a few hours. "Are you excited?"

"Yeah, I am." He set his own plate aside, a few bits left that he would get to later. For the time being, he just wanted Mercury as close as possible. He pulled up the sheet to adjust it around her, both to keep her warm and because that meant it wouldn't be in the way between them, and just held her with his arms around her back.

"Hanging out with your family makes me nervous, no reason for me to lie about that, but I'm pretty good at being on my best behavior when it matters. I'm also just mostly nervous about not somehow making a complete ass of myself in front of the Station Captain. I didn't even know they performed weddings, but your dad's strings must be pretty strong to pull that one in. I've heard she's pretty scary."

"My father insisted that I meet her when I first moved here. She's not that scary. And you don't need to be nervous about my parents or worry about your behavior. I want them to know you for you. You're important to me and that's enough for them, I'm certain." Mercury kissed along his jaw. "Just don't talk about all the things we do in the bedroom, and you'll be fine. I'm also certain my parents don't want to hear about that." She smiled as she teased him, since she knew that he would obviously avoid the topic just on principle.

"Right, that's good advice. I'll have to alter my plans. I was definitely planning on going up to your mother during the reception dinner and thanking her for passing these on to you." He reached up with both hands to get a thorough grip on her breasts as she kissed him, enjoying them, and the rest of her, as always. "But now that you mention that, maybe I'll just talk about the weather instead."

Mercury grinned and kissed him a little harder. She enjoyed his touch just as much as she enjoyed his humor. "I am glad you appreciate them so much. And that you know what to do with them too." She sighed against his lips before she kissed him again. "It's happening so fast, but in some ways, not fast enough."

"I know what you mean." He moved to get comfortable and then pulled her completely into his lap just to have her close while they talked. It was something they had gotten good at over the course of their quick relationship. He enjoyed her being naked as much as possible, but they also talked to each other more and more as the days went on, so naked conversation ended up being a pleasant middle ground between them.

"For me, I want to savor as much of this time as we can before we go into the Initiative, just make time stop for a while so I can have as much with you as humanly possible. On the other hand, I'm anxious to get moving. To be your husband, to get started with the Initiative, to get out of orbit and onto a ship headed for the other side of the galaxy, all of it." His hands continually roamed over her, caressing along her sides and her hips and the slightly tamer edges of her breasts in a constant exploration of his soon-to-be wife. "I don't know. Maybe I've been a pilot too long. We're used to being in motion."

"The ceremony won't take too long. They never do here, I'm not sure what you're used to." A few more lingering kisses were shared between them before she slowly slid off of his lap. "I want to show you your ring. If you don't like it, I don't want you to feel as though you have to wear it."

He definitely pouted a little as she pulled away, but he didn't move from his place on the bed as she went to get it. "Do you want to see yours too, or would you rather be surprised?"

"It's up to you. I don't mind either way." She retrieved a box from her desk that had arrived the day before and opened it as she brought it over to him. The ring inside was a ring made from black stone, with tiny flecks of diamond embedded around it.

"I know that we don't know each other very well yet, but when I think about you, I think about being curled up with you, looking out into the beautiful beyond with stars shimmering in front of us. I thought this looked like a little piece of the space around us, a piece you might want to keep when we're on Eleusis." She looked down at the ring again and wondered if she sounded ridiculously cheesy and insane, but she was trying to be romantic.

He took the ring from her and looked it over for a long time with his mouth partly open, just admiring the quality of the work and the detail. "That's amazing." He finally said, obviously trying to resist the urge to put it on already. When he finally looked up from it and pulled her down into a heated kiss. "It's perfect. I'm . . . completely speechless. And you know how often that doesn't happen to me."

Mercury knew from the kiss that he really meant what he said and she was happy that he loved it so much. It was expensive, but Mercury had saved her salary for a long time with little use for it. Anything made with material that came from Earth came with a steep price, but it seemed like one of the best uses of her money she could think of. "I'm so relieved that you like it. I was worried that you might think I'm crazy for spending so much time thinking about it."

"I don't think you're crazy. Not unless I drive you that way, at least." He said with a grin that reached his eyes. "Here, yours is over here." He got up from the bed with her, both of them still completely without clothes, and half-walked, half-bounced across the room to get to his belongings. Her rooms were closer to the center of Seven than he was generally accustomed to being, and the gravity was much lower as a result. It was one more thing that put him out of his comfort zone, but it had made life . . . interesting . . . at the same time.

He dug through his bag for a while, turning over his clothes inside and digging for the tiny box. He clicked it open to take the ring out so she could see it, and held it up for her between two fingers. "I saw some of your other jewelry when we first met and I thought this would suit you."

The ring was of a kind of dark rose gold that left it

looking like it had fire burning behind the brilliant sheen of the metal. Due to the speed of their relationship and the conventions of orbital culture, he had gotten her a single ring, with a fairly narrow band that looked like it was braided in on itself. There were diamonds of significant size placed throughout the braid, with a single crowning diamond in the center with a circular setting that alternated between brilliant white diamonds and deep green emeralds. The whole ring was designed so that it wouldn't be terribly obtrusive on her finger, but the stones involved were certainly significant, especially the central piece.

"I looked at some that were more elaborate, but this is the only one I could see you being able to get a glove over when push comes to shove. Literally, in your line of work. It just seemed so alive when I first looked at it. Reminded me of some redhead I know."

Her cheeks flushed as she looked at the ring. When she tore her gaze away, she looked into Orion's blue eyes with obvious awe. She really hadn't expected anything so extravagant, and just the fact that he said the beautiful ring reminded him of her left her speechless. "Orion, it's . . ." She had to force herself to take a breath because she was feeling a little overwhelmed, not only from the ring, but just the reality of everything. It was one thing to say the words, to tell someone that you wanted a future with them. It was another entirely to actually do it. "Just looking at it makes me realize how real this all is. It's not just words."

"I've never been much good with anything that's just words." He said with a grin, still holding the ring between them. "Anybody can talk a good game and make promises. I prefer more tangible results."

"Me too. There isn't much progress in the medical field without tangible results." Mercury looked down at the ring again and she touched it lightly with the tip of her finger. "Can I . . . just try it on, maybe?"

He grinned at how tentative she was being about it, and pulled her into a kiss first. "It's already yours. You don't have to ask." His lips sealed against hers as he took her hand in his and slid the ring onto her finger slowly, focusing on the feeling of the ring instead of the sight of it.

"Wow." She said as soon as it was on her finger, and they were kissing frantically, which only reminded her that they were already naked. She paused to grab his ring and then slid it on his finger, since she wanted to see a ring on his hand too. It fit perfectly. They fit perfectly. She didn't care about some official ceremony, all she cared about was their commitment to each other, and she was looking at it.

Orion clenched his fist a few times just to feel the ring on his hand, and he grinned at the way it stood out in its own unique way. He had never pictured what his wedding ring would look like aside from some plain band, but it really was the perfect thing to suit him. He picked Mercury up in both arms easily, considering the dramatically lower gravity in her quarters, and carried her over to the small dressing area just outside the walk-in closet of her unit.

The entire place wasn't much bigger than his own rooms back on Three, but every inch of it was a thousand times better maintained, every appliance new, every fixture spotless. It was the same with the floor-to-ceiling mirror that took up part of the wall beside the door into her closet. He leaned back against the opposite wall and stood her up in front of him just so they could get a good look at each other, then wove the fingers of his left hand with hers, their rings clinking against each other as his free arm laid itself across her chest to hold her back against him. His tattoo showed on his shoulder, and her vibrant red hair spilled down over his arm as he held her, leaving them as dramatic a contrast as ever.

"You think we could get away with getting married just like this? We could cause quite the scandal, but if you ask me, you're perfect exactly the way you are right now. No dress required."

"We can get married like this. Just the two of us here, however we want." She looked at their reflection and then she turned around so she could gaze into his depthless dark eyes. "I'm not taking off this ring now. I hope you know that."

"Did you think I was letting go of mine? That's not happening." He laughed as he held her against him in the corner, the world a warm place between their pressed bodies. "They'll work around it in the ceremony, I'm not worried about it. All that matters at the end of the day is that I'm yours." His hands moved up to caress her sides, up to her neck to hold her in a kiss that was almost uncharacteristically gentle before he looked her in the eye again.

"I love you, Mercury." He said quietly, and the words sounded a little strange on his lips. "I've never said that to a woman before, not like this. And it's my firm intention never to say it again to anyone but you. I don't claim to be good at it, but I'll damn sure learn. Whatever kind of love it is you need, whatever kind of husband it is you need me to be, I'll be. And it's going to be a beautiful world, whichever world it is."

Mercury was stunned to hear that kind of declaration from Orion, especially because he didn't seem the type to make a declaration like that, but she grazed her lips against his in reply. Once the kiss broke, she placed her forehead against his and closed her eyes. "I have a feeling that the future is going to be really rough for us, with all of the things that we'll be doing for Eleusis, but I still want that future." She ran her fingertips along his stubble and kissed along his jaw. "I love you too. As much as I know how to love another person, anyway. I don't claim to be good at it either."

"Well good. We can suck at loving each other together, and get better at it by way of practice." He laughed against her fingertips and turned a little to kiss them. "I look forward to it."

Mercury kissed him until her lips started tingling from the roughness of her kisses, but a light chime interrupted them. It rang throughout her unit and a very calm, collected voice spoke. "Guests Marcus and Claire Finnegan, arriving in ten minutes."

Orion pulled back just slightly at the voice. "Does that mean arriving here in this unit or here on the Station?" The way Seven worked continued to confuse him at every turn, but he was slowly learning to just roll with it.

Mercury slid away from him quickly so that she could get dressed. "Arriving at the unit. They could have alerted us sooner, but this is just a computer proximity alert. So we have ten minutes to get presentable."

Orion sighed, but followed her anyway to go retrieve at least a jumpsuit, which was the easiest thing to put himself into at the moment. "Seven doesn't have rules about allowing visitors after the wedding and the reception are over, does it? Because that's one batch of traditions that I don't think I'm gonna be okay with."

"I don't think they will stay. My father is a very busy man, but they wouldn't miss my wedding. I think they will only stay for the day." Mercury went looking for a clean dress and attempted to get her hair back in a ponytail. "We'll get married, they'll go home. Your family is coming, right?"

"I think they're all gonna be here, last I heard. My parents sent me a message last night letting me know they got in, I grabbed them and Misha a room at the hostel over on Arm Six. Khadi's coming in later today, Kam should be around, and Carl is stopping by later with my CO. But that's pretty much it for my side of the aisle." He finished wrapping himself up in his jumpsuit with a final snap, and felt comfortable in it, but meeting her parents was still more than a little nerve-wracking.

"It will be nice to meet the rest of your family." Mercury grabbed a pearl necklace to wear. It had been passed down for generations, but the act of wearing it was just another thing to distract her from her nerves about the day ahead.

She barely managed to steal another kiss before the computer notified them of her parents' arrival. Mercury stepped away from Orion to open the door and then smiled at her parents standing there. "You could have given me more warning than a proximity notification ten minutes out. That's not very kind."

"Very sorry, dear. We just thought you'd be out and about by now." Her father stepped in and took Mercury in a quick hug. Only afterward did he notice the giant standing behind her, and looked up at Orion as he let go of Mercury. "Well. Tall doesn't quite begin to cover it."

"You can say 'mildly freakish'. I'm used to it." Orion thought it was entertaining that Mercury's father was her height, or maybe a few centimeters shorter, but he kept his mouth shut on that score as he took the man's hand. "It's a pleasure to meet you, Sir. Mercury's spoken very highly of you."

Mercury's mother hugged her daughter and smiled as she looked Orion over. "He's very attractive and tall. You're lucky. I didn't actually think the program could find someone 'significantly taller' than you are."

Mercury smiled at that response and held onto her mother a moment longer before she replied. "I am lucky. Though I'm surprised you would attribute it to luck, since you and father went on and on about the science behind the matching program just to convince me to put my file into the program."

"Well, not everyone gets *this* lucky. Attractiveness isn't really a part of the program's calculations, since it's not something that can truly be quantified." Her mother continued before she turned to greet Orion. She was definitely shorter than her husband and daughter, but not significantly. "Nice to meet you. You really won our daughter over. We weren't sure she'd ever agree to marry anyone."

"Well, that would be my end of all this luck we're talking about." He agreed as he shook her hand. "Your daughter's an excellent doctor, and a very focused one. It's not my intention to get in the way of that, but I can understand her skepticism about finding a relationship that allows for that.

We want a lot of the same things. That always helps."

"That does help." Her mother agreed as she turned her attention back to Mercury. "You look very nice, sweetheart." She reached out and tucked a strand of Mercury's dark red hair behind her ear in extreme motherly fashion.

Mercury reached back and ran her hand over the hair that was tucked back before she motioned further into her unit. "Let's sit. There's still plenty of time before we need to go for the ceremony."

Her mother's attention was drawn elsewhere when Mercury motioned with her hand and immediately she grabbed her daughter's hand. "Are you sure we didn't miss it? You're already wearing a ring." She was amazed by the ring, since it was absolutely gorgeous.

"We were just trying them on before we got the notice that you were arriving. Didn't want to actually get to the ceremony itself and go to exchange rings only to find out that one or the other of us had guessed wrong about size." Orion excused smoothly, though he was still grinning at her mother's admiration. He had pretty well cleared out most of his personal accounts in getting things for Mercury in the past few weeks, but he didn't mind. What he had left, he was planning to split between Khadi and Misha, his sister-in-law.

He wasn't going to need personal finances within the Initiative or on Eleusis. There was no point holding anything back.

"Is it real gold? That's so hard to find anymore." Claire said as she continued to admire her daughter's ring. "It must have been quite a fortune." She looked up at Orion again with a raised eyebrow. "You must have a lot of faith in the match between the two of you." Claire knew that her daughter was a good woman, smart, loyal, kind. But Mercury was also a workaholic, and she had no expectation that it would change no matter where her daughter went. It was the reason why she wondered if Mercury would ever marry, since she was already married to her work.

"It's platinum, actually. Little easier to find, but actually more expensive, strangely." Orion explained with a grin at the legitimate shock on her parents' faces. *Yeah, that's right, the pilot from the Edge went all out and decked out your daughter. How do you like me now?* "But you can find just about anything on Three. Plus, the jeweler owed me a favor. I've sent him about six couples worth of business over the years and I helped him move some inventory a while ago. So he prioritized it for me."

"I didn't know that." Mercury teased as she turned her attention back to Orion. "The matchmaker part of you, I mean." She stepped away from her parents and smoothly stepped up to Orion's side. "Is it a hobby of yours? Putting people together?" She kissed his cheek and then looked into his eyes. "Your charm worked on me."

"I was only responsible for matchmaking on two of the couples. And that was mostly just helping the guy grow a sufficient pair to ask the girl out. I don't like seeing people stuck not doing what they want to do. Sometimes they just need a push." He shrugged and put an arm around Mercury easily, his left hand resting on her shoulder where her parents could easily see the band she had gotten for him.

"Well, I'm glad you needed no such push with this match." Her father said with a hesitant smile, since he didn't entirely know what to make of the giant his daughter was marrying. "I took the liberty of reviewing your flight record on the way over here. It's impressive. One of the lowest infraction rates in the pilots' corp but also one of the highest incidents of passenger complaints." Marcus seemed more amused than concerned, but it was still a strange combination.

"You'll have to give me a minute, I'm trying to decide which one of those I'm more proud of." Orion grinned back. "I tend to fly by whatever path seems best at the time. That involves things getting a little bumpy sometimes, but I stick to safe practices. Half a million moving objects circling the world within about two hundred kilometers either side of standard Station orbit, things can get a little hairy. Last I looked at it, my flight-related injuries statistic is lower than almost anybody in the corp. People may not like how I get them places, but I get them there in one piece."

"You've kept me safe." Mercury said sincerely as she briefly thought about what happened with Station Nine. She kissed him with unspoken explanation before she looked back at her parents. "They asked for volunteers to go to Earth to pick up the other half of the initiates. We decided we want to go."

"Down to Earth?" That removed the slightly bemused smile from her father's face, and in an instant, the protective man who had raised her was back in full force. "They can send automated retrieval drones for that. Why would they send anyone down into the atmosphere just to retrieve . . . them?" He guarded his tongue carefully in most circumstances, but clearly he'd had other words in mind when talking about people from Earth.

Mercury didn't have quite the prejudice her parents did about Earthlings, but she was definitely nervous about the idea of going down, even though she was excited about it too. "They have to be seen by doctors and given a first round of treatment before they can leave their planet. Not only that, but they're bound to get sick on the way up. The Initiative thought it would be best to have pilots and doctors go down who are already a part of the program since we'll all be working together."

"And put you in danger in the process?" Marcus asked sharply, but he sighed heavily afterward, since he could see the matter had already been decided without his input. "What's your assigned retrieval point, then?" He looked back and forth between them with something approaching nervousness in his eyes as he waited for the answer. The expression was so alien on his usually-confident face that it was jarring, even if it didn't last long.

"North America, Midwest district." Orion answered, since he had gotten the assignment the night before and hadn't had a chance to talk to Mercury about it yet. "We'll be leaving Sunday night for an early-morning drop-in, should make landing by 10:00 local time, half a day on the ground, departure window between 16:43 and 16:58 for liftoff and escape. Back in orbit by Third Bell Monday morning, probably a little jetlagged."

"That's six hours of ground exposure. Not to mention . . ." Marcus shook his head. "I'm sure you'll be taken care of. I just worry about the exposure you're going to pick up down there."

"It won't be that bad." Mercury promised, since she didn't want her father to be worried. "CV doesn't really start to set in until after 48 hours of exposure, and even then it's completely treatable and reversible. I'll be okay, I promise." She stepped away from Orion to put her hand on her father's arm. "You know I've been studying the virus nearly my whole life, I know more about it than most people going down to Earth."

Her mother didn't look pleased either. "Going to Eleusis is one thing. Going down to Earth is not wise, Mercury. We've done everything we can to protect you, and you're just stepping into trouble. Especially being around the Earth-bound. Most of them were conceived with the virus, for crying out loud."

"It only transfers person-to-person via sexual fluids or blood, mother. Otherwise it's completely environmental exposure, eating exposed food, drinking exposed water, eventually the air." Mercury said with a shake of the head. "And I just told you both that we're going down there to treat them and then to bring them up here. As long as they have the initial treatment, they won't pass it after 48 hours of the initial treatment. And they won't be on Earth any longer to be further exposed, though it will take some time for it to fully eradicate from their systems. After a month of daily treatments in space, they'll be fine. Almost as if they never had it at all."

"I know you know more about it than most, Mercury."

Her father's tone softened somewhat as he said so, but he still didn't sound happy. "Just be careful, and stay in contact with us as much as you can to let us know you're on schedule. We'll be worrying about you, no matter how safe it's supposed to be. Even just atmospheric entry and take-off . . ."

"That's my job." Orion chimed in with a smile. "Which we've established I'm also quite good at."

Mercury's expression softened at her father's gentle tone. "You know I will. I have no reason to make you worry, and I don't want to. But I really do feel like this will be a good opportunity. We should get to know these people." She glanced back at Orion before she looked at her parents again. "We're all going to be the first people of Eleusis. We should probably learn to get along."

"They'll have to be taught some manners first, most likely." Marcus said with a slight roll of his eyes, and Orion could almost feel the man pointedly not looking at him as he said it. Her parents were a little more judgy than even he had really anticipated, but he could live with that. After all, he was going to be several stars away with their daughter soon enough. It would be difficult for them to disapprove of him at that kind of distance.

"Dad." Mercury reprimanded softly, since she didn't want her father to think so poorly of the people that were coming up from Earth. "They're just like us, except they haven't had the resources we have. They can't be that bad." She hadn't actually met anyone from Earth, but she was trying her best to keep an open mind. She was a doctor. Every human was made equal.

Marcus turned his eyes on Mercury with a subdued smile. "I should have taken you on more business meetings when you were younger. Negotiating with Earth merchants is not my favorite thing." He chuckled and shook his head, clearly thinking her a little naive. "But hopefully your experience will be different than mine."

"I'm sure it will be. These people aren't negotiating

anything. They're coming up for the same reason that we're leaving. For a better future." Mercury looked over at Orion for a moment and heaved a defeated sigh. "This is supposed to be a happy day."

"It is a happy day." Marcus agreed apologetically, then moved to take a seat on the far side of the couch where he always seemed to situate himself when he and her mother came to visit. "So come on, is there anything that we need to do to help set up for this evening?"

"No, we are keeping it simple. The ceremony will be short, we'll have a meal afterward, and that will be it." Mercury was a bit upset that the discussion with her parents had soured the moment, but she was trying to move past it. "Can I get you anything to drink?"

"Just water's good, thank you." He smiled politely at Mercury, but it was Orion who went to go get the water for the man, with a knowing look at Mercury. It was going to be a long day.

16

Her parents remained for about an hour to chat and get to know Orion a little bit more, and while Mercury usually loved spending time with her parents, it felt different realizing she loved someone they didn't entirely approve of.

She and Orion said their brief goodbyes, and she left the unit after he did to walk her parents to their temporary rental unit so they could relax before the ceremony. Mercury walked quietly between her parents through the pristine hallways of Seven before she finally said something halfway to their guest unit. "You aren't going to tell me what you think?"

Her father smiled a little more broadly at that question, walking in step with his daughter along the corridor with his hands in his pockets, as usual. "What we think of Orion, you mean?"

"Yes, of course." She glared at him even though he was smiling at her. "I've been wondering since the moment you laid eyes on him what you think of him." Mercury glanced from her father to her mother, but her mother just shook her head, clearly not keen to offer her opinion first.

Marcus stopped in the hallway with a sigh, lowering his head for a moment before he looked back at Mercury.

"There's . . . almost an obligation in the universe for men to hate whoever their daughters end up marrying. Someday you should do a study to see if there's some kind of genetic marker for it or something on the Y-chromosome." He shook his head and shrugged it off, appearing nonchalant about it even though Mercury knew her father had never been nonchalant about anything in his life.

"I'm just . . . surprised by him, I think might be the best descriptor for what I feel about him. I hoped, with the man's service record, that the program had matched you with someone who shares your ambition, your drive for excellence. Yes, I know he's an excellent pilot and an obedient officer, but from the way he presents himself, that is all he will ever be. He just isn't what I imagined for you."

Mercury frowned and processed what he said carefully before she replied, since she didn't want to reply angrily simply out of reflex. "What did you imagine?" She didn't care to contradict her father, not because she thought that Orion had no ambition, but because she knew that even if she told her father that she knew Orion was what she wanted and the person to make her happy, her father would still view Orion as less. "Greg?"

He rolled his eyes. "Not a chance. He would have been a hundred times worse. He'd have been a puppy at your heels from the moment you said 'I do,' if not well before."

"You both encouraged me to do this and to meet him. I don't need to meet anyone else, and I don't want to. I care about Orion, and I think he's good for me *because* he's nothing like anyone I would have chosen for myself. He's funny even if I don't understand *all* of his attempts at humor, he's risky when I never am, and he forces me to see things differently than I normally would. I need that. I need someone like him."

Marcus finally took his hands out of his pockets at that tirade, and closed the few steps between them to lay his hands gently on her arms. "Then that's all that matters, Mercury." He said quietly, with the same kind of calm that she knew had pacified the Station magistrates who worked for him and just about everyone he spoke to, even if it didn't always work on her or her mother.

"When this process began and your mother and I told you that we wouldn't interfere, that we would support your decision and your priorities no matter what, we meant it. He's not what I expected or would have gone looking for in a husband for you, but I don't have to like or trust him. I trust *you* to know what you need and judge whether he can be that for you or not. You wouldn't have chosen to marry him if you thought otherwise. If he'll be a good husband to you, and make you happy, that's all anyone can ask for."

"Thank you." She said simply with a little relief, even though she felt that her father was partially saying it just to put off another argument. Mercury wasn't looking to fight, though, so she would take it as an offer of peace.

They eventually made it to the temporary rental unit, and Mercury scanned her handprint so the unit would recognize her request for the guest space. "We still have some time until the ceremony. I still need to get ready, but I'll see you there, alright?"

"We'll come find you right before. Do you have anyone else here to help you? Any of your nurses, the other doctors?"

She shook her head. "No, you know me. I don't have a lot of close friends, but that's alright. It won't be complicated, I just have a simple dress to wear. I don't want to make this into something outrageous. Simple."

That statement brought her father's smile back. "So that's why you didn't want to get married back home. You knew I'd have had the entire station in attendance." He chuckled and nodded to her, since he could respect her wanting something less ostentatious. "Well, if you do need us for anything, you know where to find us. We'll see you soon, dear."

Mercury nodded and gave each of her parents a hug and a kiss on her father's cheek before she saw them into their unit and headed back through the hallways to get back to her own unit. The residential hallways of Seven were always the most quiet, since medical professionals spent most of their time in their units sleeping or relaxing. Everything else was so busy they almost had no choice but to view their units as a kind of haven or retreat. Mercury wasn't paying much mind to the few passers-by as she walked, but as soon as she heard someone say her name from behind her, she stopped cold.

Even if she had mistaken his voice, she couldn't have mistaken the sound of his footsteps. Oh right, he did live on this level. "I didn't realize you were back already. I thought you were coming in later this afternoon, before . . ." he didn't seem able to bring himself to even say why she was back, his voice just trailing off instead as he approached.

She pulled her lips into a polite smile before she turned around to look at Greg, even though she knew he wasn't likely to be smiling. "I've been home for a few days now. I didn't seek you out because I thought it might be uncomfortable. I left here thinking that I would return the same day and be back at work again, but things happened very differently than I imagined."

"Well, there was a lot of that going around when you left." He was clearly every bit as uncomfortable about the meeting as she was, since he was actually keeping his distance for a change. The look in his eyes was no different than her father had anticipated. Mercury hadn't seen many puppies in her life, but they looked at their masters exactly the way Greg was looking at her.

"I um, I thought, for my part, that you were going to go, find out the guy was nothing like you wanted or needed, then come back to work and I could maybe convince you to stay here with me instead of going to Eleusis. Seeing as I don't seem qualified to make the trip with the rest of you."

Mercury felt a pang of guilt when he said that, since she knew he wanted to go to Eleusis. So many people did. "You know that there's more that went into the selection process than qualifications. You're an amazing doctor." Mercury didn't hand out compliments out of pity, she gave them when she meant them. His talent as a doctor was one of the biggest reasons she had been even a little attracted to him in the first place, and why she considered him a good friend. She felt like she could learn from him and that was what made their friendship so beneficial. "I don't know everything that went into the selection process, but you will get your opportunity. Eleusis needs doctors like you."

"If half of what I've heard about the Initiative so far is true, it's doctors like you that they'll need, not like me." He attempted to give her a smile, but she could tell it was just him making an effort for her benefit. "Listen, I um, can you wait right here for just a second? My unit is just up the hallway and I put something together for you, but I didn't know when I'd see you. Sort of a going-away/wedding present."

Clearly she was surprised by that. He wanted to give her a present? "Um, sure, I can wait here." She didn't know what he meant about what he heard about the Initiative or doctors like her, but she was definitely curious.

He nodded without quite looking at her, and turned around to go back to his unit. The block through which she was walking had steps and lifts to take people from one level to another, but she wasn't far from her own unit. The gravity was light enough that all Greg needed to do was take a few steps and launch himself up to the railing of the next floor, then the next and the next, climbing quickly. He'd always been fairly athletic, even if the only times she'd been able to see the evidence of his physical fitness was when he was running down the corridors to tend to a patient's emergency.

Eventually he disappeared inside his unit three floors and half a hall away, but he was only inside for a moment before he came back out. Both his hands were still free, strangely, but he swung himself down over the railings in the light gravity, catching himself on each floor on the way down to break his fall, until he landed softly on the walkway she was still standing on. He wasn't even breathing hard or sweating, since all the movement took so little real effort in such low gravity.

He reached into his pocket as he approached her, and retrieved a small data core, of the type that wasn't really necessary very often since it was only used for externally stored data. Most of their world and work was always stored on Station servers, accessible from anywhere on the orbital network.

"I've been working on a historical trend analysis for the past six years or so, ever since I finished my residency. Most of my work has been cobbling together demographic and diagnostic data from about a thousand different sources, or at least it feels that way. More like high four hundreds. Anyway, my goal of examination was a macro-analysis of all pediatric exam results charted against mortality rates, looking for patterns and trends in the data. I've never even gotten it to the point where I even know what I'm looking for, but I've always thought that if we could get all of humanity's data in one place, in one examination, then we can really start seeing some overall trends and doing something important about it. I've just been hung up on the data gathering for so long that I've never gotten around to the actual researching or analysis. But you're better than I am at those things anyway."

He handed the core over to her with the same weak smile that had been on his face before. "There's still a lot of shaky data right after Crisis in Asia, of course, since everything went crazy and a lot of the facilities housing them were destroyed, and for some reason I've never been able to pull in data from western Africa near the end of the twenty-second century, but everything else is either comprehensive or substantially representative all the way up to the last medical census of orbital and Earth populations five years ago. After the census this past summer, I was hoping to use an entire year in transit between here and Eleusis to really buckle down and do some analysis, finally write the book to put all the data out for public utilization. But it looks like I'm not going to have that kind of window any time soon."

Mercury looked down at the small core in her hands and she was speechless for a couple minutes as she really thought about everything he just told her. To her, what he had given her was invaluable, and she was taken aback that he would give it to her in the first place. Especially when he could put his name to the research and product thereof entirely himself. She stepped up to him and hugged him, even if he wasn't interested in any kind of contact. "Thank you so much, this is great. It ... I don't know why you would entrust me with something like this, but thank you. I, um, I really am at a loss for words. This is one of the most amazing gifts anyone has ever given me."

He returned the hug, and he wasn't the first one of them to let go, though he didn't try to hold onto her for too long after she stepped back from him. "You're incredible, Mercury. Incredible things should go together." He nodded down at the data core and then tried to hide a sigh as he stepped back to put some more distance between them. "You're gonna do great things. Here and on Eleusis. I wish you all the best."

He nodded as if that was satisfactory in his own mind, and finally turned away, since he knew she had things to get back to that didn't involve him, and he was off up the corridors the same way he'd come, jumping up from one level to another to get back to his own unit.

Mercury just stayed there, stunned, even after he was gone, but she eventually made her way back to her unit. She had preparations to make for the rest of her life.

* * * * *

Mercury was grateful for the hours spent alone, but she was also grateful for her parents when they showed up to walk with her to the Observatory to meet with Orion and his family. She hadn't met his parents yet, simply because she'd stayed behind to get ready, but they were kind to her and seemed genuinely affectionate even though she could tell she was not the person they would have chosen for their son.

Apparently the parents had something in common that day between them.

There was no pomp or circumstance when Mercury entered the Observatory, no music or friends in fancy dresses, there was just Mercury in a silver dress with her hair in shocking red waves down and over her shoulders, her green eyes sparkling with excitement and emotion. The dress she wore was long, the silky fabric flowing to her ankles, with silver heels underneath that added more than a few centimeters to her height. The top of the dress went over one shoulder, embellished with tiny crystals, while the other shoulder was left bare. The only other embellishment to the dress was another sunburst of crystals at her waist. She looked beautiful and dignified, and most of all, she was smiling at the man waiting for her.

Orion and the Station Captain were the only people standing at the end of the aisle between the chairs that had been set up, but Orion's side of the aisle was fairly well represented and dressed in their finest for the occasion. Orion's father was dressed in a suit that was very respectable, if not quite as embellished or ornamented as her father's. His mother and Misha were dressed in beautiful dresses, but the only part of either of them that could be seen was their faces. Little Ahmed looked like he might be on the verge of sleeping through the wedding, since he had run himself ragged earlier that day.

Khadijah was the standout of his family, not to mention a knockout in her own right. Carl was beside her, along with a few other friends of Orion's whom she hadn't met yet, but who obviously knew him through the military since they were also in uniform. His commanding officer stood out like a sore thumb, an older woman with dark skin and hair beginning to show hints of grey, with distinctly sharp features that marked her as not African by descent, but Indian, a rarity both on Earth and in orbit in the world following the Crisis.

Orion himself looked very much like he had when she first met him, and the image of him in his formal uniform made it seem, just for a moment, as though he was standing on the other side of that screen again, announcing himself to her as a stranger. But he was a stranger she knew so much better after weeks in his company. She knew what was behind the glimmer of mischief in his eyes, behind the knowing curve of his grin. Mercury could look at his hands, clasped in front of him as he waited, and remember everything that they were capable of doing when they touched her, the ease with which they handled both the controls of a spacecraft and every nerve in her body.

She knew now, as she had wondered the first time she met him, what was under his uniform, and she could see the outlines of his tattoos so clearly she could almost read the Arabic for herself and trace the lines of his unit tattoo along his shoulder. She knew what was inside the stranger she was marrying. Where his heart rested, what he wanted, what he intended to do and be in his life. She knew the important things, and he knew her.

When she was finally standing in front of him, Mercury's eyes were fixed on Orion. There were fewer people on her side of the room, her parents, a few of her colleagues, but she didn't care about any of that, other than her parents. "You look wonderful." She whispered through her smile and reached out for his hand. "The afternoon took too long."

"Yes it did." He agreed as he squeezed her hand. "You look incredible. I would ask for someone to pinch me, except I know Carl too well, he'll do it."

"I don't need Carl to come over here and interrupt." Mercury playfully chastised with a smirk before she looked over at the station captain. "We're ready, Captain."

The older woman nodded in acknowledgement and smiled. "Sometimes there are ceremonies of extravagance and sometimes there are simple ceremonies of love and affection. Today we are here to celebrate Orion Al-Jabbar and Mercury Finnegan becoming one unit." She looked between them and then smiled brighter. "Do you have anything to say to each other first?"

Orion looked down at Mercury with a warm smile, partly at the fact that they were the two tallest people in the room, with the exception of Carl. He was a fan of being a gentleman in all situations and letting women go first, but in that instance, it looked like he was the one who was going first.

"So . . . it took most of . . . these people over here," he turned and gestured vaguely to his side of the room, "to convince me that entering the Matching program was actually a good idea. It wasn't easy for them, but they eventually managed, and I showed up. Easily one of the best choices I have ever made in my life. That got me here, and I'm a fan of here." He turned back to Mercury and took both of her hands.

"Two years from now, you and I are gonna be on Eleusis, in a house that no one's lived in before, on ground that no one's ever lived on before, building a home for ourselves and a home for the rest of the world. Love is looking together in the same direction, and you and me are looking across the universe. That's a powerful thing, and it's what I want with you. I will love you from one end of this universe to the other, Mercury Finnegan."

Mercury didn't have a lot to say, but she felt touched by his words and by his emotion behind it. He really did want a future with her. That was more than enough. "I'm not a woman of a lot of words unless they're for medical purposes." That got a chuckle from the small crowd, but she didn't look away from him. "But I have enough words to tell you that you mean more to me than anyone ever has. I have so much to learn, but I'm glad that I will learn it with you, and I will learn more about you every day. Eleusis waits for us, and I look forward to our life together. I love you." Her green eyes glimmered with happiness as squeezed his hand tightly. Their love had developed quickly and had more room to grow, but she meant the words as she said them.

"The most important words are those that you can say to each other." The captain resumed with a generous smile. "In my capacity as Captain of this station, and under the laws of the Consortium, I now pronounce you man and wife." Traditional vows were not requested or required, and most matched couples didn't care to have them. Sickness, health, to have and to hold, they were words from an old tradition, an Earth tradition. They didn't apply in Orbit.

Orion grinned at the official words, since that declaration was all that was required for the legality to be completed. Most of the weddings he'd been to had some kind of encouragement afterward, or were much more involved, but he was happy that there didn't need to be much more to it. Instead of waiting for anything else, he leaned in with eagerness and kissed her with fervor, dipping her backward a little with his hands on her waist to hold her against him.

Mercury was surprised by the way he kissed her, especially being dipped backward, but she easily wrapped her arms around his neck and kissed him with just as much intensity. There were a few whoops and hollers before their kiss broke, and Mercury chuckled beneath her flushed cheeks. "That was quite a kiss."

"Well, you know. Wanted to start things off right." He responded with a mischievous grin, as the rest of the small audience continued clapping with a round of laughter. "Come on. Let's mingle and then go get some dinner, Wife."

She nodded her agreement and looked back at their friends and family with joy on her face. It happened so fast, and yet she didn't care that there wasn't much to it. It was simple, but it was everything. "Wife. Husband. Wow." She gave him a featherlight kiss on the lips. "What a day."

17

Time was ticking closer to leaving Earth. Anna was more anxious about it with every passing moment. She enjoyed her time with Logan, of course, all of which felt like a dreamy sex vacation, even after the insane wedding in the weeks following her own where Liam married all three of his loves.

The Bickford house was already busy when Anna woke, though she happened upon Liam and Brianne in the kitchen before she saw anyone else. They were only days away from leaving Earth for good. Anna and Logan were planning to go out to Doc Weber's for more bloodwork, but she was lured by the smell of bacon first and foremost.

"Didn't know you could cook, Bri." Anna poured herself a coffee and sat down at the table next to Liam.

"I'm full of surprises." Brianne said with a smirk that both Anna and Liam could hear before Brianne looked back at her new husband. True to the word she'd been promised, Brianne had a sizable diamond on her finger, and she seemed to love having it there. Each of the women had wanted something different. Margo wanted a smaller diamond surrounded with rubies, and Rachel wanted a big blue sapphire as her center stone with a diamond set on each side of it. Brianne's ring was the simplest, only a gold band, but it also had the biggest rock, though the rock wasn't accompanied by any other jewels. "I think Liam can attest to that, can't ya, babe?"

"You know, I didn't actually think you would be." Liam grinned from the table, popping another piece of bacon in his mouth mid-sentence. "But that's what I get for thinking I've got your number locked down. You come back and hit me with something I'd never even heard of before."

"That's right." She pointed her spatula at Liam with a grin and her smile didn't disappear when Rachel showed up. They oddly continued to get along, even as newlyweds. "Hey, Rach. You said you were really missing your mom's pancakes. I took a shot at her recipe."

"Thank you, that's thoughtful." Rachel said as she plopped down into Liam's lap and snagged one of his pieces of bacon. "Did you sleep alright last night?" Rachel turned and looked at Liam more directly. "You said your arm was hurting after you got down under Logan's truck to take a look."

"It's still a little sore, but it's better than it was when I went to bed. I think I just pulled the shoulder wrong or something. Nothing major." He was eating with the arm in question, after all, so it couldn't have been that major. His other arm he just kept around Rachel's waist, along the band of the shorts she wore for pajamas and her mostly-exposed ribs beneath her short t-shirt. "What about you?"

"I always sleep better when you're there." Rachel smiled and snuggled him gently while Brianne continued cooking, apparently both women completely at ease with sharing their husband.

Anna watched the entire thing for a moment in awe, since she didn't understand it all. She was just about to comment on how crazy the whole lot of them were when Logan appeared and she turned her attention to him instead, and got up to greet him with a fiery good-morning smooch. "I'm glad I don't have to share you." She whispered against his lips, since she in no way would survive whatever circus was happening in front of her with Liam and his wives.

"You and me both." He agreed immediately as his eyes darted around the room. He shook his head at his brother and his wives. Even if the entire thing had been his idea, there was no way Logan thought he'd be able to survive it himself. "Hey, Bri, any chance I could get some of that bacon on a bagel or some toast or something to go? We're gonna be late getting down to Doc's as it is. I do not want to piss off the woman who's about to stab a series of needles into my arm."

"Sure, Logan." Brianne hummed and swayed her hips across the kitchen as she whipped together a bag for breakfast with remarkable ease. She sauntered over to him with a smirk as she handed it off to him. "You always look so afraid of seeing Liam with us, as if we're just now going to discover that he's with all of us at once." She shook her head as he took the bagel sandwich from her. "Or maybe you think you're about to witness an orgy in your kitchen. Let me set your mind at ease, not everyone would be okay with that idea, so don't you worry about it."

Logan rolled his eyes and held a little tighter to Anna. "I trust you all to keep your orgies more or less to yourselves. I have to eat off this kitchen counter, after all."

Liam laughed as he leaned back with Rachel in his lap. "Yeah, well, God invented cleaning products for a reason. I wouldn't worry too much about the counter." He was rewarded with a smack from Rachel, which only led to more laughter.

The sigh that escaped Logan was mostly for dramatic effect, as Liam's two wives laughed at the situation and Logan's response. "Fair enough. I'll work on the whole not-walking-on-eggshells thing every time I see you guys."

Anna grabbed a couple pieces of bacon and a bagel for herself before she linked her arm with Logan's and they walked out. She wasn't about to linger and give Brianne the opportunity to start telling stories about Liam's sexual prowess. After rushing to the truck, Logan programmed in their destination and they both relaxed to eat once the truck was moving. Anna eyed Logan with a little concern. "You were in the shower a long time. Are you alright?"

"Yeah, just waking up. I didn't sleep that well last night." He put the sandwich down after a few bites, then leaned back to watch the truck maneuver out onto the main road, where he trusted the autopilot a little more and felt he could relax. "No particular reason, just a lot happening all at once. A lot to think about. Stayed awake and watched you for most of the night." He grinned and put an arm around her shoulders to hold her in close the way they'd gotten accustomed to riding.

Anna easily slid the rest of the way into his side and kissed his cheek before she went back to eating. "You watch me sleep? Creeper." Anna was smiling at him, though, before she took another bite. "I'm a day late, you know. I'm going to ask her to do a blood test to test for that too. A baby."

He hadn't actually been aware of that, since they'd only been together for a few weeks in total, but he realized he probably should have thought of that, since she hadn't actually been on her period for any of that time. He and his dick would've noticed. "Well that would be a hell of a going-away present from the planet, wouldn't it?" His hand moved over her shoulder to hold her firmly against his side.

"You're telling me." She smiled hopefully and gripped tightly to his arm. "I really hope I am. I want to have your babies. So bad."

"You can say that now at the beginning, and when you're in the process of pulling them out of me, but when it comes down to it, nine months from now when we're about to blast off for the other side of the galaxy, you might feel a little differently." He still looked happy and hopeful, though, as he kissed down her neck, letting her finish her food.

"Maybe I will, but I'm betting not. I've dreamed about being your wife and having your children for years." Anna ate the rest of her food quickly, even though she didn't have to, but she didn't want to make a mess in his truck. He was a little particular about his truck. "And if it turns out that I'm just late, then we'll have to try harder next month."

"Trying harder than we already have, all in lower gravity?" He took a bite of his sandwich, having regained some of his appetite. Anna had that effect on him. "God, I'm gonna be throwing you around whatever capsule they put us in. You seemed to like it when I put you up against a wall that one time. We'll see how you like it on the ceiling."

"I like it everywhere so long as I'm with you." She grinned at his returned appetite and put a hand on his large thigh so she could grip it. "I'm a little surprised that we have to drive out to Doc's again. I don't know why the Initiative would need *more* blood samples. They sure do ask for a lot."

"Doc said something about some other inoculations we apparently missed, before going up to space. She wasn't big on details, just said it was part of the Initiative's requirements." He shrugged while devouring the rest of his sandwich. "I imagine we're gonna be getting a lot of that. Requirements that don't have a whole lot of 'why' behind them, just a lot of 'shut up and do it'. The little I've ever been able to find about life in orbit leads me to believe that's pretty much their norm."

"And we're agreeing to it." She reminded him with some resignation as she remained curled into his side. "I don't do well with being told what to do. You know me. I just have to keep Eleusis in mind all the time, I guess. Just to keep myself quiet."

"I want you a lot of things, baby, but quiet isn't one of them." Logan's fingers massaged over her back as he leaned back to get comfortable for the drive down to the Webers'. "Honestly, before the meeting, I thought that was what they were trying to recruit for everybody who was going. People who would be useful, but who would fall in line. Most of the time, I think I probably fall into that definition myself. But when you told me you had been accepted . . ." he chuckled against her hair. "Yeah, falling in line and doing as you're told has never been your strong point. And I like you that way. But clearly we're not gonna be alone when it comes to civil disobedience. If they want us to be the ones going out there, then we're gonna be some of the ones in charge of how the place operates. Staying quiet isn't on the menu."

"I don't think they are interested in having me in charge." Anna disagreed. "And I don't think you would just fall in line either. You are a born leader."

"I wasn't born to it." He said quietly, since he'd never been particularly good at taking compliments when the reason for those compliments was a situation he hadn't chosen. "I was car-accidented into it. Take anybody ever born on the planet and put them in charge of an estate at ten years old and you'll eventually get somebody who's real comfortable bossing people around."

"Liam didn't step up to it. You did. It's not all about circumstances." Anna ran her fingers across his cheek. "Look at me and Ben. No one forced him into it and he is the bossiest person I know."

"Yeah, well, Ben is kind of a natural-born asshole. Shocked the hell out of me when I found out Susan went for him, of all people." Susan was almost a year and a half older than even Logan was, so when she'd gotten with a younger man, especially one like Ben, it had been surprising, to say the least. "Regardless, I'm from Earth. Nobody's putting us in charge once we get up there. From the tone of that presentation info-session, it sounds to me like they want us along because we know what a seed looks like and we understand that it requires water. I would think the rocket scientists at the Consortium would have some experts of their own on that subject, but if they want us along to help actually feed some people, I suppose I don't mind."

"I'm not going to make any guesses about what they want us up there for. If I do, I'll have expectations, and I don't think having expectations for this sort of thing is a good idea." She glanced out the window and her gaze went up toward the sky. "What do you think they're like? Do you think all of them walk around like they have a stick up their ass and like they know more than everyone else?"

"I've wondered that before." He looked up along with her, and it wasn't hard in the clear autumn sky to find a station moving across its unmarred blue perfection. How many other satellites and smaller stations were up there besides the dozen or so major ones that could be seen easily with the naked eye?

How much was the sky hiding?

"Mostly I figure they're gonna be a bunch of morons who just assume their world is better than ours because they can control every little bit and piece of it. What's really gonna freak me out is being around . . . well, old people." Two of those who had come with the informational meeting had had hair that was beginning to go salt-and-pepper, and one had even had the beginnings of wrinkles. Logan couldn't remember the last time he'd ever seen anyone with wrinkles in anything but a movie. "Who are all gonna think we're just a bunch of kids down here all playing with our parents' toys while they're permanently away."

"I don't know about you, but I don't feel like a kid." She stared up at the sky. "And I know for damn sure that we're not just playing around down here. I don't have any problem re-aligning their perspective of us. I know they're gonna need it. I bet none of them have done any real work in their entire lives. I just imagine them up there with their noses pressed to computer screens all day long."

"Sounds about right to me." He shook his head at the thought, glanced back down at her side of the truck that she never actually ended up sitting on, since she was more frequently in his lap or up against his side. "Speaking of which, I gave that tablet you found a shot the other day while you were helping Liam with his jewelry selection. I couldn't get it to turn on, since there's no charge and I don't want to hook it up to anything in case it traces itself, but honestly, I've seen tech with more of its shit beaten out of it come back from the dead. It should be salvageable."

"I guess I'll just have to wait to find the right person to look at it." She thought about the tablet for a moment as she wondered what was on it, especially since the old man had it clutched to his body like a lifeboat in the last moments of his life. "Not just anyone. Someone we can trust. Because I feel like there's probably some dangerous shit on there."

"I feel like there's gonna be some dangerous shit no matter where we go from now on." Logan responded darkly and he clutched Anna tighter as he considered possible threats. "That's why they call it a risk, I guess." He leaned her head back and swept in with a possessive kiss, while they had the time to themselves on the way down to Doc's. It was going to be the two of them against the rest of the world very soon, and he found himself really looking forward to that in ways that he hadn't anticipated when he first considered the Eleusis Initiative. There was no one else he wanted on his team the way he wanted Anna. If she was next to him, it didn't matter what was against them.

A visit to the ghost town where Doc lived was always a little depressing, but her clinic/home was bright and cheery enough. When they arrived, they were told that Doc herself was busy with a pack of boys who had gotten into some trouble on their family's ranch. There were half a dozen already in casts and still four more in makeshift splints waiting to have collarbones, arms, and legs mended by the doctor.

"That's what happens when you try to get cute at a cattle drive." Logan looked more amused than anything. They walked through the main hall of the clinic to the back office where Doc's secretary had directed them, and promptly walked in on Sierra in a doctor's coat, sitting on top of an exam table making out with Gary.

"Are we interrupting?" Logan asked with a broad grin at catching the lovers in the act.

Sierra pulled away from Gary sharply and her face was flushed when she looked toward the intrusion, but clearly her flushed face hadn't been entirely from surprise. She attempted to discreetly allow for Gary to extract his hand from underneath her shirt, but there was only so much that wouldn't be obvious.

"Anna. Logan." She cleared her throat and tugged at her shirt as Gary stepped aside so that she could jump down off the table. "I, um, I wasn't expecting any patients."

"Clearly." Logan chuckled, since it was a side of Sierra he hadn't seen before. She was a couple years younger than he and Anna, so generally the doctor's daughter was considered off-limits. "Your mom's busy with the whole pack of kids who decided to get themselves smashed to pieces out there. She told us we were supposed to come by and have some bloodwork done before we go upstairs. Did you two already do yours?"

"Um," Sierra glanced at Gary and back at Logan. "No, we decided we aren't going." She moved quickly toward one of the cabinets nearby to get supplies for blood samples. Getting back to work would diffuse the awkward interruption, right? "We decided we would be happier here where no one has the chance to mess things up except us. My mom really wanted me to go, but I guess I'm too selfish." Sierra smiled at Gary before she continued. "I want to keep his genetic code all to myself."

That chased away Logan's playful grin, even though obviously Sierra was clearly happy with her man and her reasons. "Speaking of genetic code, there's some other checks we'd like you to do while we're here, if you don't mind." He held out his arm to let Sierra get to it and gave Anna a knowing grin.

Sierra looked confused at first but she laughed once she caught his meaning. "Oh, sure. I can take an extra vial for that." Sierra was deft with getting the needle into Logan's arm. "You two didn't waste any time, did you?"

"No time to waste, right?" Anna said as she watched Sierra fill up small vials of blood and put them aside. "You two don't look like you're wasting any time either." She looked over at Gary with curiosity. "Did she convince you to stay or was it the other way around?"

"It was a little of both." Gary kept his distance off to the side of the room, but he didn't look like he was embarrassed at all about having been caught by them. No reason to waste any time being embarrassed when Sierra was just that gorgeous. "Honestly, before the meeting, I think we were both pretty excited about going. I may be a hired farm grunt, but I know a great opportunity when I see one. Then we had the meeting and it just . . . I don't know. It sounds more like they want to build something on top of us instead of giving us the chance to build something ourselves."

Anna's eyebrows furrowed as she looked over at Sierra again, but Sierra was busying herself with making sure she had taken all she needed from Logan's arm. Once she pulled the needle out and taped up the spot, Sierra started labeling the vials. "That's what you think, too?" Anna wanted to hear from them both.

"I think they spent too much time trying to woo us instead of telling us important information." Sierra replied vaguely as she briefly glanced up from her task. "I know my mom wanted me to go because she wanted me to get treated. She didn't care about Eleusis so much as just making sure I don't die, but I can still choose to believe that we'll have a permanent, Earth-based cure before I die."

"I thought Crisis research was at a standstill?" Logan knew he wasn't a doctor by any stretch of the imagination, but he had . . . well, some of his former girlfriends had been smarter and more ambitious than others. "Is that what you're deciding to get into? Not general practice like your mom?"

"It's been at a standstill here on Earth, but there are a *lot* of doctors working on it up there." She nodded upward as she finished labeling Logan's vials. Sierra then grabbed a small package and grabbed one of her mother's scanners. She held it out for Logan to place his hand on top of, so she could get his fingerprints and the scan would unlock the package with his name on it. "You better believe they don't want CV to make it to Eleusis."

When the screen beeped and the package popped open, she pulled out three syringes. "I wish I could get into the research myself, but my mom needs my help more and more these days. She's doing really well for her age, since she spent half her life up there, but she's still going to need me to help her. I can't help her if I'm spending time doing research."

Sierra held up the three syringes for Logan to see, and she tapped each one in turn. "These are your pre-treatments, we're to give them out after your final round of bloodwork. You'll get your first full treatment for CV when their doctors come down here to pick you up. The treatments aren't effective if you stay on Earth more than forty-eight hours after you get the initial one, so it doesn't make sense for us to give them to you."

She rubbed more alcohol on his upper arm once he pushed up his sleeve. "I'm told the first one burns like a bitch, the second one makes your tongue numb for ten minutes, and the third one makes your arm cold. I don't know enough about what is in these suckers to tell you why, they don't tell us what's in them. Even more reason not to want them, if you ask me, but you two have always been braver than I am."

"Great. I'm really looking forward to this now." Logan gave Sierra a slight glare, but then just balled his hand into a fist and gritted his teeth to wait for it. "Need to work on that bedside manner, Do . . . Ow!" He managed to stay still as she pushed the rest of the first plunger's contents into his arm, but Anna could see that part of his arm already turning red, along with Logan's face at the effort of keeping quiet. She hadn't been kidding. It felt like she had held a torch to his arm and the fire was just spreading outward into the rest of his body from there. It didn't help his comfort level that the plunger itself was opaque, so he couldn't even see the color of what she was putting into him. "Fucking hell, what is in that shit?"

"I just told you, I don't know." Sierra tried to fight a giggle, but his face was so contorted that she snorted just a little. "You know, you're right, I really do need to work on my bedside manner." Sierra snickered a little bit and held out the second syringe in front of him. "Ready to lose feeling in your tongue for ten minutes? I would suggest being careful when you talk, I don't want to have to stitch up your tongue cuz you bit through it."

She looked at the syringe before she uncapped the needle and tapped the tube. "They did tell us that the first syringe is meant to target the virus, so it attacks the virus in the cells closest to the injection site, which is what causes the burning, I would assume. Of course, your cells replicate the virus since it is usually in your cellular structure since birth, so it does little good except to weaken the structure of the virus for when the treatment comes. This one," she said as she jabbed Logan's arm again, though she tried to do it with more finesse this time, but there was a little part of her that was wicked enough to enjoy bringing a big tough man to his knees, even temporarily. "This one is, I think, a neurological agent so that you don't feel as much pain from the first one, but the side effect is just that it temporarily paralyzes your tongue, and the last one," Sierra nodded toward it, "is, I believe, an immune booster, so the combination of it and the neuro-agent give your arm a cold sensation."

Logan started working his mouth a little as the numbing agent set in, but she was right, the burning that had been moving through his body didn't feel quite as bad as it had a moment before. "God, I hate doctors. Well, going to the doctor, anyway. Nothing personal against you and your mom. It just never ends well." He grunted as she took the syringe out of his arm and he stretched it a little, since his arm in particular was mostly numb. "Alright, hit me with the last bit and get it over with." He mumbled as he looked over at Anna over Sierra's shoulder with a glance down at her arm. "Buckle up, baby. This shit stings."

"You roar like a lion over those things." Anna shook her

head as she pushed her sleeve up to prepare her arm. "Heaven help us all if men were left to do childbirth. We'd all be dead." Anna watched as Sierra jabbed him with the last syringe and once he was free to do so, he shook out his arm as he hissed from the cold sensation. "Oh, stop."

"I should've made you go first. Now you're just gonna sit there and show me up on principle." He glared playfully over at her as he shivered at the feeling moving through him. It was unpleasant, to say the least, and he knew it was only the beginning of the tinkering the Consortium was going to be doing with him until he was pronounced CV-free.

Anna didn't let him get away, and in fact, she went and sat on his lap before he could move from the exam table. "You're supposed to hold my hand, right? This is close."

"Your ass is close to your hand? I would've gotten slapped a whole lot more in my life, if that were the case." He put his mostly-numbed arms around her waist to hold onto her as Sierra got her kit ready to retrieve some vials of Anna's blood before injecting her with the pre-treatments. "Do you two know of anybody else who got accepted from around here? Anyone else who's going?"

"Nobody I knew of." Gary interjected with a shrug, trying to keep his mouth shut about how much of a baby Logan had been about the shots. "We didn't even know you guys were accepted until we saw you in St. Louis, and I didn't hear from anybody else. Not around here, anyway. I've got a cousin who got accepted, but he's on the east coast, and after his info meeting, he started getting really ridiculously sick, so they're revoking his acceptance."

"Revoke? I didn't know they could do that." Anna hissed at the burning sensation as it tore through her arm, but she didn't growl and yell like Logan did, though he was right, it was mostly just to show him up. By the time she was done with her pre-treatment, she was wondering if they should have been a little more curious about the Consortium and the Initiative. The injections felt like torture for someone's sick, twisted amusement. She didn't miss that Sierra enjoyed it a little bit herself, so she looked at Gary as she waited for her arm to go back to normal after turning into an icicle with the last shot. "You have a little bit of a sadist on your hands, I hope you know."

"Oh, you have no idea." Gary said out of instinct before apparently Sierra had a chance to glare at him, and he cleared his throat. "I mean, no. Not at all. She's sweet." He didn't move from where he was standing against the wall, but they could all see a slight flush run behind the stubble on his cheeks.

Logan just laughed, and gave Sierra a look of almost admiration, since he hadn't known she had it in her. "You two have fun with that."

"I am sweet, thank you very much." Sierra replied defensively as she scurried about, picking up after seeing to both Anna and Logan. She did look over at Gary again, though, with a pinched expression. "I've never gotten any complaints about being unpleasant."

"Nope. Never will." Gary answered quickly, clearly back on-script after his earlier slip.

Logan finally felt vaguely back to normal again, though he still felt a little off and his tongue was still mostly numb. "Anything else the Initiative needs from us for now before we head up?"

"No, I don't think so." Sierra finished cleaning up and finally convinced herself to look back at Anna and Logan again. "You should be all set now. The pre-treatments are pregnancy-safe, if you are expecting. I'll miss seeing you both around, especially if you do have a baby joining you soon. I was hoping to get the chance to deliver one on my own here soon."

"Sorry to disappoint you. I would say maybe the kid could hurry up, but since we're leaving in just a few days . . . I don't think they pop *quite* that fast." Logan shrugged and took Anna's hand to head out of the clinic. "I'm sad you guys won't be coming up with us. Did they give you the option of taking a second wave or something, or was it just a one-time-only kind of offer?"

"They didn't say anything about another offer." Sierra looked over at Gary and he shook his head to support her. Neither of them looked like they regretted their decision. "You'll have to keep in touch, though. Let us know what it's like up there."

"Of course. Well, until we launch for Eleusis, anyway. We'll be a little out of range at that point, for at least a little while." Logan shrugged, since it didn't seem like that long to be gone, in the grand scheme of things. If they were going to have another fifty or sixty years to live, that was ages. Spending just one of those years on a spaceship headed across the galaxy didn't seem like that big a price to pay.

"Send us wedding pictures when you make it official. And say goodbye to your mother for us. I doubt we'll be back here before we head up." He took Sierra in a brief hug, and felt the first stab of pain at leaving that he knew was going to be repeated often in the days to follow. "Liam's wives will handle sending you two a wedding present from us, I'm sure." That was a different kind of pain, realizing that he was leaving the estate in the hands of Liam and his wives. He had to trust them. That was all he could do. He just had to keep telling himself that.

Sierra gave him another brief hug before she looked up into Logan's grey eyes. "Be careful, okay? I hate to sound like I don't trust people up there, but I don't."

"Neither do we, believe me." He admitted quietly, since it still weighed on his mind, just not heavily enough to stop him from wanting to go.

Anna looked over at Gary as Logan said goodbye to Sierra. Logan had known her longer than Anna had, since Logan lived closer to the Webers than she did. "You better take care of your kinky girlfriend. She's gonna be taking care of people that matter to me too."

"I'll do my best. She takes a lot of looking after." He winked at Anna, and lowered his voice as Logan said his goodbyes to Sierra. "Honestly, I got the dream gig. Little bit sadist but also proficient in first aid. I get both sides in one."

Anna just raised an eyebrow. "And you're okay with that? You like that? I mean, she is pretty, but . . ."

"She is. And I am. I don't mind it. I've put up with a whole lot worse for much worse reasons." He shrugged off the question, still smiling, and clearly wasn't about to offer any more of an explanation of what he meant by that. "Your boy's got some of it to him too. I've played online with him enough times to know it when I see it. I don't know if he'd ever go Sierra's direction with it, but he's got it in him."

Anna actually chuckled at that and shook her head as she looked back at Logan. "You're crazy. He's never once shown me any indication that he wants to turn all bossy on me. I'm not really into that sort of thing anyway. I doubt I could do what I was told all the time."

"Yeah, I know the type, and you don't seem like it." Gary just laughed to himself, and nodded up at the sky, where there were three different stations currently in view, in their perfect line of orbit across the sky, chasing the sun. "Be careful up there. On Eleusis too. Plant a tree for us or something if you get there. The rest of us are gonna be a while."

"Not too much longer after we get there, I hope." She glanced over at Logan and nodded toward the doorway. "You ready, Mr. Bickford? We should probably head home."

"I am, Mrs. Bickford." He took her hand in spite of the rolling eyes from both Gary and Sierra, and headed for his truck with a last look around the place. It was a clinic, so he didn't exactly have fond memories of the place, especially since the last time he'd been there, he had carried Anna into it bleeding to death, but it was still a part of home. A part of Earth that he was no longer going to see, possibly ever again.

"I can't imagine what places like this must look like in orbit." He thought out loud as they got back into the truck. "Just walk into a room, press a button and some machine scans your whole body and fixes whatever's wrong with you before you can blink, I'd guess."

"Yeah, that's weird just thinking about." Once they were back in the truck and heading home, she went back to holding his hand. "We're making the right choice, aren't we?"

He nodded, but there was a deeply thoughtful look in his eyes, as he watched the road ahead of them, empty as always, with not just home at the other end of it, but the rest of the universe that they were about to go explore.

"I still think we are. I get their point, and I get it if anyone doesn't want to go. It seems like every time we learn anything about that place, we're learning more and more about all the risks that go along with going, and we already know all the benefits. I just . . ." he shook his head, and looked over at her with a sheepish, subdued smile on his face.

"Every time I think about not going, my mom's poetry starts playing on repeat in my brain. Some of the ones she wrote right before she died. She's got a line in one of them that says she trusted God to build a better world, hoping He eventually would forgive humanity for whatever we did to deserve this one. If we do get to Eleusis and make it livable for the rest of humanity, I doubt I'm gonna give God the credit for our hard work, but my mom isn't the only one who's ever believed in that kind of dream. If there's a chance of making that happen, it's a chance worth taking."

Anna nodded slowly. "I don't want to die in fifteen to twenty years because I was born on a world that wants me dead. I don't want any of my family to die for it either. That's reason enough for me. And spending fifty years with you sounds good to me."

Logan's smile broadened at her comment and he moved over to her side of the cab for a change, since the truck was set and the road was open and clear in every direction. He leaned in and placed a kiss on her collarbone, moving down over the slope of her breast as he pushed her back against the seat. "I like you selfish, have I mentioned that?"

Anna moaned softly as soon as his kisses connected with her collarbone and skimmed her breast, since she liked him selfish too. She dug her hands into his hair and held him close, silently begging for more attention from his lips. "I still feel like I'm living in a dream."

That made him chuckle against her skin, but his kisses continued their slow torture. "I've actually tried to think about what we'd fight about. I mean, yeah, I'm sure the Initiative is gonna be crazy and things are gonna get stressful, but I don't know. I guess nobody knows what they're gonna fight with their wife about at the time they get married. I'm just having trouble picturing what that would look like."

"I'd rather not think about it, mostly because I think when we do fight, it will probably get ugly. We're both pretty damn stubborn." She continued to run her fingers through his hair as his voice tickled along her skin, but it was difficult to think about them ever fighting over anything. "You don't really think that they'll force you onto someone else for genetic reasons, do you? I mean, that sounds a bit extreme up front. I don't see a purpose in that. Even if they do, it's easy enough for you and I to go off somewhere, I'll do some exotic dancing for you and they can take your swimmers in a cup. Right?"

"I figured that's how they would do it. They're not even allowed to reproduce up there until they get some kind of license. I heard that from a friend online a couple of years ago. So I doubt they're interested in anything as dirty or chancy as just spinning a genetic roulette wheel." He laughed against her breast and worked his way back up to her neck with slow, attentive kisses. "Most of their people are also supposed to be genetically altered some kind of way. Can't control your population that tightly if you just let people fuck the way God intended and let the chromosomes fall where they may."

"Too bad for them." She squirmed underneath him as

she shivered from all of his intense attention. He was teasing her in the worst way. "They're missing out on all the fun. I can't imagine living life so sterile. I mean, you and I fucked in a barn, for crying out loud. Talk about some repressed human beings."

"Hey, the barn's been a fantasy of mine since I was about twelve. Gotta check these things off while our feet are still down here on the ground." He loved her squirming, just because he loved to know the kind of effect he was capable of having on her at all times. He hoped it never went away, that they never lost the kind of easy intimacy they could share in the moments between other events in life. He knew better than to think it would always be easy to maintain, but that didn't stop him from wanting it. "Only one left on my list for the time being is the old trail we used to use when we were kids, back behind the old Williams estate."

"Mmm." She replied in agreement before she grabbed his face and hauled his lips to hers. "Once we get home, we'll have to go make sure that's checked off too. We only have a few more days and I don't think it'll hurt to give Liam and his ladies a little more space. He's learning how to work it out. Though I'm honestly surprised that he hasn't already asked for a break. Sex with three women in the newlywed stage? Yikes."

"Yeah, well, without going too far into detail, he's my twin brother." He leaned back a little and looked down at his already-erect cock meaningfully with a wicked grin and a shrug. "What do you expect?"

Anna rolled her eyes at first, but then she reached down to tease him with slow sweeps of her hand over his pants. "You sure have a lot of confidence in your cock, Logan Bickford."

"No more than you have in . . ." he looked her over, clearly having some difficulty settling on just one part of her. "Well, everything."

"Here's to confidence, babe." She smirked before she silenced any further conversation with her lips against his, since she really enjoyed the fact they could travel and enjoy each other all at the same time.

18

Rachel saw Logan's truck in the driveway in front of the house, but she didn't know when Logan and Anna had returned. All she knew was that the truck was back and they were not. Or they were elsewhere. It didn't really matter, though. She was sitting at a desk in the room that she had claimed was hers, even though it was technically hers and Liam's, though he wouldn't always be sharing it with her. Strange to think about, but she didn't find it to be a terrible thing. It would be more beneficial when they were really running things around the farm and when children showed up.

She looked back when she heard the door open and smiled when Liam walked through. Tonight was her second night in the two day allotment that the women had agreed upon, since it would mean that they would only have to wait five days before they would be able to sleep next to Liam. Two days with each woman, one day to himself. He did have his own room, and Rachel figured he would want to use it after a while.

None of the three of them wanted to break up the time by weeks, since it would mean that they would have to wait much, much longer to be with Liam, and since they were all trying to get pregnant, that wouldn't really make much sense either. "Did you see Logan? His truck is out there."

"Yeah, he and Anna decided to go out and commune with nature for a while." Liam shrugged it off as he shut the door. "I probably would too, if I wasn't gonna be setting foot on this rock for possibly the rest of my life."

He took off a pair of gloves he was wearing and a shirt that had obviously seen better days. She could tell from just the sight of him that he had been off working on the harvesters, making some adjustments that he and Logan had decided on after reviewing their performance during the harvest itself. He wasn't dirty, exactly, but he'd obviously been working hard, and there was a sheen of sweat that remained on him after he got his shirt off and tossed in the laundry basket. She heard water start running from the sink once he stepped into the bathroom to wash his hands and get the worst of it off his face. "Are you still going over accounts? What are you working on?"

"Just finished up. All of the account info that Bri told me about finally came through." Brianne had a certain amount of money on her own, and she had transferred all of it to the Bickford Estate, even though the estate didn't need it. Rachel had turned all of hers back toward her family, and Margo didn't really have much to begin with, but it didn't matter.

"Also, I transferred the money you told me to give to the Prince farm as a donation. I haven't heard from Ben, but I assume we will. I don't know if he'll be happy even though you called it 'Larissa's dowry'. Especially because nothing has been made official." She shook her head as she got up from the desk to stand in the doorway of the bathroom while he cleaned up. "There's something else I wanted to show you."

"They're gonna need to hire a caretaker for Joseph pretty soon. Ben knows that. He can get mad if he wants, as long as their dad gets taken care of." He shrugged off the possibility of Ben getting angry, even though the guy was one of his closest friends. It wouldn't be the first time Ben was angry at him, and Liam was sure it wouldn't be the last. He grabbed a hand-towel from nearby to dry as he turned to face her. "Show me what?"

"It doesn't really matter now, but I just wanted you to know." She held out an envelope, and when he opened it, he could see that it was on Consortium letterhead.

The realization hit him, colder than the water he was washing up with.

They had tried to recruit her.

"After I graduated and my test scores were so high, they sent someone to talk to me and my parents." Rachel was younger than Margo or Bri, Bri a year older than Liam, and Margo was his age. Rachel was close to two years younger than Liam, but obviously a lot smarter than she'd ever really let on. "But this is the first time they offered me a job. With quite a salary."

Liam's eyes went wide as he looked over the letter, and all the zeroes on the offer they had made to her. He looked back up at her with his mouth still hanging open. "Holy shit, they want . . ." he looked her up and down as he cut himself off, "I mean, I always knew you were brilliant, but this is some ridiculously high-powered shit they want you working on. In fact, I'm pretty sure I have no idea what I just read."

Rachel laughed weakly. "I've always been good with math." She cleared her throat afterward, since that was oversimplifying things greatly. "My parents didn't come to our wedding because they didn't want me to marry you. They certainly didn't want me to be in a polygamous marriage." She had originally lied and told him that her parents just couldn't make the travel happen, but she didn't apologize for the lie.

"They had a very specific plan for me that included having me apply for Eleusis and marrying someone of their choosing. When the Consortium visited, they basically guaranteed me a spot. But I got out here and I met you and things changed for me. I never applied for Eleusis, which is probably why the Consortium contacted me. I already replied and declined the offer and informed them that I am now married and I'm going to stay here on Earth with you."

There weren't many similarities between Liam and Logan when it came to anything but their physical appearance, but there were some mannerisms that people who spent a lot of time around them both eventually picked up that they did, in fact, share. The face they made when they were pondering something and the fact that they both had a tendency to step back for a second to let things process was one such commonality, and Rachel could see the gears turning behind Liam's eyes as he handed her back the letter.

"If they had some kind of master plan in mind for you, I can see why they'd be pissed." He thought for a while longer about it, then slowly moved to join her in the doorway to the bathroom, so that she was leaning back against the door frame with him up against her. "If going to Eleusis is what you wanted, I would've applied with you. I had no idea you were mixed up with them to begin with."

"It wasn't what I wanted." She reached up to run her hand along the side of his face. "And don't say things like that. You love Bri and Margo too, and I don't think you would have wanted to take the risk of leaving them behind." Rachel pulled him into a soft kiss.

"You should know something else." She said against his lips, but her posture revealed that she didn't want to tell him. "My parents not only wanted me to apply for Eleusis, but before I did that, they wanted me to come out here and meet Logan. The Bickford name is pretty famous in the central districts, you know. So is your money." She looked up into his eyes and sighed, but she hoped that he trusted her by now, especially because she had never once cared about his money and if he looked everything over that she had ever touched, he would see that she hadn't done anything in secret or done anything to hurt him. "They wanted me to go after Logan for your wealth."

That actually made Liam laugh, and he leaned down to kiss her roughly, his hands gripping her sides to press her spine back against the frame of the door with the bulk of him pressed against her. From the first time he'd been with her, he'd been thoroughly entertained by how small she was and how easy she was to throw around when the mood struck him, and the way he was with her showed his fascination. "If you had actually wanted me for my money, you would've asked for a bigger rock."

He turned his face to kiss her left hand where it rested against his face, and the modest ring it bore. "Why do your parents care about Bickford money? Have they got some kind of problems for themselves, or did they just want to try and make you a gold-digger for kicks?"

Rachel wasn't about to reveal too much about her parents, not because she didn't trust Liam, but because she didn't want him to get mixed up in anything that could cause trouble. "They don't have problems, they are just always looking for ways to get access to wealth." She shrugged but she was grateful that he didn't doubt her feelings even for a moment. "I'm so relieved that you believe me. I was afraid if I told you what brought me here that you would throw me out and never want to see me again."

Liam just gave her a sarcastic look and shook his head. "You think I'm new to the idea that parents want to throw their daughters at me for my bank account? Please. That's the whole reason Margo got here in the first place. Just so happened she also happened to really care. I'm not surprised your parents would set you up like that. So long as you're here because you want to be. Honestly, out of the three of you, you're the one who surprised me most when it comes to being willing to jump into this crazy three-way we've got set up here."

"Not a three-way, Liam. I am not sleeping with Bri or Margo." She clarified quickly, since apparently Bri had also made an off-the-cuff suggestion about some such idea and Rachel was *not* interested. "But why did *I* surprise you? I was the one who said 'I love you' before you did."

He grinned at her clarification on the three-way, and just shook his head. "I know that. I just . . . you always surprise me, that's all." He poked at the paper she was still holding in one hand. "You could be anywhere in the world, in the solar system or the galaxy, obviously, if you wanted. Do anything you set that brain of yours to doing. I'm sorry, but it's gonna be a while before I really manage to take it in that you've decided to stay out here with a hick from the midwest district helping run a farm."

"You're right. I could be anywhere I wanted, and I'm exactly where I want to be." Rachel tossed the piece of paper to the ground, since clearly the offer meant nothing to her, and kissed him again to prove her feelings. When the kiss ended, she pressed her forehead to his.

"I've never really felt comfortable enough with Logan to really speak my mind, but are you sure that he and Anna are absolutely set on going?" There was something in her voice that betrayed more than just open curiosity behind her question, but it was hard for Liam to pinpoint what it was.

"They seem to be." Any trace of a smile left his face at that admission and he leaned back against the other side of the door frame, holding her hand between them as he slouched to be closer to her height. "They've been packing stuff up, saying goodbye to things, getting all quiet, so yeah, I think they're really going. I don't think I've completely got my own head around it yet, even if we've known for a while. Why do you ask?"

"It just seems really dangerous." Rachel said softly, but she wasn't looking directly at Liam when she spoke. "I know my parents wanted me to go but . . ." She shook her head. "I don't think people really realize that the Eleusis Initiative is about preparing people to go to a new, unpopulated planet. That means stretching people past their limits to see if they're capable of adapting to change. It's not going to be easy for anyone who gets involved, and I don't want Anna or Logan to get hurt." When she finally met his eyes, he could see in her brown eyes that there was more behind what she was saying. She was worried, but she hadn't explained clearly why.

"Neither do I. But what am I gonna do, try and tell him he can't go? Yeah, that would go over well." He didn't press her vagueness and actually laughed at the idea of telling Logan what to do about anything. He might as well try and tell the midwest not to have tornadoes anymore. It would listen just as well as Logan ever would, even though both the Prince and Bickford families had spoken their concerns.

"They sound like they've thought it through, I just wish that they had made a different decision." Rachel pulled Liam into another kiss, her lips searing his as her tongue teased along his bottom lip. "I'm glad that you're not going, though. I want you here with me."

"Good thing that's where I'm gonna be, then. I like it when you get your way." He grinned under the kiss, but held her loosely as he looked back into her eyes.

"I know there's more you're not telling me." He eventually said quietly. She'd heard Liam angry before, and heard him suspicious, and his tone was neither, just confirming a thought. "Which is fine. I know you don't talk much about home, and I respect that. I'm glad you told me about the Initiative thing and the Consortium offer. So long as you're here and none of the things you don't talk about are gonna slide in and try to take you back, I can live with secrets."

Sometimes Rachel had moments where she realized that Liam was more clever than she gave him credit for, or he knew her better than she realized, and she immediately felt guilty and surprised at the same time. She never thought that he was dumb, but she did think that he didn't often pay close enough attention to notice things. "Nothing is going to take me away from you." She promised and then she searched his eyes again, grey, like Logan's. "I don't give you enough credit for being able to read me like you do."

That comment made him grin. "Nobody does. It's what

makes me special." He kissed her again once she'd given him that promise and pulled her in to stand between his legs as he slouched to be closer to her height. "I love you, Rach. I'm glad you chose here instead of there. And maybe one of these days, if Logan and Anna pull it off, we'll go along and see what the other side of the galaxy looks like. For the time being, I really, really like you here. And I'm gonna make it my personal mission in life to make sure you never regret deciding to stay."

Rachel slipped her small hands underneath his shirt and ran her fingers along his skin as soon as he pulled her in against his body. She enjoyed feeling every ridge of muscle along his chest, and a shiver of pleasure ran down her spine. "I love you too, 'hick from the midwest'." She replied with a wry grin, repeating what he had called himself before she kissed him intensely, full of need. "I'll tell you everything someday. Right now, it's too risky to talk about my parents in depth. But someday. I promise that too."

"Too risky, huh?" The look in his eyes was teasing, but he didn't disbelieve her. He reached up between them and began unbuttoning the loose blouse she was wearing without taking his eyes off hers. "So what you're saying is that I married a dangerous woman? Is that what you're telling me right now?"

Rachel laughed, but as soon as he pushed her shirt off of her shoulders, she wasn't really laughing. It was hard to tell if she was distracted by his determination to strip her or the fact that he was inquiring about secrets she wasn't ready to tell. "Maybe. Does that turn you on?"

"A little bit, have to be honest." He ran his hands down her bare arms and then along the band of her jeans, unbuttoning and unzipping them in turn. "So there's somebody out there, somewhere, who really doesn't want me doing this to you?" Once he had her jeans undone, he left them where they rested on her hips and slid his hand down over the panties she was wearing to tease her expertly, his hand beckoning her against him with every slow motion.

His lips found their way down her exposed skin. "Is that what you're saying?"

"Mhm." She nodded slowly, her eyes already partially closed by his touch, since he really was quite talented with his fingers and his lips. He wouldn't have ensnared three women who would be willing to share him if he wasn't good at pleasing them. "My parents definitely don't want you to do this to me. Their response to our wedding invitation was to tell me to come home."

That made him laugh, though it was just a short burst before he started kissing down over bared shoulder, still working her against him with every brush of his lips. His fingertips grazed along her breasts. "That would've been a shame. What do you think they'll do when we eventually tell them they're gonna be grandparents?"

"I hope they'll be happy by then, but also considering that I hope we get pregnant *soon,* they might not be happy." She squirmed underneath his attention, but clearly she was enjoying it. "We're going to make such beautiful babies."

"Damn right we are." His free hand snaked around to her back to unclasp the bra she was wearing, but his touch on her was slow, unhurried, as Liam had been for most of the time she'd known him. In every respect, he seemed like the kind of man who would be concerned with getting to the point as quickly as possible when it came to sex. He certainly teased enough, and there were times with him when that was true and he was greedy about it.

But most of the time, in contrast to every other man his wives had been with and most other men on the planet, Liam seemed in absolutely no rush about enjoying intimacy. When they'd first gotten together, he had spent hours turning every inch of her into a satisfied and relaxed puddle, almost entirely without any payoff on his own end. His priorities hadn't changed in the meantime. His main focus was on pleasing her, and, to hear Brianne tell it loudly and often, pleasing all of them. "If they're half as beautiful as their mother, they'll be some truly gorgeous specimens."

Rachel was a fairly straightforward woman when it came to intimacy, though they had explored each other in plenty of ways that their sex life would never be considered vanilla. She grabbed his hand and tugged him back toward their bed, since she didn't want him to have to slouch in the bathroom doorway. "You have always been the most charming, smooth-talking man I've ever met." She helped him out of the remainder of his clothes before they actually got onto the bed. Rachel mauled his lips like a sex-starved teenager before she said anything else. "Do you remember the first thing you said to me, when I showed up at that bonfire looking for Logan?"

He had to think back, since he certainly remembered seeing her for the first time, but what he'd actually said to her he was having a hard time bringing to mind. "Something about hoping you don't find him, since he's better looking, I think. And I told you to come back if you didn't find him because I was more fun anyway."

Rachel crawled on top of him on the bed and sat down on his abs, which were deliciously well-defined. There were definite perks to being with a hard-working 'hick'. She tossed her dark, glossy hair back over her shoulder as she sat there and looked down at him. "I didn't ever go looking for him. I sat by the fire and watched you instead."

"Stalker." He poked her side and pulled one of his pillows behind his head to get comfortable before he started running his hands over her legs and hips while they spoke. It was fairly dim, since the room had curtains that blocked most of the sunlight coming through and there had been no reason to turn any lights on, but Liam knew every part of her by touch.

"Can't imagine why I didn't see you." He pinched her leg teasingly, her skin dark enough that she came close to disappearing in the dim light of the room, as he imagined she must have that night by the bonfire. "I vaguely remember getting more drunk than I probably should have that night. There was a lot going on. Obviously you didn't see anything that was a deal-breaker."

"You were with Margo for a while, but I didn't know she was your girlfriend then, since she left and you didn't go with her." Margo was a difficult woman to handle sometimes, so she certainly wasn't saying it as an accusation of any sort. Rachel was still smiling at him as his hands roamed along her bare body. "You got really drunk, actually." She laughed and leaned in so her lips were dangerously close to his.

"And you run your mouth when you're drunk. You said all sorts of dirty things to me when you saw me again, and no one had ever talked to me that way. Not to my face, anyway. When you kissed me, it was all over. I couldn't stop thinking about what you said your tongue could do to me."

The look on his face was scandalized. "When I woke up that next morning, you told me nothing happened." He smacked her ass when his hands got back around to it, and kissed her roughly as he laughed. "You fucking liar. I woke up on my own patio and couldn't remember how I got there. You were sitting there curled up against me with that skirt you wore hiked up just about to your ass, and then you told me nothing happened. Bonfire's all burnt out on the other side of the front yard and there were bodies all over the place sleeping it off." He chuckled at the memory, since he had felt incredibly awkward about it at the time, but after the fight he and Margo had, he didn't feel guilty about it.

"Of course I said nothing happened." She laughed after she squealed at his smack to her backside. "I'd only just met you. And you were so drunk, I didn't want you to feel like you owed me something if you knew the truth about our heavy makeout session. I just wanted to get to know you better first." Rachel kissed him roughly in response to his kiss. "And out of all that, you remember my skirt?"

"Hey, I have a very selective memory, and ten times out of ten, I am going to remember a skirt that shows off your ass the way that one did." His hands moved over her back to press her against him in their kisses, but he pulled back after a second. "Okay, I vaguely remember now saying something like I couldn't fuck you because I'd end up breaking you in half. I'd like to formally apologize for ever underestimating you in that respect."

"I'm glad some pieces are coming back to you now." She laughed again and wiggled herself against him, since he was clearly as turned on as she was. "You really do have such a foul mouth, Liam Bickford. And I love it."

"Lucky for you, the rest of me is just as foul." He groaned as she moved against him, and his hands went back to her hips to encourage her to take him however she wanted him. So long as he had her and she enjoyed him, he didn't care what their lovemaking consisted of, vanilla or otherwise.

"Few days later when I had you to myself the first time . . . or the first time I really remember, anyway . . ." he said in halting breaths, kissing her between as she began to rock her core against him, wet and needy for him, "we should go back to that spot in the basement sometime, just for old time's sake. See if the fucking acoustics are still fucking amazing now that I know the right ways to really make you scream."

"Mmmmm. Let's do that." Rachel didn't want to tease him any longer than she wanted to be teased, and she definitely wasn't quiet as soon as she had him inside of her. She may not have his dirty mouth, but she had a noisy one. Rachel knew if Liam really wanted to know her secrets, she wouldn't be able to keep them from him, and she didn't want to. Everything, really, was just a matter of time.

* * * * *

"Here, pull this one over this way. Yeah, like that." Cory grinned as he worked in tandem with Larissa, who was sitting on his lap at the moment between him and the worktable that was occupied with their project. The fabric they were using was so strange it had taken some getting used to before they could get it to do what they had wanted, but the piece they'd conceived of together looked like it was finally finished.

"And there we go. I think that'll pretty much do it." He sat back in the chair and returned his hands to Larissa's waist to hold onto her as he looked over the fruit of their efforts. "Not his usual style, but he's not exactly gonna be working on tractors up there. I'm sure he'll like it."

"You are a man of many talents, Cory Prince." Larissa replied with a smile as she looked back at him briefly before she focused on their project again. It was a very unique coat, but she hoped Logan would like it, even though she didn't want to give it to him. Giving him the coat would mean saying goodbye.

"I can't believe they're really going to go." Her tone was soft, mostly because she didn't want to cry. Larissa had spent a lot of time with Cory recently but she was still trying to impress him, and turning into a sobbing mess wouldn't be impressive. Or, at least, not the right kind.

Cory wrapped an arm around Larissa's waist to hold her back against him, just to let her know he was there as they both dealt with the implications of their oldest sibling leaving. They started on the coat as a means of working on something together, but also as a way of dealing with the fact that they were being abandoned. Now that it was finished, the impending departure had to be thought of again. "I'm still gonna talk to Anna. I don't think it'll do much good, and she may even tell me where I can shove it, but I'm still gonna talk to her."

Larissa turned sideways on his lap so she could look him in the eye, and she looked into his eyes for a while before she brushed her lips against his. It said a lot that Cory was willing to go toe-to-toe with his sister. Cory didn't usually go looking for confrontation and normally no one wanted to go toe to toe with Anna when she set her mind to something. "I just hate knowing we might never see them again. Logan won't be here to walk me down the aisle if you . . . if we . . ."

Cory nodded against her forehead as he held her. One of the stranger things for him to get accustomed to as he got to know Larissa better was the way she viewed her brothers. There wasn't too much of an age gap between the two of them, but her brothers were almost five full years older. Most of the time it seemed like she viewed Logan as more of a father than an older brother, and Liam was the corresponding annoying uncle.

"We'll see them again. Even if it means running halfway across the galaxy to chase them down. And if they do leave, and they manage to pull it off, make it to Eleusis, then maybe Logan won't be here to walk you down the aisle. But it might give us the chance to live long enough to dance with our own kids at their weddings." He shook his head and kissed her again gently. "Still doesn't make me want them to go."

Despite the conversation about Logan and Anna, Larissa couldn't help but smile as Cory mentioned the idea of children without even batting an eye. She kissed him eagerly, her tongue teasing a few times along his lower lip. She didn't have a lot of experience with men, but she certainly liked kissing Cory and she was learning quickly. "I'm glad you see that in the future. Us. I enjoy being with you."

"You do, huh? I think I'm comfortable with that." Cory grinned up at her under her eager lips, and pulled her into another one as her cheeks began turning red. Love wasn't a stage they had gotten around to yet, with everything else going on, but Cory was certainly getting there. "I enjoy being with you too, Larissa. Most of the time I still feel like there's something I'm missing or something I'm not catching when it comes to what you need, but I like learning."

"You're not missing anything." She stole another kiss between speaking. "I don't want you to feel that way. I'm just shy. Especially when I'm with someone who I want to think the best of me."

"I do think the best of you." He reassured her with a caress along her cheek and a teasing grin. "You're probably the single most ticklish person I've ever met in my entire life, so I still have to work on not setting you off nineteen times a day, but that's funny, not a flaw. I'm starting to believe you don't actually have any of those."

"I definitely have flaws." Larissa tensed up slightly at just the thought of being tickled, but she tried not to be obvious about it. Thinking of flaws had her comparing herself to whoever she thought Cory might want, and the girl he'd waited for before her came to mind. She knew about the girl because Anna warned her about Cory's past interests. "Why didn't you apply to Eleusis?" She asked abruptly, but she wondered for a while now and just never asked.

It was Cory's turn to tense up at the question, and his smile faded as he shrugged, as he tried to look casual again. "I did. I was rejected just a few weeks after the application deadline. They didn't even wait until they sent out the rest of the determinations. Something about them finding anomalies in my genetic code that gave them concern, blah blah blah. I went to Doc Weber and she did a full workup on me afterward, said she didn't find anything they could've been talking about. So I don't know."

"Oh." Larissa replied softly, since she assumed he hadn't applied. She felt bad the truth was he had applied and was rejected. "Why don't you want Anna to go if you wanted to go?"

Cory actually blushed at that question, but he held onto her a little tighter as he considered how to respond to that. "I um, didn't really want to go to Eleusis when I applied. I only applied because a girl I knew applied and I thought I'd have better chances with her if I was accepted and went." He shook his head.

"It was the wrong reason to apply and it would've been the wrong reason to go. I'm fully aware of how stupid I was being. Especially because it was a pretty classic example of a girl really and truly not being that into me. But that's a long story. Anyway, I don't want Anna to go for the same reasons I thought it was stupid of me to apply in the first place. It's dangerous, there are no guarantees, it's too far from family, and overall . . . I just . . . I don't trust it. Any of it. Maybe I've been hanging out with Ben too long, but there's some places I've read online that people don't even believe Eleusis even exists. That this whole Initiative is just a cover for something else. They make some pretty compelling arguments, even if I'm not a hundred percent convinced either way. No matter what the truth is, it's shady enough that I don't want to be a part of it, and I sure as fuck don't want anyone I care about to be involved."

"Anna told me about the girl. But I didn't know you cared about her so much that you wanted to go." She cleared her throat in nervousness and Larissa wondered if she was just a choice of convenience. Would it be bad if she was? Convenience wasn't the worst reason to start a relationship. Larissa nodded after she considered his explanation about not wanting Anna and Logan to go, though, and she attempted to ignore her self-doubt. "I agree. I think it's too dangerous. But I also don't think that Logan will let anything happen to Anna. Even if you can't change their minds."

As much as he had a hard time getting to really know Larissa, there were some things he knew for certain. When she looked away to talk about his former acquaintance, he reached up to gently pull her face back to look at him. "It would have been a mistake. Because I never would have gotten to know you. If it was you who was running off to the other side of the universe, I would go with you. I'd try and talk you out of it first, probably, but I would go with you. And if I had been really pumped to go to Eleusis for some reason, I would stay here for you, if that was what you wanted. She pretty well showed whatever regard she might once have had for me when she decided to leave without me, and I've hardly even thought about her since the day they got their acceptance. I'm not looking up and wishing I was there. I'm looking at you, and grateful I'm here."

Larissa blushed but she didn't look away, since she felt like her chest was going to explode with happiness and reassurance. It was rare for a woman on Earth to find someone who would say such things, especially without a pregnancy first. Larissa pressed her hands to his cheeks before she pressed her lips warmly to his and turned completely into him with her legs winding around him and the back of the chair. Her fingers slipped into his hair as she kissed him, but when it broke, she was back to looking into his eyes again.

"I'm glad, Cory." She replied between quick breaths from the intensity of the kiss. "I would do all of that for you too. I care about you. I wish I had gotten to know you sooner." Larissa had never felt this way about anyone in her entire life, and it was the most amazing feeling. It felt like nothing in the world could be wrong as long as Cory wanted to be with her. It was incredibly fast, but everything about life on Earth was fast.

Those who took their time were taken by time.

His hands caught on the hem of her blouse as he moved them to hold her tightly against his body, and it made his heart skip a little as he kissed her again. Was she going to think he was just sweet-talking her to get something from her because it felt like he was trying to do something to her shirt? He hoped not, but he had no idea. They just hadn't been with each other long enough for him to know what she would think when certain things happened or when they didn't.

He also had to move a little to adjust himself after the way she kissed him, but with her in his lap, it would be impossible for her not to know why he was moving her around a little to get himself comfortable. Would she think that meant he had just a one-track mind? There were a lot of things in the world he had little idea about, and he was learning that most of them had to do with Larissa.

"I'm glad I get to know you now. But I'm with *you*. The last couple years I've spent a lot of time on people that weren't worth the expense. I wish I'd been spending them with you." He shrugged slightly, his usual grin starting to return. "Although this way, I'm past the whole acne-ruining-my-life phase, so you get a much better-looking me than I was a few years ago."

"I've always thought you were good looking." Larissa assured him as she kissed along his neck and put one of his hands back where it had brushed along her side, but underneath her shirt so he would know she was okay with it. He could touch her anywhere. "A few years ago I didn't look like this either. Thank goodness for puberty and maturity."

He let out a low moan he was immediately self-conscious about, but then he kissed her again and traced a caress along the skin beneath her shirt as his eyes looked obviously down into the cut of her neckline. "Amen to that."

"Ahem." The two young lovers were interrupted a few moments later by Logan clearing his throat from the doorway, though when they frantically turned around to face him, he was smiling rather than scowling, leaning against the doorframe with Anna beside him and his arms crossed over his chest. "This looks cozy. Did you text me to come out here with the intention of getting walked in on? Because that was poor planning."

"No! No." Larissa said quickly as Cory slid his hands back down to a safer area on her waist. She had forgotten all about texting Logan after she got all caught up with Cory telling her how much she meant to him. Her brain was all scrambled for a moment as she tried to remember why she had texted her brother. "I, um, we . . ." She looked around and saw the coat on the work-table. "Oh! We have a gift for you."

"A gift?" Logan wasn't entirely sure how to take that, since anything anyone gave him would be his for maybe the next few days, but it was Larissa. He wasn't going to say no.

Larissa got up off of Cory's lap slowly but then grabbed the coat off of the work-table and walked it up to her brother to present it to him. "You can take clothes with you, right? We made this for you. Cory and I, together."

Logan held up the coat with a surprised look at the two of them, and shook it out to get a good look at it. It was a great deal lighter than it had looked at first glance, but it was comfortable against his skin and certainly felt sturdy as he tossed it around. The coat would fall roughly to his knees when he had it on, a dark brown that was eminently practical when working on a farm but which he was sure would stand out like a sore thumb up in space. It had a multitude of pockets on it both inside and out, and when he shrugged it onto his shoulder the fit was perfect.

"How the hell did you two . . ." he looked up at Larissa with a smile. "Liam helped, didn't he?" It was the only way they could've gotten the size right without involving him directly.

"Maybe." She replied with a smirk. "Also, you live like a pig sometimes. You leave your clothes everywhere. Liam and you aren't exactly the same, after all. I won't say who is bigger-chested, because that'll just start a fight." Larissa smiled as she teased Logan. "Do you like it?"

"I do." He adjusted it around his collar and gave Larissa a grin. It was more formal-looking, somehow, than almost anything else she had ever seen him wear, but it suited him nonetheless. He didn't look like he was going to be crawling under any engines or changing any oil, but he did look like a man about to do business, and a man who meant what he was about. He pulled Larissa into a tight hug, closing his eyes against her hair. "Thanks, sis. It'll go across the universe with me."

Larissa held him in a death grip and buried her face into her brother's embrace. She mumbled into his shoulder just so she wouldn't tear up in front of him. "I don't want you to go."

Logan held onto her even tighter, but moments later let her go slowly, setting her feet back down on the floor. "Come on, Anna and I were talking about it on the way over here. You and me are doing omelettes for dinner tonight, like we used to do." He kept one arm around her shoulders as he let her go, with a look over at Cory. "If I can steal her away for a while, of course."

"Oh, yeah, sure, that's . . . yeah, that's fine." Cory nodded at Larissa, obviously uncomfortable at being deferred to by the older brother who had arranged the match between them.

Anna hung back so she could walk with Cory on her own, since she wanted time with her brother as much as Logan wanted time with his sister. "Looks like things are going really well." She teased with a knowing smirk as she jabbed her brother in the ribs with her elbow. "If we had taken any longer to show up, I'm wondering how far you would have gotten." Anna was relentless, mostly because she liked to see her siblings squirm.

Cory gave her a sideways glare as they made their way out of the house to meander around the estate. "We've gotten . . . a ways. We decided early on that we want to get to know each other before we get . . . . well, we kind of commented to each other on our first date that as soon as we start having sex, we're not likely to want to stop, so . . . yeah." He shrugged, but he was still smiling confidently. "Things are good. I finally talked to her about Holly today. That was easier than I thought it would be."

"Easier for you or her? Or both?" She asked curiously. "I know what Holly did to you was extremely hurtful, but I really did hope that being with Larissa would make you forget all about someone who didn't think twice about hurting you."

"I actually haven't thought about her lately. Ever since I started hanging out with Larissa. So your diabolical plan seems to be succeeding." He gave her a sheepish smile and turned up the driveway toward the street, since there was plenty of ground to cover even on the main portion of the Bickford estate. "I do, however, have a really, really angry letter that I wrote to her right after she told me she was going up to Eleusis with the other guy. So if you'd be willing to deliver that for me when you see her up there, I'd be grateful."

"I can definitely do that. In fact, it would make me happy to do that." Anna reached out to loop her arm through her brother's. "I'm sorry I won't be here to see you and Larissa make it official. But I'm sure you can send video to me. I'd love to see it any way I can."

Anna knew him well enough to tell just from the way he shoved his hands in his pockets that he was going to say something he wasn't completely comfortable saying. "Or you could just, you know, not . . . go." He wouldn't or couldn't look at her as he said so, but he eventually tore his eyes off the ground to look up at her. "You know. To Eleusis. Or up to the Initiative. You can still say no."

"Cor . . ." Anna said with a tone that was both sympathetic and stubborn at the same time. "I can't pass this up. This isn't only about me and Logan, but you too. Do you only want twenty more years with Larissa or fifty?"

"I want all the years I can get with Larissa. But I want all the years I can get with you too." He gave her a look that was just as stubborn. "I spent a lot of time talking Eleusis through with Holly. Mostly pretending to be excited to go if I ended up getting accepted, which I didn't. But if this first mission goes, with everybody who just got accepted, and it only takes them a year to get there? Then we're gonna find out that whatever crazy transportation system they've worked out actually does work, and then the whole planet is gonna lose its mind. Within a generation, this whole planet is going to be empty. People are gonna pour money and resources into getting to Eleusis like they're giving away free beer. The whole world. And we can all still be a part of that. Hell, knowing the Bickfords, they could probably buy their own ship to make the trip. My point is, I want Eleusis too. I want that kind of life, not to die when I'm only halfway to where we should be. But you don't have to risk your life for us all to get there someday."

"I think I do, and it's worth the risk. They told us our families get priority after we get to Eleusis. That's enough to convince me to go. Watching Mom die and now Dad . . . I don't want to watch anyone else die like that. I refuse. Logan and I are going to go, and we're going for ourselves as much as for anyone else. We want a long future together, and we want a future for our families too."

Cory didn't want to ask the question he was about to ask, and he kept his mouth shut for nearly another twenty paces. Eventually, he decided that asking the question was less terrible than not asking it. "So what if it's not true? What happens if you get up there and you find out that the whole thing is some hoax the Consortium's been pulling on the entire world for years? You'd be going up there for nothing. Both of you."

"So the risk of it not being true outweighs the reward if it is?" She clearly didn't agree with that sentiment and she shook her head. "It's real, Cory."

"You're betting your life on that." He could hear the condescension in his sister's tone, and he was used to it, since he was younger than she was, after all, but that didn't mean he tolerated it well. "You're betting Logan's life on that. Your life together. Your children's lives, if it turns out you are pregnant."

"And I'm condemning them if I stay. Condemning them to a short life and a long, painful death. A life where they don't have time to accomplish much, a life where the whole thing is a race to make babies as soon as you can. I'm sorry if you disagree with my methods to facilitate change, but this kind of life isn't okay, Cor." Anna stopped, grabbed her brother's hand and turned him toward her. "You've trusted me until now, right? Why can't you give me the benefit of the doubt?"

"There's a difference between giving you the benefit of the doubt and watching you run off the planet without telling you what I honestly think about it." Cory was getting mad as she got more confrontational, but he didn't back away. He was enough like Ben not to stand down once he was standing his ground on a subject.

"We love you, Anna. All of us. And you're asking us to watch you walk away with no guarantee that we're ever going to see you again. With no guarantees of anything. Just like that. You're stoned if you think we all believe in Eleusis as strongly as you do. For all we know, you're walking into a firing squad, and there's nothing we can do about it."

"I have to believe there is a better future out there for all of us, and I'm not going to run away from the risk that might be involved to get it, Cory." Her tone softened, but she was still as determined as ever. "I love you. I love you all. I'm grateful you're concerned, and I'd be stupid to think there's no possibility you're right. You could be. That's possible. But I have to try."

"You keep saying that. But you don't." Cory said quietly, obviously defeated, but still not convinced away from his standpoint. "You don't have to try. You're choosing to."

He was quiet long enough afterward to try and pull himself together to keep from crying. "I don't want to see another fireball coming down from orbit and have to know that you're inside it. That's what you're risking." He shook his head and turned to look along the path they'd walked down, unable to look straight at her. "I hope you're right about all of it. It's just hard to hope for that when there's more we don't know than we do."

"I know." She pulled him into a hug so she could hold onto her brother and try to convince him that everything would be alright even if she had no idea if it would be. "Someone had this same conversation with their sister back when the first space station went up into the sky. And now they are everywhere up there. Even if some other piece of a station comes crashing down into Earth, don't assume I'm on it. Because I can promise you, I find trouble before it finds me. I'll be back, Cory. I will be."

He met her eyes and nodded, unable to actually say he believed her, since he didn't. But she was his older sister. What she said was gospel, as far as he was concerned. "Dad got the numbers back from the marketplace earlier this morning. Our crop ended up higher than it's ever been, plus we didn't have to pay out any extra labor, so profit margin was off the charts. Dad and Ben were still gawking at it when I left."

"That's awesome. You're gonna need that for Dad. And Ben's new baby. Even your babies, when they come." Anna hugged him once more and urged him toward the house. "If Larissa is cooking, we don't want to miss it. Come on."

Cory followed, looking dejected, but he attempted to pull himself out of it and looked over at his sister with a hopeful expression. "You also realize you're gonna be eating, like, pre-packaged, flash-frozen, super-enriched, stupidly-processed space food for the next, like, at least five years, right? Maybe *that* could convince you to stay? No?"

"It's not *all* that way, but yes, I'm aware." Anna sighed loudly. "You're really not going to give up, are you? We made our decision, Cor. Please."

"Well, if you're not gonna stay for the food, then you must really mean it." He made another attempt at a smile as he walked beside her, but mostly he left his hands in his pockets, since he didn't really feel much of an appetite himself, even for Larissa's cooking.

"Don't be sad for me. Be happy. It's a big deal." She kissed his cheek and jabbed at his side playfully. "Or we can talk more about what I just saw in the barn if that would make you even more uncomfortable."

Cory rolled his eyes, but that mention did bring a smile back to his face. "Please. I walked in on you giving Jamie Martin head. You really wanna play the who-can-embarrass-who-more game with me? I see all."

"You see all?" Anna fought the heat creeping into her cheeks but she could only imagine what else he might have seen. Or heard about. Anyone else talking about her sexual exploits didn't matter, but her family . . . that was different. They undoubtedly knew her reputation as well.

"I've seen a lot." He looked over at her sheepishly, and a little apologetically. "You probably don't want the full list.

But if it's any consolation, most of the times I saw something, it wasn't you, it was Ben and Susan. They've always been around the house a lot more than you, and it's really not that big a house. You know how loud Susan gets sometimes."

"I've told Ben that like fifty times. He always tells me it's against the law to attempt to silence a satisfied woman." She shook her head, but she had to laugh a little. "Good luck with that."

"Anyway, my point is, you can hardly make me feel guilty for you walking in on second base when I've walked in on you blowing the outfielder." He grinned at her and opened the door to the house for her, which was not just a gentlemanly gesture, since it was a massive and heavy door and he struggled to get it open himself. "That, at least, shouldn't be a problem up in orbit, I'm guessing. You all are probably bolted down and soundproofed and all kinds of secured up there. Won't have to worry about anybody laughing at you from half a house away or waking up the neighbors across an open field."

"True. You're right, it will probably be a lot different. And at least you won't have to worry about defending my honor anymore, right? Not that I had much to begin with." She laughed as she they headed toward the kitchen where they could hear Larissa laughing. "I went a little crazy after Logan and Mel got serious."

"A little?" Cory said immediately, then shook his head and put his hands up. "Not judging. No right to judge. I just hope I never go your kind of crazy. It was hard to watch there for a while."

"Okay, it wasn't *that* bad." She only got blackout drunk a couple of times and tried a couple of drugs, but mostly it was a ton of sex. Lots and lots of sex. "I don't think you would experiment with your own sex just because you were so angry with the opposite sex that you felt it was worth a try. You seem pretty straight to me."

He shook his head. "Yeah, that's not likely. I had a

couple guys from farther up north come onto me at our last school gathering. I kissed one of them, found out very quickly that it's just not my thing."

"You did not!!" She laughed and stared at him incredulously. "You still haven't hooked up with Larissa but you kissed another guy? You are full of surprises."

Cory just shrugged. "Wasn't like I was gonna get a whole lot of other opportunities to experiment with things. Figured I might as well see if I was into it while I had the opportunity. Definitely not into it." They could see the kitchen at the other end of the long hall they walked down, massive and well-stocked, since it was the main one in use at the moment. He smiled as soon as he saw Larissa in the distance, and nodded toward her. "That, I'm *very* into."

"The Bickfords are some very beautiful people, aren't they?" Anna smiled and pushed her brother ahead of her. "Go on, I'm right behind you."

Logan was sitting at the table as they came in, leaning back and watching his sister work while throwing barbs at her from time to time about her methods, but when Cory came in, the joking stopped. Logan watched for a moment as Cory fell in with Larissa easily, not asking if he could help or even where anything was. He just got to work, and handed off a packet of cheese to her when she got to the right point in making omelettes.

The smile that passed between them at the small moment made Logan smile in turn, and he felt his heart twist at the fact that he wasn't going to be around to see such moments continue to evolve into something even more.

He looked up at Anna afterward with the same conflicted look on his face, and sighed as he scooted over to make some room for her beside him. They were making the right choice. He knew that. They made the choice together, so it couldn't be wrong. He had to trust that. He had to trust everyone he was leaving behind to make the best of their lives, and he had to trust himself to do the same with his own. It was just harder than he thought it would be.

19

Mercury still wasn't completely accustomed to flying. Going down to Earth was completely different than hopping from station to station as she started to get used to in Orbit. Orion wasn't the pilot who had flown them down to Earth, but he would be the one flying them back up to space, so she was enjoying her time with him while she had it before they would have to go about their own duties.

Orion helped her get out of her seat and the entry webbing when they finally reached the ground and got the all clear, but it was all incredibly strange. Earth gravity, as much as they tried to simulate it in space, still felt different. "My whole body feels heavy. This is unsettling."

"No kidding." He and several of the other passengers, along with Mercury, had never been inside the atmosphere before, and Orion actually found that walking required some conscious effort. "I lived in an apartment on the very outer rim of Three for about six months in flight school. It was supposed to be twenty percent above Earth norm. I don't remember it feeling like this. It's just . . . it doesn't move right."

"It doesn't move at all, moron." Carl brushed past Orion and slapped him on the back of the head with a teasing grin, clearly having no difficulties himself with the change in gravity. "Once you're done getting your land-legs under you, get out there and breathe deep. Might be the only chance any of us get." The big man headed out to what would normally have been the airlock, opening out onto a tarmac instead of connecting to a decent dock as it would have in space.

Everything about the place so far made Orion stop and stare. Pictures could never have done justice to the kinds of blues and soaring views they had seen out the windows on the way down over the past hour. It was all so rich it almost hurt his eyes just to remember.

"Are you okay to walk?" He asked Mercury once Carl was out of sight. He was Orion's best friend, but he could be a bit much sometimes.

Mercury slipped her hand into his and held tight as she stared out at her first view of Earth from the ground. "Yes, I'm fine. It's easier with you here, even though I'm a little doubtful you would catch me if I fell at the moment."

"Hey, hey. I resent that. I've carried twice you, and for much worse reasons." He squeezed her hand as they headed out of the airlock, but he pulled to a dead stop as soon as they were standing out on the small platform at the top of the steps for disembarking.

The airport where they landed was far from a busy place. Due to the ideal takeoff and arrival windows the site offered, they had landed in a place he recently learned was called The Waste. From the air, he certainly understood why it had gotten the name. There were pockets just like it all over the world, places where civilization curiously seemed to come to an abrupt halt and nature took over.

Of course, nature had only taken over because such places had once been large, metropolitan cities, before they had been wiped off the face of the Earth during the wars that had followed the Crisis centuries earlier. The Waste where they were standing had been known, before the Crisis, as Kansas City, in the former United States of

America. Orion could only assume that was a former name of the midwest district in the Americas, but he hadn't looked deeply enough into the historical record to find out more about the long-defunct nation.

As far as the eye could see, the Waste was covered in wild vegetation, unfit for farming due to the risk of exposure to whatever might be left over in the soil from the wars of the Crisis, and left almost completely uninhabited for the same reason. The airport was on just enough of a rise to make the rest of the landscape visible for several kilometers in every direction, and it was enough to make Orion feel a little lightheaded after just a glance.

He realized suddenly he had never looked at anything so vast and empty before in his life, with nothing standing between his eyes and the empty world. Wind whistled over the broken plains, ignorant of and apathetic to the events unfolding with their shuttle and their reasons for visiting that particular scrap of nowhere. The air was a mix of a thousand different scents he couldn't even begin to identify. Each of them hinted they had a name, a story, a source, a destination, even if he would never know them.

Mercury's voice was hushed, as if she had to be quiet in the face of the wind. "It's so strange to be here." Strange was the only word that kept coming to mind as all of her senses seemed to be on fire with every new sensation. "Humanity was born here, our ancestors walked on land like this, and yet you and I have lived our whole lives without even once feeling the wind on our faces."

She looked around and then let go of his hand to wander a few steps away. There was a patch of autumn flowers blooming nearby, though some of them looked worse for wear since they had been in such close proximity to their shuttle when it landed. Mercury plucked a couple of them and walked back over to Orion. "Real flowers. Just out here for anyone to see, for anyone to pluck. It's never so simple up there for something like this. A couple of flowers."

Orion shook his head and took a few of the small flowers

from her, twisting some of the stems together as they walked. Even the crunch of the tarmac under his boots was jarring. He'd walked over some floors on Three that had been less than meticulously cleaned, but this was stone. Grass. Dirt. Pebbles. Nothing about the world was smooth, and yet everything was, somehow, at the same time.

"Do you think they ever consider it in those terms? How free everything is? How open it is? I mean, seriously. Someone could just come along and build a house a hundred meters from here, and decide they're going to live there. Who's going to say no? There's no one here." When he finished weaving the spray of tiny flowers together, he turned Mercury toward him and tucked them behind her ear, winding the stalks with her hair to hold them in place, since her hair was tied back tightly in a braid for traveling.

Mercury smiled at the simple action and she leaned in to give him a gentle kiss. "I'm sure they don't. I'm sure they don't realize what they have, or maybe they even see it as desolate or lonely. No one really thinks about what they have until they're faced with something very different. Like this." She looked around and she wondered all sorts of things as they moved slowly toward the Consortium's facility. "I wonder if there is a river or a lake around here. Haven't you always wondered what water looks like here? So much water in one place?"

"I always thought skinny-dipping sounded like a lot of fun." He grinned at the idea, but shook his head as he squeezed her hand. "I don't know if there is or not, but I doubt our schedule will give us much time to find out. The rest of the Initiates should start arriving in about half an hour, and it's gonna take most of the afternoon to get them all processed." He looked up past Mercury as he said it, looking out over the Waste and the lone road that led up to the Consortium facility, seemingly in the middle of nowhere. "It does make me wonder what we'd find if we could just run off across the world. Swim in a river somewhere, see a beach, climb a mountain, who knows?"

"I wouldn't want to linger too long, though. I'm not interested in catching CV, and it only takes about a week to fully set into your body and start causing microscopic destruction. Tiny bits of damage every day until your body shuts down in your forties." She shook her head, but she was still admiring the landscape. "All the more reason to figure out how to eradicate it. There is no reason for all of this to go to waste."

"The more I learn about what happened back then, the less I think reason had to do with it." The wind picked up a little as they walked through the grass, and the sudden gust stopped Orion in his tracks. He closed his eyes just to appreciate the feel of it. The instincts he had honed as a pilot told his senses there was unimaginable power running through the atmosphere all around them, just to push such a volume of air. The chaos of currents he knew were there above and around them unseen, the spinning of an entire planet that could generate that kind of force . . .

"When I was a kid," he started quietly, then had to raise his voice because of the wind. "When I was a kid, I tried to imagine Earth like just another Station, only a hell of a lot bigger than the others and a lot more complicated. But it was a place where people live, which is in constant motion, drawing energy from the sun, providing nutrition and life to those who live on it . . . it sounded like a Station to me, so that was how I made it make sense."

He shook his head and looked around again. "Nothing people build is ever gonna come close to this. Not if our species lasts a million years and colonizes a thousand planets like Eleusis."

"Well, I would like to think Eleusis is something like this. I would like to think it is beautiful and windy and vast." She watched him as he enjoyed the wind, the way he reached out as though he could grab it, the look of awe on his face, it only made her fall in love with him even more. "You are so cute to watch."

He opened his eyes and looked down at her after that

comment, and gave her a playful glare. "That might be the first time anyone's ever called me cute. I kinda went from lanky and awkward straight to hot at some point in puberty, so I think I skipped cute." He squeezed her hand and spun her around once whimsically in the middle of the breeze. "Also, of the two of us, I thought we determined *I* was the one who liked to watch?"

"Hey, I can watch you if I want. I like watching my husband." She smiled as he twirled her a few more times, and she giggled as he pulled her close. "Come on, Awkward and Lanky, I need to go get instructions about what they need me to do."

Once they got inside (strange concepts to deal with, inside and outside), things felt a great deal more like home, but Orion couldn't find anything particularly comforting about that fact. The world adhered closely to the colors he had been accustomed to his entire life, steel and stone and glass. Dark, neutral colors covered everything with the exception of carefully-placed panels of brilliant color and very little artistic substance hanging around the main gathering area of the center.

The building was primarily a shipping depot, or had been until it had fallen out of use a few decades earlier. It had since been renovated as an orbital hub for passenger transport, but saw very little use. Some pieces of furniture were still under drop-cloths and there were parts of the building that obviously hadn't seen use in some time. Crewmen from their shuttle were already at work with some of their ground-dwelling counterparts to set up screening partitions off to one side of the large room, and everyone quickly received instructions on how to access processing protocols on their communicators. The Initiative had received a hundred and nineteen affirmative responses from the midwest district's invited applicants, with forty-six negatives and two hundred and ninety-seven outstanding with no response.

Orion gawked at the numbers for a moment once he saw

what they were going to be working with. Nearly five hundred people from across the continent offered a place on Eleusis, and they were only forecasting to process half of them? Maybe even fewer?

"I hope for their sake most of the undecided get their heads on straight and come along." He said in a low, irritated voice as he strapped his communicator onto his arm so he could use it easily as he worked. He grabbed some chairs out of storage racks and set them in place around the room for people to wait for liftoff. Nearly everyone in Orbit would kill to take the spots that the Earthlings so casually ignored.

"I'm not surprised, actually." Mercury was looking over her instructions and the supply list that outlined what she would have available to work with and a few patient charts. Simplified charts, of course, for her current purpose, but she still needed to know a few things about a patient before attending them. "A lot of them don't trust the Consortium. They would rather take their 'safe' life, short as it is, and keep that than take a risk."

"Well that's a damn shame, then." Carl said nearby, reviewing his own instructions, which were mostly geared toward him keeping watch on the security of the place in the event of some kind of hostility toward their proceedings, though none was expected. "Nothing happens for people who aren't willing to take *some* risk once in a while. Especially when there's something like this sitting in front of you." Carl shook his head, clearly not as conflicted about their objectives as some of the other crew members.

Orion gave Mercury a sympathetic look as Carl adjusted the body armor and several weapons on his body. The armor he wore was subtle, and he looked like he could have been wearing an overly-complicated flight suit, but Orion knew different. A man like Carl, in the gear he was wearing, would be an unstoppable force against most situations Orion's mind could conjure. "Well, let's hope Earth surprises you today and you can go back to being a bright and shiny optimist along with the rest of us."

Carl laughed and clicked a baton into place at the back of his belt, shaking his head at Orion. "Not fucking likely, buddy, but nice try."

"Do you think she'll be here?" Mercury wondered with a playful grin, since they had speculated several times what Carl's match might be like. It was hard to imagine what kind of woman could handle such a beast of a man. "Maybe she's from Earth. Your match."

Carl's head snapped up at that, since that wasn't an option he had really considered previously. They had talked about maybe some nerd from one of the data stations, maybe another security officer from a different station (that conversation had involved many iterations of Carl theorizing about what it would be like to be with a 'warrior woman,' usually with a wicked leer on his face) or maybe a scientist like Mercury who would keep Carl humble with her very different focus of work. All Carl cared about was, in his words, not completely fucking things up within five minutes of meeting her, whoever she was. "You think? I would've thought they would, you know, pair things up more or less along orbital/earthbound lines, you know? Reduce the possibility of inheriting some kind of susceptibility to CV? Or does it not work like that?"

"I don't see any reason why they wouldn't mix things up, especially if they are that concerned with genetic diversity. Anyway, you don't need to worry about CV. That's why I'm here. Once they have their first round, they can't pass it after 48 hours. It will take about a month to eradicate it from their bodies, but as long as you don't sleep with her in the first two days, she can't pass it on to you. Anyway, even if you couldn't keep it in your pants, you could get a treatment too and it would wipe it right out of you in one treatment. They've been exposed to it since their conception. It takes longer for them." Mercury knew she probably gave him more information than he cared for, but he *did* ask.

Carl looked momentarily worried, but then he shook it off and finished with his check of his gear. "They're not gonna put me with somebody from down here. Nobody down here could handle me."

Orion looked back and forth between Carl and Mercury as an idea clicked in place. "You feel like putting some action on that?" Orion had his own weapon for the purposes of the flight, but checking the handgun was a quick process for him, he made sure it wasn't actually chambered and the safety was securely on. "You've got about a fifty-fifty on being matched with somebody Earthbound instead of Orbital. If you're so convinced you won't get paired with anyone down here, put a price tag on it."

Carl took the challenge in stride and beamed right back at Orion as he crossed his arms. The man couldn't help but put up a defensive stance. He was always in intimidation mode. "I get paired with somebody from down here, I'll build your house on Eleusis." Carl scoffed, then reconsidered. "Half your house. I'll go in on it with you. I get paired to somebody back home, you help me build mine. Ours. Mine and hers."

"I'm gonna make sure we design a big fucking house, then." Orion agreed, and shook Carl's hand on it to seal the deal, and both of them looked supremely confident as they puffed out their chests at each other.

Mercury couldn't help the laughter that escaped her lips and she shook her head at the two best friends together. "You two are too much. I need to get to work." She grabbed Orion's hand and hauled him into a fiery kiss to yank him away from the testosterone-fest. She needed a 'see you later' kiss before she went to work. "Try not to get into too much trouble? I don't want you to get locked up into some Earth prison. Then where would I be?"

"Hey, do I look like somebody who just gets into trouble like that?" Orion gave her a confident nod with a knowing smirk as she released him from the kiss. He watched her backside as she walked away, sexy even in a jumpsuit. Their first batch of Earth-colleagues had started to trickle in to be processed, so they all needed to get to work. No one was actually due there until later that day, but Orion could understand people being over-eager about the process more easily than he could understand people passing up the chance altogether.

* * * * *

Kazuo couldn't bring himself to get out of the car immediately as they drove up to the Consortium facility, even though it was obvious they were some of the first to arrive. Their trip had only been a three-hour drive, and their parents hadn't wanted the two of them to be late for the first day of the rest of humanity's existence.

He managed, for the thousandth time just that morning, to suppress a shudder at the pain he had almost gotten accustomed to feeling as a constant companion in his life. Most of the time he even managed to hide it from his sister, though he sometimes wondered if she just permitted him to think that. "*Haha*," Kazuo said quietly, unable to quite bring himself to look at his mother in the front seat, "what happens if they change their mind about accepting us? Or one of us? The last physical they drew was last year at the application. They don't know. . . what if they change their mind?"

"They won't change their minds." His mother reassured him sharply, but she didn't look back at her children. "They had too many from Earth decline their acceptance, and too many that may not show up at all. They need bodies more than they can afford to be picky." She finally forced herself to look back at her children with a reluctant sigh. "And we have been informed that they're only doing blood draws today to test for pregnancy and to match you up with an acceptance and your file. Nothing more. You'll be fine."

"They'll know eventually." Kazuo said in the same low voice he felt like he'd been speaking in for months. He gave a final sigh, though, since he wasn't going to speak against his parents. He was anxious and he hoped it didn't show too obviously. "I'm sure you're right about their treatments. It'll be alright. That's why we're all here, right? To make things better?" He saw the people inside the building working, and he couldn't think of any reason to delay any longer. They had arrived, and they had said their goodbyes more formally and completely back at home in St. Louis. There was no reason to delay things. "Just . . . don't drive home until after launch, please? Just in case?"

Their mother nodded and promised silently they would stay until after the launch.

Aiko, as usual, was quiet during the whole exchange but she felt comfortable speaking to her brother once they were out of the car and the doors were closed. "You don't have to be worried. We have each other to depend on."

Especially walking together as they were, it was obvious that Kazuo and Aiko were siblings. As people of Japanese descent, they already stood out in any crowd they were in, but Kazuo had gotten accustomed to that since childhood. The Crisis had taken a disproportionate toll on South and Eastern Asia compared to the rest of the world, and the years that followed had only barely been kinder. Their features marked them as a rarity that most people in the world went their entire lives without meeting personally, and their parents had already confirmed that the two of them would be the only people of Japanese descent participating in the first wave of the Initiative. It was something that had Kazuo feeling both honored and even more nervous at the same time.

"If they do a complete scan, they're going to leave me behind, Aiko." His fist tightened in his pocket, clenching against a surge of pain in his chest that thankfully passed quickly. "I would, if I was them."

"Hush." Aiko said as she dug into her pocket and pulled out a couple of tiny blue capsules. "Take these. I made them." He paused when she put the pills into his hand, but she kept talking. "They're made from an Eleusis/Earth herbal hybrid, so the medication won't be recognized on their scans and they'll have to claim a technical failure and toss any blood samples if they take them. They can take a handprint to prove your validity. And they'll help with the pain without making you high. I made sure."

He took the pills and only examined them briefly before he popped them in his mouth. She could have told him they were from Neptune and he would have trusted her word on it. She was the best at what she did, and Kazuo had no reason to disbelieve anything she told him. Especially about her medical creations.

"I hope they don't scan some of your cargo too closely. They might think you're trying to come along and poison everybody." He managed a weak smile as he looked at her and the bag she was carrying. Initiates had only been permitted to take so much with them, but he knew most of the contents in her bag had to do with her work. That was just the way she was.

"I'm a botanist and pharmacist. At most they'll think I'm a crazy health nut with all of my herbs and plants." She wasn't worried. Her plants were the reason she had gotten accepted in the first place, after all. "And who says I'm *not* trying to poison anyone?" Aiko didn't have any plans of injuring anyone, but she hadn't shown up unprepared to protect herself and her brother.

"Shush. You're gonna get us arrested." He was smiling again by the time they reached the doors, and he held them open for her with a last look back at their parents, waiting in the car as they had promised they would. He waved, then turned away without waiting for them to wave back. He and Aiko knew what was expected. It was up to them to get it done.

Aiko looked around at the empty space inside the building and sighed as they walked up to the desk to sign in. The sheer quantity of security inside was distracting. "They sure are paranoid."

Kazuo just gave her a sarcastic look. "Says the woman who packed cyanide powder in her carry-on?"

"Well, guns aren't going to protect anyone from being poisoned." She reasoned as she sat down next to her brother to wait. "Anyway, have you seen the size of some of those guards? They don't need guns, their orbital growth hormones have done enough."

"If that's all it was." Kazuo said suspiciously as he eyed a few of them. He and Aiko were small people to begin with, Aiko nearly head and shoulders short of two meters and Kazuo only a few centimeters taller, but the men who were guarding the place looked like they could have eaten him and his sister both for breakfast. At least, that was his impression before another huge specimen of Orbital humanity came past the desk toward them. He was easily the largest human being Kazuo had ever seen in his life, and he flinched a little just by instinct at the first sight of him.

The huge man looked around the waiting room and flashed what looked like a ready and open smile. "Silly question, I'm guessing, but I have to make sure. Kazuo and Aiko Tanaka?" He read their names off the tablet in his hand smoothly, and with the right accent to their names, strangely enough, then looked back up at the two of them with the same welcoming grin to wait for confirmation.

Aiko nodded at the same time her brother did, and they got up from their seats and headed toward the large man. "How did you guess?" She asked sarcastically, but not with malice.

"Just lucky like that." He kept smiling down at them as they stood, apparently amused at just how far down he had to look to meet their eyes, but then nodded back past the desk. "Come on, you two get first shot at the doctors, seeing as you're the early birds."

"So what's your name?" Aiko asked in open curiosity as they were led back to the doctors. "Or is that a secret?" She had enough secrets of her own, so open conversation seemed the best bet.

That got a laugh from the big man, and he turned to offer her his hand as he walked. "Sorry, gotta get used to meeting new people I don't already know, I'm guessing. Carl Espinoza, at your service. Formerly a security contractor, recently drafted to the E.I. security staff."

Aiko placed her hand in his, even though hers was completely swallowed up in it. "Nice to meet you. I didn't expect there to be so much security around here. You look like you can handle anything that comes your way, though." She looked him up and down in an appraising perusal before she continued. He was a wall of muscle, attractive with his confident-as-fuck smirk, but she wasn't here to notice those things. "Obviously you know my name. Aiko Tanaka, Experimental Botanist and Pharmacist."

"Knew the name, not the title." He glanced over at her brother, who didn't seem talkative, which was fine with him. The sister was more interesting than anyone he'd met in a long time. "Forgive my saying so, but Experimental Pharmacist sounds like you're either the person to go to for recreational drugs or somebody I'm not sure I want pouring my drinks for me at a party. Which way does that tend to go?"

"I've never really had time for many parties. As long as I can remember, I've been studying. There's not much time to waste down here." She didn't say it as a criticism, just as a fact of her life. "Maybe I can enjoy it a little more now that I know I'll get to live a little longer." She purposely dodged answering his question, even though she could tell it was meant to be a joke. He had no idea, though, that she could be as dangerous or as fun as anyone wanted her to be. Aiko had experimented with many different things, mixing all kinds of concoctions. The Consortium was very interested in her work.

"Here's hoping we all live a little longer than we previously thought we would." He agreed wholeheartedly, and strangely, she couldn't detect any note of sarcasm or offense in his tone. They stopped in front of a row of hastily-cleaned offices where several other people in Initiative uniforms were waiting for them, one of them a diminutive Indian woman with a huge smile on her face, the other a tall and imposing redhead with a slightly more sedated smile for them both.

"Here you go. Ms. Tanaka, you'll be seeing Dr. Patel, she'll take good care of you. Mr. Tanaka, this is Dr. Finnegan, she'll be processing you. Don't piss her off, I know her husband." He grinned and patted Kazuo on the shoulder to get him going, then waved at Aiko. "Nice meeting you, Ms. Tanaka. I'll go get your kits and some uniforms. You'll look like you belong before you know it."

After Mercury processed her patient, she was back out in the hallway when Carl showed up with orbit kits, having already passed on the uniforms. "Dr. Patel said Ms. Tanaka was asking more about you after you left." She smiled at Carl teasingly, mostly because the woman was half his size.

Carl's lips broke into a grin before he could clear his throat and attempt to look unaffected. "Oh yeah? What kinds of questions? I think Dr. Patel knows a little more about me than I would want given out, generally."

"Personal information, where you are from, how long you've been in security, those kinds of things." Mercury laughed again at his grin. "You look so pleased. I didn't realize that Ms. Tanaka had interested you so much."

"Man's got a right to be glad when people ask questions. So long as they're not the wrong ones." He looked around for any sign of the Tanaka siblings, but they went to get changed and briefed for the next phase of orientation. "She said she was a botanist *and* a pharmacist. What is she, fifteen? Sixteen?"

"I think she's twenty." Mercury said as she looked up at Carl. "I've read some of her pharmaceutical research. She's very good. Most of the people we're going to see here today won't be much older, if you ask my guess. Maybe early twenties at the most, if any. They're adults so young down here, and it shows."

"Yeah it does." Aiko and her brother appeared in the hallway shortly after, still obviously getting accustomed to their nondescript Eleusis uniforms. Things were kept simple in space for a reason. Fewer distractions, fewer liabilities. But minimalism showed off people's assets in striking fashion, in Carl's opinion.

Aiko seemed constantly aware of her surroundings, and as soon as she looked around and noticed the redheaded doctor and Carl looking at her, she gave Carl a small wave but walked the opposite direction with her brother to continue with processing.

"She waved at you." Mercury teased in a singsong tone, but she looked away as soon as she realized more patients were incoming. "I don't think she realizes that making friends with you might not be a good idea. Both you and Orion are trouble."

"Hey, you *married* trouble. Of your own free will and choice. What does that say about you?" He teased right back, shoving her with one elbow as he brushed past her to go back to the front desk. "Let's get you another victim, Mrs. Trouble."

* * * * *

As soon as Jessie stepped into the building, she wondered if she was making the right decision, actually joining the Eleusis circus, but she also felt like she had little other choice for her life. Her mother was being cared for by professionals now, the previous man in her life was a mistake, and she was too old to really hang around and look for a real prospect on earth. Life on Earth would give her nothing at this point, not with her life half over already. She needed Eleusis more than it needed her, and doubts and misgivings were not something that she could really afford.

Once she checked in at the desk, she realized she had a bit of a wait before she would be called into her medical exam. They weren't allowed to eat because it could cause major issues during takeoff, but she wasn't hungry anyway, so she sipped at a bottle of water. It was a nerve-wracking kind of day, but looking around, she clearly wasn't alone in her anxiety.

There were only so many doctors and so many people working through the supply lists, and clearly they were approaching the busiest part of the day. When Jessie found a seat, it was one next to the glass walls that someone had just barely vacated, with a clear view of the rolling plains outside and the cloudy sky that had moved in over the course of the morning.

Just outside the window, in the far corner of the facility's parking lot, there was a lone car with someone lying back on the hood against the windshield. It was an ancient-looking thing, from the first century when mankind had just begun to travel by automobile, all hard lines and solid metal framing. It might have belonged in a museum, except that it wasn't even pretty enough to deserve that kind of placement.

The man lying back on the windshield was wearing jeans and a dark, long-sleeved t-shirt. In the intermittent cloud cover, it was hard to tell if he was even alive at first, since he was so still, but as she looked at him, he took a deep breath and stretched his arms and legs wide, apparently just relaxing in the cool autumn air. He looked vaguely familiar, but it took a moment to place him in her memory as the man who had spoken to her during the Initiative information session, still looking every bit as collected and confident as he had then, just under the eyes of heaven rather than anyone else more local.

The wait was long enough that Jessie was sure her newly issued communicator would alert her when it was her turn to be examined. She wove her way through the crowd and out to the parking lot, but she didn't say anything until she was half the distance from the building to the car. "Still weighing your options?" What had his name been? Jordan? Gordon? She wasn't sure.

He seemed genuinely surprised to be approached, but then gave her a broad smile and shook his head. "What is there to think about? When somebody gives you a choice between Heaven and Earth, you choose Heaven." He shrugged and looked around again at the nothingness all around them, then scooted over on the hood and patted the dented metal next to him. Up close, the ancient car looked even worse than it had from a distance, and obviously if it was Gordon's, he wasn't exactly obsessed with taking care of it. "Looks like a hell of a crowd in there. Care to join me as I say goodbye to everybody's second-favorite planet?"

Jessie looked at him and his car at the invitation, but she only moved close enough to stand next to the hood. She was definitely a woman with curves, not that she thought of herself as excessively large, but she didn't really get many invitations to sit on cars with anyone. She was not the type where men wanted to fantasize about her on the hood of a car. "I don't think you want me to get on top of your car."

"It's only mine for a few more minutes. After that, it belongs to whoever comes along to steal it after lift-off." He turned his head to look her up and down, and smiled a little more mischievously. "And yeah, I'm pretty sure this is exactly where I want you."

She glared at him for his comment and decided to climb on, though she didn't look over at him as she laid back against the hood. Jessie still had mixed feelings about how he both angered and excited her at the same time. Her eyes fixed on the sky and stayed there. "You know, I don't know what to think about you. You make suggestive comments like that, but I can't tell if you mean them or if you're just making a joke at my expense."

"That kind of humor isn't really my style." He sounded almost bored at the response, obviously not surprised at her questioning tone. "I really don't make fun of people all that often, at least not to their face. If I have a problem with you, you'll know it because I'm either yelling at you or telling you at length exactly what kind of a moron I think you are. It gets a little tedious, since I think most people are morons. So I try to keep my vocalized criticism to a minimum." He smiled at the sky again and turned to look over at her, no trace of a smile or a joke on his face. "I'm sorry about your mother. That can't have made it easy to come today."

Jessie paused briefly, still unsure how a relative stranger knew so much, but he seemed the type to know more than he should. She knew trouble when she saw it.

"It's actually a relief in some ways. Nothing is going to save her now, and the drugs they have her on keep her happier than she ever was when she was healthy." She didn't look over at him for more than a moment before she looked away again. "It's not that I want her to die. It's just freeing to only have to worry about myself and to not have to hear her criticism about my disappointing life. If she only knew the extent of it, she probably would have been ecstatic to see me leave for Eleusis."

Gordon shook his head as he looked back at the sky. "Never had that problem. Never really had parents to disappoint. Older brothers, but not parents." He sighed, putting his hands up behind his head as he relaxed.

"I was reading the other day on some of the social networking hubs. There are already people who are talking about Eleusis like it's the cure to all of life's problems. Leave everything behind and go, you'll be a different person, a new world, a new life, blah blah blah. I'm not saying it can't be true, but I think it's only going to be as true as we make it. I'm still gonna be an asshole, even light years away. It would take more than interstellar travel to change that, I think."

"From what little I've seen of you, you enjoy it too much to actually want to change anything about yourself." Jessie didn't look at all relaxed, but she wasn't moving around to get comfortable either. "Are you nervous at all?"

"About going to space? I'm terrified." His tone still sounded just as casual, but he didn't laugh afterward or give any other indication that he was joking. "For starters, I hate flying. No matter where, no matter why. Just hate it. Being cooped up in a metal can moving a few thousand kilometers per hour . . . space just feels wrong. So yeah, I'm a nervous mess."

Jessie's eyebrows raised in her surprise, since he didn't look like a mess. He looked calm and collected. "You hide it well, then." She actually turned her head towards him, followed by the rest of her body. "I'm sure they have medication they can give you. Not that I think you would trust whatever they would give you."

"I wouldn't. It probably wouldn't work too well on me anyway." He shrugged, and turned his head toward her, his eyes raking up and down her body as she turned a little toward him. "I'm glad you decided to come along. The one acquaintance I have on this flight headed up today, well, the only non-business acquaintance, isn't exactly speaking to me right now. It's always nice to have friends around."

She laughed at the idea of them being friends and shook her head as she remembered the only conversation they had about being friends in the first place. She still wasn't entirely convinced that they would make good friends. "You're wasting your time with whatever you think you're trying to accomplish with that look. We'll be assigned to a match as soon as we get up there. Even though I know my breasts usually catch people's attention. Big girl, big boobs. That's how it works."

"All anyone ever accomplishes with a look is a look. Not too much harm in that, is there?" He looked down at her breasts and gave her an approving nod. "And they are gorgeous. Well worth all the attention I'm sure they've gotten in recent years."

He smiled knowingly and laid back on the windshield again, reaching up to dig at the collar of his shirt for a moment before he drew out a solid-looking chain necklace with what looked like a small data core on the end of it, smooth black and obviously worn from long use. "What are you hoping to get in your match, do you think? You have any specific requirements in mind? Traits you'd prefer over others?"

He reached over and set the data core down on one of

her thighs, holding it steady for a moment to make sure it balanced before he snapped his fingers above it and an entire display of lights appeared in the air in front of them. It was difficult to see the holograms under the bright overcast sky, and it would have been impossible to see them at all from the building a few dozen yards away, but Jessie could make out what looked like a roster of names and a few subordinate panels for demographics and biographical data, a few medical tabs for past charts and genetic scans, everything that could be known about whoever the people on the list were.

He scrolled through in mid-air, and looked over at her playfully as he did. "Don't let it fall. I live and die by that thing." He finally got down to the Rs, and stopped as he got to her name. "Let's see who they've got picked out for you, shall we? You want to peek into the future a little?"

Jessie was surprised by his touch on her thigh, since she was wearing shorts and his hand had grazed her smooth skin at first, but then as soon as he gave her a warning not to let the data core fall, she felt like she wasn't able to move. "You hacked their list?!?" She replied with a harsh whisper as she tried to bat the hologram away, since she didn't want him to get caught. "No, I don't want to know. It doesn't matter anyway, they're going to put me with whoever they want despite whatever preferences I may have."

All her batting managed to do was to send the hologram spinning, which made Gordon laugh as he brought it back to being in focus for the two of them. "Relax, if anyone was paying attention to what I have on this thing, I'd know about it. I'm not gonna go flashing this around inside, of course, but still, what's a little shared information between friends?"

He gave her a grin as he stabilized her portfolio and sifted through a few parts of it to get to her matching profile. "Matches are still unstable at the moment, since the program is waiting on a final roster of everyone who actually showed up today before making final determinations and reviews.

Nothing is fixed. Well, I shouldn't say nothing. A few things are fixed. Not yours."

He pulled up the profiles of the top five men she was potentially about to spend the rest of her life with on another planet, and left their faces hanging in the air for a moment. Two of them were barely men, both from midwest districts who looked both skinny and scared. One was an overweight man from somewhere in Europe, by his profile tags, one was a man with sharp features that looked like they had never smiled in the entirety of their history, from Station Seven. The last had grey hair but no wrinkles, a mechanical engineer from Station Two.

"Well." Gordon said with a click of his tongue. "Those are some very seriously sexy options."

"Don't you know how to listen?" Her glare was fierce this time, and she contemplated throwing his damn data core in his face. "I told you I don't want to know. It doesn't matter. It's not like I came here looking for true love. It doesn't exist. At least none of them are already married." She hissed at him before she looked away. Old or young, it really didn't matter. She didn't figure her 'match' would really last anyway, since the whole purpose was genetic diversity, not happily-ever-after.

He didn't shut off the display right away, still playing through the images of the men who might be a part of her future as if he was just talking to himself. It was unclear if he was genuinely curious or really just eager to piss her off. "The boys aren't bad, I suppose. You could sort of train them however you like, make sure they know who's boss. This older guy, though . . . divorced twice . . . I wouldn't want to take my chances. The other two . . . well, that's anybody's guess."

He dismissed the images of the men's faces and returned to the list of names by itself, changing every moment as people checked in or failed to do so across the world. He reached over and adjusted the data core a little on her thigh, where it had begun to slide a little too one side, and his touch lingered on her skin for a little longer than it absolutely had to. "Wouldn't you rather choose for yourself?"

"What difference would that make? I don't know any of these people, I can't choose anyone better for myself than a computer can. Clearly. Otherwise I would have already been married by now. I'm not some fresh, young thing. I'm twenty-five. Halfway dead already." She sat up so she could reach for the data core. "I didn't show up here to find someone to love me, or to find someone to love. Who did it pick for you, huh? Some exotic-looking tiny thing? A beautiful woman with long hair and curls? Did you hack it to pick whoever you wanted?"

"Among other reasons. Mostly I'm just an inquisitive son of a bitch who likes to know everybody else's business before they do." He grabbed her hand as she reached for the core on her leg, and his grip was surprisingly strong, for such a lean person. His hand was rougher than his almost-frail first impression would have led her to guess, and his grip on her didn't waver. Neither did his smile as he looked over at her. "Are you always this angry?"

"Are you always this incorrigible?" She snapped right back at him as she attempted to free her hand from his. "Do people where you're from not get angry when you blatantly ignore them?"

"Almost always, I just figured it's best to ask right up front. And yes, I'm always this incorrigible." His grin was unwavering as he held onto her hand, and he actually pulled her just a little closer to him as she struggled to free herself. "If you're going to get this angry every time I offer you a chance to choose what you want, you're gonna spend a lot of time angry." His look softened slightly as he looked back and forth from one of her eyes to the other, as did his voice. "Though I'm gathering quickly that being angry most of the time wouldn't be too far a change for you from what you're used to."

A slow sigh escaped from Jessie's lips and she stopped struggling to try to pull away. "Listen, the only reason I'm here is because I want to have a life of my own that isn't tainted by the life I already have here. You can judge me however you like, I don't care. Just don't . . . just don't ruin Eleusis for me, alright? I thought that you said we were friends."

He had just thrown a lot into her face quite unexpectedly, her potential matches the least of it, but the knowledge that he had the ability to hack the Consortium was huge, and all she could think was that he was trying to get her in trouble somehow by showing her. Why else would he trust her, someone he barely knew?

"I'm not trying to ruin anything for you." He released her hand slowly, and reached down to take his data core off her leg, the hologram winking out along with it as he replaced it on its chain around his neck. "No one in this Initiative wants Eleusis to be a successful home for us more than I do. I don't want to ruin that for anyone, or allow anyone to ruin it for everyone else."

There was a flash of anger behind the last statement that didn't have an obvious source, but he kept going instead of stopping to explain. "I'm not judging you, for anything. In fact, past your basic file to show that you've never been married, never had any kids, are Type B positive and a Scorpio, I haven't read anything farther into your history. I looked over your mom's quickly, that's how I knew she was on hospice. And I glanced over your sisters'. Interesting women, but they sound like some fairly heinous bitches when they want to be. The one article about the time Jenny burned down part of your high school over an ex-boyfriend said a lot about how crazy she can get in a pretty short span of time. Kind of impressive, in its own way."

"Yeah, well." Jessie looked down at her legs before she said anything else. "I'd hate to think what she would do if she found out I was sleeping with her husband. I'd rather not find out." She shook her head and looked back at him, expecting to see judgment in Gordon's eyes over what she'd said now that she had revealed something so personal. The fact was that her sister was a bitch and Jessie was lonely, and those things didn't help one another. "You're the only person I know here, even a little, and while I have no idea why you're trusting me with knowing your secrets. I can't choose for myself. I'll just fuck it up."

"I don't think you would." He gave her a small smile and leaned back on the windshield beside her with his arms stretched out wide, one of his hands moving to pull some of her hair back over her shoulder as if the two of them had been the most intimate of friends for their entire lives. His grin widened a little before he spoke. "Although now you do have me halfway questioning your taste in men. Her husband isn't exactly a glowing specimen of humanity. But, then again, if he'd been that good, then you wouldn't be here leaving him behind, I suppose."

He chuckled and put his hands back behind his head to relax. "If I had it to do over again, I'm pretty sure I wouldn't have . . . well, I've slept with three different women. I can't bring myself to regret the first one, though she's nobody I would've chosen if I had really been thinking it through at the time. She was married for most of the time we were together. The second one was a nobody who just happened to be nearby and willing, so who knows, maybe she was married too. I have no idea. The third . . . well, I really shouldn't have gotten involved with the third one, but that's hindsight for you."

Jessie ran her hand over her hair that he touched and leaned back as well, as though it didn't bother her, his little touches, but they did. She was unsure exactly how much they bothered her, though, and why. Did she *want* to like him? "Do I look like a woman who can afford to be choosy?" She let out a bitter chuckle and looked up into the sky. Earth was sparsely populated as it was, her hometown was even less populated, and she wasn't exactly the cream of the crop. "If I regretted it and went back and changed it, I'd be a virgin instead."

He looked her over after her confession, and they sat on

the car in silence as the wind picked up around them to roar in their ears and remind them of the world they wouldn't feel again until they walked on a different one. Eventually, he turned to look at her, then slid off the hood and walked around to stand by her side of it. He was taller than his slouch gave him credit for, nearly her height exactly, which meant that as she laid out against the classic straight lines of the car, his face was near hers, and when he spoke, he leaned in with one arm across her waist to rest at her hip, his eyes only a few centimeters from hers.

"You are gorgeous, Jessie. You can have anything and anyone you want, in this world or any other. All you have to do is choose what and who that is." He looked her in the eye afterward, just to let her see the complete confidence he had in what he was telling her, then drew back slowly, his hand lingering on her waist and trailing down over her leg casually as he backed away from the car. "I'll see you inside."

Jessie watched him go and leaned her head back against the glass before she shook her head. Whoever Gordon was, he was crazy. And he was driving her crazy in more ways than she wanted to think about. Clearly someone with that kind of power could choose whoever and whatever *he* wanted, and she wasn't about to admit to him that maybe she'd choose him instead of the men that were potentially her match. There was so much unknown about him that it intrigued her, but she was too afraid he would laugh in her face, even though he said he wasn't the type. He was too unpredictable for her to figure out what was truth about him and what wasn't.

She stayed outside until her new communicator alerted her that her turn was coming up, then slowly slid off the car to go inside. She just needed to keep to herself and move forward. That would get her to Eleusis, right?

20

Anna and Logan sat in silence for a solid fifteen minutes just staring at the Consortium building before they finally emerged from Logan's truck. They'd taken as much time as they could saying their goodbyes back at home before leaving to report, so much so that they were nearly about to miss their only chance to get to Eleusis.

There was less than an hour before the shuttle would leave, and it was obvious from the lack of people sitting in the waiting area that those who wanted to go were now waiting elsewhere in the building to board the ship and prepare for takeoff. Anna immediately slid to Logan's side and took his hand closest to her before he reached out for the door with his free hand.

When he hesitated to open the door, she leaned in and kissed his cheek. "We've stewed over this enough. This is it. If we don't go in now, they'll leave us behind."

He nodded quietly in resignation and agreement, then reached into the bed of the truck and pulled out the two small bags they had packed with the few possessions they decided they would take with them into orbit. They would never have enough of home with them, and even bringing such a small selection seemed more like a tease than anything, but Logan knew he'd be glad of the reminders once they were out of the atmosphere.

Once they had the bags over their shoulders, Logan reached back into the truck, checking to make sure the fuel was still sufficient for a trip, then finally keyed in the instructions for it to return home without a driver. As soon as he stood back and closed the door, the truck eased into motion, carefully avoiding the two of them as it pulled out of the parking lot and started back the way they had come, quietly rumbling out of sight.

Logan squeezed her hand as they watched it go, standing alone for a moment on the asphalt. The wind whipped Anna's hair into her face and kicked up some of the dust from the Waste around them to pelt their arms and sting their noses just enough to notice.

"Alright then." He let out the last sigh he would allow himself. No easy way home, no way but forward. He leaned down and brushed Anna's hair out of her face before he kissed her soundly, closing his eyes with his forehead resting against hers for a breath. "Let's do this thing."

"Let's do this thing." She repeated against his lips and walked hand-in-hand with him toward the facility. They stepped inside to a mostly-empty waiting area and then walked up to a desk where there was no line. They had clearly waited until the last minute. Logan signed in first, then Anna after, smiling just a little that she wrote Anna Bickford on the paper instead of Anna Prince. "Still hard to get used to, seeing Bickford after my name, but I like it."

"It suits you." Logan beamed beside her as the man who'd taken their names headed away to get them processed. A moment later when someone came back, Logan's eyebrows shot up in alarm at whatever was behind Anna, and when she turned around, she was face to face with the single tallest human being either of them had ever seen in person, striding toward them with a tablet tucked into one long-fingered hand and a friendly smile on his face.

"Mr. and Mrs. Bickford. Fashionably late, but still right

on time. Orion Al-Jabbar." He offered his name along with his hand, shaking first Logan's and then Anna's as they craned their necks to look up at him. "Welcome to the party. Come on back, we'll get you in the works."

"The party, huh?" Anna replied as she looked back at the now-empty waiting area, since the few stragglers had been seen ahead of them. "I'm not sure you know the definition of party. There are usually more people, definitely more booze, and typically pyrotechnics."

Orion actually grinned at that comment, walking beside Anna to escort them farther into the building. "We try and avoid the pyrotechnics on the stations, but the rest, yeah, I'm familiar with that. Pyrotechnics tend to get a little out of control with oxygen supplies and all that. Doesn't prevent the occasional flaming shot, though."

"Bummer. But I get it." She bantered with a laugh as she looked up at the man again. "You know, I didn't think of myself as that freakishly short, but you do a good job of making me look that way. You are taller than I ever thought the human race could get. So either you are descended from giants, or science played a role. Go science. Or giants, if that's the case."

"The popular story when I was growing up was that my feet got caught in a centrifuge and the rest of me got whipped around until I stretched." He smiled down at the woman, who was admittedly on the shorter side when it came to the women he'd spent most of his time around. "So no, no giants involved that I'm aware of. And it turns out the human race can get quite a lot taller. My doctor tells me I'm actually in the middle of a growth spurt. Hopefully my last. Time will tell."

"Growth spurt? What, are you fourteen?" That was the last time Logan could remember really popping upward with any kind of speed, though he'd gone from six one to six two in the last year.

"Twenty-four." Orion gave the man a smile and a shrug. "Science just has me taking my time with it, I guess."

"Good God." Anna said in response to that. "You're going to get taller? And you're twenty-four?" Anna noticed the ring on his hand and she looked at it before she looked up at him again. "I hope your wife is some sort of Amazonian woman, because . . . yikes."

"Well, Amazons were darker, I thought. Little closer to my coloring than my wife's. But otherwise, yeah, she manages." Orion grinned just at the thought of Mercury, and they came around the corner to where the medical offices had been set up, where Mercury was making some final notes on a tablet about a previous patient. "This would be her, Doctor Mercury Finnegan." He said loudly enough for Mercury to hear herself announced, then went up to her side. "These look to be our last stragglers, Mr. and Mrs. Bickford."

Mercury looked up and gave a polite smile as her fingers tapped once more to save the patient file from the last and get the next one. "I'm very glad to see that you two made it in time. We wouldn't want to leave anyone behind that actually wants to be a part of such an amazing opportunity." She looked over at Orion and smiled brighter with pride before she kissed his cheek. "It looks like I pulled up Mr. Bickford's file next. Do you want to wait with Mrs. Bickford until Dr. Patel is finished with their patient?"

"Sure. I'll take her out of order to go get geared up, we need to start pre-flight soon." He left a hand on Mercury's back as he pulled away with a smile, then nodded off to one side to direct Anna away. "Right this way, shorty. Time to meet your new wardrobe."

"Shorty? I take offense to that, it's not my fault that you're genetically altered to be a giant. That does not make me short, that makes you tall." She paused to consider her argument. "Not the best argument I've used to make a point, but it'll do."

Mercury chuckled a little as they watched Orion and Mrs. Bickford walk away before she turned her attention back to Mr. Bickford in front of her. She had loosened her hair from the braid that she had it in earlier, which had left her with some exhausted waves in her hair, but she was attempting to push it back as she motioned toward the exam room. "Your wife seems like quite the personality, Mr. Bickford."

"Wait till she gets going." He gave the doctor a smile as he stepped inside, not entirely sure what to expect from an exam, since he had thought all of that was already taken care of. Still, he surveyed the place like he owned it and was only there because he was permitting himself to be.

He looked over the woman who was about to look him over, and couldn't help but think that Anna's assessment had been about right. Apart from her pale skin and striking red hair, the doctor was everything Logan had imagined an Amazon would be when they'd learned cursory stories about mythology in school. "She can be a handful, but that's got its own virtues."

"I'm sure. Both of you wouldn't be here unless you had something important to bring to the table." Mercury tapped her tablet a few times as it brought up everything she needed to know about her patient and what she needed to administer.

"It looks like I just need to do a brief physical exam, take a finger pinprick, and give you an immune booster along with your first round of CV treatment. Your iron count was a little low at your last draw, so that's why they want me to take a sample so you can be tested again. Nothing that can't be fixed with a little dietary supplement." She smiled and nodded toward the curtain standing up in the corner of the room. "You can undress over there, or I can step out. Do you think that you'll want an anti-nausea for the trip? I've recommended it to everyone, but it's up to you."

"I haven't had any trouble with motion-sickness before now. I don't think it'll be a problem." He declined, and left his bag near the door to head over to the curtain and get undressed. He felt a slight awkwardness about it, a stranger close to his age as she was, but he'd gotten exams from Sierra before too, and she was a great deal younger and less professional than the woman in front of him.

Still, he was going to need to keep his eyes on other parts of the room, otherwise the medical gown provided was going to show a little more definition than was probably appropriate.

"Have you and the giant been married long?" He asked from behind the curtain as he kicked off his boots and tucked his socks inside them just outside the curtain.

"No, actually." She finished typing in his order, and then waited for the appropriate supplies to dispense from a large box sitting on one of the counters. "We're newlyweds. We got married only a few weeks after we met." Mercury looked over the syringes that were dispensed as she waited for him. "We were matched and hit it off really well, and the rest is history, as they say. It's been an exciting time, getting married and getting ready for Eleusis at the same time."

"Oh, well congratulations, then. Anna and I were just married a few weeks ago too, after we both got our acceptance." The rest of his clothes followed one piece at a time, but after some cloth rustling behind the curtain, it eventually became clear that Logan didn't see the point in actually tying the medical robe entirely over himself. He came out with it folded down and tied around his waist like some kind of single-use kilt, hanging to his knees and leaving the rest of him exposed for examination.

He wasn't the first person that day to either be incredibly comfortable exposing himself or attempt to come onto her by appearing almost completely naked for their exam (Earth-people could be fairly vulgar, it seemed, when they wanted to be) but Logan didn't appear to be doing either. He knew they were in a bit of a rush, and he wanted to expedite things as much as possible. Him and every single one of the muscles that stood out on his arms and chest as if they had been sculpted out of marble.

Mercury felt fairly immune to the human form, having learned to look at people more scientifically than sexually, but being with Orion had changed that for her somewhat.

She noticed people more, noticed things about them that weren't necessarily medically relevant, and she had mixed feelings about the change in perspective. It didn't help her focus, but it made her think of her patients more as people, which was a good thing.

She definitely did notice, however, Logan's muscles and form as she approached him. It was a trend among most of the earthlings, to have well-defined bodies, but not all of the men that she had seen that day looked like the one in front of her. Most of them did hard labor for a living and their bodies proved it.

She met his eyes with her emerald green ones for a brief moment before she put aside her tools to perform the medical exam first. "Have you had any injuries or alterations in your physical well-being since your last submitted exam?"

"Nothing major. Had a few burns and gashes when the station arm came down a dozen clicks from my house, but those healed up just fine." He indicated the patches on his arm and shoulder where the skin was shaded slightly differently in the wake of being scorched and regrown and not yet tanned to match the rest of him, though it was a subtle variation. "Nothing lasting, though, no."

Mercury stepped in closer to look at his arm and shoulder, and she traced her fingers across the burned area just to make sure everything looked alright. "I'm sorry to hear that you were so close to that." She replied softly as her touch lingered because she was distracted by her thoughts of the incident. "We were on Station Nine right before the accident. We're lucky to be alive, Orion and I."

Logan shook his head as he looked her over again. She seemed like the definition of an indoor-girl, and picturing her in the middle of a crisis was difficult. "I'm sorry you were near it. There was a family living on the farm it came down on, but I can only imagine how many more people were actually on that thing when it fell. It was a terrible thing to see."

Mercury's hands moved away from his scars so she could

continue with her exam, but she didn't meet his eyes as she continued. "The worst for me was being held like a criminal afterward, as if I would do anything to harm all of those people. Just the idea makes me sick."

"Well, I'm glad there's one doctor in the universe that takes the whole 'do no harm' thing seriously." He smiled at her, then shook his head before he explained. "Sorry. My doctor back home has a daughter training to replace her who has a bit of a mean streak. Your bedside manner is already a world and a half better than most of what I'm used to from the medical community."

That brought a smile back to Mercury's lips and she shook her head slowly before she gently pulled his head a little closer so that she could check his ears and his mouth. "Usually my expertise is babies and the women that carry them. You really don't want to get them riled up, or else *you're* the one in trouble."

"No kidding." He was glad to see the woman smile, and stood still for the rest of her examination, though it was a little strange to have someone checking him out whose last name wasn't Weber. "Might have to start actually being nice to my wife, then, if that's the case. Our physician ran a pregnancy test on her a few days ago, but they told us there was something wrong with the sample or something, they couldn't get an accurate test. I'm sure she'll ask you to re-run it here in a minute when she gets in here."

"Dr. Patel will take care of her, I'm sure. They were almost done with her previous patient." Mercury smiled up at him again before she gave him a nod and stepped back. "Most everything looks good." She was brief about checking over the parts of him covered up with the gown and made her notes on her tablet quickly afterward. "That would be amazing, having your baby up there in Orbit before we go to Eleusis. I hope that she's pregnant. I miss my maternity patients."

That made Logan smile again, even though he had to clear his throat as she finished checking the parts of him that were covered with the medical robe. "Always a pleasure to meet someone who enjoys their work. How long have you been doing it? Your husband said he was twenty-four."

"I'm twenty-two, but I've been working on my education since I was fourteen. I just finished my residency last year." She smiled warmly right back at him as though she hadn't just seen every part of him. When she approached him again, though, it was with needles. "I love my work. I love seeing the miracle of life. Cliche or not, it *is* a miracle. A messy one, but still." She held up one needle and gave him a polite smile. "Quick prick first, then the two syringes. I'll do my best to make it painless."

"The Messy Miracle. There's a title for the first book of your memoirs." He smiled and offered his arm, bracing himself slightly for the needles. He wasn't going to let himself act bothered in front of a complete stranger, and an Orbital to boot.

True to her word, the blood draw was only a pinprick of pain, the two shots afterward were similarly simple and painless. She tossed the used syringes into a biohazard box and gave his shoulder a reassuring pat before she tucked her hair behind her ear. "You can get dressed, we checked off all the boxes for you. I'll wait outside while you dress so that I can take you to get your new uniform and finish the rest of the registration process. We'll need to rush a bit, though. They're strict about takeoff times."

When he did redress himself, he didn't bother putting his shirt back on, since he had gone a fair percentage of his life without wearing one anyway, and as she'd said, they were in a hurry. He could feel the anti-CV drugs she'd given him working their way through his system, but it was nowhere near as excruciating as the initial dose had been, a slow sizzle rather than internal combustion.

They passed Anna and Orion on the way out, and she was already wearing a flight suit and standard-issue boots. The change in outfit made him grin, since it seemed to make things a little more harmlessly real, especially when it was

Anna who was wearing it. "Very sexy."

Anna stopped to make some ridiculous modeling poses before she grinned and moved away from Orion back to Logan's side. "I'm sexy? Look at you, walking around shirtless. You're supposed to save that for me."

"We're in a rush. Go get checked out by somebody other than me." He pulled her close for an instant, then sent her on her way with a smack to her backside before spinning to follow Mercury to pick up his own uniform.

The whole exchange made Orion laugh. "Yeah, you're newlyweds alright." He went to lean against the wall outside Dr. Patel's office as they finished up. "Somebody somewhere has surely done a study about how soon after marriage the ass-slapping stops, but I haven't dug it up yet. I'll have to see about finding that. My guess would be a year, maybe a year and a half?"

"Who says it has to stop?" Anna watched Logan walk off with the tall, redheaded doctor. "My parents were crazy in love all the way until my mom died. Even now he talks about her like she was the best thing in the world."

That made the grin on Orion's face fade, since he couldn't imagine having lost his mother so young, but he knew he had to keep in mind that most of the Earth-born he was going to be working with would have lost their parents by their late teens or early twenties. If they still had living parents, they weren't likely to still be living when they came back from Eleusis for the first time.

"Well I'm sure she was. Crazy in love doesn't always mean ass-slapping, though. It definitely should, in my opinion, but that's not an opinion shared by everyone." He shook his head to clear it of an image he didn't want. "I think if I ever saw my father slap my mother's ass, I would have him arrested until we could figure out what kind of demon was possessing him. Very much not their style."

"Well, my husband better always enjoy slapping my ass. Even when we're old." She smiled as Dr. Patel came out to retrieve her. "Excuse me while I get cured and felt up by your friend here. I'll be back."

"Dr. Patel gets frisky. Fair warning." He smiled at her and went to sit down by the wall of windows that faced out toward the shuttle, relaxing in the few minutes he was likely to have left before he had to get back to work hauling everybody up to space. He knew all the theory and had simulated the entire thing dozens of times, but the actual doing was always going to be something unique.

He heard static click through the receiver he had tucked into his ear, and narrowed his eyes a little, reaching up to tap the pod inside his ear canal. "Somebody trying to check in? Your mic might be blown."

There was silence for a moment on the other end of the open connection as he and apparently the other five security officers posted to the retrieval waited for one of them to check in and answer, but no one did. Voices started chiming in quickly after a five second delay, all of them following protocol.

Carl's deep voice was first. *Espinoza code 10 on the tarmac, eyes on Fitch and Adebayo on board, confirming code 10, no touch on Johnson, St. Pierre or Mikkelson. Talk back.*

St. Pierre code 10 on the front approach. A young man's voice came across, sounding nervous. *Eyes on Mikkelson, confirming code 10 on the south side. Saw Johnson a few minutes ago sweeping north parking lot, no eyes for maybe five minutes. Talk back, Johnson.*

There was nothing further from the communicator, and as the seconds stretched on, Orion got up and got moving. He could see Carl already moving out the windows, closer to the north lot than he was. "Johnson, if you're getting this, come inside and switch out that mic, you've got a dud. St. Pierre, Mikkelson, Fitch, and Adebayo stay put. Eyes up."

He moved quickly through the facility, ignoring everyone else nearby as he did his best to look out through any available window to get a look at the north lot, but the exit wasn't in a convenient spot. He could've broken through the glass in a window somewhere, but causing a scene when there might be nothing to cause a scene about wasn't something he was willing to risk.

By the time he got outside, he heard the yelling, and realized that making a scene would have absolutely been the right risk to take. A single shot was fired before he could see who might be shooting, and his hand was immediately back on the mic in his ear.

"All points, code 2, north lot. Fan back, cover down, unknown targets." He crept up to the corner of the building, and saw Johnson on the ground before he saw Carl come up from between two abandoned cars. His friend's face was a mass of blood, as if he'd just gotten bludgeoned by something out of nowhere.

A figure swinging a bat was wearing a flight suit as if about to get on the shuttle, but Orion didn't recognize them from the crew heading down that morning. An Earth-born man, from the look of the scruff on his face and the slightly wild look in his eyes. Orion didn't see a gun in the man's possession as he continued to swing away at Carl, so he took a step away from the corner of the building with his own gun raised. He knew how to use it, even if he'd never fired it at a living person before.

Knowing how and doing something suddenly became much farther from each other than he had ever before given them credit for. "Drop it!"

The man with the bat swung around to look wildly at Orion, and the moment's distraction was all Carl needed to grab one of the man's arms and snap it with an audible crack and a screech of pain from the assailant. The next few moments were a blur, as the man collapsed to the asphalt but came back up with a knife directly into Carl's ribs through the seam of his flight suit.

As soon as Orion saw the stab coming, that was all he needed to push him across the space between knowing how and doing. His bullet sailed straight through the assailant's brain, spraying blood partly on Carl and mostly on the window of the car next to them.

"Fitch, go get the doctors. Two down, single stab wound

and possible shattered jaw on Carl, no assessment on Johnson. Move it! Adebayo, St. Pierre, Mikkelson, sweep the lot, row by row. Talk back every aisle. Eyes *in* the cars as well as around them."

Orion continued to approach slowly, his eyes on the assailant and the surroundings just to make sure the man had been alone. Once that was verified and the other three started their sweep, Orion holstered his gun and ran to Carl first to apply pressure to the wound in his stomach. The hit to his face should have knocked the big man out, but Orion helped ease him to the ground next to a car as Carl groaned in pain. "Easy, pal, just hold pressure on the stomach. Can you talk?"

Carl shook his head, blood pouring from the side of his mouth where it looked like his jaw had been broken. He couldn't even open his eyes through the pain, but he pointed his broken chin toward Johnson, and Orion took his meaning.

"Hold pressure on the stomach. If you bleed out while I'm in command, it looks bad on my resume. Remember that." He patted Carl on the arm once gingerly before scurrying away, staying low to the asphalt as the other three reported that their first aisle was clear.

Johnson was barely breathing, with multiple gashes on her arms that looked like they might have been defensive wounds, and a single spot of blood dripping from the side of her head where it looked like she had been struck with the bat. She was out cold, and Orion had to wonder what kind of insane concussion a hit like that could produce.

He gave the attacker himself only a cursory glance to make sure he was actually dead, but kept his attention between binding up the gashes along Johnson's arms and making sure Carl wasn't bleeding to death. Luckily it was only a few moments before Mercury and Dr. Patel came running out of the building, though it felt like the entire thing had taken much longer than the ninety seconds or so it had actually been.

Mercury was immediately in action, kneeling at Carl's side with her medical kit. With him apparently stable, the first syringe she gave him was a triage mix of painkiller and antibiotic. She didn't even wait for his body to relax before she started ripping at the fabric of his clothes to get to the stab wound, since it was bleeding the most. Dr. Patel was at Johnson's side, though she was frantic. Apparently working in a situation where she might get attacked wasn't going well for the other doctor, but she was doing her best.

Since Anna had barely finished up her treatment, she came stumbling out of the building behind the doctors, clearly all too willing to barrel into a situation that was hostile. She looked around and narrowed her eyes a few times before she looked back at Orion. "They wouldn't attack the security for no reason. It's a distraction." No one had asked her advice or her opinion, but she gave it anyway. "Did anyone stay near the shuttle?"

Orion looked toward the shuttle as she said so, and there were a few people standing outside on the steps leading up to the doors to watch the entire scene, whispering to themselves about what they could barely see from the windows. Anyone could have . . . but they were alone, in the middle of nowhere. He hadn't seen anyone else, and the others were radioing in that they found no one else in their sweep of the parking lot. Somehow, that didn't make Orion feel any more at ease.

"Adebayo, St. Pierre, back to the shuttle, talk down the bystanders. Fitch, go start pre-flight checks. Run them twice. Mikkelson, sweep the interior of the building, tell everyone it's time to get in the shuttle and get strapped in. Time to go." He took his hand off his earpiece with a sigh as he watched Mercury work on Carl, then turned to look at Anna.

"Idiot with a baseball bat and a kitchen knife doesn't seem like a terrorist threat to me. More like a psycho chip on his shoulder against the Consortium. You think somebody's trying to sneak on board?"

Anna shrugged, since she didn't know what someone would do. "Wouldn't that be the best cover-up, to make you think it was a one-shot? I mean, it's no secret that Orbit . . . some people think that Earthlings are idiots. It would definitely make it easier on someone if everyone thought that one crazy person was the biggest threat."

Orion nodded his agreement, looking to the shuttle and waiting to hear from Adebayo and St. Pierre, who had taken the gawkers back inside. "Mercury, how long would it take to DNA-check everybody on board? What's our passenger count, two hundred nineteen? Something like that?"

Mercury didn't look up as she attempted to stitch Carl's wound closed, her hands already covered with his blood. She needed to check his jaw as well, but she was trying to hurry. "Check everyone? How quickly? The scanners are fast, but I don't know that we could check everyone and make it in time for takeoff. And we really shouldn't linger or we could get grounded." Mercury looked up at Orion at that. "If they feel the threat is great enough, they might not allow us to go back for a long time."

Orion looked back and forth between Mercury and the shuttle, weighing the possibilities and the risks of the launch. "Is he going to be stable enough to get him on board and secure him?" He needed more information, and looked back at Dr. Patel as well. "Is she?"

Mercury finished sewing Carl up and she nodded. "There are medical transport pods on every ship. We're going to have to use both of them." She wiped her bloody hands on her scrubs. "But we have to move fast. I don't know if he's bleeding internally, and this building isn't equipped with what I need. There should be a scanner on the shuttle, though. We need to get him on the ship."

Orion nodded and started off toward the shuttle, waving Anna with him. Logan came out a few moments later with Mikkelson and one of the other crew members, and Orion waved them over as well. "You're with me, big guy. Two medical pods on the shuttle to get back to these two. We need to move fast." He was jogging toward the far side of the shuttle where they could get to the medical pods. "Mikkelson, is everybody out?"

"Not many left to begin with. Diego and Abha are rounding up the rest." He looked back at the building and hastily did a sweep of the parking lot as well just to make sure there were no other threats coming out of the woodwork. The emptiness of the world around them seemed suddenly less peaceful than it had just a few minutes before. "Diego said there are reports from some of the other sites. He didn't have time to say what kind."

Orion shared a suspicious look with Anna, since if there were attacks happening around the world, all at Eleusis launches, then it certainly wasn't just some random psycho with a baseball bat. "All the more reason for us to get in the air. Now."

They ran on board through the cargo doors and quickly dislodged the medical pods Orion had always known were there but had never had a reason to use. He and Anna got one, and Mikkelson and Anna's husband got the other, carrying them quickly out of the shuttle and across the lot to Mercury and Patel. He just hoped it wouldn't be too little too late.

While Orion and the others went to get the pods, Mercury set Carl's jaw and put him in a neck brace before she examined his eyes to see if she could see any obvious signs of brain damage. His eyes dilated appropriately, which was a relief in itself. He was out of it due to the painkiller, but she still ran a gentle hand over his cheek.

"Hang in there, big guy. Orion doesn't need to lose another brother." She sighed before she looked over at Dr. Patel, who was still shaking out of shock, so she scurried over to help Johnson. The woman's breathing was shallow and her pupils were not responding at all. "Come on, we've got to get her in the pod, alright? Just take a couple of deep breaths, Doctor, and pull it together. We can handle this."

Dr. Patel nodded, but she was still frantically looking

around as if someone was going to jump out and attack them. In her entire life she had never once faced any kind of bodily harm or threat, certainly not on her home station or on Station Seven where she had been trained as Dr. Finnegan had. Violence and attacks were so unheard of that what happened on Station Nine had been a cruel wakeup for all of them. There were still people out there that wanted to hurt them. "I . . . what if . . ."

Mercury just shook her head. "Here they are with the pods. Did you give her pain medication? A sedative?" Mercury looked at the kit at Dr. Patel's feet and saw that most of it was intact. She immediately grabbed it and pulled out the necessary items and injected Johnson before she looked up when Orion came back with the pods. "Hurry. We need to get her on oxygen."

Orion's instinct was to help his friend first, but he knew Mercury wouldn't have just left him on the ground to help Johnson unless he was stable or dead, in which case he would be beyond help. He and Anna brought the pod down next to Johnson and helped to lift her, gingerly, into the containment unit while the few remaining people streamed out of the building nearby, Diego and Abha whipping them in haste toward the shuttle.

"Mercury." Orion called quietly, working with Anna to get Johnson secured in the pod for transport, "I want you and Dr. Patel once we're out of the atmosphere, to go through every passenger and check on their zero gravity nausea. Do ID checks as you go. If we can't delay take-off, then we can do the sweep while we're in the air, we'll have about four hours of hang time before we're supposed to dock with Nine. Is that do-able?"

Mercury nodded, since she knew they would have enough time in the air, but it made her feel queasy just thinking about potentially taking someone who wished to do harm with them up into the air. "Yes, we can do that." She looked over at her colleague who still looked shaken up, then sighed before she went to help with Carl and the other pod.

Once Carl was strapped in and she had oxygen flowing for him, she went up to Orion. "Maybe I should do it alone." She said in a lowered voice. "I don't think Dr. Patel can handle it right now."

He just nodded, and kept from looking over at Dr. Patel. "You're senior, do whatever you think is best." He put a hand on her shoulder briefly just to let her know he trusted her judgment, then got back to work lifting up one end of Carl's pod. To his surprise, Anna got the other end, and lifted it with him until the wheels could get under it to roll back to the shuttle. Mikkelson and Logan had the other one handled between them.

"You're stronger than you look." They walked the pod quickly back toward the shuttle, leaving the assailant with the bat on the asphalt behind them. No amount of medical attention was going to help him.

Anna choked on a broken chuckle as she helped move the pod along. "Nobody's exempt from hard work on a farm, it just doesn't work that way." She kept an eye out as they moved as quickly as they could without further injuring his friend. "I guess things really do work differently down here than they do up there. Dr. Patel looks like she's never been in a dangerous situation in her life."

"She probably hasn't." He agreed, though from the sound of his tone, he was much less surprised at that fact than Anna was. "She's a doctor. They typically come in *after* the dangerous situation."

"Maybe up there. The doctors I know have seen it all." Anna replied as she helped him get the pod secured, and though it wasn't as easy for her as it was for him, Anna didn't struggle too much. "It looks like one of your friends might be okay. The other . . ." Anna had seen enough people die to know, more or less, when someone was on their way out. His tall friend was beaten up pretty bad, but he was still breathing better than the woman. "Does the ship look okay?"

"I've got one of my people running double-checks on everything. I've flown enough of these that I'll know if something feels sketchy. Did I mention I'm the pilot?" He wasn't honestly sure if he had mentioned that or not, but he kept moving once Carl was secure, running through the cargo bay of the shuttle toward the passenger section, where there was a lot of buzz and a lot of very concerned faces, all of which seemed to look back at him in unison as soon as he was through the door.

The space was set up for maximum efficiency of personal transportation in zero gravity, and as such there were three tiers of seats stacked one on top of the other and interwoven so that more people could be packed into the negative spaces allowed by human comfort. It looked like the entire bay was full of people sitting on each other's laps, but they only had to stay in that configuration until zero gravity. The seat configuration in orbit was much less crowded, since people could be turned upside down to get out of each other's way.

What he was left with at the moment, though, was a beehive of people all looking at him in some kind of accusation. He saw Diego and Abha at the other end of the room looking like they were trying to pacify the situation, but obviously not doing that great a job.

"Two of our officers were assaulted." Orion said in a booming shout that silenced everyone else in the corridor. Apparently his lungs were as freakishly mutated as his growth plates. "They are both seriously injured, but will be monitored for the trip up to Nine where they can be hospitalized. The assailant attempted to use lethal force on them, and was shot and killed. We do not, at this time, have reason to believe he was anything but an anti-Eleusis protestor acting irrationally and alone. There have been reports of similar assaults at other project launch sites."

He strode through the cabin, unimpeded by the people gawking at him and his candor, whereas Diego and Abha had obviously been talking sideways about the whole thing to try and keep people quiet. "I'm your captain for this afternoon, Lieutenant Orion Al-Jabbar. If you got on this shuttle thinking you were headed somewhere without opposition and without risks, then let me speak on behalf of the Eleusis Initiative and invite you to please get the fuck off my shuttle and stay home."

"We're on our way to take the biggest risk any person's ever taken in the history of mankind. If you're not on board with that, then you shouldn't be on board." He turned around once he reached the front of the cabin and looked everyone over, most a little shell-shocked at his speech. He took note of a few who weren't. Resolute faces, committed, even amused. A thin man with a larger brunette sitting next to him, a few of the earthbound he'd seen earlier who still seemed to think the universe revolved around them, a brave and devout soul here and there. He hoped he would be able to remember those he saw. One of them could have been an accomplice of the man with the bat.

"Takeoff is in ten minutes. You know where the door is, and you know where your seatbelt is. That's how long you have to decide." He ducked into the cockpit where Fitch was working at pre-flight checks, and finally let out a deep sigh when he was out of sight, balling up his hand into a fist to keep it from shaking.

Fitch didn't look away from the screen as she continued to get them ready for takeoff, but on a different monitor where they could see certain spots of the passenger area, she saw some people were unbuckling and getting off. She shrugged and kept tapping at the screens in front of her. "Fewer bodies we have to worry about. You okay, Cap?"

"Yeah, I'm good, my best friend is just bleeding to death in the back. Another day in paradise." He shook his head and stepped in to help with the pre-flight checks, but he could see that she had already run the full gambit on everything. "If there is more to baseball-boy, then it at least doesn't look like it was sabotage. Any ideas?"

"It looks like someone tried to get in to mess with wires,

only to find that they're not easy to get to. Everything else looked alright." She pulled a flask out of a pocket on the side of her leg and handed it to him. "At least take a drink if we might die. It'll calm your nerves."

Orion gave her a sarcastic look for the offer, but he took it anyway and took a swig, letting out a grateful sigh afterward as he handed it back to her. "Figures you'd be the smart one who remembers to bring alcohol to Earth. I'm glad one of us has our priorities straight."

He saw all the flight systems go green one by one, as the ship began to recalculate its take-off and atmospheric escape needs based on the current mass on board. Everyone had been instructed during processing to shed everything possible to keep their weight as light as they could. Orion wasn't worried about making it off the planet, just efficiency in doing so.

"Finish off checks and let Nine know we're about to be under way, I'm gonna check through the cabin and see about getting us a backup to replace Johnson. You alright up here?" It had been a first for everyone, actually running into resistance or being attacked, and he knew that was the only reason why Johnson and especially Carl had been harmed at all. He didn't want any more surprises with his team or anyone folding the way Dr. Patel seemed to have done.

"Yeah, I'm alright." She looked over at Orion for a second and then she tapped the gun on her belt before she said anything else. "Do you think we can trust any of the mudders? Maybe you can haul one of them into this mess."

"Might not want to call them that where they can hear you." Orion said with a slight glare in her direction. "And yeah, I've got my eye on a couple I plan to snag for backup on the way up. Unless they hauled ass off the ship the moment I gave them the out, but they didn't seem like the type." He got to the hatch leading back toward the passenger compartment and paused. "Keep the door locked until I get back. Just in case."

"As you say, Captain." Kameron walked up and locked the door behind him and went back to work. She wanted to get the hell off of Earth and back up in space where her life wasn't in so much danger.

21

Mercury made sure her two patients were as comfortable as unconscious, injured people could be in the medical pods, then cleaned up and grabbed a tablet, scanner, and a bottle of anti-nausea medication. She was nervous to go wandering through the crowd of people, but it needed to be done. They had to know if another threat was on board.

Before she could do checks, though, she needed to be strapped in for liftoff, and so she took the seat next to the medical pods to monitor both patients. The vitals for both Carl Espinoza and Allison Johnson were lit up in the air above the pods, and Mercury could reach out and swipe through the hologram if she wanted to access more information. For now, they were stable, but even if they hadn't been, she didn't exactly have the kind of supplies an operating room would have if it came to that. She hoped it wouldn't.

Orion walked back through the passenger portion of the shuttle, looking closely at the people he had picked out earlier just to make sure their faces were fixed in his mind, but he brushed past them until he found the couple he was looking for. The Bickfords appeared to be getting settled in their seats, and he breathed a sigh of relief they were even still on board. They were the only groundlings whose whereabouts he had been personally certain of at the time of the attack on Allison and Carl. "Glad to see you two didn't take the out."

"We don't have a ride home. Going to space is better than walking back to the plains district." Logan teased without quite smiling up at the taller man. Things had been more interesting than he had really hoped they would be for their very first hour as a part of the Initiative.

"That'd be a hike, I'm sure." Orion looked down at the seats they occupied, the next rank of seats just a few centimeters from their faces, especially for Logan, who was built much bigger than was typically considered normal for people who used the shuttles often. "I've got temporary jobs in mind for you two. Wouldn't come with many perks or any pay, but I can at least give you better seats if you're willing to help out for the next few hours."

"Why not?" Anna replied as she shrugged and looked over at Logan, always one to jump into the fray. "Doing something to help would at least distract me from the fact that I'm not sure what the hell is going to happen now."

"Well, a few things are gonna happen now." Orion stood back to let them out of their seats and into the aisle, then waved them to follow him back to the cargo area, where he was glad to see Mercury already strapped in and busy monitoring her two patients. No one else was back there with her, which didn't make him happy, but the others were all busy helping people get strapped in and giving instructions for liftoff safety procedures. They all had known groundlings were going to take a lot of looking after, they just hadn't known they were going to be in a hurry.

"We're about to lift off and we're down two security personnel with a situation that may very well require some security personnel. Should I assume a farming background also comes with comfort and familiarity when it comes to firearms?" As he spoke, Orion was working through a case strapped down farther along the compartment and he entered security codes to reveal a store of handguns and ammunition cartridges.

"I mostly stick with bows and arrows, just by personal preference, but I'm a fair shot with a rifle or handgun." Logan answered hesitantly, since he had never seen guns of the design Orion was pulling out.

"Same basic principle, point and shoot, just don't expect a recoil." Orion closed and locked the case after pulling out a couple weapons, loaded up a cartridge in each sleek gun, and handed them over to Logan and Anna before pulling out his own and twirling it into his palm. Even in dire situations, he was incapable of taking things completely seriously.

"Safety's here, trigger it slowly the first time, release immediately unless you want a sustained shot. You'll feel the trigger set the gun humming before you actually reach the firing point. Feels pretty weird the first few times, but you get used to it. Cartridge is good for a few hundred single-shots or a couple dozen brief sustained ones. Use sparingly." He put his own gun back in its holster and pointed out the spots on their flight suits that were designed to hold firearms securely out of the way along their ribs.

"Doesn't sound too complicated." Anna replied as she looked over the gun. "Logan has always been more about the sport. I'm more about the kill, so I'm a little more familiar with guns. Certainly not these, though." Anna looked up at the tall pilot again. She was familiar with hunting animals, not people, but guns didn't scare her. "We can handle security detail. Just tell us where you want us."

Orion gave her a raised eyebrow. "Well, now you're making me nervous, so work on making me not nervous about having just given you a high-powered firearm, please." He wasn't actually that nervous about it, but he had just met the woman, after all. If she was trigger-happy, handing her something to be happy with wasn't something he wanted on his list of things he'd accomplished that day.

"I want you with me up front on watch between the

flight consoles and the passenger compartment. That's usually Johnson's job." Orion looked over at Logan afterward, though he still looked back at Anna and the gun he'd given her just to make sure she knew he was nervous. "You, I'd like to stay back here and accompany Mercury when she goes to administer the nausea supplements and ID everybody. I'll have Mikkelson and St. Pierre stay near you guys as well, but honestly, if we do find somebody's ass on board who shouldn't be here, you're gonna be better suited to kicking it than they are."

"I can manage that." Logan agreed, nodding at Orion and then back over at the doctor, to let her know he'd take care of things.

Mercury looked at the man from Earth she'd just met, then looked at Orion afterward, everything about her usually-placid demeanor unsettled. "Be careful. Please." She pleaded, since she didn't want to be tending to Orion next. "I don't want to see you hurt."

"I've got the easy job. Unless trigger-happy over here has it out for me, which I doubt. Normally people know me at least a week before they want to kill me." He went over to Mercury and gave her a quick kiss to reassure her. "You be careful too. You find anybody who shouldn't be here, don't make a fuss right away. Get away somewhere and let me and the rest of the crew know. We'll handle it." He left a caress along the side of her face, then stood back up and headed for the passenger compartment, where he stopped to wait for Anna.

"Guess it was a good idea to send the truck back. It would look pretty tempting right about now." Logan said quietly with a hand on Anna's waist. "Don't fall asleep up there. Somebody's on this ship and shouldn't be, they're gonna want access to the flight deck, maybe try and take a joyride."

Anna pulled Logan in for an intimate kiss, since she wasn't about to walk away from him without taking that, especially if there was even a tiny possibility it was her last kiss with him. "I love you." She looked up into his grey eyes after she said it, just so he would be sure to listen to her.

"I love you too. Reach out if you need me." He tapped the communicator in one of the front pockets of his jumpsuit.

Anna followed Orion back to the cockpit and sighed once he showed her where to sit and keep watch while he prepared for liftoff. They needed to get into the air as quickly as possible, but she was oddly calmed and fascinated by all the controls. "I've certainly never seen something like this before. Looks like fun."

"Fun, huh?" Orion smiled back at the odd woman and chuckled nervously as he worked, looking over everything Fitch had done approvingly before he actually strapped himself into the pilot's seat and reached for the intercom. "You've got an interesting idea of fun. Lock down that door for us and run a final pressure check on the hull. Back panel by the door. If you think the rest of this looks like fun, you shouldn't have trouble finding it."

After giving the order, he picked up the intercom and sighed before he clicked it on. "Alright, everybody. Preflight is clear, the exit window is open, and we're about to get this bird in the air. I still show a dozen of you not locked down back there, so either get latched in the next twenty seconds or it's possible you're gonna end up a stain on the rear bulkheads. I would prefer that not happen, but at this point, it's your ass. Hold on tight and just settle in, this next part gets bumpy."

He put the intercom down and nodded approvingly as the number of unbuckled passengers began dropping quickly. "How's the pressure looking?"

It took Anna a little bit to familiarize herself with what he wanted her to figure out, but it wasn't too complicated. "Pressure is stable. You should be good."

"Keep an eye on it. Basically if anything starts yelling at you back there, yell at us. Ship's systems do most of the work for you when it comes to monitoring. And keep the hatch locked." He let out a deep breath once she confirmed the pressure was stable, and looked up to set his eyes on the airstrip ahead of them. "Alright, then, everybody, time to kiss the planet goodbye."

He hit a few switches that brought the engines on either side of the shuttle roaring slowly to life, then closed his eyes and brought his fingertips up to his lips in a quick gesture, tapping them against his mouth, then his forehead before returning his hand to the throttle and drawing it sharply back to throw the ship into forward motion. WIthin seconds, they were hurtling down the runway at a breakneck pace, and seconds later they were tilting upward into the sky at an increasingly steep angle, shoving everyone and everything on board back into the deep padding of their seats as the engines pushed harder and harder toward the clouds.

Anna had never experienced anything like the feeling of the thrust of the shuttle roaring skyward. She'd been on a small plane, a helicopter, but this, this was something all its own. It both terrified and thrilled her with the speed and power behind it, even though she was glued to her seat by the pressure of it all. "Wow." Was all she could mutter through the pressure on her body, but she was clearly enjoying it while most probably weren't.

Orion did his best to keep from being obvious about the fact that it was the first time he'd done a liftoff of that nature as well. He needed to look like he was a professional, otherwise the whole situation would fall apart in a hurry. "Really wakes you up, doesn't it?" He managed to turn his head slowly to look back at Anna in the corner of the cabin, grinning even though his entire body was shaking under the throttle. "Remember not to hold your breath. The cabin is re-pressurizing as we go higher, so if you hold your breath, you'll end up collapsing a lung."

"Good to know." She said haltingly as they continued up and up, and it felt like it was no time at all before they had broken through Earth's atmosphere and they were leaving it behind them. Anna kept working to breathe, but it was getting easier.

"What a rush!" She eventually said breathlessly as she stared at Orion. "No wonder you're a pilot!"

He smiled back at her as they finished their initial break-out, nearly ten minutes later, which he knew was the most difficult part, not to mention the most energy-consuming. Their acceleration was starting to taper off, and he could feel that they were about to be back in near-zero gravity once they were finished with the initial burn.

"Mrs. Bickford, there's a seating realignment panel by your right hand. Move through that and realign them for null gravity instead of ground-based. Fitch, start checking our position and replotting our course, I'll handle engine disengagement and redeployment." Orion started shutting down the engines by degrees, and looked back at Anna with a grin. "This is nothing. The real fun starts when you don't have gravity to deal with. Or at least not as much."

Anna looked over to her right and started tapping around on the screen without making any changes at first so she could just explore and learn a little bit more about what was in front of her. Every computer had some kind of "are-you-sure?" feature before any changes were made, and the shuttle was no different.

Eventually she got around to realigning the seating as he told her to do, it just wasn't immediate. "Not having gravity will definitely be an adjustment, that's for sure." She looked up at him and smirked as she thought about something she definitely shouldn't think about in a potential life-or-death situation, but as a newlywed, sex with Logan was always somewhere in the back of her mind.

"It's more complicated than you might think." He said once he saw her smirk, and let out a brief chuckle as the acceleration of the ship began to dramatically slow, until they were barely being held in their seats. "And yes, I'm talking about sex. I know a smirk like that when I see it."

Anna laughed and she noticed when Fitch looked back at her, but she didn't look ashamed or embarrassed. "I imagine it is pretty complicated. Some men have a hard enough time finding the right hole on the ground."

Fitch couldn't hold back a laugh after that kind of comment, since she wasn't expecting it, but she looked over at Orion and shook her head. "See? This is why I like women. So smart."

"Calm your tits. That one's a newlywed just like me." He finished the preparatory steps to disengage the engines, then cut the throttle completely, which left the cabin feeling strangely silent after the rumbling that shook them for the duration of the initial escape. The lack of shaking added to the loss of gravity was something Orion was accustomed to, but he knew it would be incredibly disorienting for the rest of the passengers on board. "And this would be the part where everybody in the back starts puking. What do you think, Fitch? We've got two hundred plus Earth-born in the back. I'd be willing to put money down on . . . let's say seven percent of them losing their lunch. What do you think?"

"Only seven? I'd take higher than that." Fitch glanced back at their Earth-born passenger, but the woman didn't seem to be too bothered by the change. "Really? Married? Damn it. Didn't even notice the ring before." She lowered her voice before she continued. "I heard that they don't really care about that down there, though."

Orion gave her a warning look before he glanced back at Anna. "Old and married and bored, maybe not so much, but I'm pretty sure every newlywed, on the planet and just off it, cares about it at least for a little while."

Fitch shrugged and looked back at Anna again too, but the woman seemed too distracted by everything around her to notice.

Anna heard the conversation, the space was too small not to, but she wasn't sure what she should address. Certainly she had her own preconceived notions about Orbitals as they did about her.

"Marriages matter." She eventually said out loud, since she felt it was necessary to say. "Who you spend your time with before you get married, not so much, but it does after. On the note of talking about what we've heard, I've heard that you have to get government permission to fuck up there. But I doubt that's true, or else I would suspect that your penitentiaries would be full. Heaven knows I wouldn't be able to abide by a law like that."

Orion looked back at her with an appraising expression, looking her up and down to reassess her and, by extension, Earth-born in general. "No government permission needed to fuck around however you want, only if you plan to get pregnant. Outside of that, they don't really care. Otherwise, yeah, everybody would be a felon."

"You have to get permission to get pregnant, and yet down on Earth, it's illegal to buy, sell, or use birth control. Funny how that goes, huh?" She looked around at all the different screens but stayed in her seat. "I'm sure we have all sorts of differences."

Orion certainly hadn't considered that possibility for people from Earth, and he couldn't quite wrap his head around it. "I'm sure we do. Aside from, you know, height." He chuckled over his shoulder at her and began unbuckling himself from the chair so he could move a little more freely.

The shuttle was still being thrown around a little as they adjusted their course to move safely upward into orbit without flinging themselves completely loose of the planet's gravity. "You can unstrap now. Just be mindful of what's around you, since we'll be making adjustments. If you're gonna puke, there's a bag under your seat. Otherwise you get my cleaning bill."

"Sucks for you, I left most all my possessions back down on Earth, including cash." Anna unbuckled slowly, mostly because she couldn't really remember how to get out. When she did, though, her look sobered as she turned toward the hatch. "I hope everything goes okay out there."

"That's why you're here, help keep an eye on things while we get the course set." Orion pushed himself up out of his seat gingerly, and spun deftly in the air to re-orient himself toward Anna, using the toe of his boot to push off a spot on the control panels that didn't have anything dangerous nearby. He looked as comfortable in null gravity as a bird in flight, pushing himself around with perfect balance and the grace that could only come from long experience.

Within a few seconds, he had settled himself close by, upside down with his feet hooked into a stray exposed pipe in the ceiling. His fingers moved over several of the control panels near her that had been dark during liftoff, and they came to life to show half a dozen shots of the passenger section in its reconfigured seating arrangement.

"This is real-time, but they're recording on a constant feed. Have been since we took off. You see anything that needs looking into, circle it on the screen so we can reference it later. Don't be shy about it. Though I get the impression shy isn't something you'd be much good at."

"Definitely not shy. You could ask just about anyone in my hometown and they'll tell you. Though if you do intend on asking about me, steer clear of most of the male population. They tend to embellish." Anna didn't look up from the feed, her gaze first focusing on Logan. It wasn't easy being away from him at a time like this, no matter how fascinating the shuttle was, or how calm she seemed to be. Joking around was her defense mechanism.

"Well, the only one here from your hometown is your husband, and I doubt he's likely to do much embellishing." She seemed like she was settled in with the monitors, so he went back to hover near the pilot's seat, moving from one set of controls to another as he and Fitch set the ship on the course that would get them to Nine the fastest, bickering like old friends the entire time.

Once they were able to unbuckle from their seats safely, Mercury checked over her patients again and looked over at the large man that was now her assistant/bodyguard. "Well, Mr. Bickford." She said politely as she looked down at her tablet. "I can tell that some people are not handling things as well as they thought they would. How are you feeling now? Do you need medication for nausea?"

"Flying doesn't usually bother me, Doctor. I'm alright." He took his time getting out of his seat and started to float around the cargo space, though, moving gingerly through the air to look things over and get accustomed to weightlessness. "This . . . I can only imagine this takes some getting used to. Though I guess not for you."

"I'm not as used to it as you would think. I'm a doctor. I'm used to working in a space that's closer to earth-gravity." She looked up at Logan again, even though he was only slightly taller than she was. Without gravity, everyone was always looking up. "Come on, let's start scanning our passengers."

He followed her toward the passenger compartment after a last look back at the two unconscious assault victims, and immediately had to dodge someone floating through the space to clean up the result of someone not getting to their barf bag fast enough. He saw another few pieces heading for Mercury ahead of him, and reached out to grab her by her waist to yank her out of the way with one hand still braced on the bulkhead.

One of their fellow passengers floated by, apologizing profusely, with a bag in which they were working on cleaning up the mess, and all Logan could do was shake his head. "Very glamorous thing, space travel." He actually chuckled once and moved with Mercury toward one of the closest rows so they could get started.

Mercury shook her head, since while unpleasant, vomit was not the worst thing she'd ever seen floating around, certainly not after dealing with childbirth. She smiled at him, though, since she was grateful for his quick reflexes. "Thanks for the save. I would not have appreciated getting vomit all over myself this early in the flight." She laughed softly and got to work, pleasant as ever as she moved from person to person, scanning, offering whatever she thought would help people feel better. It was going to take time, and she was nervous about what they might find, but she was doing her best to keep a calm composure and even head.

Gordon was sitting calmly near the front of the passenger section, without showing any signs of nausea or difficulty with traveling in null gravity. He was still strapped into his seat, since he didn't see the point in floating around aimlessly. He looked over at Jessie floating next to him with a smile. "Having fun?"

"Well, it's certainly different." She was holding onto the straps of her seat just to keep herself close. "And I'm glad I took the doctor up on the meds before I even boarded the ship. I would not be doing well right now otherwise."

"It takes some adjustment. But once you've been doing it a while, you get used to how everything moves. Or doesn't, as the case may be." He smiled at her as she tentatively let go, but his eyes were constantly darting around the space to make sure they weren't about to get vomited on. "I've always thought it felt rather . . . freeing, if I can say that?"

"It feels scary too." She admitted as she eventually reached out for one of his straps so she could keep herself anchored, but misjudged and pulled herself a little too close to him. "Sorry."

"You should be more sorry." Gordon said as he reached up to tug one of the straps of her suit to pull her even closer with a smirk. He certainly didn't mind her proximity. "You want me to shove you off? Throw you across the room so you can feel what it's like to fly?"

"And what, watch me crash into five other people first?" She looked directly into his eyes and examined the color of them a little bit now that they were so close together. "I think I better stay here."

"I think you'd better." Gordon's tone was teasing, but his grip on her suit didn't relax. His eyes were a strange kind of brown that kept teasing at her mind that it was hazel without ever actually proving it with the presence of other colors. There were shades in them from amber to earth and everything between, his pupils narrowed almost to single points in the bright light of the passenger cabin.

"The main thing is to remember not to jump off something as if you're on the ground. Good way to break an arm when you try to land on the other side. Goes for a lot of things in life, really." He let go of her suit just long enough to adjust his grip along her side and pull her in closer, until she would have been sitting on his lap if sitting had meant anything in their present situation. "Comfy?"

"Um, sure." She said hesitantly, since she didn't expect him to be so . . . openly touchy-feely. "I guess in space I don't have to worry about crushing someone like you." Jessie had curves in all places, hips, large breasts, and an ass that was more than a handful, and Gordon was wiry, even if he was taller than she was.

"Give me a little more credit than that. I may be skinny, but you'll find I'm not weak. Or easily crushed." He said with a grin, moving his hand over her leg as he held her in his lap. He was a little surprised that she was comfortable with him so quickly, or at the very least wasn't moving away. He knew how off-putting he could be, and while he made no apologies for it, he also wasn't surprised when people swore off his presence on account of it. "In fact, the first lover I ever had was about your height, and not a small woman. Her breasts were far less impressive than yours, though I didn't quite have an adequate appreciation for that at the time."

Jessie rolled her eyes and looked away from him, but there was heat that crept up her neck and into her cheeks. "Didn't know you were a tit man." She mumbled sarcastically, since he'd made no secret previously about her breasts.

"I'm more of a brain-man, really, but tits are a pretty close second." There was a vibration that came out of nowhere against her leg from a pocket on his own, and he grinned at the way it made her jump, then went to retrieve his communicator to see what caused it. As he looked at the screen, though, his teasing smile changed to a deep look of serious concern, and his eyes flicked up quickly to look around the passenger space once he was done reading.

"Interesting." He almost growled as he looked past her across the space to where Mercury and Logan were going around checking people for nausea troubles. "They're smarter than I gave them credit for."

Jessie turned her attention to the Orbital doctor and Logan beside her. She raised her eyebrows before she looked back at Gordon in confusion. "They're smart to go around and give people medication to stop the puking madness? Yeah, I'd say that was pretty smart. And necessary."

"They're checking for stowaways." Gordon said as he pulled out the data core she had seen him use earlier, anchoring it as best he could between his leg and the side of his chair so it could emit its holographic interface. "Here, get comfortable." He put one hand on her back and pulled her down so that her face was resting against his shoulder. It put the two of them much closer together, and also blocked any sight of the small interface from being seen by Logan and Mercury as they made their way through the rest of the population.

Jessie wasn't sure how she felt with her face against him, not to mention the rest of her, but she was trying not to dwell on it. He was using her to cover him, that was all. She lowered her voice as she looked at the different bits of light moving faster than she could follow in front of her face. "Are you a stowaway?" She didn't previously think she was befriending someone illegal, just someone who knew too much.

"Not exactly." Gordon's fingers moved quickly through the interface, but he had to pause and do some detail work when he got to something that looked like a projection of DNA structures. As she watched, she saw letters come up on the screen from someone apparently named Jeffrey.

What do I do? Are you handling it? Stop messing with that bitch and answer me!

Gordon's chest heaved in a sigh as he pointedly ignored the message that came through. "Poor Jeffrey. He never could quite understand priorities." He made no move to hurry the message off the screen or keep her from seeing it, he just continued to work, now with two genetic sequences. From his gestures and the few nuggets of code she could see as he worked, it appeared that he removed one string of DNA and inserted a different one. As he cycled through the information, the name Gordon White came up with Gordon's picture on it for identification. At that, he seemed satisfied, and dismissed most of the program, to access Jeffrey's message and reply.

Tell them whatever you want when they detain you, Jeffrey. By the time you finish reading this, your communicator will be fried. Have some dignity, and remember, you are on the right side of this, even if they can't understand that.

Gordon finished the message and sent it off, then pulled up another program that Jessie could follow easily, navigating through some of the technical components of the ship all around them until he isolated the communicator that appeared to belong to Jeffrey. A few pokes at the hologram and she could see the device's status turn from green to red to black under some kind of programmed assault that rendered it useless.

Jessie wasn't sure what she had just witnessed, and she was trying to piece it together in her head, which just meant she was lingering against him even longer and not really even thinking about it. "Do you know who attacked those security people?" She whispered when she looked up, but part of her was also wondering what he meant by Jeffrey and priorities. In no way, if she was dealing with some kind of fugitive, did that make her a priority, but it almost sounded like he'd meant it to sound that way.

"Difficult as this may be to believe, no, I actually don't." Gordon said with a brief chuckle, even though he realized it would take a specific kind of psychopath to chuckle at the fact that someone had just died. "I saw him approach Johnson with the bat, saw her begin to engage, and decided the distraction was a good opportunity to unload the actual bag I wanted to bring with me from my vehicle in the lot, but Jeffrey and I were on the shuttle before things really escalated. I have no idea why he had such a bone to pick with the Consortium. All I can really say is that he didn't plan ahead very well. He should have brought a gun, at the very least, if he wanted to do any real damage."

Jessie leaned back slightly, but she realized she might expose him with his data core, so she leaned back in sharply, and bumped her nose against his face. "Am I going to get kicked out of the Initiative or worse for being with . . . for being friends with you?"

"I don't know what you're talking about. I was invited." He pointed to the hologram with a grin. "See? Got a letter and everything. I was just, you know, being considerate. Making sure the Initiative's data on my DNA matched what was actually in my veins."

He finished with what he was doing and put away the data core, though as he reached up to put it back inside his shirt, it put his hand quite close to her own chest, and he wasn't careful about keeping himself from brushing the front of her flight suit in the process. "No, the Initiative won't do anything to you for being with me." He said without correcting himself as she had. "So long as they don't know who I am. Which they won't for a long time, if I have my way with it."

She narrowed her eyes at him and pulled back as soon as he had put away his data core, since there was no other reason to remain close if she wasn't helping him be secretive. She didn't need to tease herself or tease him, since as soon as they got to Station Nine, they would be matched with some random people they'd never met. And she wasn't even sure she liked him. Did she? "I don't know why you're trusting me." She pulled away a little bit more. "But I won't tell. Just be careful. And don't leave me out of the loop if something serious happens."

"I'll do my best. It's a big damn loop." He smiled up at her, but pulled her in closer as Logan and Mercury finally got close to include them in their sweep.

"Oh look, two people who aren't puking. How refreshing." Logan said with a teasing grin at the two of them. "You two look like you're adjusting fairly well."

"Yeah, I really thought it would bother me, but I hardly notice. It's easier when you stay strapped in, I feel like." Gordon said amicably, one hand still bunched in Jessie's suit to keep her on his lap, even if she wasn't exactly snuggling any more.

"I took the smart route and got the meds before even leaving the ground, right Doc?" Jessie said to the redheaded woman who just smiled back at her.

"Yes, I remember. Jessica, right? Rogers?" Mercury scanned Jessie and nodded as she looked over the dosage she'd given the woman. "Do you still feel like it is enough? I can give one more dose if you need it."

Jessie shook her head. "Nope, I'm good." She looked over at Logan and raised an eyebrow. "Got appointed to bodyguard already, huh? Is the pilot afraid someone is going to hit on his wife?"

"We're down a couple security personnel, in case you didn't notice." Logan said without sounding angry about it, and actually gave Jessie a smile. "Just taking precautions."

"The kind of precautions that involve drafting the farm-boy." Gordon agreed as he turned his face to help accommodate Mercury's ID scan. "I don't need any nausea meds, Doctor, but thank you. How are the two who were attacked in the parking lot? Were you able to stabilize them?"

"They're stabilized for now. But it's not exactly a short trip from the surface to Station Nine, so let's just hope they stay that way." Mercury looked over her scan and then looked past Gordon and Jessica. "I better keep moving. You know where to find me if you need more medication."

"We do. You and your bodyguard stand out just a little." Gordon said with a final smile, waving at them as they started away. Jessie could see his eyes settle on a man farther up the section from them, who was looking back at Gordon with panic in his eyes, but with a resolute set to his jaw. It would be a while until Mercury and Logan reached him, but from the looks of things, the man was already feeling the countdown deeply.

Jessie leaned in close again so she could whisper in Gordon's ear. "Why is he going to get caught but you didn't? That doesn't make any sense."

"He came to get caught." Gordon said almost sadly, holding Jessie close even as he watched Jeffrey sweat out the moments before Logan and Mercury got to him. "That's his whole reason for being here. I know he was hoping it would happen later instead of right here at the beginning, but it's really for the best. He was useful on Earth, but he's too unstable."

Gordon shook his head and sighed quietly, then turned to speak in Jessie's ear. "The Consortium took his father six years ago, seized his research, destroyed his lab, all of it. He was getting close. Jeff has been waiting ever since to get nabbed by them and see if he'll have a chance to find his father, or at least find out what happened to him. He was a good colleague to have back in the mountains. Revenge is a solid motivator, so long as it lasts."

"The mountains? You're really full of secrets, aren't you?" Jessie found she didn't mind being close to him even though she knew it was a waste of time to entertain the thought. "I find myself more and more attracted to you. Probably because you showed me all of those other men and proved you are intelligent or because you're so mysterious. I can't explain it."

"The human race has a love for secrets and the people who carry them. I'm not sure I can explain it either." That made him laugh, and his hands got bold, moving down over her back and running up her thigh to her hips to hold her close. "But the ones who don't really have secrets are the ones that act like they do, and the ones who really do have secrets are usually the ones that act like they don't. I've got plenty to hide, but you'll see it all eventually, if you decide you really want to."

"Really? Why me?" She shivered a little when his hands went over her thighs, but at least he wasn't disgusted by her and her ample curves. "What about your match? Won't she be jealous that you're confiding in someone else?"

"Oh, absolutely." He laughed as his hand continued its caress, though not much by way of intimacy was possible while wearing the flight suits. "I hope that she's a deeply jealous woman who goes into fits whenever I so much as look at another creature. I have a habit of choosing intensely possessive women. It tends to backfire if the relationship goes badly, but it's great fun while it lasts."

Jessie furrowed her brows and pulled back again. Clearly she had hoped for a different kind of answer, but she barely knew the man. He was very cavalier. "I'm not really interested in sharing anyone with someone else again. I didn't come on this journey to make another woman want to kill me." She pulled out of his lap completely and moved back toward her own seat, but it was slow going in the null gravity.

"No. You came on this journey to have a new life." He grinned a little brighter as he watched her get back in her seat, then unbuckled himself and arched his back to slide into mid-air deftly, one hand still resting on the arm of his chair to anchor him as he spun easily to face her. "And I'm gonna really enjoy watching the look on your face when you get it." He moved in against her just as she got settled, and anchored his hands on the sides of her flight suit to hold himself close in the kiss that followed.

His lips tasted like something sharp enough to draw blood, a kind of tart mint that was difficult to place at first taste. He wasn't shy about the kiss and clearly wasn't trying to hide it from any of the other two hundred people in the room, but as intense as it was, it lasted just barely long enough for the more conservative passengers around them to start getting uncomfortable before he pulled away. "I need to go check some of the bags I brought on board. I'll be back soon."

Jessie was stunned into silence after a kiss that intense, and it was almost instinct for her to reach and grab his arm before he could get too far out of her reach. She hauled him back for another kiss, since no one had kissed her like that in her entire life and she wanted at least one more.

He had no problem with being hauled back, but she could feel him smiling under the touch. His hands gripped her thighs to keep himself stable as he kissed her, and his fingers digging into the stiff fabric of the flight suit were just a tease for what his fingers might feel like digging into the rest of her.

"Like I said," he finally said quietly, once the kiss ended momentarily, "I like my women possessive." He tightened his grip on her suit by way of illustration, chuckling once against her lips.

"I'm already jealous of whoever she is." She admitted softly before she dared to look into his eyes again. "No one has ever kissed me like that."

"Which just means I'll have to help you make up for lost time." The tone of his voice was a promise on its own, but the genuine intensity in his eyes might as well have been swearing on something holy. There was nothing inherently striking about the man except his eyes, and the contradiction in him only became more apparent the longer she spent with him.

As he pulled away, she got another good look at him in his flight suit. Nothing to be too excited about, more of a uniformed stick figure than anything else, shaggy hair in a halo around his head in zero gravity and flowing back from his face as he moved as if he was swimming rather than floating. His features weren't unfortunate, by any means, but there were easily a dozen men more objectively attractive within a dozen paces of where she sat. Everything about him was in the eyes or behind them. Everything that seemed to matter, anyway.

Even after Mercury scanned someone that didn't show up in the database, she acted as though nothing was wrong and moved down the rest of the row treating patients until she could pull Logan aside. He had seen the screen when she scanned the man. He knew. "How do we prevent a scene? Is that possible?"

"Not forever." Logan said with a sidelong look back into the passenger compartment, not looking directly at the man, but pretending to be very intent on someone a few rows away from him, in case the man was watching to see if he'd been discovered.

"What we need to decide is if we make a scene now or we make a scene later. If we make a scene now . . . I've never fought somebody in zero gravity before. This guy might have. So there's no guarantees on that. If we do it later, that gives him the opportunity to do something else while he's still on board. We can watch him, but we can't watch every single thing he does. Without knowing what he's planning, it's hard to know what we need to prevent."

"If you think you can detain him somehow, I have plenty of sedatives I can use to keep him from causing any more trouble. We can't give him any more chances to hurt anyone."

Logan clearly agreed, and looked back over the rest of the passengers with a sigh. "Alright, let's hit the row across from him, let him think we're going about business. If I get a chance to see that he's distracted or just relaxing, I'll grab him. Just have something ready to stick him with in your kit when I do. We've only got the two rows left to do, so once we're sure he's the only one we're worried about, I'll bag him."

Logan allowed himself to look directly at the man again, who wasn't small or weak-looking, even if he was nothing particularly impressive either. Once he'd gotten a chance to size the man up with a solid glance, he looked back at Mercury. "Don't step in until I tell you. Keep your distance."

Mercury nodded as she looked at Logan, since she was grateful that he was going to help her. Orion had enough to worry about with piloting the ship, and the farm-hand next to her looked as though he could handle himself well enough. "Thank you for helping me with this. You don't know me and I don't know you, but I'm grateful that we at least have one thing in common. We want this project to succeed and to get to Eleusis. I doubt you would be so willing to throw yourself at this man otherwise."

Logan shrugged without taking his eyes off the passenger compartment at first, but then turned his stormy grey eyes back on her. "We've both got a lot to lose if this project fails, and a hell of a lot to gain if it succeeds. If throwing myself at somebody is gonna help with that, then that's not a problem."

"I've spent my whole life working toward getting to Eleusis and spending my life there. Especially now that I have someone I love and I want to build a family with. Eleusis has never meant so much to me as it does now. I know you want the same thing with your wife. We're on the same team." Mercury gave him a resolute nod and then turned her attention to her kit. "I'll be ready when you are."

Checking through the rest of the passengers went about as easily as the first part of their task had, though they still had to stop and clean up a few messes from people who hadn't quite adjusted to their lack of orientation. When they finally got to the end of the row again, they settled in talking with a pair of sisters who were fawning over Mercury and asking where she dyed her hair to get it to look that color, to the amusement of all. Logan was legitimately entertained by the entire exchange, mostly because Mercury seemed so confused and taken aback by it, but the entire cabin was set at ease one laugh at a time.

Keeping "Jeffrey" in his peripheral vision was fairly easy during the conversation, and it was similarly easy to anchor himself on the edge of one unoccupied seat, rocking to gauge the momentum he would need to get to the imposter before being spotted doing so.

Mid-laugh, he launched himself in the man's direction and managed to barrel into him hard with his shoulder while simultaneously grabbing the man's forearms. To his credit, "Jeffrey" recovered quickly, head-butting Logan as he attempted to move the fight out of the seat and into mid-air where things would be more confused.

Logan was having none of it, though. He hooked his feet around one bolted chair leg and shuffled the imposter around until Logan could grab one flailing leg and slam the man hard against the floor of the compartment. In the disorientation that followed, he launched himself at the man's back and managed to pin both his arms, with his legs locked around the man's waist.

"Calm down, pal." Logan said as the man attempted to struggle in vain with still more head butts that Logan easily dodged. "You're gonna go to sleep for the rest of the trip. We'll talk more when you wake up. Just get comfy. Doc's got something for ya." He had to twist himself as they flailed together in the air due to the man's struggles, but there were a few individuals nearby who had presence of mind enough to take Logan by the back of his shirt to stabilize him in such a way that Mercury could approach without getting bitten or kicked.

Mercury acted fast and had a lot more practice with orienting herself quickly and correctly, so she was at Logan's side almost too soon. She had the sedative ready and even though the man was wiggling, she managed to get the needle securely into his arm. Somehow afterward, he was able to get the arm free, and he elbowed her hard in the cheek. Mercury could already feel the bruise that would show up on her pale skin, but she managed to catch herself on someone's seat before his blow to her face actually pushed her further away.

Logan wrenched the man after he threw the elbow,

slamming his flailing leg into a nearby seat with an audible crack that had the man roaring in pain rather than defiance. But even as he wailed, he began to settle and go limp, and within a few moments, his groans of pain gave way to grunts as he tried to stay conscious and failed. Once it was clear the man was out cold, Logan released him to float in the open space between the passenger rows and went to tend to Mercury.

"Let me see it." He reached up to turn her face toward him, looking over her cheek and the side of her face with a touch that was every bit as tender as his hold on the imposter had been rough. "Nothing broken?"

She reached up and touched her cheek with a wince, but ran her tongue along her teeth inside of her mouth to make sure that there was no damage. Mercury shook her head slowly with his hand still touching her skin gently. It was strange that he could be a hulking fighter one moment and gentle the next, but she had seen the same with Orion. Men were such strange creatures sometimes. "Nothing feels broken. Though it hurts a lot. Does it look bruised already?"

"It'll ring for a while, and yeah, it looks like it's gonna bruise something awful, but it should be gone in a day or two, if you heal up here the way we do down below." He held onto her face for another moment just to finish looking over her cheek, then let it go. "Sorry about that. He's not that strong, but he's a slippery bastard."

"It's alright." Mercury said as she tried to smile, though she winced again. "It'll make me look tougher than I really am." She looked over at the now-unconscious man and then she sighed heavily. "I'm going to put a cold pouch on this. Can you update Orion?"

"Sure, just as soon as I get this guy tied up." He had to use Mercury to push back a little bit just to get himself in motion back toward the man's body, leveraging with a hand at her waist to push himself toward the deck and push Mercury gently back against the seat where she had ended up.

"Nothing to see here, folks, everybody go back to gazing at the stars. Just taking out the trash." Logan grabbed the man by the back of his flight suit and began carefully floating with him through the air toward the cockpit, towing the man's body with one hand. An hour in space and he'd already had to beat someone unconscious. That didn't bode well for the rest of his time in the Initiative.

22

After Logan had subdued the passenger masquerading as Jeffrey Wurtz, the mood on the ship turned pointedly sedated, as if Mercury's syringe had been intended for everyone, not just the fraud. Everyone else on board had checked out, their identities secured and verified, and there was plenty of sedative to keep the imposter unconscious for the rest of the trip to rendezvous with Nine.

Orion looked over his shoulder at Anna, who was still looking through the various controls for the ship after she had promised not to blow them up by touching anything she shouldn't. Fitch had long since decided to sit back with a book just to forget everything that happened prior to launch, which left him watching the instruments and Anna playing with the machine.

"If you're wondering, the answer's yes." He eventually said as he leaned back to stretch in mid-air, nearly breaking himself in half as he arched his back in zero gravity. "Yes, it's always this level of boring. Ninety percent of the time, anyway. Maybe ninety-five."

"It's not boring." Anna said as she continued to explore, since she was having a good time, even if the situation was somewhat dire. "And if you're really *that* bored, then come over here and teach me some more about this shuttle. That's got to be more exciting than just floating there watching screens, right?"

"You really are the cat that curiosity's gonna kill." He laughed and twisted slowly in the air to grab onto the wall of the cockpit and move himself toward her. "We should be about half an hour out, so that's how much education you get. What are you looking at?"

She glared at him for his comment about her curiosity, but he wasn't the first one to say her curiosity would get her into trouble. On the other hand, most of the men in her life hadn't been complaining that much when they realized all the experience her curiosity gave her.

"Well, when I look at this screen, I think I'm looking at the other stations nearby, right? Smaller stations. Even though they're not that close, I realize. But what are these others? Satellites? And how do you orient yourself up here? I mean, North, South, East, West, they all still apply, I guess, but . . . everywhere you look there's nothing. It's not like going off of the sun, or land masses, or the river . . . Technology is great, sure, but what if things go to shit? Surely you can pilot this thing without a computer telling you what to do, right?"

"Yeah . . ." he affirmed, but he sounded doubtful about it. "It's not so much about piloting things up here. If you think of it like that, you'll run out of fuel in a hurry and wind up stranded somewhere. You've gotta think of it in terms of inertia, trajectories, and all the shit that's potentially in your way. It's all the other shit in the sky that ends up being a problem."

"So yeah, you could fly without instrumentation, but it's the computer that keeps an eye out for the stray . . . I don't know, there were some fuckwads a few years ago who got their hands on a big box of golf balls and were hitting them out of the airlock of their station for kicks, joking about who could hit the moon with them. Turns out, about two hundred of them managed to stay in solid orbit and four people died because of station impacts that couldn't be avoided. So, it's shit like that most likely to kill you up here."

He oriented himself so he was behind her as she looked over the panels, just because he was accustomed to being so much larger than everybody else around him that reaching over people's shoulders wasn't a problem. He reached past her and pointed to the right commands for her to get data on the other, smaller objects that she had correctly pointed out. "This is a running Little-Shit catalog of everything within three hundred kilometers or estimated to be within three hundred clicks in the next hour. That's why it's changing like that."

He left the list up and moved so he could look down at her, even if he was still in a position to walk her through the screens with other questions. "You fly down on the ground? I thought I would've remembered seeing another pilot in the registry for this pickup."

"Legally?" She asked with a laugh as she tilted her head back and to the side to try and look back at him, though it wasn't working very well despite how much taller he was. "I'm not a pilot, just like I'm not a lot of things. You know, by title or profession. But I like to learn and I like to deal with machines. It could be my small-er-person complex." She laughed again and turned her attention back to the screen. "I don't know, when people tell you your whole life that there isn't a lot of time to learn much of anything, sometimes it makes you want to learn everything."

That was clearly heavier than Orion had thought she was going to go with the conversation, but he just nodded his agreement. "Well, if you're good with machines, then you're gonna be good with everything up here. As far as I know, they've got some of you set for certain positions in the Initiative, but most of you are gonna be under an open skill set until you decide what you're into. You want to be a pilot, you could certainly take a run for it."

"Really? You think they would actually give me a shot at that?" She was surprised he thought she could be a pilot.

"That would be fun. Think you would be my teacher?"

"I don't know. Maybe. There's maybe thirty of us in the Initiative, against almost three thousand people, mostly from Earth, so I expect we'll be training a few more of you to help us out." He reached out and smacked her hand when she was about to hit something that wasn't what he knew she was looking for, and he indicated the right one before he let her continue.

"I've trained before. If you manage to actually ask a decent question about the controls instead of just dicking around for twenty minutes trying to find your way back to the central prompts screen, then you'll be easy."

"I don't know, I like dicking around." She replied with a wry grin, even after he smacked her hand. "You're a little bit pushy. Lucky for you, I'm not ladylike enough to get offended." Anna was always absurdly sarcastic. It was part of the reason why Ben acted the part of the oldest sibling, he was always more serious about everything than she was.

"You think *I'm* pushy, just wait and see if they give you a *real* instructor. If you're not questioning your own existence within the first week, they don't feel like they're doing their job." He showed her a few more screens where she could track the progress of inbound objects and watch for current mapped trajectories of just about everything in the sky, but there was an alert in the middle of one of his commands, letting them know it was time to start prepping for final approach to the station.

"Alright, this is the fun part. Watch and learn." Orion gave her a final smile and contorted himself through the air back into his own seat, though the ship lurched a little while he was away from everything and sent him against the front view-window. He just rubbed the back of his head and glared at Fitch. "You know, someday that's gonna get old. For both of us."

"Nah." Kameron said with a grin and a satisfied chuckle over at Orion before she looked back at Anna. "It was twofold anyway. I get a better view of her when the restraints have to do their job."

Orion just rolled his eyes as he got himself back into his seat and into his restraints. "You're hopeless. You realize that in about . . . an hour and a half, you're about to get matched with somebody possessed of a penis, right?"

Kameron definitely did not look happy about that, her wince was obvious but her gag at the idea was well-contained. "I hope he expects to get cheated on, because dicks are disgusting." She looked him up and down once and shook her head. "I can't be the only woman that definitely does not want to get involved with a penis, and I'm going to find however many of those women that I can. Somehow I'm going to have to tolerate it for reproductive purposes and I really don't know how to make that happen."

"Hey, we're going to a new planet. We're all about new experiences." He grinned over at her, even though he sympathized with the problem. "Besides, like you said, you're getting matched with him to reproduce, it's not like you're legally required to fall in love with the guy. Just set expectations right off the bat and you'll be fine. Who knows, maybe you'll get paired up with a gay guy who's just as unhappy about it as you are. That way you can both get incredibly drunk, go at it, then move on with the rest of your lives afterward."

Her expression still looked incredibly sour as she contemplated the idea and looked back at Anna longingly. "So not fair. Can't they just inject me with some sperm and let me have a beautiful woman?"

"I can still hear you, you know. Especially when you turn your head and look at me." Anna replied as she peeled her eyes away from the screens. "I'm flattered, and I bet you're a lot of fun, but I'm still married. And honestly, I actually do like penis much better than tits and a vagina. I've had a fair sampling. Penis wins."

The whole exchange had Orion laughing as he worked on the controls to adjust the pitch of the ship to bring them into rotation with Nine as they approached. "Alright, well, as much fun as it is to listen to how either disgusting or amazing my equipment is, it's time to get back to work. Bickford, you think you can go back and help get people in their seats? Docking gets bumpy sometimes, I don't want people getting pancaked against the hull if I have to move fast and dodge somebody here in a minute. It's sure to be a pretty busy dock right about now."

"Doesn't look that busy, actually." Fitch said as she turned her attention back to her reports, though her expression didn't look happy about it. "This news feed coming in says some of the ships didn't get clearance to come back." She gave Orion a sideways glance. "A couple were destroyed."

He was worried when they found an imposter aboard that there was something larger going on, but he hadn't wanted to admit it. He made a final few adjustments to make sure they were on course to match up with the station, then sighed and lowered his head without looking over at her. "How many? What pickup sites? Anyone from our unit?"

"Four ships didn't get clearance to come back. Another was completely destroyed, fifty-five passengers killed. The other destroyed was just the ship, no one had boarded it yet, they're sending another down to pick people up, but obviously they'll be a few days late." Fitch was starting to feel sick to her stomach as she read over the information several times as quickly as her eyes could read. "It looks like the ships were mostly on the Asia continent. One in Africa." She shook her head quickly. "We can't think about this right now. We need to get our passengers safely aboard Nine. We'll get the full story once we're inside."

Anna was quiet as she listened to Kameron explain the severity of the situation, then unbuckled her restraints to go do as Orion had asked. "I'll be back once I've made sure everyone is ready for docking." She eventually said out loud, but she didn't pause to hear a response as she slipped out of the control room and floated haphazardly out into the general seating area.

She immediately saw Logan near the doctor she knew was Orion's wife, and she made a beeline for him, since she needed to talk to him. Fortunately for her, his reflexes were like a cat. She'd pushed toward him too hard and nearly crashed into the wall next to him before he reached out and grabbed her. "Hey, you. Nice save. My skull thanks you."

"Your skull is welcome, along with the rest of you." He pulled her through the air to set her down on the seat next to him so she could get her bearings, but didn't take his hands off her afterward. "How much longer till Nine? People are starting to get antsy back here."

"We're nearly there. I'm here to tell everyone to get back into their seats so they don't become splatter on the walls." She buried her face into the side of his arm, though, as soon as she was sitting next to him.

"Logan." She said softly, and when he leaned down to get closer to her face, she kissed him first and then spoke in a whisper in his ear afterward. "Two shuttles were destroyed, one with fifty-five people on it. Four others weren't even cleared to leave. This shit is bad. What are we doing here?"

That was clearly a lot worse than he had imagined it was going to be, and it took him a moment to take in that kind of information before he just sighed and kissed the top of her head as she rested her face against his arm.

"Trying to make a difference." His voice was low as well, and he didn't sound as thoroughly convinced as he had a few hours earlier when they had been trying to talk themselves into getting out of the truck. "Any claim of who did it? Angry people who didn't get accepted? Terrorists? Religious freaks?"

"I don't know, the other pilot didn't say if her information specified. That's . . . a very well-planned attack, Logan. I mean, six different launch sites compromised, seven, if you include ours? At least our shuttle wasn't blown up." She held tighter to him afterward. "This is terrifying. Who knows what the fuck could happen next?"

"Whoever's doing the blowing up, I would guess." He looked across the cargo bay to where he had secured 'Jeffrey' against a wall with half a dozen different cords after searching him and finding nothing but a fried communicator. "Maybe he'll have some answers for us once we get to Nine and turn him over to the Director."

"Maybe." Anna replied as she looked over where Logan had secured the infiltrator. Eventually she looked into Logan's eyes and pressed her lips against his in a desperate kiss. Her tongue traced along the seam of his lips in a velvet tease before she pulled away. Fear of death apparently made her want him even more. Logan kept her grounded, and reminding herself that they were in this together was keeping her sane. "I love you. I would be lost here without you with me."

"I love you too." He pulled her into his lap to kiss her once more, since he knew she had to go and get everyone else secured for docking and he wanted her as close as possible for as long as possible. "We'll handle it. Whatever this is that's going on up here, we're in it now, and we'll handle it. Whatever it takes."

She nodded in agreement since it was all she could do and they had no other option. They weren't going home, and now they might never get the chance, certainly if people were out to kill them for being associated with the Initiative. All they had was whatever was ahead of them with Eleusis itself, and they would have to figure it out somehow.

Anna stole another heated kiss before she took a deep breath and slowly started to move out of his lap. "Stay secure, alright? I'll see you after we dock." Anna ran her fingers over the side of his face and gave him a small smile before she pulled away completely.

Mercury hadn't intended to watch Logan with his wife, but they were sitting close enough that even though she hadn't overheard the conversation, she couldn't miss how he was holding his wife and the way they kissed each other. "We're lucky people, aren't we? We get to be a part of this

Initiative with the people we love."

Logan nodded, smiling sadly after Anna as she floated out to start bossing around some of the passengers to get them back in their seats. "We applied for this program for completely different reasons than the ones that actually got us to accept. World was a different place for both of us a year ago. I applied because I couldn't stand watching her with anyone else any longer, and things had kind of taken a turn for me that left me without much reason to keep moving. I'm glad it's a different world." He smiled, then nodded over to Mercury. "What got you and the giant to apply?"

"We both have been working toward this our whole lives." Mercury replied as she looked over Carl's vitals one more time before docking. She was glad to see that both of her patients were still alive and stable, but she had no idea how extensive the damage was for either of them.

"I didn't think there were so many people out there that hated it, or that wanted to destroy something good for humankind, but I still want what I wanted when I applied. I grew up hoping to be a great doctor and to live on Eleusis. I want to develop a permanent cure for CV. I want to protect Eleusis from CV and to help Earth. All of that was all wrapped up into one big dream, and now Orion is a part of that too."

"He seems like a good man. I've never had much use for military types before. Out in the districts, they tend to just be the reason kids leave home too early and get killed earlier than they should have for being somewhere they shouldn't. He at least seems like he knows what he's doing."

"He does." Mercury nodded confidently and looked over at Logan briefly. "It'll be good to get on Nine where things can settle down. Everything will get sorted out. Hopefully these two will make full recoveries." She glanced over at the vitals and then back at Logan. "I just didn't imagine it would be like this."

"I knew space was going to involve expanding the

capacity of my imagination." He said sadly as he looked over Johnson as well, since she was closer to him, then turned to look out the window at the Earth as they rolled to match the station, spinning slowly through the dark at a scale that made him shake his head. "Doesn't mean I'm prepared." He floated over to check the imposter in his restraints again, then went to Mercury to make sure she was strapped in tightly for docking. He had been told to look out for her, after all, and he took that kind of job very seriously.

"Thanks." She said politely as he tugged on the restraints over her chest to make sure that they were tight and secure. Her cheek still ached from being hit in the face, but the cold pack had helped. "You've helped me a lot today. I'm grateful. You're a good person."

"I try to be. Just like everybody else. At least most of the time." He gave her a conflicted smile as he headed back to his seat, strapping himself in tightly with his eyes going back and forth between the restrained redhead across from him and the passenger compartment where everyone was attempting to get settled. Over fifty people dead, shot out of the sky, another ship destroyed.

He had his doubts about how hard some people were trying to be good.

Compared to the rest of the trip, the docking into Station Nine was probably the smoothest part. Mercury sighed in relief as soon as she heard the hissing of the landing clamps, even though she knew that there was probably still more headache to come. Especially concerning her patients. Orion made an announcement for everyone to remain in their seats until the two injured could be taken off the shuttle, and as soon as they were locked in place and the airlocks opened, a medical team came swarming into the shuttle.

Mercury barely had time to say anything before they uploaded the information they needed from her monitoring and rushed Carl and Johnson out of the shuttle. She was stunned by how quickly her patients were gone, and how little regard she was given about it. She wasn't even out of her own restraints in time to follow the team, and then a security team came in to remove the unconscious prisoner before anyone else was allowed to do anything at all.

"I . . . um, I hope they keep us updated." She said to Logan, though she wondered if he would even care to continue talking to her now that they were docked and he didn't need to work beside her any longer.

"Well, the two injured are a part of the Initiative, right? We'll see them once they're out of recovery. As for the other guy . . . I wouldn't figure on seeing him again." Logan had seen the look of the security detail that came to collect the imposter, and they hadn't seemed like they were even interested in hearing anyone's version of what had gone down on the ground. They were interested in getting the guy out and nothing else. "Those didn't look like the type you come back from once they decide they need you locked up."

"They don't, you're right." Mercury fully disengaged herself from her seat, but she had to grab onto Logan's arm for a moment to orient herself correctly. "We should go find our spouses. I don't want to give the Initiative any chance to separate me from Orion because they want to question people. Being treated like a criminal once was more than enough."

It wasn't difficult to find Orion and Anna, but the rest of the passengers were busy getting out through the airlock as Logan and Mercury wove their way through in mid-air. The other security officers had gone ahead to lead the way for the Earth-born passengers to get where they were supposed to be congregating, but Orion and Anna hung back with Fitch to make sure everyone got off safely and the ship was secured.

Orion hovered in the upper corner of the passenger bay, watching everyone get out, but put out a hand to pull Mercury in against him once she was close enough. "I missed you."

Mercury instantly melted into Orion's embrace and she

kissed him with need behind every press of her lips. "I'm so glad to see that you're alright. They rushed in and took Carl, I was hoping they might let me go with him, but they didn't even talk to me. I'll try to get more information once we're settled."

"I'm sure they'll take care of him." Orion said mostly to convince himself. "I would've felt better with you looking after him, but he'll be alright. He's a tough son of a bitch, if nothing else." He squeezed her tighter against him as they waited for the shuttle to empty. "Are you alright? After everything on the ground?"

She nodded as she kissed him again, but then leaned back so he could actually see her face, since she had jumped into kissing him as soon as she could. "The prisoner hit me pretty hard when I tried to sedate him, though I'm pretty sure Logan broke the man's leg. Or arm. It was hard to tell where the sound came from." Her cheek was definitely turning purple.

"Ouch." He ran his hand around the edges of the bruise, but didn't touch it directly. "I mean, I'm glad it wasn't anything worse, but that looks like it's gonna sting for a while."

Mercury nodded, but she was a little surprised his reaction wasn't anger like Logan's had been, and Logan didn't even know her. "Come on, let's get inside. I hope they have some answers about something."

"So you're basically telling me you're the one who flew us here." Logan joked as he pulled Anna onto his back with her legs wrapped around his waist. It was easy to navigate with her attached to him that way, and he liked having her hanging on at every available opportunity. "What was the hardest part, would you say, the actual flying or the lying to your husband about it afterward?"

"I'm not lying!" She defended with a laugh as she held tighter to him, mashing her breasts into his back and kissing his neck every so often as he floated them both into the space station. "Just ask that Orion guy. He'll tell you. I totally owned that shuttle."

"That's a useful skill to have." Logan said with another laugh, but his tone grew a little more serious as they gained some distance on everyone else around them. "Might come in handy sometime before we're done with everything up here. Be good to know how to take one of those things and run with it in case there's a need."

"I know." She agreed quickly, since the same thoughts had crossed her mind. "I still want to be able to get home." Anna whispered into his ear before she nipped at his earlobe. "He says I might be able to get into pilot training now that we're here. It will be good knowledge to have."

"Really? Wow, that would be pretty great for you." Four hours in the air and she was already lining up a career for herself. Just when he thought he couldn't admire his wife more than he already did. "Only thing I'm likely to get trained in after today is how to use a gun. Not sure I want to make a career out of that, but I guess if they need me on that kind of detail, that could come in handy someday too."

"They're going to need you for more than a gun." She said as she teased the side of his neck with her teeth. It wouldn't matter if they were dying, bleeding out, she would still want to be touching Logan, kissing him, just be near him. As it was, he randomly reached back and grabbed her backside to make sure she was still firmly in place on his back, but she knew that wasn't the only reason. "You have so many skills. Half the stuff I know, I learned from you."

"Let's not talk about where you learned the other half of the stuff you know." He teased back at her, turning his head to kiss her and having to flail a little to correct their balance as they floated down the corridor afterward. "And most of the stuff I know, I only know because I messed around with things until I broke them, then kept messing around until I got them working again. I doubt we'll be given that kind of freedom to fuck around up here."

Anna just shrugged, since she wasn't sure she could agree. "Orion let me mess around with the shuttle. You know, under supervision, but still. I imagine they want us to learn how to figure things out for ourselves, right? I mean, there's no IT support on Eleusis."

The entire dock was like something out of a hallucination for Logan, people pointed every which way, drawing their luggage with them, all in the same iron-grey Eleusis Initiative flight suits. There was a woman pushing a pallet of supplies that Logan estimated had to weigh at least five hundred kilos, but she guided it through the air by way of a pair of thin lead ropes and the occasional kick or shove, heading down to a supply room of some kind just off the dock. It felt like watching a school of incredibly disorganized fish in a bowl, except he was one of the fish. "At least Eleusis will have gravity. This is . . . I'm not sure I'm ever gonna get used to this."

Anna nodded in complete agreement as she continued to hold on like a monkey on his back. "It smells weird up here, too. Everything is so . . . sterile." She wrinkled her nose as they drifted further in the direction of the light-up arrows. As they moved, every so often, she could see their names light up above them, which disconcerting. They were monitored everywhere they moved, but it looked like everyone was, so they could be guided in the right direction by the station itself. "And there's no breeze. There's just nothing."

It took a little creative maneuvering to get them heading in the right direction, but they eventually got one of the smaller lifts, and Logan was about to touch the button for the appropriate level written on the wall when the button lit up on its own and a sign was displayed to warn them they were about to begin descending.

For the first part of the descent, they were sitting with their backs to the ceiling, and Logan just shook his head. The day couldn't get much weirder. "I always thought when they got up here, they would try and replicate what was down there, you know? Throw some green in somewhere, a flower box, something. But if this place is any indication, they walked away from Earth and never looked back."

"Why would they want to leave Earth behind for all of this?" Anna questioned softly, since nothing about the place appealed to her except that it was the only way for them to eventually get to Eleusis. "You would think they would have put a little more effort into saving Earth all those centuries ago if this was the only alternative."

When the lift slowed down, Anna could tell there was a little more gravity pulling them away from the ceiling. They were closer to hovering over what she considered was the floor, but it was still hard to determine floor from ceiling. "It's much better than this."

The gravity wasn't quite enough to make it easy to walk, but it was enough to make it possible to bounce with long strides across the floor in the direction the lights were indicating. "There's certainly more to it. This just seems . . . dead." There were others in the corridors with them, all heading the same direction, but the place was still mostly deserted. Logan wasn't sure if that was for their benefit or if there was some kind of population shortage in space as there was on Earth.

Anna didn't recognize anyone as they bounced through the corridor, and she didn't like the fact that most expressions weren't happy or hopeful, but full of worry and concern. Clearly they weren't the only shuttle that had experienced some difficulty getting up into space. "God, it feels like we're going to a funeral."

All Logan could do was agree as they looked around at all the grim faces, but within a few moments, there was much more to see. The corridor ended in a large set of double-doors, on the other side of which was a meeting-room that was . . . strangely beautiful. From the doors, the floor fell away in broad tiers into a wide amphitheater, with a wide stage at the far end of it.

The wall behind the stage was completely clear, as if they had stepped out to a room that was actually exposed to space, even though Logan knew there had to be glass there.

The Earth was visible beyond it, but they were spinning steadily, and the part of the world they were looking down on changed with every passing moment. The ceiling of the chamber was patterned in subtle colors, like metal worked in a fire at different temperatures, bringing out patterns and rifts in the structure above their heads.

There were thousands of chairs already set up through the vast space, individually bolted into designated spaces, and hundreds of people already settling in for whatever came next. "Looks like this is the place." He looked down at himself and shook his head, squeezing her hand tightly. "If this is a funeral, then I forgot to get dressed for it. And I'm pretty sure I left all my handkerchiefs at home."

"The only person I would mourn here would be you. And I'm not letting you go, so if you're dying, you're taking me with you." Anna gripped his hand even tighter as they moved to find some seats, and it was only as they moved slowly through the empty seats that they happened to see a few people that they recognized from their own ship. Not friends, really, but people they knew from Earth, at least.

It was clear who was from Earth and who wasn't, not only because of the way people fumbled around or didn't, but also how awkward people behaved in their uniforms, or how haggard they looked based on a rough ride or a simple ride from one station to the next. Clearly both sides, Earthlings and Orbitals, were wary of each other.

Logan noticed people at the same time Anna did, and after squeezing her hand, they took a tentative jump over a few rows of seats to land near some of the other passengers who were still looking around at the place half in wonder and half in trepidation.

"Aiko, right? Tanaka?" He said to the tiny woman in the next row. "Sorry, I saw your name when we were coming around with the meds. You two kind of stuck out." He tried to give the woman and her brother a smile, and reached out to shake their hands once they were planted, a few more people from their shuttle gathering near them in small groups. "Logan Bickford. Didn't get a chance to introduce myself earlier."

Aiko gave him a small smile as she shook his hand. Her hand was easily enveloped by his, but that seemed to be the case with a lot of the men she had met that day. She felt like she was surrounded by a half-giant race. Maybe they made a mistake in accepting her in the first place. "Nice to meet you." She shook Anna's hand after and was grateful that at least Anna didn't look like a giant.

Aiko glanced over at her brother and sighed as she looked around the room. "You were watching over the injured guards, right? Were they okay? Was anyone else hurt?"

"They were stable the last I saw them. And no, nobody else got hurt, thank god." He shook Kazuo's hand afterward and sat down awkwardly, since it felt like he was barely being held to the seat. Every little move he made to get comfortable set him bouncing in the air. "Not on our ship, anyway. There were other ships that have had . . . problems. I'm sure they'll talk about it here in a minute. They have to."

Aiko's expression was hard to read as she considered what he told her, she then looked back toward the staging area where she assumed the leaders of the Initiative would speak to them when everyone had arrived. "I'm not sure we'll get the whole story."

"I'm sure we won't." Logan said darkly, but he sighed and put an arm around Anna to hold her tight against him while they waited.

Some people had an easier time moving in the low gravity than others, but Gordon wasn't one of those who seemed bothered by it. He walked/bounced next to Jessie as they headed into the seats, scanning the crowd for everyone he knew he would know.

"So this is what the beginning of the end looks like." He said with a half-dreamy kind of smile on his face as he looked around the room. "Nicer place than I would have thought."

"The beginning of the end? Don't you sound positive and upbeat." Jessie mumbled as they found seats. The kisses they had shared were something she wanted to repeat, but she knew in less than an hour she would watch her name pop up on some kind of screen or announcement and it would match her picture with someone else. Someone she wasn't really interested in kissing, not like her sudden interest in Gordon. "It's nice enough."

"It's the nicest place we're likely to see for some time." He seemed quite positive and upbeat about it. He smiled at her as they moved into a row of seats and settled, but something a few rows away caught his eye as he followed Jessie.

He hadn't seen her at the airstrip, or on board the shuttle, but there had been over two hundred people all jostling about, so missing just a few was hardly surprising. He stopped when he saw her, and watched her eyes as they moved constantly around the room to take in her surroundings and the other people.

It was only a matter of moments before she would keep scanning and see him. He briefly considered turning away and letting her miss him, since he kept himself as nondescript as possible, but instead he waited for her to meet his eyes. She had to have known he would be there, just as he had known she would be.

Aiko froze when her eyes crossed over Gordon, and when his eyes met hers, her stomach sank. Aiko reached over to her brother subtly and poked his side so that he would look as well. She knew that *he* would be here, but seeing him was another thing entirely.

Kazuo looked up when she poked him, and when she didn't look away from whatever had her transfixed, he followed her eyes and froze himself. He was quiet for a moment, but moved to hold his sister's hand to let her know she wasn't alone with the guy so close by. "I was hoping he wouldn't show up." He whispered, half in Japanese, half in a growl.

"We knew he would." She whispered back in Japanese, and he could feel her hand shaking slightly as he held onto her hand. "He wouldn't miss this. Not now."

Kazuo's grip on her hand tightened when Gordon had the audacity to actually smile back at them on his way down the row toward a seat. Once the man sat down, Kazuo finally let out the breath he hadn't realized he was holding, and tried to force himself to be calm, for his sister's sake. "He can't hurt you here. He can't risk it."

Aiko watched Gordon for a little while longer but then forced herself to look away. "I was never as worried about getting hurt by him as I was about other things." She shook her head slowly. "Let's sit down. Here. Away from him."

Kazuo kept glaring at the back of the man's head, even though he never turned around to look at them again. Kazuo kept tapping his fingers on his knee as they waited and the room filled up, watching Gordon and the others on the stage.

Part of the broad windows looking out on Earth turned opaque at a few gestures from some of those on the stage, and the logo of the Eleusis Initiative came up in beautiful detail. All Kazuo could think of as the screens came on was what would be put up there. Their matches among them. His fingers clenched as he looked over at Gordon again. If they tried to match Aiko with Gordon . . . he closed his eyes and shook his head. That wouldn't happen. He wouldn't let that happen.

Orion and Mercury were some of the last to enter the room, floating in with long, easy strides to find seats for themselves where they could see those up on the stage. A group of other pilots trailed in behind them, people lingering in the docks to make sure everyone had disembarked.

It was clear the room was well shy of its originally-anticipated capacity, and empty seats abounded. "If there was this much movement against us even picking people up from the surface, the Consortium should've known about it before they sent the shuttles down. I don't know why we weren't given more of a security detail for this if they expected to run into resistance."

Mercury didn't say anything until after they sat down, but she slid her hand into his. "If they knew about it, they didn't want the rest of the world to know there was that much resistance. Or they wanted to do it regardless of threat. I don't know." She looked around carefully before she held tighter to Orion's hand. "I'm worried. And scared."

He pulled her hand up to his and kissed her knuckles before he put his arm around her. "You already know I'm gonna take care of you no matter what." He kissed her cheek and leaned his head against hers, taking in the scent of her and attempting to let go of the stress of the day so far. "There's still a better world out there. And I still want to see you smiling on it by the end of this. We'll get there."

She nodded as officials filled the stage, but she didn't look away from him or move her forehead away from his. Orion became so important to her in such a short time that she wanted to be close to him as often and as long as possible. "I love you."

"I love you too, Mercury." It was still a little strange to say such a thing to someone he'd known for such a brief time, but he didn't feel the worry about it he had always thought he would. He had imagined he would have reservations, doubts, that he would always be holding something back. He didn't want to hold back with Mercury. He wanted everything.

"Please take your seats, friends." The speaker at the front of the stage spoke, his voice rumbling pleasantly from every corner of the room at once. "And we'll begin."

23

Director Vance stood in full uniform, looking over the assembled group, several stragglers still headed to their seats under the gaze of his dark eyes. He waited for everyone to be seated and settled before he continued, but he didn't move away from the edge of the stage while he waited. His presence was like a weight hanging on the collective attention of the crowd, lifted only when he finally began to speak again.

"We have lost, at my most recent information, seventy-four brothers and sisters today." He let the heaviness of that number sink in, and looked down at the stage for a moment, bowing under the pressure of the deaths the day had seen, before he looked back at everyone resolutely.

"They were not the first to give their lives for this project, and all of us gathered here know that they will not be the last. Shuttle Nineteen touched down outside of Bombay this morning and was permitted to load its full complement of passengers. During take-off, a sabotage device ignited in its fuel compartments, ripping the shuttle to pieces and killing all on board. This afternoon, threats were made to seven other shuttles out of the twenty-eight that were sent to Earth. Shuttle Six was permitted to touch down in Cairo and was destroyed during passenger processing. Twenty-six people were injured, but none have been pronounced dead as of this time. In Moscow, Johannesburg, Boston, and Lima, credible threats were issued and investigated. The shuttles in Johannesburg and Lima have since been able to review their passenger manifest and run thorough checks before taking off. They are en route. Moscow and Boston are still grounded until we can send additional security teams to verify their status and secure the passengers' safety."

"Shuttle Thirteen, in central North America, had some of its personnel attacked just prior to take-off, one of whom is now in critical condition. Further, they discovered an imposter on board, who has been detained pending interrogation. It is our hope that Moscow and Boston will be in the air within the next twenty-four hours, and all members of this Initiative will be present on this station, ready to begin work."

He sighed after the long report, looking around the room to meet each and every eye in the audience as he was able. "We do not, at this time, have firm information on the identity of the saboteurs and attackers at each of these sites. What we have are many of the same conjectures and theories many of you already have. The Home Alliance, the Earth First Coalition, these are likely candidates for accusation. We will not report, however, until we know for certain who is responsible. They will be found, and they will be brought to justice for the pain they have caused."

A woman moved to stand next to Director Vance and while her face was just as somber, something about her walk up to stand next to him said everything it needed to say about her confidence and determination. She was clearly Vance's second-in-command, and he looked pleased to have her standing next to him. "We don't have all the answers we want or need, but we do have all of you here, and we are grateful for your presence."

For those who didn't recognize or know the woman, her

name flashed on the giant screen behind her. Victoria Gehrig, Junior Director of the Eleusis Initiative. She was older, with grey hair and eyes that were such a light blue they blended in with the silver strands that framed her face.

"Our hearts break and we mourn for those we have lost. But they would want us to press onward toward Eleusis, and we cannot give those who would destroy us the power to stop progress." She turned from side to side slowly as she surveyed the crowd. "We have a lot to prepare, a lot to learn, and honestly, not that much time to do so before we launch." The screen changed to show the projected timeline of events, and despite what had happened that day, the timeline was not altered. Clearly they meant business about getting to Eleusis and letting nothing get in the way. Not even death.

"We're still waiting for some of our friends to arrive, and we need time to recover, certainly. The next few days will allow for that. Matches have been adjusted and established based on the people still involved with the project. This is a time to get to know each other, socialize, mourn together, and develop relationships. Look around. You're all going to Eleusis. It's important that you hold on to each other and value the faces around you. The success of Eleusis depends on all of you."

Two more faces stepped forward from the back of the stage to look over the crowd, both a great deal younger than Vance or Gehrig. Their names and faces appeared on the screens to introduce them to the audience, along with their titles. Stephen Kaplan, Manager of Operations, and Maria Santos, Chief Medical Officer. It was Stephen who spoke, in a vaguely Australian accent.

"We know the next few days are going to be filled with a lot of adjustments for everyone, even those of you who have lived in orbit for most of your lives. As Vice-Director Gehrig said, now is the time to start up the relationships we're going to take with us across the stars. No pressure." He gave the crowd a tentative smile, obviously one of the more light-hearted of the bunch, though his clean-cut appearance and clear-eyed stare didn't hold the warmth his voice was trying to showcase.

"To help everyone get started on that, there are two pieces of information that we want to give you all in this meeting before we let you all get settled in your quarters and start getting ready to jump into the real work next week. First, each and every one of you has been assigned a department and a position within that department."

"Keep in mind, these positions are tentative, every last one of them. They've been assigned based on your strengths and the application materials we received from you, and it is likely that they will change at some point in the next few months as we see different strengths and weaknesses from all of you. This group, this room, together with those of our friends we're still waiting on, is going to begin civilization on a new planet. That's no easy or simple task, and it depends on all of us working together as well as we're able, where we are best able to do so. That's the first piece."

"The second piece is the match that was just mentioned as well. It was discussed at length in pretty much every information session that took place down on the planet and up here in orbit. So if any of you had any misgivings or worries about that, I assume they've all been dealt with by now, or else you wouldn't be sitting here listening to me jabber on." He gave everyone another attempt at a smile, and did manage to get a few chuckles from around the room, but only a few.

"Rest assured that everything has been taken into careful consideration." Dr. Santos replied after Kaplan spoke. "We want everyone to be as happy as possible, to lead fulfilling and productive lives, here and on Eleusis. The Match program has had decades of data poured into it, and has been wildly successful, especially in recent years. The positions have been assigned with the same kind of consideration. We ask that even if you disagree with either aspect that you give it time, that you put forth an effort, and that you look toward the bigger picture and the biggest reward."

"We all want a full and productive life on Eleusis. The Initiative has built this entire structure to make it happen. These are the last stages of truly centuries of work to get to Eleusis, and you will be the ones to finally reap that reward." She smiled brighter than anyone else as she looked around, the smile of someone who believed in what she was saying.

"By now, your questions should have been answered. If they have not, there will be time for all of you to approach an Initiative official after the matching and position placement has concluded. Also, each of you has already been assigned a communicator. All of our contact information is there at your fingertips, and you are more than welcome to contact us directly."

Orion wasn't completely comforted by the speeches that had been given, but he was still trying to be optimistic about the entire process. As the leaders on the stage got the screens ready to start going through people, he looked down at Mercury. "Maybe they'll decide you'd be better suited as Medical Director than Santos up there. She looks like she's about sixteen."

"And I don't look sixteen?" Mercury teased, but she was feeling too uneasy to keep up the banter. "She's very well-known in the field of psychiatry. One of the most-often referenced and researched in her field. She's almost thirty, actually."

"I see." Orion still sounded like he didn't quite believe her, but he shook his head and looked back up at the stage. They were discussing the way the rest of the meeting would go, with people's names, faces, and future assignments up on the screen opposite the picture and information of the person with whom they were going to be matched. The leadership was talking about living arrangements, the fact that they were all being given the option of having private quarters to themselves or immediately moving in with their match. "Looks like they've thought all this out pretty thoroughly. More than I can say for their travel plans earlier today."

Mercury stared up at the screen and without saying anything she got up from her seat and moved to sit in his lap, though the seats really weren't wide enough to accommodate it. She closed her eyes and turned her attention solely onto Orion even while the leadership continued speaking on stage. "My stomach is all twisted in knots. What if they re-match us?"

"We talked about this." He hugged her against him tightly and kissed her shoulder as they waited. "Whoever's genetics end up whichever direction, all that matters is that I'm yours and you're mine. That's for life."

Mercury nodded but it was hard not to feel worried or scared. Her life had been built on trusting and utilizing the Consortium and the systems within it, but it was hard to remember that when fear weighed heavily on her mind. They could put another man's sperm in her, but she didn't want that. She wanted her husband. Only Orion. "For life." She repeated the words to give herself some kind of comfort, but it wasn't really working. "I can't pay attention. I don't want to."

The four heads of the Initiative took turns reading off names as the process started, looking around the room for each of them as they did. "Francis Adebayo. Security officer. Misha Angou, Communications." Orion looked up at the mention of the man who'd been on his security detail earlier that day, and actually smiled as the man stood up and found the woman he'd been matched with across the room. She was from Earth, which Orion thought was interesting, but he didn't have long to dwell on it before they moved on to the next name, and then the next, and the next.

Aiko, in the middle of the room, just clutched her small bag of personal items as she waited to hear her name. She was hoping to hear Gordon's first to set her more at ease, but hers came up early on. Too early.

She stood up as soon as her name was called, then she

glanced down at her brother. It took all her energy to stop herself from rushing to the bathroom just to keep herself from throwing up in public. She was afraid of being matched with Gordon, afraid of being matched with someone who would mistreat her or someone she couldn't protect herself against without exposing herself and her secrets. Aiko pleaded silently with any gods that would listen that she would get a good man.

"Carlos Espinoza." Vance said, as the face of one of the guards she had seen earlier that day came up on the screen, with the title of Security Officer under it. "Ms. Tanaka, as of just a few moments ago, we've been informed that Mr. Espinoza is out of surgery and expected to make a full recovery. He'll be informed of being matched with you once he wakes up."

She stared up at the screen, since she was surprised, but the man had seemed nice enough, even though he was easily three times her size. How did that make sense? Aiko nodded and continued staring at the screen until her picture and Carl's disappeared. Was he a good man? She didn't know, but he had been working to keep them all safe when he was injured. That had to mean something, even if the match itself was confusing.

More names came and went on the screen, people from every part of the world and every station in the sky getting matched with each other. People took up the pattern of standing and moving to sit with the person they were matched with after their names were read, or at least most people did. Some of them were obviously more reluctant than others to be matched, and some people refused to even stand up, though they were obviously there in the crowd. "Dr. Barry Woods, Medical Unit, Pediatric Director." Kaplan read out as the young pediatrician's face came up on the screen, and he smiled down into the crowd as he continued. "And Erebi Woods, Data Support."

Mercury looked back at the screen as soon as she heard Barry's name, since she considered him an ally in her field, and she felt a rush of relief when she saw that he was matched with his wife. "Oh, that's so good. I'm so happy for them."

There was actually some applause at that, since people seemed happy to see that a married couple had been left together. They could see Barry and Erebi in one of the front rows with their arms around each other, exchanging quick, furious kisses of celebration that they would be together without complications. The directors allowed for a moment of applause, smiling down at the group, then continued on with their list. "Kameron Fitch, Navigation and Security." Vance called out, nodding at the woman once she stood up. "Kazuo Tanaka, Engineering."

Kameron looked up at the screen and looked around for her match before she sighed and looked over at Orion before she moved away, since she was sitting close to Orion and his wife. "I was really hoping they would change their mind about the whole penis business."

"Go get him, girl." Orion smiled at his friend, even though he knew she really wasn't looking forward to what was coming. The Japanese man she'd been matched with didn't look thoroughly excited about it either, but he did manage to give Kameron a smile as she got closer, and the names continued to rattle on through the list.

"They must be saving the best for last." Gordon said as he leaned back in his chair with one arm still around Jessie's back. He looked almost bored with the entire proceeding. "You think?"

"There's still a lot of people to go through." She watched another set of people matched, and she couldn't peel her eyes away from the screen but it was giving her more anxiety than she could manage. "I feel like they're toying with me."

"It's actually worse than that." Gordon said without changing his tone, still flippant and relaxed as he had been ever since they got on board the station. "It's not that they're toying with you, it's that they don't know enough about you to even care enough to toy with you. They know some, and they know what they care about knowing, but it's not enough. They're messing with all of us. But they're like a researcher with a lab full of monkeys. They don't do it because they hate monkeys, they just don't care about monkeys, so they use them. They certainly don't care about making you wait to find out what your future's gonna look like. So long as they control that future."

Jessie finally turned her attention away from the screen after listening to what he said, and she looked him straight in the eyes. "Why do you have to say things like that? God, you could turn people suicidal that way. I mean, why even tell me something like that? Do you care about me any more than they do? You kiss really well, but otherwise, you have absolutely no reason to care about anything or anyone up here either."

Gordon didn't meet her eyes immediately after that kind of accusation, then slowly began looking around over the crowd of people surrounding them, half a dozen of them in the process of walking over to join their new match as the names continued rolling on.

"I care about Eleusis." He finally said, still looking around the room. "I care about Earth. I care about the human race as a collective whole. There are a few individuals I care about for their own sake, but it's everyone that I care about." He reached up to run his hand over the back of her neck and pulled her into another brief kiss just to keep her against him and ease her mind.

"And yes, I do care more about you than the rest of these fuckers. Worlds more than I care about any of the assholes up on that stage, that's for damn sure. Which is why I'm never gonna bullshit you about what I do and don't know. What I know is that we're all monkeys in a cage to them. What I know is that Eleusis isn't the salvation of humanity to them. It's a business opportunity. But they're the ones who hold the means to get there, which is part of the reason I'm here. I care about Eleusis, I care about Earth, I care about my friends, and I care about you."

His grip on her tightened a little just to squeeze her against him firmly, and he raised his chin a little to look her straight in the eye. "If you stick with me, no matter what else happens, no matter how far south this whole Initiative ends up going, I will do everything in my considerable power to get you to Eleusis. To make sure you get the new life you want. If you stick with me."

Jessie wasn't sure what to make of that speech, and it was hard to think with names being called in the background along with her own continued anxiety. She eventually nodded, not necessarily because she trusted this man she barely knew, but because she trusted him just a little bit more than the rest of the strangers she barely knew. Jessie needed a friend, for more than just to get to Eleusis, but because she needed to have a relationship with someone who didn't halfway hate her for whatever reason.

"Alright." She replied in a whisper. "I'll stick with you. Whatever that is supposed to mean."

That brought a smile back to Gordon's face, and he kissed her thoroughly, his hands bunching into fists in her flight suit to hold her tight. "Wise choice. And I think I'm going to like having you on my side." He grinned and actually chuckled, out of place as it was in the otherwise severe atmosphere that had been brought about by the mass matching. He kissed her a few more times, heedless of the crowd around them, then set her back in her seat with his arm still around her. "I hope, for his sake, that your match is a singularly understanding human being."

Her cheeks were flushed by the time she was in her seat again, but the high from the kisses was severely dampened by his last comment. "I said that I didn't want to choose, but I didn't want to choose any of the men you showed me. I would rather choose you." It was difficult for her to admit it, since he still frustrated her and riled her up in many different ways, and she barely knew him, but it was the truth. His mysteriousness and his kisses had somehow won her over.

"I would choose you too." He said with a lingering caress along the back of her neck beneath her hair. His eyes raked her up and down, but it was only when he looked into her eyes again that he smiled.

It looked like he was about to say something else, but Kaplan spoke again before Gordon could open his mouth. "Jessica Rogers, Catering Operations." Kaplan looked around for a while, obviously waiting to see if Jessie was there to join them.

Catering Operations. Of course. Jessie refrained from rolling her eyes before she stood up in response to her name being called. She had hoped for a more exciting job than a 'cook', but she wasn't going to make any waves about it. At least not now, not in front of everyone else.

It seemed, imagined or not, like there was more of a delay in the other screen lighting up with information, but when it did, a face she recognized came up on the screen. "Gordon White." Kaplan intoned, still looking around the crowd for the man. "Data Support."

Gordon stood up where he was right next to Jessie, as if the two of them didn't know each other, and he just smiled over at her as they got a small smattering of applause from those around them who had assumed they were already together. "Well, will you look at that?" He grinned at her and sat back down as the list went on and he put his arm back around her shoulders. "What are the chances?"

Jessie was stunned into silence even as she sat back down with his arm around her. She blinked several times as their faces left the screen and the list moved on. "Did you do that?" She eventually asked as she turned her face into his so she could whisper into his ear.

The grin that spread across his face at her question was all the answer she really needed, and his caresses resumed along her back and neck. "An honest, law-abiding citizen like me, break in and fuck with the system for my own gain? I'm scandalized. It's like you don't know me at all."

She let out a heavy breath she didn't know was trapped

in her lungs. Jessie leaned her forehead against the side of his head, and closed her eyes. Clearly she was happy to get what she wanted. Mysterious or not. "I hope you know what you're doing, getting tied to me. Now I get to see you naked, and I want that *really* bad."

That statement chased away the smile from his face, but he didn't move away from her. "I'm glad you want it now. You might change your mind when you get what you want." His tone was back to being dark, but he moved to kiss her cheek as his fingers massaged her back. "If we're off for the next few days, though, then I see no reason for you to get back into anything at all once I get you back to our room and out of that flight suit. Not for days."

"I won't change my mind." She assured him as she stole another kiss from his lips, since a kiss on the cheek didn't satisfy her, though her cheeks were definitely burning after he said he wanted to keep her naked for days. "I don't have to share you. That's more than enough, to have someone I want all to myself."

"Like I said," he whispered back as he kissed her, "I like my women possessive. Own me all you like, just know that I expect the same in return."

Jessie nodded since she had no desire to be owned by anyone else, not now when she had someone to herself and someone who wanted her. At least it seemed like he wanted her. He was hard to read. "I'm all yours." She kissed him several more times, though clearly they were one of only a few couples who felt so enthusiastic about their match.

Anna wrinkled her nose as she saw Gordon and Jessie making out, and she turned her attention back to Logan, while she looked at the screen every so often. "I didn't even think that smug asshole would actually make it onto the shuttle after the first meeting, and I certainly didn't think his match would be so enthusiastic."

"No accounting for taste sometimes." Logan let out a short laugh, but he was getting more nervous the longer the list of names went on. He thought when the obviously-married couple had been announced that there would be a whole run of all the married couples in the room, just to set people's minds at ease, but so far he hadn't seen anyone else either get upset about being separated from their spouse or rejoicing over staying with them. If other married couples had been kept together, they were keeping it to themselves, and if they had been split apart, they didn't seem too broken up about it.

They found Orion and Mercury off in another section of the room a while earlier when following the people who stood up and moved from one place to another, and Logan could see the two of them looked just as nervous as he and Anna felt, though they were still sitting together.

"There's not that many left." He said as he watched the screen and listened to the constant listing of names and occupations. They had been there for nearly an hour, but Logan couldn't imagine they had too many more to go through, as quickly as people were being read off.

"So that means this horror is almost over." Anna said as confidently as she could manage with her nerves. Another couple was matched and they moved to sit together across the room before anything happened, and Anna nearly broke her neck when she whipped her head around to look back at the screen at the sound of her name.

"Anna Bickford, Mechanical Operations." They put her married name up on the screen by her picture, so that had to mean something. Anna stood at the sound of her name, staring at the screen, willing Logan's face to appear next to her. Director Vance scanned the crowd looking for her, and nodded once when he located her before turning back to the tablet in his hands to pull up her match.

"Orion Al-Jabbar." He announced, as Orion's face and name came up on the screen opposite hers. "Navigation Officer."

It felt like Anna's whole body was dropped in ice water as soon as she saw the pilot's face and name appear on the screen next to hers, and she couldn't even look away from the screen, let alone move her body at the sight. This was a joke, right? She'd met the guy, he'd taught her a few things on the shuttle, so someone was playing a joke on her. It had to be a joke. When she looked over at Logan's face, though, she realized that it wasn't.

Across the room, Orion closed his eyes when he saw his name come up across from someone who wasn't Mercury. He squeezed her hand and looked over at her, no trace of a smile on his face as he let the weight of what just happened settle over him. "I love you." He said quietly, since he didn't want her to doubt that at any time. He held her hand for another moment and slowly looked across the room at Anna to see whether she was coming to him or he needed to go over to her.

Mercury was just as stunned as Orion or Anna or anyone else in the room, but she held his hand as long as he would let her before she replied with a whispered "I love you too."

Anna stared at Orion across the room before she shook her head and then sat back down, since she wasn't going to leave Logan. She had nothing against the pilot, he seemed like a nice enough guy, but she wasn't going to move. Anna waited her whole life for Logan to be hers, and she wasn't about to fucking walk away from him because of some computer program. "Fuck that shit. A computer doesn't know what I know. I'm not moving."

Orion squeezed Mercury's hand one more time before he started walking through the rows to get over to Anna. There were plenty of open seats around her, but as the list continued through a few other people's names, he ended up taking one a few seats down from her on the same row. Neither of them were happy about it, but Orion and Mercury had talked about what would happen. Nothing was going to change the way he felt about Mercury. Certainly not some arrangement of convenience or genetic benefit. That didn't have anything to do with a person's choices. He sat in the chair and leaned forward with his elbows on his knees, just listening for the one and only other name on the list he cared about.

Mercury felt ridiculous and alone sitting by herself once Orion had moved, and she felt sick to her stomach most of all. The list of reasons why she had resisted a relationship for so long was playing insistently through her thoughts. Relationships had the power to do harm, to distract, even though Orion hadn't done anything himself to hurt her. Just her feelings for him gave him the power to do so, and the Initiative had done the hurting for him, though she wanted to believe she wasn't split away from her husband because someone was twisted enough to want it to happen.

She knew she and Orion were already genetically diverse, but the woman he had been matched with was genetically similar to her own Earth-born husband. So if Anna and Logan Bickford had to be split up, then they had to be put with other people. It was logic. Wasn't it? Mercury ran her hands over her cheeks to try and calm the heat that appeared, but nothing would chase away the sick feeling that was heavy in her stomach. Especially not when she knew her name was coming. There weren't many people left.

Logan felt like he couldn't even blink as he watched the screens and listened to the names continue to roll through the room. No one seemed to be clapping for anyone after Anna had obviously been matched with someone who wasn't her husband, and as he watched, he saw more existing couples split up, matched with others who were new to the Initiative.

One older woman, obviously an Orbital with maturity to her otherwise-attractive features, was paired with an Italian man Logan knew had to be his age or younger. A distinguished-looking man from Kenya was paired up with an Australian girl who had been sitting with a girl who could have been her sister but might also have been her girlfriend from the way they were holding onto each other. People were being moved around like trading cards in every direction, and it had his heart thumping in his chest until it was almost painful.

"Logan Bickford." Kaplan finally got around to reading out, his eyes jumping up to look straight at Logan, after having located Anna there earlier. "Agricultural Operations."

Anna looked back at the dreaded screen once she heard Logan's name, and already she wanted to throw something at the stage because she knew her name wouldn't be there. She turned her attention quickly to Logan, though, before anyone else's face could be matched next to his. "We're still in this together. No matter what." She reminded him, since he looked about as sick as she felt.

"Always." He promised quietly, his huge hand resting on her leg to let her know he wasn't moving, though he did stand up to let himself be recognized.

Kaplan actually paused when he looked down at his tablet again, and his eyebrows went up just slightly as he read the next name, but there was no other trace of a reaction on his face to explain the reason for the pause, at least until he read it out. "Dr. Mercury Finnegan. Medical Unit, Obstetrics director."

Mercury had a harder time convincing herself of 'logic' when she was matched with the man she'd met only hours ago, whose wife was now paired with her husband. She stood up slowly as soon as her name was read, but she realized he wasn't moving, just as his wife hadn't moved. She felt as though she had been played a fool somehow, but there was no reason for her to sit alone. Slowly, she made the move to sit somewhere near her match, even though he wasn't making anything easier for any of them.

There was certainly no one clapping for that particular match, and the fact that the two married couples had been cross-matched was lost on no one in the room. Mercury could hear people whispering their opinions of the situation as she passed, but more names were still coming through to drown out the sound of the voices. Logan didn't move any closer to her when she got close, but he did remain standing until she got to his row and took a seat near his. He looked over at Anna once he sat down, and took her hand again tightly, then looked over at Mercury with a slow sigh, since he could see she was no more excited about the match than any of them were.

Mercury barely glanced at Logan before she looked over at Orion where he was also sitting by himself nearby, and there were tears in her eyes as she stared at him. Mercury told herself over and over that it didn't matter, that she would have this stranger's baby and it would be nothing. She told herself it was genetic diversity. Logical diversity. It wasn't nothing, though. The officials had already explained they could have rooms together with their match, so clearly they wanted people to remain paired together, but for what reason, she didn't know. Why would that matter, if the only reason was genetic diversity? Why live together if procreation could be accomplished in a more civilized way?

Anna held even tighter to Logan's hand as soon as the beautiful redheaded doctor sat on the other side of him, since she was not going to share her husband with anyone else. Certainly not a busty redheaded doctor. "We're going to do something about this. They're going to switch us back." She said loudly enough to be heard by the people surrounding them, including the pilot that was her 'match' and the doctor. "They have to switch us back."

All the four of them could do in the aftermath of that statement was look back and forth among themselves, each meeting the eyes of the other before looking away. None of them could look at any of the others without mixed feelings of fear and rebellion and resignation. Their worlds had lost the option to be simple.

As the names went on, all four of them turned their eyes away from each other and focused on the platform ahead of them, thoughts spinning in circles that had no readily-available escape, only a prescribed path forward all of them had somehow chosen and yet none of them were about to walk by choice.

The directors reached the end of the list of names at last,

and Director Vance took center stage again to give his closing remarks, his hands folded in front of him and his dark eyes taking in everyone in the crowd at once.

"One thing I would encourage all of you to keep in mind today and in the days to come, is that this is a beginning. The roles you have been given may change as we go through the preparation process to leave for Eleusis. Our systems have done the best they can, but people can always do better than machines, at most things, at least.

"For tonight, and until we can convene again in a few days with all of our colleagues from the remaining shuttles, I encourage you all to think on this: you have chosen to be a part of a new world. Choose to be fully a part of that world. Some of us here in this room have dedicated our entire lives to the pursuit of Eleusis, and it is finally within our reach. It is worth all of us. It is worth all we have, all we can give."

"Let us make this Initiative the beginning of a new home for our people, a new reason to hope, to dream. Let us be the reason those dreams survive. Keep that at the forefront of your thoughts in all things, and everything else will fall into place."

He concluded with a smile that took in the entire crowd, and an authoritative nod that put the seal on his words of encouragement. "You are dismissed to quarters. Further meeting and scheduling information will be sent to you by your communicators regarding your individual operations. You are free to explore all of the unrestricted areas of Arm Four, where we currently are and where all the operations of this Initiative are now housed. The Arm is ours alone, so remember that everyone you meet is a part of this Initiative, working alongside you. Treat them accordingly."

"I wish you all the best, here and across the galaxy, my dear, dear friends."

The story continues in

The Rebels

ABOUT THE AUTHOR

D. Brumbley is a husband/wife duo from Kansas City who spend most of their time in each other's heads. In suburbia the duo lives in a simple house with a dog and two feisty kiddos. One half of the duo loves football, baseball, libraries, and romance. The other half of the duo likes D&D, Fantasy novels, Marvel Comics, and cheesecake. A country girl and an east coast boy met online, became best friends, fell in love, and somewhere along the way decided that telling stories together would be fun.

Best. Decision. Ever.